This is a work of fiction. Names, characters, places, and incidents either are the product of the author's imagination or are used fictitiously. Any resemblance to actual persons, living or dead, events, or locales is entirely coincidental.

(If real life were like this book we probably would, instead, read about mundane things like cutting the grass and going to the grocery store.)

Author Info:
Website: http://www.SeanRFrazier.com
Facebook: https://www.facebook.com/SeanRFrazierAuthor/
Twitter: https://twitter.com/TheCleftonTwain
Email: cleftontwain@gmail.com

i

DEDICATION

To those who strive to do amazing things—don't stop. Don't merely *see* the magic, BE the magic.

ACKNOWLEDGEMENTS

To Kristin, Gillian, and Tanith, who have always helped me be the best that I can be, and continue to love and support me when I fail. To my inspirations: there are too many of you to name, but know that you have awed me with your awesome talents and skills. Lastly, Brickton keeps me caffeinated. They are true heroes.

Thank you to Gretta Geheb for the fantastically mind-blowing cover art.
http://grettasgraphics.com

Thank you to Scott Ziolko for the wonderful map of Cygil!
http://scottziolkovscomics.tumblr.com/

Titles by Sean R. Frazier

The Forgotten Years:

The Coming Storm

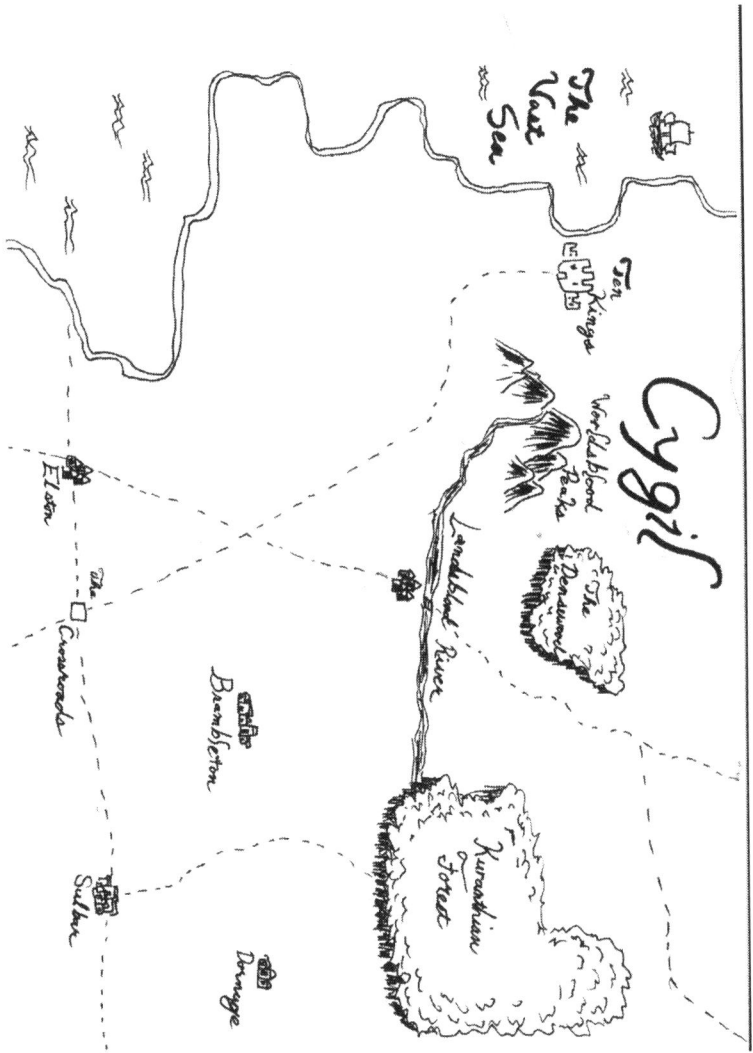

Cygil

The Vast Sea

Ten Kings

Worldblood Peaks

The Denauven

Landsblood River

Brambleton

Elam

The Crossroads

Kunathian Forest

Sulhre

Drauge

v

Sean R. Frazier

Prologue

When Alannin Stormbriar awoke, the sun was just beginning to show itself over the horizon. Droplets of water clung to the leaves, lingering from last night's rain, and the air was wet and heavy, but there was a pleasant chill that made up for the discomfort. He rose carefully, avoiding the branches under which he had made his crude bed of leaves, and stretched.

It was a beautiful morning. He hoped to see many more, but he knew that they would not be in this place. He did not belong here, and he knew that fact very well. As far back as he could remember, he felt out of sorts in this place—not out of place, but he knew there was somewhere else he *should* be. He was far and away not the only one. All elves experienced what they called "The Longing" and it eventually drove them to become nomads, forever moving. Forever trying to find that one place they could call "home."

Sadly, many elves never found that place. Some even perished—simply refusing to eat or drink, and eventually wasting away from their desire and despair. It wasn't by choice. It was a drive, an instinct that could not be denied. What mattered was how much they let it affect them.

It was unique to the elves. Though he had not encountered many, Alannin had never met a dwarf or gnome who had the same drive. They had their own problems, of course, and both were usually too wrapped up in their own strife to share in that of another people.

He buckled on his two swords, shouldered his quiver and bow, and took one last look at the lush, beautiful forest around him. He sighed, filled with both uncertainty and excitement, and left, clearing the tree line soon after.

Sometimes he had second thoughts—that he should have gone with the rest of his brethren. They were, after all, from the same village and he was very close to some of them. But they had

1

felt a pull in a different direction than he, and he felt compelled to follow his own path. There were no hard feelings, because everyone understood the pull of The Longing. Still, he should like to see them again, someday—particularly, his friend Aref. That possibility was slim, but he held onto small hopes.

Alannin stopped at the edge of a cliff and looked down. Somewhere beneath the canopy of trees below was his destination. He felt a sense of urgency, now—that was new. It was almost as if he needed to hurry because, if he didn't, it wouldn't be there anymore. *That's silly. The trees aren't going anywhere. This is to be my new homeland and it certainly isn't going to disappear.* No matter how thoroughly he tried to convince himself to the contrary, the feeling of urgency was still there, nagging at him and pushing him forward.

The sun rising behind him cast a soft glow down upon the trees in the distance while leaving the area directly below him still in shadow, though his keen elven vision could see enough detail to know that the cliff itself would be an impossible climb.

Upon closer inspection, he noticed an easier way down. It would still require some climbing, but the wall was less steep in some areas. And, still, the feeling of urgency nagged at him. It was near impossible to resist, driving him to expediency. *Well, unless I am planning on taking a couple of days to walk around and find a decent path into the valley, this is the best I am going to get.*

It didn't take long for him to reach the spot of descent. He carefully slipped over the edge and worked his way along the cliff wall. At certain points, there was almost a path of sorts that he could walk down. Other times, it was a straight climb, but he could almost always find a ledge that made the climb a lot easier. Though the descent was slow-going, he eventually reached the treetops and, once he was close enough to the trees, he left the cliff and easily climbed down the branches instead.

Upon reaching the ground, he found himself in a beautiful forest with towering oaks and sprawling maples. The canopy was so dense that the area beneath was much darker, with isolated rays of illumination poking through, some creating only small points of light on the forest floor.

The forest was alive with the sounds of birds, and it smelled damp. Alannin took a deep breath, savoring everything about his surroundings. He then walked forward in the direction that he knew was right. Though he tried to be leisurely about it and enjoy himself in his new surroundings, he found his pace quickening.

He stopped at a creek for some water and noticed a deer upstream. Another doe was close by with two babies. *Hopefully there will still be deer in my new homeland. Surely there will be. The Longing wouldn't lead me to a desert or plains, would it? The forest is where elves belong.*

He deftly hopped up onto a rock and used a fallen tree to quietly cross the creek, trying not to disturb the deer. Once on the other side, he walked up the gentle slope of a hill and headed further into the forest.

He didn't know where his family was. They had all followed their own urges. The Longing didn't always feel it necessary to keep families together, nor did any elf feel that way. Elves were a very independent people. Families raised their children until it was time to wander and, once that time arrived, they may never see each other again. But an elf's life was long—hundreds of years—and anything was possible.

Alannin could feel his destination getting closer. Excitement filled him with each step that he took, but he still tried to take it slow. He had never been one to hurry unless there was a specific reason to. While he was anxious to arrive at the end, he was still mindful of everything around him.

Not every elf felt The Longing. Some wandered late in life while others went their entire existence without feeling the urge at all. Still others miraculously resisted and lived happy lives in one place. The experience was different for every individual and, it being rather personal, it was rarely discussed—even among friends and family.

Alannin ascended a hill that was littered with fallen trees. They looked as though they had died quite a while ago but, there being so many, they made the way difficult. When he reached the top, he paused a moment to catch his breath. He could not see much except that the terrain leveled out a bit up ahead.

What concerned him most was the wolf to his right. Obscured well enough by trees so that Alannin could not see it, the beast was hunting him and had been for the last five minutes. The wolf was doing an excellent job of remaining concealed, but Alannin could still hear it moving and, very occasionally, snarling.

His hands remained at his sides. He saw no need to draw a weapon. *Fear is a great motivator, but it can too easily consume someone and lead them to hasty decisions. No mistakes shall be made here today.* He continued his journey, preferring to let his stalker make the first move.

And it *did* make the first move. Soon after, it showed itself, emerging slowly from behind a clump of bushes, growling and baring its teeth. From here, he suspected that the wolf was female, judging by her size. At first, he thought that he may have wandered too close to her lair but if he had, she wouldn't be following him. No, she was hunting him, not protecting her home.

She was large for a wolf, and obviously well-fed. Her coat was light gray with a white underbelly. Her face was also gray and white with black around the eyes. She was beautiful, but still belligerent toward Alannin.

She inched closer with her hackles raised and her teeth bared, drool dripping from her jaws. What happened next would depend on just how hungry or desperate she was. Alannin's experiences with wolves had taught him that they usually preferred to prey on animals smaller than they. *So why is she confronting me?*

He stood his ground and began walking toward her. She never took her eyes off him, but made no move to advance. Her stance slowly began to change as if she was confused. *Most hunters will not expect their prey to fight back. When challenged, they will sometimes back down.* This summer would be Alannin's 84th. Though relatively young for an elf, he had dealt with plenty of predators and had emerged from every encounter without a fight. A few situations had been close, however.

He didn't see why this encounter should be any different. Slowly he pulled a *sarashrum* from one of his pockets and held it out to the wolf who was now just a few feet from him. The animal sniffed the air, obviously smelling the dried meat wrapped inside the leaves. She continued snarling, but licked her lips and panted. Then she cautiously, and slowly, approached.

Once she was just a mere foot or two away, Alannin let her take the *sarashrum* from his hand. She dropped it and inspected it, sniffing and licking it. After several moments, she finally ate it.

"Tasty, huh girl? I've never been very good at making them, but this was my most successful attempt so far." He reached into his pocket for another and pulled out one of his remaining two. "I've only got this last one for you—I need to save the other one for me. But you can have it."

The wolf once again took it from his hand, inspected it on the ground, and then gobbled it up. Alannin noticed her tail wagging slightly as she stared up at him, no longer hostile toward him.

"Well, that didn't take long," he continued. "Alright, then, off with you. I'm sure you have pups to tend to, or a nap to take." Alannin turned and left, letting The Longing guide him once more.

But the wolf followed him, remaining a few steps behind. When he stopped, she stopped. Every time he looked down at her, she looked back up at him. *Well, now I've somehow managed to acquire a pet. What exactly am I supposed to do with her? And is she really being friendly or does she just hope I have more food?*

He reached down to put a hand on the top of her head. To his surprise, she let him. In fact, she sat and watched him as he stroked her fur. It was soft and fluffy—no, this was not an animal that was struggling to get by. She was strong, majestic and, for the moment, quite friendly. *I guess I've got a traveling companion. There are worse things that could have happened, I suppose.*

He scratched behind her ears a bit and she responded with a playful whimper, leaning into his fingers. This was the easiest encounter he had ever had with a wild animal. Admittedly, he was glad to have the company.

"Well, girl," he said, kneeling so that his face was at her level. "I've no idea where I am going to end up, but you are certainly welcome to get lost with me. And I can't just call you 'girl' all the time. You need a name. But what name would you like? I've never had a pet before—if I can actually call you a pet."

The wolf panted and licked his face once.

"How about Belle?"

She simply stared at him.

"No? Okay, how about Trelania? No? Liera? Tania?" None of them sounded right. He rubbed his chin for a moment, cycling through every female name he could think of. Finally, something clicked.

"Ilvania," he said. The wolf licked his face again. "Oh, you like that name?" he laughed. "Very well, then. *Ilvania* it is! You do know that means 'damsel,' right?" He received another wet tongue in his face. "I don't know if that's a 'yes,' but I'll assume so."

He stood up and continued his trek through the forest, his heart a little lighter now. He could sense that he was nearing his destination. Ilvania happily traipsed through the undergrowth, sometimes playfully bounding over obstacles or splashing in a stream. Like it or not, they were a team now. It felt good to have a friend along for the journey, even if that friend was unable to speak to him. He'd trained several animals in the past but they were working animals—horses and oxen mostly. This could prove to be more interesting, and definitely more entertaining.

"Something tells me that I should have named you 'Silly.'" Ilvania stopped and looked at him, and he half-expected her to laugh. She quickly resumed her playful behavior. *If I didn't know better, I'd say that she* does *understand me.*

6

That night was spent sleeping under the forest canopy. At first, Ilvania had found a pile of leaves out of which she had made a nest of sorts. After just a couple of hours, however, Alannin found himself rudely awakened as she made herself at home, snuggled as close to him as she could get. In fact, she had pushed him halfway out of his own makeshift bed! He tried to move her but soon realized that it was a lost cause. She looked at him with one eye cocked open before quickly closing it and going back to sleep.

Despite the cramped conditions, Alannin got a good two to three hours of sleep before he awoke. *One of the problems with not needing a whole lot of sleep is, when traveling, you get bored at night when it's too dark to see anything.*

Since he could feel his close proximity to the end of his journey, Alannin was even more anxious for the sun to rise. He—*they*—were so close now! He found himself hoping that Ilvania would follow him all the way to his destination.

When the first rays of light finally penetrated the forest ceiling, Alannin was quick to get moving. Ilvania, on the other hand, woke up very slowly. When Alannin urged her to get moving, she simply looked at him through indifferent eyes and rolled over to go back to sleep.

It was only a few short moments after he left, though, that she came tromping through the woods to catch up to him. She looked both happy to see him and irritated that she had been forced to wake up.

"Serves you right for pushing me out of my own bed," he joked. "You and I are going to have to work this out eventually."

Ilvania replied with a blank stare, panting.

"Alright, then, come on. Let's see where we end up today. We're close."

Alannin estimated it was a little after midday when he suddenly stopped walking. Ilvania stopped, too, and sat at his side, nibbling on her shoulder to scratch an itch.

Alannin's urge to wander had suddenly ceased, but something still didn't feel quite right. It was as if he was where he wanted to be, but not where he *should* be.

"Well," he said, "here we are." He looked around at the forest—there was nothing remarkable about where he was and he felt a pang of sadness. "But where is here?" He had held out hope that, when he finally reached the end, he would find something magnificent—a town or beautiful scenery. At the very least, he had hoped for something *different*. Yet, here he was, in the midst of the same forest in which he had been traveling for a while already.

And this was definitely the spot. His wanderlust had suddenly ceased, as if it were a torch that had been abruptly dunked in a bucket of water. Alannin was most assuredly where he was supposed to be.

"This is where we shall live now, Ilvania. It is our home," he sighed. Though he tried to convince himself otherwise, he was disappointed. He was, however, also relieved that he had found his true path. But there was still something nagging at him. He knew he was supposed to be here, but he also felt like he needed to be somewhere else. *I cannot be in two places at once. Why am I still feeling The Longing? The feeling is there, but it's also not.*

He looked around him, at the trees, the leaves, the bushes and the ground. There was nothing different about this part of the forest—nothing unique. He closed his eyes and concentrated, letting his emotions take hold. He knew there was something still yet for him to find.

Like a flame springing to life, something awoke inside of him. He opened his eyes and turned to his right. Something nearby shimmered and distorted the forest around it. It blinked in and out sporadically, and when it did so, the trees and bushes behind it seemed to bend and twist.

"There," he said, pointing as if Ilvania understood. "*That* is where I'm supposed to be." He felt excitement welling up within him. He knew not *what* this strange area was, only that it was where he needed to be. It felt right. Nothing he had ever experienced had ever felt so right.

But he hesitated. It would be one thing if he had encountered a cliff or a fire, but it was another thing entirely to simply walk into the unknown without caution. Ilvania, however, didn't seem to notice. She was busy chewing on one of her hind feet, unconcerned with much else.

With slow, cautious steps, he approached the shimmer. It made no sound, produced no heat, and didn't seem dangerous. Standing just a few feet away, Alannin could detect nothing unusual about the area until the shimmer briefly appeared. Once it disappeared it was as if it had never existed. The Longing was unbearably strong here. He was incredibly close to his destination but still not quite there.

He stood before the oddity for quite some time, staring at it. He walked around it, giving it a wide berth. It looked the same from every angle. It *was* the same from every angle. He was now certain that The Longing was compelling him to that *exact* spot. He was going to have to step into the shimmery area.

"Ilvania!" he shouted. The wolf stopped what she was doing and looked at him. "Ilvania, come!" She hesitated briefly, but then trotted over to his side. He was surprised that she so easily obeyed, but most of his attention was consumed by the oddity before him. He stared into the shimmer, still unsure. *But this is where I am* supposed *to be. Has The Longing ever compelled anyone to harm before?*

It was a good question, one for which he did not have an answer. He'd certainly never heard of it happening but that meant very little.

"Well, Damsel," he mumbled, "it looks like this is the place."

He'd hesitated long enough. He took a deep breath and relaxed. Abruptly, he and the wolf stepped into the shimmer.

"Do not fear that which is different. I once came across an orc who not only did not wish to kill me, but he wished to travel with me. I politely accepted and we journeyed for a spell, parting ways at a fork in the road. I found myself confounded by his demeanor, and I thought about him as I was confronted by a less cordial orc tribe much later.
—Darian, *Out and Beyond*

Chapter 1

The world had changed; this was no surprise—at least, it wasn't to Cor'il. He had known it would—had been *told* that it would—and he accepted the consequences.

Just *how much* it had changed and in what ways—those he could not have predicted. And, though many months had already passed, he had probably only experienced a small taste of the change that was yet to come.

Thus far, it seemed about on par with what he'd seen before both stones dropped into the well. Orcs and their brethren flooded the land, permeating every corner of the Realm. Most of what Cor'il knew now, he had gleaned from conversations in a tavern or on the street. It sounded bad. Everyone now knew, and they were in shock.

He'd not seen an elf, though he'd heard the tales—most of them from children or drunken sellswords claiming to have encountered one. The truth was, he didn't know much because there really wasn't much to know. It sometimes took a while for word to spread. That Blacksmoke fellow often had information, but Cor'il had only encountered him a couple of times in the last seven months. Even then, he wasn't sure he trusted the man. Kendra always appeared very cautious around him.

Nobody knew what had *really* happened. Not Kendra, not Orvaril, not anyone except Cor'il and Dalinil. The people of Elston continued with their lives, now aware that the myths—the stories they had grown up with—were very real. Some appeared to be handling it well but, by far, most citizens were troubled. "The Battle of Elston" they were calling it. Not terribly original but descriptive enough, he supposed.

Dalinil had been having a much tougher time coping. He'd sporadically show up for a day or two, then he'd disappear for weeks—or even months—on end. When Cor'il *did* see him, he was distracted and agitated.

Orvaril continued being Orvaril. He performed nightly at Lady's Luck, a tavern in the western portion of the city. Cor'il often thought about going to see him perform, but he rarely ventured out of his room at the inn. He had gone into hiding after The Blacksmoke had informed him that there were certain interested parties looking for him. Apparently, his display of magic at the city's walls had aroused fear and suspicion.

As for the city itself, it was recovering slowly. The attack had done major damage to Elston and it would take time to repair. The first thing to be rebuilt was Elston's great walls and the gates. After that, progress seemed disorganized and haphazard.

Winter had been brutal, further slowing progress. Cor'il wasn't sure if the extremely cold temperatures and snow were normal for this area, but everyone he had asked had told him that they were not. He still felt a longing to live among the trees of The Densewood, but had opted not to travel until the weather had warmed.

What intrigued him more than anything was the Threads, which seemed more energized than before. Several times now he had almost had a mishap while channeling them. He had to use less of their power than before when performing simple weaves and it had taken him a while to become accustomed to it.

Sitting on the bed, Cor'il turned the page and focused on the new symbols. The book he had carried with him—the one he had eventually finished—now held new passages. As before, it only offered up a page or two at a time and, when he had pored over each page, it returned to illegible scribbles and unintelligible symbols. He had noticed the new information only a few days ago, but after having read just a few pages, he had already learned so much!

Kendra left most days—to do what, Cor'il did not know, and she wouldn't tell him. She always had coin for lodging, though, and she gladly paid for the room. On the rare occasion that Cor'il *did* leave the room he did not roam far. He had returned to the habit of keeping his cloak's hood up when he was out in public and he always felt as if everyone was staring at him. After seeing his image on a poster nailed to a pole, he was convinced it was unwise to stray out into the city. Nobody had recognized him yet, but someone eventually would.

It was time to leave, now that the weather was warmer. Cor'il needed out of the city, and tomorrow was as good a day as any. After some thought, however, he decided it was time to return to his homeland and not The Densewood. He did not belong there anymore—he knew that much, and he had come to terms with that quite a while ago. Even if, by some miracle, they asked him to stay, he would not. He wished to at least see everyone again—possibly one last time. Surely, they would welcome him as a guest—if they knew he was eventually leaving, of course. Still, something told him it may not be that easy. When he thought of home now, there was something foreign about it.

"Foreign" may not have been the right word. He felt as though he was forgetting something. Lately, when he thought about his homeland, he would feel queasy. He couldn't shake the feeling that this hesitation was because of something he was not remembering—possibly something he had done.

The scribblings on the page filled his mind more quickly than he could understand them. This was normal. He absorbed the information and his mind made sense of it all soon after. He still wasn't at all used to it; he simply knew what to expect.

He looked at the next page and found that it did nothing. "It appears that I am done for now," he sighed. "The Goodness knows I could use a break." His head swam with everything he had just learned. The book creaked as he closed it. *So, tomorrow, I will set out for Kuranthas. I do hope, in light of recent events, that they are all alive and well.* He saw the irony—that he had been cast out as a danger, but now he could help if they came under attack. *But I was a danger back then. What would I have thought, were I in their place?*

He'd asked that question many times. He *wanted* to believe that he would have decided differently, but the truth was, he probably would have been just as scared as they had been. The things he had accidentally done back then were terrifying. The things he could do *now* were even more so. And, now that the Threads provided even more energy, he was fearful that something awful would happen if he lost control.

He was much more careful now, though he quickly remembered when he had hurled himself into the air back in Listerville. It had been an accident during a stressful situation and had, fortunately, been beneficial. It also could have just as easily ended poorly.

When he and Dalinil had returned to the city streets during the invasion, he hadn't been able to locate Kendra and, though he tried not to admit it, he had been frightened and angry. The power he had drawn from the Threads and had unleashed upon the hordes of orcs had been devastating. Dalinil had been a one-man army, cutting down enemies in a rage-induced frenzy. And when his axe finally broke, he had continued fighting with his bare hands, enjoying every minute of it.

While Cor'il did not enjoy harming other creatures—even orcs—he had to admit that, when emotion took over, he lost some control. He could very easily see himself swallowed up in the power of the Threads, hurting friend and foe alike with reckless abandon. He wasn't sure he could live with that. He certainly didn't *want* to. He was frightened by the notion.

Dalinil seemed less concerned. Cor'il had to admit that he was constantly confounded with how Dalinil wove the Threads. Cor'il's own method was much different from his, and not surprisingly, produced vastly different results. Dalinil felt much the same, admitting that he was just as confused by how Cor'il did it. They were completely different talents.

This led Cor'il to surmise that Dalinil, might *feel* the Threads differently, too. He still had a lot to learn about his new friend. Cor'il almost believed Dalinil *enjoyed* fighting and killing, but he found that difficult to stomach.

He stared at his sheathed sword, leaning up against one of the corners of the room. It had seen more use than Cor'il had expected—or wished. He hadn't used it since he helped drive back the horde, but he had trained a little on his own and his skills had improved. He never really believed he would *have* to use it when he left Kuranthas. He'd hoped it would be more of a deterrent, just having it with him.

The weapon was certainly nothing fancy—a plain, steel crossguard with a leather grip and a spherical, brass pommel on the end—but it had served him well when he needed it. During his fight to reach the Elston wall he had relied heavily on the Threads, but there had also been a level of fatigue that had eventually crept in. His sword had kept him alive long enough to perform another weave or to get to safety.

His father had given it to him on the day he had left Kuranthas. He'd said it was his, but that Cor'il would need it more. It was the one act of true kindness from his father that Cor'il clung to. Of course, his father didn't convey to Cor'il that he had any confidence in him. His voice had given him away all too easily. It had been cold and unfeeling, without any hint of compassion. He and his father had never been close, and he always felt as if his father had never even known him.

His biggest problem now was whether he could get Kendra to come with him. At first, he hadn't been sure if he wanted *anyone* to come along with him, but he did enjoy the company and he thought she might like to see his beautiful homeland and meet his childhood friends. More than that, though, returning home would be emotionally difficult and it would be nice to have someone to support him.

He wanted to find Kendra but, having no idea where to look, he had to stay put until she eventually returned. She rarely stayed away for longer than a day, so he expected he would probably see her tonight sometime. Until then, he would relax and let his mind acclimate to the new information it had just absorbed.

He sat at the window, looking out at people moving about the city. A few of them he recognized, having observed them over many months. Some of those individuals even followed patterns, visiting certain shops on certain days and whatnot.

He had a dull headache—something that was expected after working with the book. It was a marked improvement from the first time he'd stared at the pages and it seemed to get a tiny bit better after each reading. But it was still uncomfortable. It felt as if his mind was rearranging itself in a rather painful way. Thankfully, it didn't happen every time.

He'd let Dalinil try to read the book a couple of times but he could make no sense out of the symbols. He told Cor'il that several of the pages were blank, even though Cor'il could see the scribbles on the page before him. Cor'il had become frustrated the last time they tried because he couldn't understand why Dalinil couldn't see what he saw.

This, in turn, had angered Dalinil. He had eventually calmed down, as did Cor'il, but his friend had been quick to anger. After the last time nearly ended in a fight, he decided not to try to get Dalinil to read the book anymore. Dalinil didn't seem at all curious about the book, which further perplexed Cor'il. *You can't force a square peg into a round hole, you can't move mountains, and you can't get Dalinil to read the book,* he joked to himself.

Cor'il found it difficult to occupy himself today—more so than usual. He was nervous, excited, and apprehensive all at the same time. At the very least, his path was clear, and it truly *was* the path he would follow. Even if Kendra tried to stop him.

The sunlight was becoming duller as it continued its descent toward the western horizon. The crowd below had thinned out a bit and shopkeepers were beginning to clean up. He wasn't sure how long he had been sitting at the window, staring blankly out into the city, but the headache was beginning to subside.

Kendra eventually climbed up to the window and unlocked it before Cor'il had a chance to help. She somehow slid the pin out of its slot using a thin piece of metal. Of course, she'd done this before and it amazed Cor'il each time how easily she accomplished the task.

"Um," she started, "Are you going to move and let me in?"

Cor'il got up and moved the stool, setting it down at the foot of the bed.

"Many thanks!" She laughed, as she climbed through the window and locked it behind her. Then she pulled the curtains and peeked out from behind them. Cor'il had also seen her do this many times. He wasn't sure if it was just a force of habit or a necessity.

"Are we expecting someone?" he asked, laughing.

"Mayhaps." She wasn't laughing. She continued looking out the window for a few more minutes until finally turning and falling onto the bed, landing on her back. "Not anymore, thankfully. Raynar must have hired a couple of decent men to be his goons this time. These last three guys were more difficult to lose, but they also weren't very fast." She sat up and inspected her skirts—for what, exactly, Cor'il was not sure.

"I'm not sure I even want to know what you've been up to."

"Oh, nothing unusual," she laughed, brushing the strands of brown hair away from her eyes. She wasn't wearing her hair tied back today, and it looked a bit disheveled. He could tell that she was being more cautious than usual—not afraid, but careful. "So, where are we going?"

"I'm afraid I don't understand."

"Sure you do, treeboy!" She stood up, grabbed his satchel, and held it up. "You're nicely packed. Even that book is in here. You're going somewhere and I'm going with you. I'm merely curious as to *where* we are headed." She pulled a brush out of her satchel and ran it through her hair several times before putting it back.

"You don't wish to stay in Elston?" He grabbed his satchel and put it back down on the ground.

"I think you know me better than that." She grinned and tossed her hair behind her head. Then she paused, her grin slowly fading, and turned to the door.

"Well, I guess—"

She shushed him and put her finger up to her mouth, eyes still affixed on the door. Walking cautiously toward it, she continued listening, and pressed her ear against the solid wood. Then she slowly cracked it open and peeked into the hallway.

"What are you looking for?" Cor'il whispered. Kendra waved a hand his direction, still peering out into the hall. He watched her for a moment longer before she pulled her head back into the room and locked the door behind her. "See anything interesting?"

"Actually, yes," she whispered back. "Three of Raynar's goons. It would appear their skills are more advanced than I gave them credit for." She glanced around the room, and settling on the window, moved to unlock it. "And I think they saw me."

There was an angry rap on the door immediately after she said that. Cor'il looked at Kendra who shrugged and began climbing out the window. There was no balcony, so Cor'il considered his options. He could easily create a weave to either launch him to the next roof or cushion his fall, but he was not prepared to attract attention to himself.

"Be patient!" he yelled. "I'm coming!"

Kendra glared at him, as she jumped back into the room, and tried to keep him from opening the door. *I'm not entirely sure*

I know what I am going to do, but I might be able to give her time to escape. He unlocked the door and opened it, making sure to stand squarely in the doorway to block the three men from entering the room. Kendra jumped to the side, hiding behind the open door. *Why hasn't she left yet?*

Three men moved to rush into the room but, using a subtle weave of a couple of white Threads, Cor'il applied force to gently push back a little.

All three of the men were rather rough-looking. Two of them had dark facial hair and the third had a wicked scar that went from his chin to the left corner of his mouth.

"Where is she?" the scarred man in the middle demanded.

"Where is who?" Cor'il replied, his voice cracking a bit. He was trying to sound as confused as he could. From behind the door, Kendra was making faces at him. She had a dagger in each hand.

"The wench who came in here through that window." The man pointed. "Our boss wants to have a little talk with her."

"There is nobody here but me." Cor'il gestured around the room. He then got an idea, though he wasn't sure if it would work. He just needed to stall them for a moment. "So, as you can see, she obviously isn't here. You may want to try another room, mayhaps further down the hall?"

"We know she came in here," the man on the left piped up. He was missing several teeth and held a short sword in his left hand. "We saw her go through that window over there."

"Aye, we did," the middle man continued. "Now let us in, boy."

"I'm not so sure." The man on the right appeared confused. He looked around almost as if he had forgotten where he was. "It may not have been this room."

"Quiet your tongue, Gofrin." The man in the middle with the scar stuck his elbow in the other man's ribs. "Or I'll cut it out."

"I'm serious," the man called Gofrin wheezed, obviously in pain. "I don't think this is the right room. It doesn't look right."

"What do you mean it doesn't look right?" The man on the left reached behind the middle man and smacked Gofrin on the back of the head. "You're a bloody idiot, you are!"

"No, wait," the man in the middle barred the way with his arms. He looked closely at the room, obviously trying to figure something out. He paused for several moments.

Cor'il tweaked his weave a little, removing one of the white Threads. After another moment, he removed another one. *Don't push too hard. Be subtle and hopefully this will work.*

A moment later the man snapped back to reality. He looked back out into the hallway and once more at the window.

"I think Gofrin is right," he finally said.

"Bloody Hell! How could you imbeciles mess this up?"

"But Ralgrim, I really thought—"

"Shut up already!" the scarred man—Ralgrim—smacked Gofrin on the back of the head. "Raynar is paying you too much for your incompetence!"

"In fact," Cor'il continued, "Mayhaps you should try another inn?" He grinned, working his weave in minor, subtle ways. "I might suggest the Lusty Maiden Inn."

"I knew it!" The man on the left snapped his fingers and smiled. "That's the inn I saw her duck into! I must have gotten it mixed up with The Panting Calf!"

Ralgrim looked at this other man and, for a minute, Cor'il wasn't sure he would believe him. All three of them looked rather flustered. Cor'il decided to stop manipulating his weave for fear that he would go too far.

"Right, then," Ralgrim finally piped up. "Let's go. She can't have gotten far!"

All three turned and ran back down the hall, their footfalls and clattering weapons making a racket. Once they were out of sight, Cor'il shut the door and released the Threads. For a moment, a rush of cold washed over him as the energy dissipated. He shivered.

19

"Quite clever, treeboy." Kendra moved back to the bed and sat down on it, gathering her satchel. "I can only assume that was your handiwork somehow?"

"Mayhaps." He slung his satchel over his shoulder and started buckling his sword back onto his belt. "I wasn't quite sure what would happen."

"You're learning new things quickly. I cannot even begin to understand what it is you do, but it is quite impressive." Kendra moved to the window, its curtains still drawn, and peeked out.

"Sometimes," Cor'il finished with his belt, "even I don't understand what it is I am doing. And that is a little frightening."

"Well, it appears to have worked. Those three goons are in a hurry."

"Good. Hopefully they won't bother us again." Cor'il moved to the door and opened it, checking the hallway first for safety. He motioned to Kendra, pretending to usher her out the door. She exited the room and he followed, closing the door behind them.

"So," she continued. "Where exactly is the Lusty Maiden Inn? I am unfamiliar with it."

"Sulbar," he replied, grinning, as he pulled his hood over his head.

Chapter 2

Cor'il and Kendra stepped inside the Old Tabard Fest Hall and gazed at the crowd before them. It was a large, open room filled with long tables and benches, most of which were occupied. Smoke hung heavy in the air as patrons puffed on cigars and pipes. It was a bizarre, spicy mixture of different tobacco varieties that made Cor'il's eyes water. It was not a pleasant odor, but he had certainly smelled worse. He remembered the pungent, sour smell of the Scorovian hog juice. The very thought turned his stomach.

"This is the place," Kendra stepped out in front of Cor'il. "And there is Orvaril." She pointed to the stage at the other end of the room where, sure enough, Orvaril was perched on a stool playing his lute and singing. "We may as well make ourselves comfortable." She began muscling her way between patrons and past full tables.

Cor'il followed her as she made her way toward the stage. There were not many empty seats, but he managed to find a bench that could probably accommodate the both of them. Space was cramped and Kendra was nearly sitting in Cor'il's lap by the time they got situated. She didn't appear to mind much but Cor'il felt uncomfortable. He wouldn't be surprised if she was making him squirm on purpose.

"Don't get too used to this, treeboy," she scowled. Cor'il nodded, unsure of whether she was completely serious.

They were situated just a few tables away from the stage. Though the room was crowded and noisy, Orvaril's voice carried quite well above the din and Cor'il could understand each word perfectly. Cor'il had never before heard the song Orvaril was singing—something about a hawk stealing a cow and flying away with it—but the tune was catchy.

"He's quite talented, you know." Kendra was enjoying his song. "I've been here several times to see him perform. And the ladies absolutely *love* him."

"Probably because they've never actually traveled with him," Cor'il joked. He looked around and noticed that quite a few women were seemingly entranced by his friend on stage. Every so often, one of them would toss a coin at Orvaril and continue gazing at him. "I'm sure, if they heard him snore, they might think very differently."

"Mayhaps," she continued, grinning. "They enjoy the 'missing all hair on the left side of my head' look." Cor'il couldn't help but laugh. "Whatever it is, he definitely has their attention."

"What about you?" Cor'il asked jokingly.

"Oh, he's quite charming," Kendra replied. "But if you're going to go bald, don't only go halfway."

Cor'il started to try to explain that mayhaps it wasn't Orvaril's choice but he stopped, realizing that she most likely was joking. So, instead, he laughed and so did she. There was a small part of him, however, that was curious about it.

They sat, watching Orvaril's performance. He truly put on an entertaining show for everyone. The men sang along, pounding their mugs on the table while the women swooned. Kendra sipped on a glass of wine and watched, though she did not appear to be as captivated as the rest of the ladies.

Orvaril winked their direction and nodded which saved Cor'il the trouble of trying to get his attention. Kendra nodded back. Cor'il's urge to get on the road faded somewhat, though he was very eager to begin the journey to Kuranthas. It was not the same feeling he had about The Densewood. Instead, it was extreme curiosity and the urge to reconnect. But it was strong— strong enough that he could not ignore it.

"And if you leave me today," Orvaril sang, strumming his lute and making lovey eyes at the crowd, "You know I will find you. Should the world end tomorrow, we'll be together today." Several coins clattered onto the stage.

As Orvaril sang, Cor'il very subtly moved his hands beneath the table.

"*Verisoc*," he whispered.

Colorful sparks exploded behind Orvaril, popping and crackling and showering down from the ceiling. The crowd gasped, then erupted in a cacophony of clapping, shouting, and whistling. Kendra shot Cor'il a sharp, disapproving gaze, but Cor'il merely shrugged and grinned.

Orvaril finished his song and then got off the stool. As he took a bow, coins littered the stage, thrown from the exuberant crowd.

"Thank you!" he shouted, taking another, deep bow. As the audience continued cheering, he knelt and quickly snatched up every coin, stuffing them into a coin purse on his belt. Then he took another bow, waved, and left the stage.

"Come on," Kendra whispered. She quickly guzzled down the remainder of her wine and left the glass on the table. Cor'il followed her out the door and around to the back of the building where Orvaril had just emerged from the back door, slinging his lute over his shoulder. He appeared quite pleased with himself.

"Well, hello my friends!" He gave them both hugs. "It is good to see you both. I do hope you are well."

"Indeed," Cor'il replied.

"And, might I add," Orvaril whispered, "those were some mighty fine... whatever they were you did in there. Probably made me 15 extra coppers!" He clapped Cor'il on the back. "We should develop an act together! We could be rich!"

"I do not understand what you're referring to."

"Of course you don't," Orvaril laughed, winking.

"Yes, yes," Kendra interrupted. "The treeboy is quite talented at almost getting himself noticed. Don't worry, Cor'il, I let Orvaril in on your little secret." Cor'il nodded and nervously adjusted his hood a bit.

"You and me, Cor'il. We could put together the most stunning performances. We'd be famous throughout the land! But... you sort of already *are* famous, I'd imagine—even if nobody truly knows who you are. I hear your exploits during the Battle of Elston were quite impressive. Almost on the scale of my own talents!" He laughed and clapped Cor'il on the back again. Cor'il wasn't sure he enjoyed it but laughed along anyway.

"Yes," Kendra scoffed, "you two would make a *wonderful* team. You'd probably end up getting yourselves killed within a week. You *do* know that there are people out looking for you, right Cor'il?"

"He can't stay hidden for the rest of his life. Besides, if my guess is correct, this kid is going to be the least of the Realm's worries in the coming months."

"Fine." Kendra crossed her arms and grunted. "Regardless, we're leaving—today."

"Excellent! Where are we going?"

Cor'il instantly felt better. He had missed Orvaril and enjoyed having the man with them. He was good at diffusing tension. He hadn't been sure that Orvaril would want to accompany them, what with his comfortable situation in Elston. But he also knew that it would be impossible for him to resist the lure of traveling to Kuranthas—a place he had never been.

"Back to Kuranthas—my homeland."

"Very well. Off with us!" With a dramatic flourish, Orvaril pointed to the road. It was very much the wrong direction, but it didn't matter. Cor'il was surprised that Orvaril was ready to leave at the drop of a hat. The man was truly unpredictable at times.

"Your adoring fans won't miss you?" Kendra's tone lightened up a bit.

"Pssh!" Orvaril waved her off. "This will just make them happier to see me when I return, of course! What is that old saying about too much of a good thing? Besides, it will give them time to store up more coin for me!" He jiggled his coin purse. It sounded awfully full.

"We have one more stop to make before we go." Kendra began walking.

"Oh?" Orvaril appeared quite curious.

"We need to tell Dalinil." Cor'il followed Kendra into the street where they turned to head deeper into the city. "I should like to see him again."

"You may change your mind," Kendra replied, "when we get there."

"Is he not well?"

"Oh, he's fine," she continued. "But he's had a rough time of it, I suppose you could say."

• • •

The sun was well into setting when they arrived. Kendra stopped abruptly, nearly causing Cor'il to run into her. They were somewhere on the western edge of Elston in what appeared to be an affluent neighborhood. The houses and shops were immaculate and sturdy while the architecture was cleaner and more ornate than what Cor'il was used to.

"That is his smithy." She pointed ahead of them to a building on their right. It was a one-story brick building—smaller than those around it, and it lacked much of the ornate décor and fancy facades, but it certainly looked as if Dalinil was doing well for himself. Cor'il could hear the sounds of clanking metal from within.

It would be good to see his friend again. They had shared so much in so little time and then, even though they lived in the same city, they had seen nearly nothing of each other. Cor'il had barely seen Dalinil since the Battle of Elston. He missed him, almost as if Dalinil was his brother. They shared a unique bond that nobody else could possibly understand.

When he and Dalinil had resurfaced from the chamber beneath the castle, they had found that the battle was raging further into the city. Every street and alley had been crawling with the creatures of Chaos. But with Dalinil's and his help, the tide had slowly turned against the orcs, and the forces of Elston—both city guard and townsfolk—had eventually been able to drive the creatures out of the city.

The orcs had never fled. They had fought until the last one fell, leaving a battlefield covered in corpses—streets and alleys alike were crowded with the dead. It was a grizzly memory to recount. After that day, Cor'il had retreated into hiding and Dalinil had apparently settled over here on the western side of the city, having become somewhat of a celebrity for his fighting prowess. The same power that had made Dalinil a hero had created a monster in Cor'il.

"It doesn't appear as though he is having a rough time of *anything*," Orvaril observed. Kendra grunted a reply and resumed her approach.

Before they walked through the archway Cor'il could feel the immense heat—a sudden change from the chilly spring air. It was like a wall of fire that they had just walked through. He wondered how someone could work in such conditions every day. *I suppose, during winter, it is quite welcome. But during summer it can't be pleasant.*

Dalinil was busy striking a large, two-headed axe blade with a hammer.

"Hello, friend," Cor'il said. Dalinil continued hammering and did not look up. But he paused momentarily when he heard Cor'il speak.

Cor'il paused, waiting for Dalinil to reply. When he realized that no response was forthcoming, he continued.

"Um," he stammered, unsure of exactly what he should say. This was not the companion he once knew.

"We are leaving the city tonight, Dalinil," Kendra chimed in, her voice soothing and soft. "We are here to either ask you to join us or to say goodbye for a while."

Her words sounded very official—as if she was signing a contract rather than addressing a friend. It all seemed... cold.

Dalinil paused again. He set his hammer down and, using tongs, moved the axe head off his anvil and back to the fire pit which he then stoked with a metal pole. He stared up at the group, obviously looking them over. His gaze was frigid and unfeeling.

"Then," he finally said, his voice cold, "goodbye it is. I wish you well on your journey to wherever you are headed." He paused a moment before turning away to inspect the axe head, completely ignoring the group.

"You do not wish to come with us?" Cor'il asked. He was both shocked and disappointed.

Dalinil did not respond. Instead, he stoked the fire some more, then pulled the axe out of the fire and resumed hammering on it.

With the blazing coals throwing off so much heat, Cor'il found it disconcerting that cold crept into him. He did not feel welcome in this place, which made him both sad and concerned— almost as if he were in danger. He was suddenly very uncomfortable. His friend had changed, and he wasn't sure why.

Nobody spoke for what seemed like a year. Cor'il fidgeted and looked nervously at the floor, hoping that Dalinil would somehow warm up and agree to accompany them after all.

"And we wish you well, also," Kendra replied in a similar cold demeanor. She turned and left, which surprised Cor'il.

"Goodbye, friend." Cor'il reluctantly followed her back through the archway, still hoping that Dalinil would come to his senses and tell them to wait. But he could not have left quickly enough for his liking—he felt very uncomfortable here. Upon exiting, he felt the cold wash away in the crisp spring air and his spirits lifted. He was warmer outside than he had been around the fire. It was as if a weight was taken from his shoulders—a weight he hadn't even noticed until now.

"Well that was pleasant!" Orvaril exclaimed, stepping out behind Cor'il. "What a nice fellow!"

"Yes, he is quite the conversationalist," Kendra tried to joke, but there was no levity to her voice. "I told you, he's changed. He's grown... cold."

"But why?" Cor'il didn't understand. Dalinil had never been the most jovial individual, but he certainly had a better disposition when he and Cor'il had traveled together. "Has something happened to him?"

"Not that I am aware of. I visited him a few times during the colder months and, each time, he seemed more... troubled. Mayhaps he has some skeletons in his past to deal with."

"I would think," Orvaril interjected, "as much as this other boy has been heralded a 'Hero of Elston,' that he would be living the good life. I know that I certainly would!"

"I don't have an explanation," Kendra responded. There was sadness in her voice. "In the days following the Battle of Elston, he withdrew—I watched him. Yes, he has a successful smithy, but he keeps to himself. Townsfolk stopped paying him attention once he discouraged their visits. These days, he appears to be all business and, surprisingly, turns away a lot of customers."

"I should go back and talk to him. Just me." Cor'il started to turn around, but Kendra grabbed his arm.

"I would not recommend that," she said in a faint voice. "Several individuals have ended up with broken bones for angering him. I would leave him be." She began walking further west. Cor'il paused a moment and then, eventually, followed.

"Shouldn't we be going the other direction?" Cor'il pointed eastward.

Kendra stopped and turned around, then she walked over to a lamp post, a dull glow illuminating the area around it.

"You'll want to read this," she said, pointing to something affixed to the post. Cor'il approached.

"Wanted: On authority of the Red Swords," he read. "For treason against the Realm and for unnatural acts."

"So," Kendra continued, "if you'd like to walk back through town and draw attention to yourself please do. I am pretty sure there is at least one Red Sword office between here and there. Otherwise I would recommend we leave town through the nearest gate and keep to the wilds."

"I would tend to agree with the lady," Orvaril added.

Cor'il nodded and they proceeded west through the city, keeping to alleys and side streets. The sun cast long shadows across the streets, providing them with convenient and much-needed cover from city watchmen and other prying eyes. Cor'il, of course, kept his hood up as they traveled, but he was becoming apprehensive about how they were going to get out of the well-manned gates.

"I have heard talk of the Red Swords," he said, keeping his voice down. "But I am not sure I understand their purpose. Who are they?"

"After the first siege here at Elston, word spread rapidly to nearby towns." Orvaril sounded matter of fact. "Of course, after that, it didn't take long for fear to follow. This leader of the Red Swords—Captain Forsch—hails from Sulbar. He has been recruiting soldiers for his Red Swords army—defense of the Realm is what they claim."

"Under nobody's authority," Kendra added.

"Correct. He has gathered quite a few men and they answer to no king."

"What about King Alzine?" Cor'il asked. "Surely he—"

"Alzine has done everything short of supporting the Red Swords." Orvaril adjusted his lute and rucksack on his shoulder and sighed. "There are some who believe Alzine fears the Red Swords. But, if he is wary of them, Alzine hasn't come out and condemned the Red Swords. Their numbers are supposedly thousands strong already."

"That is quite obviously an untruth," Kendra replied. "How could such a force grow so fast in such a short amount of time without any actual support from the King?"

"Captain Forsch supposedly repelled an orc invasion of Sulbar by singlehandedly killing one of those trolls. Or mayhaps it was an ogre. To be honest, I have a difficult time telling them apart. I think trolls are the ugly ones."

"Word travels quickly," Kendra added. "If Captain Forsch became an overnight hero for his actions, it probably didn't take long for the Red Swords to hear about *your* actions, Cor'il."

"I suspect *everyone* knows about you, my boy." Orvaril clapped Cor'il on the back. "As to how Forsch knows what you look like, well, those drawings are pretty terrible. That could be virtually anyone. I swear I saw a drawing of you with a beard!"

Cor'il found that amusing since he had never been able to grow a beard. Being half elven probably had something to do with that. Since learning of his heritage, he yearned to know more, but his only source of information had vanished with the two crystals back at the well.

"Actually," Orvaril continued as Kendra started walking again, "if you ignore the orcs and such and forget about the fact that a kid wields unimaginable power, the cities of the Realm are experiencing a rather prosperous period of peace! Most have stopped their bickering while everyone scrambles to figure out how to survive."

"But I don't understand." Cor'il moved to catch up with Kendra, having just noticed that she had resumed walking.

"Cities are communicating with each other," Kendra explained. "They normally leave each other alone, I'd imagine. But now there is a common interest. Cities and even noble houses have allied for a defense against a common foe instead of trying to sabotage one another."

"Aye." Orvaril slid his lute into his hands and started to strum, but stopped when Kendra shot him a dirty look. He continued holding it and pretended to strum. He sneered at Kendra, daring her to say something. When she looked away he winked at Cor'il and grinned.

"So those pictures of me might be posted in other cities?"

"I would think so. I wouldn't be surprised—"

"Would you two pipe down?" Kendra whispered. She pointed ahead of them to the city gates. "We need to think about how we're going to get the treeboy here past the guards."

The city gates loomed ahead, well-lit by many lanterns as the sun's last rays dappled the streets in a slightly rusty hue. Ten well-armed city guards, clad in leathers, manned the area and inspected travelers as they entered and exited—though, at this time of the evening, there was nobody leaving with the exception of Cor'il and his friends.

"Do you think they will recognize the boy?" Orvaril asked.

"Mayhaps not all of them will," Kendra replied, "but it only takes one of them to notice before we find ourselves in trouble."

"You know," Cor'il piped up, "that I am older than both of you, right? I'm not quite a *boy*."

"Only in human years," Kendra joked. "From what you've told me, you're still technically around my age." She stuck her tongue out at him and then went back to inspecting the situation. "Do you think you could vault over the wall?"

"Easily," Cor'il replied. "But the wall is rather well-guarded as well." Cor'il could see that there was a guard with a torch about every 20 feet. He was still not graceful with landing, and he was confident that he would probably cause a commotion.

"We could probably defeat them all," Kendra continued.

"No!" Cor'il shouted. Kendra slapped her hand over his mouth and shushed him. "We are *not* going to harm them," he whispered.

"Well, then, treeboy. What do you suggest?"

"Surely," Orvaril interrupted, "there is an option we are simply not seeing."

"But of course there is," came a voice from behind them. Kendra spun around, daggers instantly in her hands.

"Hello Blacksmoke," she growled.

"You always make me feel so welcome, my dear." The man stood just a mere few feet behind them but held no weapons in his hands. Kendra looked slightly nervous but, after several moments, slowly put away her blades.

"What brings you around on this fine night?" she asked, sarcasm dripping from her voice. Cor'il rested his left hand on his sword. He had observed Kendra's behavior around this man and, while they had never fought, she was always very cautious around him which he took to mean that he should be as well.

"Oh," he replied, "the usual. Just keeping an eye on my city. It wasn't difficult to find you three. You're sticking out like a gortog in a goat pen."

"If you are going to help us then be quick about it, kind sir." Orvaril seemed to have both complimented *and* insulted The Blacksmoke in the same sentence. "We wish to be off hastily."

"Right," The Blacksmoke grumbled. He adjusted his hat, pulling it down a bit over his face. "Of course you do. And because I am such a giving individual I am going to help you out of the city without raising a big stink with the guards."

"And why do you want to help us?" Cor'il inquired. He certainly did not trust this man even though The Blacksmoke had yet to try to harm him.

"My reasons are my own. Do not concern yourself with them." He turned and began walking into an alleyway. "But if you follow me I can most certainly get you out of the city."

Cor'il, Kendra, and Orvaril looked at one another. Kendra shrugged and followed after The Blacksmoke, with Cor'il and Orvaril close behind.

"One of these days," Cor'il whispered, "we are going to put too much trust in this man."

"Let's hope this is not that day," Kendra whispered back.

Chapter 3

Captain Jarel Forsch sat at his desk, staring into the mirror on the wall. His brown hair was growing a little long for his liking. He preferred to keep it extremely short, but he had not the time lately to have it trimmed. *When I actually get time to breathe I will have one of the servants take care of it. Should that ever happen.*

There was a lot to be done. There was *always* a lot to be done. Even with as many lieutenants as he had put in position, he still had more to do than there were hours to do it in. With every day came more new recruits and, with more recruits came more problems. He was having difficulty housing and supplying them all within the walls of Sulbar. No matter how many squads were out patrolling the surrounding lands, the Red Swords' numbers within the city still swelled.

Since the orcs' attack on Sulbar last summer, Forsch had had no problem finding soldiers to fill his ranks. The Council was more than happy to house the soldiers—at least for now—to make certain that there were enough eager blades to defend the city should another attack occur. But the Council thought small. Forsch didn't think they understood the wider implications of the first invasion. His scouts reported wandering tribes of orcs and, more frighteningly, other strange creatures roaming about the hills outside the city. It was entirely possible that they hadn't seen even a fraction of the danger they faced.

There was a knock on his door. He stood and walked across the room to stand by a small end table.

"Come in," he said. A rather short, round man with receding black hair walked through the door and shut it behind him. Forsch filled two goblets with golden mead and handed one to the man, who received it but did not drink.

"Thank you, m'lord," he said, adjusting his ornate, white robes around him. Emblazoned on the front was a sword with a red blade pointing downward, surrounded by a golden circle—the symbol of the Red Swords. "What do you require of me?"

"Well, Fordaril," Forsch sat down and reclined in a plush, black chair and pausing a moment to gaze into his glass. "I hear we have found a boy with, shall I say... unique abilities?"

He knew that every step he took had to be filled with caution and, while he placed some trust in Fordaril, he also knew that the man was extremely intelligent and not without his own agenda. Through word of mouth, he learned that Fordaril had earned the nicknames "The Snake" and "Forktongue" among Forsch's soldiers. However, while Forsch was wise to be suspicious of him, the man did have a way of providing useful information.

"Aye, m'lord."

"Come, sit with me."

"I would much rather stand, m'lord."

"Very well."

They remained in silence for several moments. Forsch wondered if the little man distrusted him as much as he distrusted Fordaril. He suppressed a smile as he sipped from his goblet. He then swirled the mead around in his cup and watched it play with the lamplight.

"So," Forsch continued, "this boy..."

"Aye, the boy." Fordaril paced, staring into his goblet. No doubt he wondered if there was something in it. A man in his position always survived longer if he was suspicious of every little thing. It must be a tiring existence, though. "Yes. He has exhibited quite extraordinary ability. Unfortunately, he also has exhibited a frightening lack of control."

"Oh?"

"Aye, m'lord." Fordaril stopped pacing. "My sources report that he nearly destroyed an entire barn by shaking it to its foundations."

"And what leads you to believe it was accidental?" Forsch took another sip from his goblet. The mead was sweet, with subtle hints of hibiscus. It was much preferable to the last few bottles he had acquired.

"He was inside the barn cleaning out one of the stalls," Fordaril continued. "When the building started to shake, he fled, screaming. He was obviously frightened—not a common reaction from someone who would've known what he was doing..."

"Could it have been someone else nearby?"

"There was no one else nearby, m'lord." Fordaril finally drank from his goblet. Forsch suppressed a grin. There was nothing in the mead, but he did so enjoy toying with the man. They had only known each other for a relatively short amount of time, but it often felt as if they were old friends with a tumultuous relationship.

"Interesting." Forsch put his feet up on a small stool. He set his goblet down on the table beside the chair. "And where is this boy now?"

"We are... not sure, m'lord." Fordaril bowed his head, refusing to make eye contact. "He spotted one of my agents and fled into the forest. My agent felt it prudent not to follow in case another accident should occur."

"That is unfortunate, Forktongue." He wasn't sure why he used one of Fordaril's nicknames but it seemed to carry more weight—as if Forsch knew more about the man than Fordaril expected. Hopefully it conveyed his frustration. "Since the inception of the Red Swords," he continued, "We have found three—now four—individuals who dare to commit blasphemy through abilities which they derive directly from The Abyss. They spit in our very faces and threaten to destroy us all. You have let two of those four slip through our fingers. Thus, I would say, your record of apprehending these targets is lousy at best."

"M'lord," Fordaril stammered, "you must understand that apprehending these people is not easy. It is impossible for us to know how much power they wield or what they can do with it. They have all been unskilled which, despite what you would think, makes them even more difficult to capture."

"Our numbers are growing." Forsch abruptly stood, nearly knocking over the goblet next to him. "The city is bulging at the seams, and every day brings in more recruits. If it is more men that you require, then all you need to do is ask. I've got roaming bands of orcs to deal with, not to mention there are reports of other... things causing problems." He approached Fordaril, stopping within inches of him. "We are at war on every front, Fordaril. It is our duty to keep the Realm safe. We can't do that if we have these cursed individuals roaming about, using power that could decimate all of us. They *must* be dealt with."

"I," Fordaril stammered, "understand, m'lord. The safety of the Realm is of the utmost importance. I will ensure that none of my agents travels alone."

"A wise plan." Forsch replied, backing off a bit. "And what of the individual we *did* apprehend last week?" He walked to the window and looked out. The city went about its day, blissfully unaware of the danger lurking in the lands beyond. They had no inkling as to the delicate peace they clung to.

"We interrogated him extensively."

"And?"

"He was inexperienced, m'lord. He could not tell us how he had set fire to... water. Once we were sure there was nothing more to learn from him, we had him executed as per your orders, m'lord."

"And? What did you learn from him?"

"Sadly, very little." Fordaril looked disappointed but did not divert his gaze this time. "The man called himself a... Threadspinner."

"A *Threadspinner*? What in The Abyss is that?"

"I know not, m'lord. He said that he had just recently come into his abilities. He had little else to say before his head was removed from his shoulders. But he said it was a gift, not a curse."

"One man's gift is the rest of the Realm's curse, Fordaril."

The two stood in silence for a spell. Forsch continued gazing out the window at the innocents outside. Any one of them could be cursed and not know it. Ever since that boy had surfaced in Elston, blasting everything around him, these *Threadspinners* had started popping up. Was there a connection?

"We need a castle."

"Excuse me, m'lord?"

"We have outgrown Sulbar." He turned to face Fordaril. *Yes, this is what we need. Better organization and consolidation of power. We can show the Realm the might we have at our fingertips.* "The Red Swords require their own fortress."

"M'lord," Fordaril replied, uncertainty dripping from his lips, "We don't have the coffers for something like that."

"Then *find* the coin!" he growled, balling his fists tightly. "If the people of this Realm wish to be safe, then they are going to need to make some sacrifices!"

"But, m'lord—"

"Understand this." Forsch looked Fordaril in the eyes. "I watched good soldiers die because we were completely unprepared when orcs attacked Sulbar. Elston was nearly overrun and ransacked last summer because the city was unaware of the threat. We can no longer live as we have in the past. There is a storm on the horizon, Fordaril, and it will sweep us all away if we sit idly by and let it. Procure the resources we need. I don't care how."

"Aye, m'lord."

"And find a suitable location to build me what I require. I don't care how you do it."

"Aye, m'lord. It will be done."

"And, Fordaril?"

"What is it?"

"Make it happen *quickly*. We've no time to waste."

"Aye, m'lord."

"You are dismissed."

Fordaril set down his goblet and promptly exited. Forsch watched the people of Sulbar walk past the window. Forsch knew a little something about Sulbar that many did not. Sulbar sat atop an extensive supply of gold—a fact about which he was eventually going to make Fordaril aware. First, however, he had to make sure that his secret would be kept safe.

The Council of Four would have to be swayed, of course. If he could convince them to supply him with the gold he needed, then the Red Swords would be able to protect the Realm. If they did not share his vision, however..."

Then I will simply have to take over the operation myself. I will not allow innocent people to die at the hands of orcs or Threadspinners or whatever else is out there.

After the attack on Elston, the boy had simply vanished. All the leaflets his men had handed out and posted had done no good. Either nobody knew of his whereabouts or they weren't telling. Many people he had talked to had said that they thought the boy had *helped* the city by defending it! They obviously had no idea how preposterous that sounded.

There was supposedly another who quite obviously *had* helped in the defense of the city. Forsch had heard hundreds of reports of a boy who used his axe to great efficiency, cutting down orcs and trolls as if they were mere weeds in a garden. Unfortunately, Forsch didn't know where this boy had run off to, either. *But if I could locate him and bring him under the wing of the Red Swords, he would be a monumental addition to our forces. We could use a warrior like that. The Realm could use a warrior like that.*

If he truly *was* just a boy, then he could very possibly become a more ferocious warrior. Men unquestioningly followed great warriors into battle. Those great warriors inspire and lead not just with words but with their deeds as well. Fordaril's agents could find him. Until now, Forsch hadn't pursued this avenue very aggressively, but mayhaps it was time to explore it. *If it's not just hearsay, that is.*

There was a lot to be done. Even without his new initiatives, the daily administrative tasks required of him were almost overwhelming. He knew that he should offload many of them to advisors or underlings, but he didn't trust anyone enough... not yet. *Hopefully, once the foundation is sturdy enough, I can trust others to build the walls.*

A fitting analogy since his agenda involved constructing a fortress. He had no set plans for an actual structure yet, but he knew that it would have to be secure and it would have to support thousands of soldiers within its walls—hopefully tens of thousands. It quite possibly could become the largest keep in the entire Realm. With a solid base of operations, the Red Swords could more easily defend The Realm. It would be a symbol—a symbol of might. It would inspire confidence and, yes, fear if necessary. *And Sulbar could be just the beginning.*

It was a start, but it would take much more than a keep to combat the evils encroaching upon The Realm. It bothered him that these people were out there, commanding energies straight from The Abyss itself. They were a threat to everyone in The Realm—including themselves. It was bad enough that they didn't seem to have control of their abilities but, what if they *did*? Forsch had heard the tales—how the one boy was able to rain destruction down upon Elston, breaching its walls and decimating man and orc alike. To combat abilities like that, mayhaps he needed similar abilities.

That kid had seemed to command complete control of his abilities, and he had used them with brutal efficiency. For a brief moment, Forsch pondered the possibility of bringing *him* under the command of the Red Swords. With that kind of power at their command they would be a serious force, able to defend The Realm much more easily.

But that kind of raw power could ultimately not be contained. It needed to be stamped out—to be snuffed like a candle. No, his hopes lay in the other boy—the warrior. He couldn't very well lead the Red Swords against these so-called Threadspinners if he had them among his ranks, could he? And he could make an example by eliminating this target. With that show of might, who would oppose the Red Swords then?

It was a puzzle, and right now all the pieces were scattered about the table. But they would come together. Unfortunately, time was not on their side.

Chapter 4

Sparks showered the forge as Dalinil's hammer struck the white-hot metal, the clatter of metal on metal ringing in his ears. Sweat ran down his face as he raised the hammer and brought it down again several times before he inspected his work. He stared into his forge's fire, watching embers glow and flames burst into the air. The amount of heat given off was astounding, but it was beginning to wane.

No, that won't do. It must be hotter.

Dalinil reached out, embracing the Threads around him as he had seen Cor'il do many times. His surroundings blurred as the Threads came into view, shining like beacons on a foggy night. They ran from one object to another—bricks, stones, the ground, the sky, and plants. He noticed several red and white Threads, but those were not what he was interested in.

The black Threads were few. They were scarce here in Elston and sometimes Dalinil had to work to find them, but they were the most useful to him. He located three black Threads nearby and singled them out. When he called out to them, they obeyed and snapped to him, filling him with glorious energy. He reveled in their simultaneous warmth and cold, feeling them flow through his entire body. No matter how many times he embraced them, he always enjoyed the feeling of immense power.

This method of using the Threads was still foreign to him. This may have been how Cor'il used them, but he was different. Dalinil could only describe how he used the Threads as "melding" with them. He became them and they became him.

He channeled that power into the fire until he *was* the fire. He felt it burning, lapping at the air above it, and he commanded it to burn hotter.

And hotter it burned. He saw the massive bricks around the fire glow and backed off a bit—not wanting to damage his forge. Once he was sure it was hot enough, he begrudgingly released control of the Threads and resumed hammering.

This would be the finest weapon he had ever created—possibly the finest weapon ever created by *anyone*. Smithing had always been his strength, and he knew it. His weapons and armor had been the pride of Ten Kings but he felt he never received the credit he deserved. Here in Elston people appreciated his work.

It was true—he used the Threads to help him in his endeavors. He could produce a hotter fire and cooler water, but he could also bolster his own strength. Each clatter of his hammer was unmatched by any other smith in The Realm—of that he was certain. And he had already gained recognition for the quality of his wares. Was it possible that he had *always* been using the Threads and simply hadn't known what he was doing?

He was very young for someone so skilled, a fact that had surprised everyone he knew in Ten Kings—including himself. If he had all along been using the Threads, then that would explain a lot. With his abilities, he could shape his creations as he hammered them, using the Threads to flatten or bend each project. There was nothing he couldn't create.

His current project, however, was proving more difficult and he was forced to shape it with hammer and fire.

He brought the hammer down on the two-headed axe blade. Iron ore from the Worldsblood Peaks had been scarce until recently, when its supply had begun flowing again. Dalinil had procured a small amount for special projects and requests. It was rumored to make the finest steel and, thus far, was living up to that reputation. Blood iron could be made into a weapon so sharp and durable that it supposedly could cut down a steelwood tree without breaking or even dulling the edge. Its red tinge made it easily identifiable. It also appeared to be resistant to the Threads, which meant that Dalinil had to craft his axe the traditional, slower way.

The trouble was, it was also much more difficult to work with and required a considerably hotter fire to shape. Thus far, Dalinil was the only smith who could produce more than one piece a month. In fact, he could churn out one or two a week. This had steadily filled his coffers with more coin but, in the case of his own weapon, had slowed him down considerably.

He could have had this axe head done already if it weren't for his quest for perfection. He had eschewed all other projects for days just to get this one finished. The shaft alone had taken him weeks to perfect—steelwood with a blood iron pommel on the end. This weapon's might would truly be unmatched.

He was fashioning the head of the axe in the form of dragon wings. Though he had never encountered an *actual* dragon—he still did not believe they were real—there were plenty of pictures in children's books to work from. This would truly be a work of art.

And then... well, then I will clear my name. He felt rage welling up inside him from the very thought, but he suppressed it, channeling his anger into each hammer strike, instead.

That particular task would be more difficult. He wasn't quite sure how he would accomplish it. What he *did* know was that he grew tired of always looking over his shoulder and trying to remain hidden. Two trackers had managed to find him, and both had met with death quickly. The men of House Emory did not appear to relent, it seemed, and he began to wonder if it was not easier to simply eliminate everyone in it rather than try to clear his name. Intrigue was not his arena; combat was. He felt a grin cross his lips.

He had hoped his reputation from the attack on Elston would keep any would-be assassins or trackers at bay. And mayhaps it had. It was entirely possible that, instead of just two trackers, there would have been more. Even two, however, was too many for his liking. He wanted to be left alone, but it went even deeper than that. He had grown tired of being challenged by those who sought to take advantage of him.

No, he did not kill Lord Emory. But someone had, and Dalinil had somehow taken the blame for it. When the city guard had come for him, he had been caught completely unaware and he had fled, probably confirming his guilt in the city's eyes. He was the least of The Realm's problems now, and yet Emory's men persisted. *Hopefully some of them have ended up in orc stew pots during their quest to find me.*

He brought the hammer down on the axe head with furious anger and strength—a force that would have shattered any other weapon. He reveled at this metal's strength and durability as he hammered again, shaping it into his most beloved creation.

The natural red hue of the metal was intriguing to Dalinil. Iron itself could normally hold a slight reddish tint, but blood iron went beyond that. It was not the normal ruddy, rusty red, but instead, it was a more vibrant shade—subtle but obviously there.

The color itself seemed to vary. Of the various chunks Dalinil had acquired, some of them were of a color that seemed a bit more muted than other pieces. Whether the quality of the ore was related to the color, Dalinil did not know. To him it all seemed the same, and it was beautiful.

The sun was beginning to rise. Its first rays shone directly into the forge, forcing Dalinil to shield his eyes and switch his direction. The fire was waning again and Dalinil was getting tired. Not only had he been up all night working, but he was fatigued from both keeping his strength up and from keeping the fire so hot.

He'd broken two hammers. Blood iron was stubborn, and it took its toll not only on Dalinil but on his tools as well. Twice he had shattered the hammer's handle and had been forced to replace it. This slowed down his progress, and it irritated him, building up anger within him. He had to be careful how much strength he channeled from the Threads. Take too much and it could result in another broken hammer or, worse, a shattered axe blade. He did not like the idea of completely starting over, especially since his supply of blood iron was limited.

He was getting close, though. The axe blade was taking shape nicely. Mayhaps one or two more days and it would be ready to affix to the steelwood shaft. For a moment, he stopped to ponder the situation. He had been focused for quite a while just on creating this weapon but, as he now realized, he didn't know what his next move was—how was he going to clear his name?

Obviously, the best place to start would be Ten Kings. It would also be the most perilous. He was certain the city guard and the Emory family would be watching for him. But he knew the city well and he might be able to find a way to remain concealed from prying eyes. He would have to stay hidden while he investigated, and he had no idea where to start. He was certainly nowhere near as adept as Kendra in these matters. Subterfuge and hiding in the shadows were not his proficiencies.

Upon recalling Kendra, his thoughts turned to Cor'il. He had some nerve, asking Dalinil to travel with them, and to where? His homeland? How did such matters concern him when he had more important things to tend to? How dare they interrupt his work with their petty requests. Obviously, they had no respect for his situation.

The streets slowly began to fill with people as the sun continued its daily ascent into the sky. The noise around Dalinil did not distract him, however, as he continued to shape his masterpiece. It wasn't until a good two or three hours later that a man approached him. He was a rather stout man, well-muscled with dark hair and a thick mustache to match. Dalinil remembered him—Luke Malick.

"Good morn," the man said, stepping under the roof.

"Good morn, Luke," Dalinil replied. He did not stop his work, and he put forth effort not to sound annoyed at being disturbed. "What can I do for you today?"

"I wanted to check on the five swords I asked for. How are they coming along?" The man was looking around as if trying to find the weapons. His nosey glances only served to irritate Dalinil, but he kept both his composure and concentration. "You seem to be taking longer than usual. I feel that your work is slipping."

"I've not started on them yet, sir," he replied calmly, holding up the axe blade to inspect it. "This particular project has been taking all of my attention." He could feel his irritation growing.

"When do you think they will be done? You know I came to you several weeks ago. Any other smith in the city would have gotten them done by now. At the very least they would have *started* on them by now!" The man was annoyed. Dalinil could hear it in his voice. He tried very hard to remain calm.

"I am not any other smith, sir."

"What?"

"You obviously value my craftsmanship, else you would have gone to another smith by now, correct?"

"Aye, but that—"

"Well then, sir," Dalinil growled, "I would advise you to be patient. If you do not like the current situation, then you have two options."

"Oh really? And what are those?" The man inched forward, now standing very close to Dalinil who was unfazed by his advances.

Dalinil sighed, setting the axe blade down on the side of the forge. He turned to the man who had his arms crossed and a scowl on his face.

"You can simply wait a while longer until I get your order completed, or you can obviously take your order somewhere else." Dalinil turned back to the forge.

"And what if I don't like either of those options? I demand that you start on my weapons *now!*"

"If neither of those two options are to your liking," Dalinil continued, still with his back to the man, "then you have a third option."

"And what would that be, boy?"

"You can kiss my ass."

"Did I hear you correctly? Did you say—"

"Aye," Dalinil growled, turning to face Luke. He was at least a head taller than the man, so he had to look down a bit—a fact that amused him at the moment. Anger warmed him, flowing through him as if it were his very blood.

Luke's arms bulged as he balled his hands into fists, flexing, and the scowl on his face deepened as he stared at Dalinil. He was quite sturdy, but he would be making a mistake if he thought he wanted to get into a fight of some sort.

"How dare you—"

"No," Dalinil shouted, taking a step forward. He was now mere inches from the man. "How dare *you*! How dare you try to tell me how to run my business! This particular project I am working on is very important! If that is not to your liking then, as I said, you have other options!"

A few people in the street stopped to watch the spectacle. Thankfully, the city guard appeared to be absent.

"You're a bloody crook!" Luke shouted.

"Do not besmirch my name!"

Dalinil could feel his blood boiling. He had embraced the Threads without realizing it, channeling black and red together in a braid that flowed through his body, filling him with fire and emptiness. He stepped even closer, his nose barely touching Luke's, and stared into the man's eyes.

They held fear and surprise. It wasn't until a few seconds had passed that Dalinil finally realized his hand was gripped securely around the man's throat, squeezing. It would be so easy to squeeze just a little harder, to kill this ungrateful man. He felt the urge—it beckoned to him, begging him to squeeze harder and snap the puny man's neck.

Calmly, and without a word, Dalinil lifted Luke off the ground as if the man weighed nothing. Luke choked and gasped but otherwise uttered no sound as Dalinil moved out of the smith, carrying the shocked man.

Once Dalinil reached the street he flung Luke into the air like he was a mere child's doll. The man hit the ground hard, choking and coughing while massaging his throat. He slowly got to his feet and tried to yell something but choked on his words and dropped to one knee.

Dalinil didn't wait. He returned to his forge and stoked the coals, heating the axe blade. He paid no attention to anything around him except for the hammer that shaped his future weapon. Luke had gotten what he deserved and would, no doubt, not forget this. He had spoken an untruth about Dalinil and, therefore, deserved punishment. Dalinil felt that he let the man off easy.

I shall no longer be forced to suffer lies and hatred against me. I'll show them all—especially anyone who would sully my name or stand in my way. Still, it would appear that I need to expedite things a bit.

No doubt the city guard would be paying him a visit sometime soon. He would need to be ready for that—it wouldn't be pleasant. But Dalinil was prepared to do whatever was necessary. If he worked through the night again he *might* be able to leave Elston with a finished weapon before sunup. If he could just lay low until then it would make things much easier. He would not settle for anything less than perfect, even if it meant that he had to take on the entire city guard by himself.

His hammer struck the axe blade. With every swing Dalinil felt satisfaction as he heard the ring of metal against metal and watched the sparks fly. He knew it might be a while before he would be able to practice his trade again and that saddened him. *I will have to leave all of this behind but, then, it wasn't mine anyway, was it?*

He was consumed with purpose and single-minded in his task. At first, he had questioned his own plans—whether there was another way to prove his innocence or even if he should bother. He still thought that he could escape far south to Scorovia and mayhaps live without worry. However, the more that he thought about it, the more he became angry that everyone believed *him* to have actually committed the crime. He wanted vindication. He wanted *revenge*. The hatred burned brightly within him and he let it consume him, fueling each swing of his hammer.

The man he had killed so that he could take over this smithy had not been difficult to dispatch, and Dalinil simply told anyone who inquired that he had left for another town. Mallory had been his name. Dalinil was unsure if that had been the man's first or last name. It didn't matter. He was gone and easily disposed of. Someone else would probably take up shop after Dalinil left the city. Of course, he had plenty of orders which would go unfulfilled but, then, he'd never intended to complete them in the first place. The only important item would get done tonight, hopefully.

And then I can return home.

Chapter 5

Arcturas looked out his window at the forest beyond. The sun's rays dappled the foliage below the canopy, creating patches of light and shadow. He clasped his hands behind his back and sighed, unsure of where he was today. To be sure, it was always an odd feeling, but certainly not something to worry over. It did not take long to get used to and, in the end, it really didn't matter. He was always exactly where he needed to be. The Great Machine saw to that.

Obviously, that did not mean that he always understood his purpose. In fact, when he stopped to think about it, he *rarely* understood his purpose. He never let that hinder him, however, and everything became apparent with time. He was patient, and that was crucial to his—and Ilathri's—purpose.

They were on a hill—that much was apparent. He could see the gradual slope and the tops of some of the shorter maple and elm trees below. For a moment, he thought he recognized this place, but that moment was fleeting. He had felt that before. Mayhaps he *had* been here in the past, or mayhaps he merely wanted to believe that there was some sort of familiarity.

The front door creaked a little as he pulled it open and walked outside into the sunlight. The trees of the forest grew in his yard, in the road, and on sidewalks. Sometimes Ilathri supplanted itself in exchange for the terrain and sometimes it appeared in harmony with it. Arcturas wondered what happened once the city vanished and moved on to another location. He always found it ironic just how little he knew about many things when he himself was supposed to instruct others.

Arcturas closed his eyes and leaned his head back, taking in the morning's warmth and the wonderful scent of the forest. He stretched and yawned, feeling a pop in his back. *That's a new one. I guess I can add that to my collection of old body noises.* Several people were up and tending to their daily chores already. The city, of course, looked quite different from the last time he had seen it. It never surprised him, but it *was* a little unnerving at times.

The buildings were the same—white and pristine and looking as if they were priceless works of art. The roads and sidewalks, however, were a drab grey dotted with black. The layout of the city was different than last time and, though this was normal, it created quite a difficulty when one needed to find a particular person.

Braelus approached from down the Main street. He stopped next to a house, picked a flower, and smelled it. Arcturas grinned when he realized he did not know whose house it actually was. Most likely it was an empty house. There were too many of those these days.

"Good morning, Braelus." He clapped a hand on the boy's back, nearly causing him to drop the flower—a daisy, if Arcturas was not mistaken. The petals were white but the center, instead of being yellow, was a dull gray.

To most, this would seem to be merely a freak of nature— something odd but nothing of consequence. Arcturas knew better. Very few things in the world were without meaning. He took note and filed it away in his head for future consideration.

"Good morning, sir," the boy responded, twirling the flower between his thumb and index finger.

"It appears we're in a forest again."

"What do you mean, sir?"

Arcturas often forgot that not everyone saw Ilathri the same way. In fact, as far as he knew, he was the only one who understood even a few of the secrets that Ilathri held. He had insight, yes, but very little understanding. He may have been the only individual who noticed that the city had changed both in layout and in color.

It was as if everyone else had no memory of Ilathri before its present incarnation.

Sure, sometimes someone would notice that there was something askew, but they could never point out exactly what it was. There was a time when Arcturas would try to puzzle it out of them, but eventually, he grew tired of the effort and simply moved on.

"Never mind, Braelus. It's of little consequence."

"Oh, okay then."

Arcturas began slowly walking down the street with Braelus quickly following. The air was fresh and fragrant with the many scents of the forest—leaves damp with the morning dew, flowers, and grass. Sometimes he felt a little guilty that his people lived in perfect harmony and peace within the walls of the city while, outside, the world struggled to find equilibrium.

"It took me a little while to find your house this time," Braelus finally said. He looked a bit troubled and confused.

"Oh?"

"Aye, sir." The boy paused for a moment. Arcturas could tell that he was having difficulty finding the words to explain himself. "It doesn't make sense but, your house wasn't where I thought it should be."

"No, Braelus," Arcturas responded, "it indeed does not make sense." The fact that Braelus had this problem intrigued Arcturas. Nobody else ever displayed that kind of confusion. He was a remarkable boy—Arcturas had always known this, but he was surprised by Braelus at every turn.

"I apologize, sir." Braelus sheepishly bowed his head a bit. "It was silly."

"There is absolutely no cause for apologies, my young friend," Arcturas laughed. "Simply because something does not make sense does not mean that it is imaginary. Your instincts are sharp. You would do well to listen to them."

"I will endeavor to do so, sir."

They walked together in silence for a few minutes. Braelus repeatedly glanced at the flower he held and, though Arcturas was not sure if the boy noticed the deviant color, he was certain his pupil was suspicious of something. The boy kept looking as if he wanted to say something but, every time, stopped himself. *He is advancing. He is touched by the Great Machine and his knowledge will only grow as he gets older.*

"There is another," he blurted, "isn't there?"

"You never fail to surprise me, Braelus. You are truly extraordinary."

"I am but a grain of sand on a vast beach compared to you and your knowledge, sir."

"My knowledge will seem miniscule to you someday," Arcturas laughed. "You will eclipse what I know."

"That is kind of you, sir, but—"

"And humble, too." He laughed some more. The boy nervously laughed with him, but Arcturas could tell he wasn't really sure what was so funny. "But you are indeed correct. There *is* another. His arrival is imminent."

"But... how? How is there more than one?"

Arcturas stopped and looked around. *I do not remember this place. I have no memory of it.* The buildings themselves looked almost alien to him. He recognized his fellow brethren but the surroundings were completely foreign.

"It is often not our place to ask *how* or *why* but merely to play with the cards which have been dealt to us. Truthfully, I wish I knew, but I have my theories. I will fully admit that it is quite unexpected. I do not believe the world has ever seen two Threadweavers sharing it at the same time."

"What do you think it means?"

"If we were to look at life as a game we could simply say that the rules have changed. I believe something big has been set in motion. It cannot be stopped but it can be guided along its path. But, with it, there is uncertainty and danger. I fear dark times ahead."

"So, what are we to do?" Braelus' confusion now turned to a look of worry.

"We will welcome him and, hopefully, the purpose will reveal itself to us. The Great Machine's designs are rarely clear, but there are clues that we can see if we look hard enough."

"But there is... something else," the boy continued, "isn't there? You've felt it as I have, right?"

Arcturas, once again, felt both surprise and pride.

"Aye." Braelus' connection to the Threads and the Great Machine was maturing at a phenomenal rate. It astounded even Arcturas. When he thought back to his own abilities and advancement, he remembered their ascension as being quite rapid, but not at the level that Braelus was experiencing. *Not only have the rules of the game changed but it appears that there are several new pieces in play as well.*

"Do you know what it is?"

"I have felt it," Arcturas continued. He paused and tried to coalesce his thoughts into something that would make a modicum of sense. Most of what he had experienced were feelings and senses on the fringe of perception—certainly nothing tangible. He considered them to be dots of light in the vast darkness. There were, however, most definitely a few things he knew for sure. "If I am correct, then there is still much yet to be learned about the Threads and our world."

"What do you mean?"

"Well," Arcturas began, resuming his pace down the street. "As with the day there is night, correct?"

"Aye."

"They are counterparts. It appears that the Great Machine has its own counterpart—a sibling."

"The Dark Machine."

"Aye." Arcturas could not hide his surprise. "Your perception serves you *very* well. What else do you know about it?"

"That is all, sir. I can't explain fully how I even know that is what it is called except that... it *told* me, somehow. But I can't feel it or sense it at all."

"Nor can I. Despite searching through all the relevant texts I could find, I could uncover no additional information about it in any of our archives. As it would happen, I do have some insight into its nature."

Arcturas stopped and sat down on a nearby bench. He recognized this area. It was good to know that not everything had changed.

"I can only assume that the Dark Machine is as timeless as the Great Machine. It provides its own Threads and I believe these Threads are utilized by the Great Machine to some extent... and vice-versa. How much it touches or affects our world, I do not know. We are only custodians of the Great Machine because the construct wills it. Obviously, the Dark Machine does not."

"But what are we to do about it?"

"Why, nothing!"

Braelus sat down on the bench, obviously perplexed. Arcturas watched as worry crept into the boy's eyes, replacing any curiosity that was left. The boy sighed and bowed his head.

"The Dark Machine means us harm," he finally said, "doesn't it?"

"What leads you to believe that?"

"Extrapolation. The Great Machine is the light and the Dark Machine is, well, the opposite. One is good and one is evil."

"Now, see," Arcturas argued, "that is where I believe you are incorrect."

"How do you mean?"

"I do not believe that there is a good and evil side to either construct. Those concepts are for men to squabble over. I think it is more accurately explained as order and chaos. Essentially, as we've always put it, The Goodness and The Abyss—these are not accurate concepts. They are ideas invented by people who had little understanding of the Realm. No, the Great Machine and the Dark Machine are no more good or evil than a rock is."

"A rock?" Braelus laughed nervously.

"Aye, a rock can be used as a tool to hammer a nail or to be a part of a wall. But a rock can also be thrown at someone as a weapon. The rock has no choice in how it is used; it is neither good nor evil."

"The Dark Machine spins the black Threads, doesn't it?"

"Aye, that is what I believe. Those black Threads have a rather unique effect on the world as well as on those who use them. However, once again, they are just a tool and the Dark Machine is the tool's creator. Until now we always thought that the black Threads were a part of the Great Machine like all other Threads. Apparently, we were mistaken."

"But why are we just *now* learning this?"

Arcturas could tell that the boy was becoming frustrated. He himself was unsure how to treat the situation. He had to remind himself that it was not their place to act, but rather to observe, and to guide others. This made things slightly less frustrating.

"Again, the *why* often doesn't matter. Our knowledge of the Threads expands when it is meant to. Mayhaps it is related to our impending visitor. It certainly would be a wild coincidence if these new developments are completely unrelated."

"So," Braelus posited, "you think that having two Threadweavers and the discovery of an entirely new source of the Threads are related?"

"Did you not feel the tremors? When she died, did you not feel the Threads—"

"They amplified, right?" Arcturas could see the excitement in Braelus' eyes. He was assembling a puzzle and had just found an important piece. "When the Threadweaver—Antina—died, the Threads became even more powerful, didn't they?"

"You are correct, my boy. Her power returned to the Great Machine but some of it escaped. I wasn't sure at first, but it is undeniable now."

"What is?"

"Not only do we have two Threadweavers about, but I have felt... others—Threadspinners, they are called, and they have apparently not existed for quite a long time. They now command a small portion of the Threads' power, and mayhaps only one or two colors. This means that the Threads' power is now available for all with the potential to use it, which means that the world just became a much more dangerous place."

"And what of the first Threadweaver—Dalinil?"

"A storm is brewing in the West and I fear that he is the center of it—whether he knows it or not."

They sat in silence for a spell. Arcturas, as always, turned many thoughts over and over inside his mind. Braelus looked to be doing much the same thing. Arcturas could almost see the thoughts coalescing in his pupil's head as the boy tried to grasp the new world that was being shaped.

"What now?" the boy finally asked. Through nervous compulsion he had completely destroyed the daisy. It was nothing more than a stem, now. The petals all lay on the ground at his feet.

"We've got an unexpected second Threadweaver seeking us out. We must be ready to do whatever we can for him. So, for now, we do what we've always done."

"We wait?"

"Aye," Arcturas replied. "We wait."

"I have always made it my business to know who my enemies are before it is necessary."
—The Wisp

Chapter 6

Kendra crouched behind a wagon, watching an orc slowly sift through a garden, inspecting the plants by pulling them out of the ground and sniffing them. The brute obviously didn't like what it had discovered, because it uttered a disgusted grunt and promptly discarded the vegetable, which landed near a goblin who also sniffed it and decided it wasn't worth eating.

She sat down, her back to the wagon. From here she could see her friends hiding on the other side of some trees. They were doing a very poor job of it, sticking out like a razorbeast in a room full of kittens. The moon provided bright illumination in a cloudless sky, making them easy to spot. Fortunately, it made the orcs and goblins also easy to spot.

They had only been on the road for a day, but that day had been fraught with danger. Their travel was constantly hindered by the threat of enemies and, though they had thus far managed to avoid confrontation, Kendra had a feeling their fortune would not hold out forever. It appeared that orcs and their kin were becoming more common, making life in the Realm more perilous, let alone travel.

This was the third farm that they had visited and, so far, the only farm with orcs roaming about. The other two farms had been occupied, and the inhabitants had been suitably prepared for invaders. In fact, at the last farm, the family had almost attacked them when they tried to approach. Orvaril had suggested that they waste no time in moving onto another farm.

This one, however, appeared abandoned. *Or the people who lived here are dead. At this point, is there a difference?*

It had been Orvaril's idea—to find horses for faster travel. They certainly did not have enough coin to buy one horse, let alone three. And Kendra didn't think the idea of *stealing* horses would go over well. That left them with only one option, even though it was wildly improbable—find horses that had been abandoned. Given the state of this farm, that probability had just gone up.

There was, however, the complication of the orcs and goblins. Kendra had seen only a few, but she was sure there were probably more lurking about. They usually didn't wander around in small numbers unless they were scouts.

At first, she had pondered the idea of asking Cor'il to simply use his abilities to take care of everything, but he probably would have fought against that. He insisted that he did not wish to kill, but Kendra wondered if, mayhaps, he was afraid of what he could do—either accidentally or on purpose.

There also appeared to be limits to what he could do. Her observations had led her to believe that, whatever his powers were, they eventually wore him out. They were too valuable a resource to waste on a few simple orcs. Besides, this type of task was more suited to her talents. No, she was not an assassin, but she was the only one of the group who could catch them by surprise and dispatch them quietly.

She once again peered out from behind her cover and saw that the way was now clear. There were still several orcs and goblins about, but they had all wandered out of her path. She quickly moved through the garden and snuck behind a chicken coop, pausing behind it to formulate a plan.

She heard noises from within the small structure. The door was on the other side of the building but there was a window next to her. She peeked inside to see a goblin eating what appeared to be a chicken—probably long since expired, judging by the odor coming from inside. That fact apparently mattered not a bit to the filthy creature.

These beasts will eat anything, won't they? Her morbid curiosity got the best of her, and she watched it eat for a few moments before she finally decided it was wise to move on. There was a fence ahead and, beyond that, some piles of rubble or trash. She darted around the coop, vaulted over the fence and stopped behind the first pile.

She noticed the smell immediately.

It was a pile of neither rubble nor garbage. It was a pile of bodies, mostly orc but she saw a few human bodies as well. She inspected the next mound and found the same.

Kendra emptied her stomach as the smell assaulted her. *Pull yourself together. Now is not the time.* She forced herself to recover and, holding her breath, she scanned the area. Only one orc was visible from here, but it was chewing on something next to one of the other piles. She wanted to throw up again. *Whoever lived here apparently did a respectable job defending their home. I wonder how long they held out.*

Instead, she prepared to kill the creature. She drew two daggers from her sleeves but, just as she was about to make a move, she was interrupted when the goblin emerged from the chicken coop. Without a thought, she flung a dagger at it.

The blade missed its target and clattered harmlessly off the side of the building, attracting the goblin's attention.

The Abyss damn me!

She awkwardly flung the second knife, this time barely hitting the creature in the neck. It fell immediately but was still moving and screaming loudly. She closed the gap in an instant and finished the job. After she retrieved her daggers she ducked into the chicken coop to catch her breath.

I know you have never been good with throwing knives but that was terrible! You'll have to do better than that if you are going to survive!

A grunt from outside alerted her to an approaching enemy. The orc she had just seen had apparently heard her and felt the need to investigate further. *Great. I'm an amateur and clumsy! This is shaping up to be a fine evening. The Blacksmoke would've probably eliminated a dozen of these things by now. And, I'm sure, he'd never let me forget it.*

She waited a bit as the brute drew closer. She watched it approach and stop to... eat the dead goblin.

You know what? To The Abyss with all of this!

Kendra leapt from the chicken coop, onto the back of the hunched-over orc. In an instant, she had buried her daggers deep into it—one in its back and one in its neck. It thrashed about for a moment, shrieking through a mouth overflowing with blood, before it stopped moving altogether and collapsed to the ground.

"At least I did *something* right tonight," she muttered angrily, cleaning the blades and sliding them back into her sleeves. She quietly moved amongst the pile of corpses again until she spotted a large barn. Hope swelled up inside her, but she would have to cross an open field to get there.

"Alright," she muttered to herself, "this shouldn't be too difficult. There are only... one... two orcs and a goblin between here and there."

While Kendra did not relish the idea of having to deal with one, let alone multiple orcs, the problem was compounded by the fact that they were all three together and they weren't moving. It appeared they had found something to eat or were just lazy. That didn't matter. What *did* matter, however, was the fact that they were directly between her and the barn.

She briefly considered going around them, but that option wasn't much better. There was still no cover and there were other shapes wandering around in the darkness. At least she could take these three by surprise. She cursed Cor'il for refusing to use his power to make this easier. By now he probably could have had the entire farm cleared of any danger. *And possibly burned everything to a crisp in the process. Mayhaps that wouldn't be such a great idea after all.*

Kendra was unsure what degree of control Cor'il had over his abilities. He insisted that he indeed still had issues, though

Kendra had never seen him lose control. *Come on, Kendra, just figure this out and then you can investigate the barn.*

She was going to have to fight at least one of them face to face and that thought scared her. She was not a warrior or a soldier. She certainly wasn't an assassin! She used shadows and surprise to get the jump on her targets and, while she had occasionally fought face-to-face, her adversary had never been an orc. She didn't see how she could eliminate three enemies without any of them fighting back. Even being able to take out two of them that quickly was a stretch. *I'm afraid of a fair fight. I'm not sure whether that's funny or pathetic.*

Fortunately, she did not see any weapons on them. That was, however, an assumption based on her vision at night while they were at least 20 feet or so away. *So, I guess I can take out the biggest orc first and then—*

To her surprise, she found herself already running at the group. She often found that she best worked when she didn't stop to think about her actions. Sometimes it was as if her body reacted before her mind knew what was happening.

The first orc fell without a fight, stabbed in the back of the neck several times. The goblin immediately squealed and jumped to its feet. Kendra swung at it but, in its flailing panic, it slapped Kendra's hand away. She moved to the other orc and attacked it but was rebuffed again. She began to worry as fear set in. This fight was not going well for her. Any fight that lasted more than a few seconds immediately put her at a severe disadvantage. She attacked the orc again while trying to formulate a plan.

But the orc wasn't a "him." It was still muscular and repulsive but it had a slenderer build and its clothing suggested that it was not a warrior. *Was she his mate?*

A closer look at the goblin revealed him to be not a goblin at all, but an orc child. Kendra stopped, dumbfounded, and unsure what to do next. Killing a family—even orcs—seemed wrong somehow. *Of course, The Blacksmoke would have no qualms about it. He'd dispatch them no matter who or what they are.*

62

But, then, he probably would've killed them all without a fight. She hated the fact that she compared herself to him. He was a gortog's ass... but he was also very good at what he did.

And she was not The Blacksmoke. She wouldn't hesitate to rob a family blind and steal the tunics off their backs, but this was entirely different.

Before she could come to a decision, she was knocked backward several feet. She landed hard on her back and tried to catch her breath. Her chest ached from where the orc had just slammed into her and, before she could react, the creature had pounced on top of her. Kendra, still in a daze, barely managed to scramble out of the way and to her feet, narrowly escaping.

Her daggers lay somewhere on the ground, but she hadn't the time to find them. She slid two more out from her dress and took a deep breath.

The orc swung wildly at her, uttering pained grunts and cries, trying to grab Kendra, but missing her target. It was all Kendra could do to back away from the fury of blows the orc savagely threw. No, she was not a warrior orc, but she was a female whose probable mate had just been killed. That was much more dangerous.

Kendra clumsily swung her daggers, but she felt like a baby fighting a giant. Her blows were easily cast aside by the orc and it was all she could do to hang onto her weapons. She dodged as best she could, but was being forced backward toward the barn. The one time she tried to parry the orc's attacks she'd nearly broken her left arm. It now throbbed with sharp pain.

The fight was going poorly. She'd lost track of the child, and hoped that they had not attracted the attention of any other orcs in the area. Her focus was solely on the she-orc who still savagely advanced.

Kendra dodged another swing, ducked under another, and jumped to the side. Her foot caught on something and she staggered backwards, dropping both daggers as she struggled to stay upright, eventually tumbling to the ground. The orc took advantage of the situation and leapt into the air again, yelling in anger and triumph.

"Damn it!" Kendra yelled, trying to scramble away, but there was nowhere she could go. She could not reach any of her other daggers so she desperately grasped for something—anything—to use as a weapon and suddenly felt a familiar blade land under her palm.

She grabbed it and pointed it upward just as the orc landed on top of her. Kendra felt the orc's warm blood run down her arm and soak into her clothes. The she-orc's yellow eyes showed stunned surprise for a moment, but she quickly came to and flailed at Kendra who squirmed and dodged as best she could. Unfortunately, with a heavy orc on top of her, she could not dodge every blow, and the orc's clawed hands pummeled and raked at her.

Kendra jabbed the wicked knife further into the orc's stomach and twisted. The orc howled in pain, blood now running out of her mouth. Kendra continued, desperately trying to do whatever damage she could until, finally, the orc went limp and motionless.

Kendra sighed. She was sore all over, and she struggled to get out from under the heavy corpse. Finally, soaked in blood, she emerged, gasping for breath. Then she dropped to her knees and sobbed quietly, as much out of sadness as fear. The orc child was nowhere to be found. *Good. I don't wish to make the decision whether a child lives or dies. Even an orc.*

Kendra got up and looked around. She was alone in the quiet darkness. She cleaned off the dagger, using her skirts, and searched for her lost weapons. After finding two of the three, she quickly moved toward the barn which, except for a goblin outside, appeared completely empty.

"To The Abyss with you," she muttered, slinging the black dagger at the goblin. This time, her aim was true and, with only a slight gurgling sound, the goblin fell dead. *Get back here, dagger. I may have lost one of your friends but I'm not losing you.*

Just as she was about to pull the dagger out of the goblin's eye socket it jumped out on its own, somehow putting itself back in her hand. *Oh, now, that's handy! But how? Never mind right now. You've got to move quickly!*

She wiped the dagger off on the goblin's rags, tucked it back into its concealed sheath around her wrist, and then ducked inside the barn. A few glowing coals—remnants of a now dying fire—cast an eerie light about the otherwise dark barn. Kendra heard a horse's whinny and her spirits lifted.

She found a small, half-burned log that still glowed. Using it as a torch she fumbled around the barn and nearly tripped over the half-eaten body of a horse. She carefully stepped over it and made her way to the stalls. To her surprise, four of them were occupied. *The Goodness smiles upon us this night with great fortune! At least* something *is going right tonight.*

She got to work fitting bridles on three of them—a chestnut mare, gray stallion, and a brown stallion. There was no time to try to find saddles, so this would have to suffice. Once she had the horses ready she led them out. They were exceptionally well-behaved and eagerly followed her lead. *And my fortune continues!*

The fourth horse—a white stallion—whinnied and snorted as she started to leave. She turned around to see it trying to escape its stall.

"Oh, don't worry," she whispered. "I am not about to leave you here to become dinner." She quietly unlatched the door and it creaked open. The horse slowly walked out of the stall, following her to the entrance of the barn. "Alright, boy. You're free to go wherever your legs take you."

Kendra climbed up on the mare—a chestnut with white splotches—and, holding the reins of the other two, urged her new steed forward. The horse obliged willingly, and Kendra brought her to a slow trot. It was dangerous to ride a horse in the dark, but she didn't see that she had any other choice.

The two stallions also followed without any effort on Kendra's part. *Whoever these horses belonged to, they trained them extraordinarily well. I've never seen such behavior—not even from professionally trained animals back home in Alarantha.* That was saying a lot, since her parents had always hired the best trainers for their horses.

The white stallion was following them. He kept in stride with the other horses as Kendra urged hers to move a little faster. In the distance, she saw orcish shapes but, fortunately, they were too far away to notice or even catch up to her.

It wasn't long before she found the road and her companions. Both Cor'il and Orvaril looked a bit surprised. Obviously neither of them had expected her to find *one* horse, let alone four. Truth be told, she herself had felt much the same way.

"This one's mine," she said, pointing to her chestnut mare. "But you can certainly take your pick of the other three. The white one followed me home, so to speak."

Orvaril inspected the gray stallion and quickly chose him. Cor'il took a liking to the white horse. Once they had all gotten situated, they rode largely in silence, leaving the brown horse behind, until they found a good spot to camp.

As Kendra stared up at the stars, she replayed events in her head, trying to make sense of it all. Everything was no longer as black and white as she'd tried to believe—at least, not for her. Thinking of orcs as actual living creatures with families—and children—that altered her view. It was so much easier to think of them as mindless savages.

But they now had mounts which would hopefully make their travels both easier and safer. Hopefully they could avoid most danger from here on out, and Kendra wouldn't have to worry about what to do if they encountered another family of orcs.

Chapter 7

Dalinil awoke to a clap of thunder overhead. His eyes shot open and his left hand grasped his dragon wing axe, but he quickly relaxed once he saw no danger. He had fallen asleep sitting with his back up against a tree. His neck was stiff but he felt otherwise rested—a fortunate condition, given that he had a long road ahead of him.

Elston was behind him—for now, just a memory along with all the people within. He had plenty of money, but he preferred to travel on foot rather than on horseback. He wasn't that fond of horses and saw no need to waste coin on one. Instead he kept off the road in case any interested parties were out looking for him—Lord Emory's men or otherwise. He wouldn't be surprised if The Blacksmoke wanted him dead for some reason. He did not trust that man, even though the two had never butted heads.

Thunder rolled. While there was no rain yet, the sky threatened to pour at any moment. Occasionally, he got a peek at the clouds through the forest canopy—gray and dark. Lightning sporadically lit up the area as if to warn him of an impending downpour. It all kept him on edge.

Dalinil leaned back against the tree, closing his eyes and trying to relax. His thoughts wandered to the situation in which he found himself, and ultimately, what he was going to do once he reached Ten Kings. He had thought about it a lot and, even now, he still was completely unsure of what he was going to do.

It wasn't that he didn't feel confident in a fight—quite the opposite, actually. He was not afraid of battle. In fact, combat was where he felt the most comfortable. But he needed to make it to Ten Kings quickly and quietly. It would all be made much easier if he did so secretly so that he had time to formulate a plan.

That being said, he was not opposed to fighting his way into the city. If he commanded any kind of an army, that is exactly what he would do. He was prepared for anything; as not even trolls or ogres gave him much pause anymore. That faceless creature, however, was an entirely different situation. And the skeletal monsters that sometimes showed up when he channeled the Threads were an unwelcome adversary as well. He had learned, for the most part, to overcome the paralyzing fear he had once felt when they were around. They still had an effect on him, but it was nowhere near as strong as it used to be.

Mayhaps fighting would not be necessary at all. *What if word of my battle prowess during the attack on Elston has spread through the Realm? Mayhaps the people of Ten Kings will respect me. Or fear me. Either way it can't be a terrible thing, can it? I could be a legend in my own time and nobody would dare stand against me.*

After he had finished eating some cheese and dried meat from his rucksack, he got up and stretched. There would be no navigating by the sun today, but it was no matter. He had a decent idea in which direction he was headed. He slid his axe into the loop on his belt and headed deeper into the woods as the gray sky overhead began to slowly brighten.

He knew it was silly to fear running into one of the faceless creatures a second time simply because he was in a forest. For the most part, he didn't expect to encounter one of them again. He was, however, cautious about what *else* he might encounter. He expected to run into orcs or goblins—they seemed to be everywhere now. Most reports that had come into Elston were of scattered bands of wanderers and not sizeable armies of any kind, but most encounters with them had spurred brutal violence.

When in Elston he had routinely heard stories from passersby discussing how small villages were being ransacked by hordes of orcs. While Dalinil believed there was truth in there somewhere, he wondered just what was considered a "horde" by different individuals. He'd seen a true army of orcs, and that was *his* definition of the word.

Still, it probably did not take many orcs to overrun most of the villages in the area whose inhabitants were largely unarmed.

68

They relied on the larger cities like Elston or Ten Kings to provide defenses. Of course, early on, those defenses had been overwhelmed. Now that the cities had begun forming armies of their own, they could fight back. And this group in the East—The Red Swords—seemed very promising. Dalinil had briefly considered joining them. Even now, it was not out of the question.

Dalinil was well aware that those soldiers would likely attack him if they were aware that he used the Threads. They did not, however frighten him. In fact, he believed that it was *he* who frightened *them*! He would certainly not hesitate to swat them like biteflies if they opposed him in any way.

The forest was alive with birds singing. Several times he saw rabbits flee in front of him. Twice he saw deer who, unlike the rabbits, appeared largely unconcerned with him. But what made him stop in his tracks was what he saw that afternoon.

He saw it first during a flash of lightning. It was an animal—a white horse mostly shrouded by the trees and bushes about 30 feet to his right. At first Dalinil thought his eyes were playing tricks on him but, yet, there it was. He desired a closer look so, as quietly as he could, he slowly moved toward it.

As he got closer he noticed a horn protruding from the horse's head. *Not a horse. A unicorn! Finally, a creature from myth that won't try to kill me! Assuming the stories are true, that is.* For a moment, he was dumbfounded—completely taken aback by the fact that there was an actual *unicorn* standing mere yards away from him. The animal was majestic and regal and he felt a sense of tranquility as he watched it.

The unicorn was beautiful. Dalinil stopped behind a tree to admire the creature. Its coat was as white as newly-fallen snow and it shined with almost a silvery sheen. A gold stripe spiraled up the shaft of its pristine, white horn, ending at the tip. Just looking at this fantastic unicorn sent a wave of serene happiness through him. He felt lighter and safe. He was compelled to get a better look.

Dalinil started to move closer, but he was certainly not a stealthy individual. The unicorn stopped chewing on some grass and looked directly at him. The two locked eyes for a moment as Dalinil froze, hoping not to startle it. He was about 20 feet away now, and he half expected it to charge him. Everything else he had encountered wanted to kill him, why not a unicorn? For reasons he couldn't explain, this thought brought a smirk to his lips. No, this creature would not hurt him, he was sure of it.

The unicorn indeed did not attack. It continued looking at him as if inspecting him. Suddenly it fled in the opposite direction.

"No, wait!" Dalinil yelled. It was instinctual—he in no way expected the unicorn to understand him. He pulled the Threads to him—green, white, and black, and took hold of them, bolstering his strength and stamina. Then he ran after the creature.

It was difficult for him to run too fast in the forest—there were too many trees and rocks to get in his way. Twice he destroyed two small trees, ramming his shoulder into them when he couldn't maneuver around them. His shoulder now throbbed, but he kept up his pursuit for several minutes until, ultimately, the unicorn proved too fast for him and it disappeared further into the forest.

Dalinil kept running for a little while after he lost sight of it—just in case—but he never found it again. Disappointed, he stopped beneath a large oak and released the Threads. He braced himself for the wave of fatigue that hit him, but it did no good. It was as if the air was sucked out of him all at once. His wobbly legs gave out and he gasped for breath. His spotty vision darkened as he rested, trying to stay conscious, and slumped against the tree. Finally, after several minutes, he was able to support himself again. *It's getting easier to recover, if I use the Threads wisely. Hopefully it will get to the point when I won't need to sit and recover at all.*

He was both disappointed and fascinated by what he'd seen. As a child, he had invented an imaginary unicorn protector to keep himself safe. When other children would call him names or push him around, he had pretended that his magical companion would come to save him and teach the other children a brutal lesson.

Today, though, he'd seen one—a *real* unicorn! It was beautiful but, now, he felt empty. He wanted nothing more than to pet the majestic creature. Mayhaps, someday, he would get another chance.

It wasn't long until he heard more noises coming from up ahead. Hoping it was the unicorn, he carefully and, as quietly as possible, sneaked from tree to tree in hopes of getting another look. He moved behind a large rock and peeked out from the side.

His heart filled with glee and anticipation. He laughed at himself for being so giddy—like a little boy seeing his first firefly or... *or seeing a unicorn. How many people can say that they have seen a unicorn?* But part of him still rejected the notion. Of all the things he had been through these past months, he still found it difficult to believe what he had seen—what he had chased through the woods. Certain things just took some getting used to, he supposed.

Dalinil moved to another tree, pressing himself up against it to stay hidden. He laid his hand against the soft, green moss, its musty scent permeating the air. He still felt very out of place outside of a city, but at least he wasn't frightened of every little thing anymore. A year ago, he would have jerked his hand back and made sure he wasn't hurt. He was quite different then. *Everything was quite different then. And I no longer need an imaginary protector anymore, do I?*

Making sure to move whenever thunder roared overhead, he made his way up to another tree, then descended a small hill with a dry creek at the bottom. When he crested the hill on the other side, he knelt behind a large, fallen tree and looked around, hoping to catch another glimpse of the unicorn.

Instead, what he saw was two goblins.

He rested his left hand on his axe but stayed his advance, deciding to watch the two squat creatures. One was dressed in ragged furs and the other appeared to be wearing a tunic and breeches—both of which were way too large for it and were stained with blood.

They had killed a rabbit and were squabbling over it. Each one had a firm grip on part of the animal and tugged at it, grunting, snorting, and screaming loudly in their high-pitched, whiny voices. But their words, though difficult to understand, were in the Common Tongue.

"Give rabbit, I kill," the slightly larger one screamed. "Give back to Torgath—be hero!"

"No!" the other one shouted, tugging back on the dead animal. "You no kill! *I* kill! My rock hit rabbit, not yours! I give rabbit to Torgath! He reward *me*!"

Intriguing. These creatures must be smarter than the goblins I've encountered in the past. Mayhaps this is a more advanced tribe or a different creature altogether? For them to learn Common so quickly is remarkable!

Any remaining thoughts of the unicorn vanished, replaced by his curiosity over these goblins. They were still simple, stupid creatures that he could effortlessly slaughter at any moment, yet they were intelligent enough to speak!

Dalinil continued observing them for several minutes until both creatures agreed to share the credit for killing the rabbit. They proudly, each with a firm grip on the animal, carried it away through the trees. Dalinil followed, trying to be quiet, but he was sure that his endeavor was failing. Were it not for the continuous thunder and the incredible amounts of noise the goblins were making, they most likely would have discovered him.

Several times, the goblins stopped to figure out where they were. They squabbled over whether they were lost and, on multiple occasions, tried to part ways in opposite directions. Dalinil wasn't sure whether he wanted to laugh at the hapless creatures or just kill them outright. He was beginning to grow bored and the latter option was appealing more to him.

But he stayed his axe a while longer, following at a distance. He became so transfixed by the goblins that he almost failed to notice a group of orcs to his left. He came within just a few yards of the slumbering orcs and abruptly stopped, ducking behind a tree. His axe was soon in his hand as he held his breath, trying not to make a sound.

The orcs thankfully stayed asleep, grunting and snoring. The two goblins moved further into the woods, down a slope and out of sight. Dalinil cautiously moved forward, using the trees as cover and keeping an eye out for any more unexpected surprises. The pace was painstakingly slow. He saw no movement and heard nothing but his own loud footfalls as he continued his advance. He hadn't noticed earlier, but the birds had fallen silent. He could hear activity ahead, and he smelled smoke.

As he approached the edge of the downward slope, he slid his axe back onto his belt, confident that there was no more immediate danger. Without a tree nearby to hide behind, he crawled to the edge and looked over. Below him was an army. *Not an army, a horde.* Orcs literally covered the forest below, with makeshift shelters and fire pits littering the area. There were hundreds of them. He could see numerous goblins as well—tending to the fires and cooking meals. The two he had followed were nowhere to be seen.

The throng of bodies writhed and rippled over the landscape below. Orcs sparred with each other, training for battle. Some were building shelters or, more appropriately, instructing goblins on how to properly do so. What he hadn't expected to see were orcs crafting, cooking, and even sewing. There were women and children in the group and, though they appeared just as ugly and savage as any other orc, they were going through the same menial tasks that any human would perform in a similar situation.

His curiosity got the best of him and he watched for quite a while, both astonished and entertained. He wondered if this was the beginnings of an orcish settlement, or worse, a possible invasion forming. Thankfully he saw no trolls or ogres in the group—they were formidable enemies, even for him. *Now, if I see an ogre or troll mending clothes, I will have seen it all.* He chuckled.

What kind of an army brought along its women and children? Mayhaps a *horde* wasn't specifically an army? Either that or mayhaps the women and children were just as savage and bloodthirsty as the males themselves. That was a frightening thought.

With the exception of the goblins, the camp appeared to run smoothly. There was no bickering or fighting that he could see—again, except for the goblins. Any goblin fights either resolved themselves quickly or were abruptly quelled by the orcs— usually resulting in the death of one or more goblins. It didn't take Dalinil long to discover that those goblins soon ended up in orcish cook pots, which made him slightly ill.

There was another burst of thunder overhead and it finally began to rain. Dalinil heard grunts behind him and felt a sharp kick in his ribs. He rolled over on his back, wincing and clutching his side. It was all he could do to gasp for breath. Four orcs, all wielding crude axes and swords, stood over him. The orc that had kicked him had drool dripping from his two tusk-like lower fangs—one of which was broken.

"More food for tonight," the drooling orc grunted, pointing to Dalinil. One of the other orcs nodded. They were all clad in rather haphazard rags and furs—no armor of any kind, but they were big and very muscular. Three were bald and the fourth had sparse, coarse strands of hair protruding from the top of his head.

"Wait!" Dalinil groaned. All four orcs showed surprise and one of them gasped. None of them made any motion to attack.

"It speaks," he heard one of the orcs whisper, apparently surprised.

"Should we kill it here?" the one with hair asked.

"No!" the broken-tusked orc blurted, holding his arm out to keep the others from advancing. "I have a feeling Torgath may want to talk to this one first—and possibly kill it himself."

Sean R. Frazier

Chapter 8

Dalinil was led down the hill to the orc camp, his arms at his sides. He wanted to reach for his axe but, of course, the orcs had taken that from him as well as his rucksack. He felt naked without his weapon, and it made him feel very uncomfortable. He could have already killed these four orcs with his bare hands, but his curiosity had gotten the best of him. There was also the problem of the hundreds of orcs below him that would probably retaliate.

His left side throbbed. He wondered if something was broken—the orc had kicked him hard with its heavy boot. For the most part, they had not touched him since then except to shove him when they felt that he was walking too slowly. They kept quiet mostly, but Dalinil could hear them mumble occasionally to one another, though he could not make out what they were saying.

These orcs seemed to have a decent grasp of the Common tongue. They were the first orcs he'd encountered that didn't simply grunt, snort, and wail. This fact further intrigued him, and it kept the orcs alive a little longer.

He felt a sharp jab in his back as the orc behind him used Dalinil's own axe blade to urge him forward. Though it was difficult, Dalinil resisted his urge to attack the orc, balling his fists and gritting his teeth. He did, however, take note of the orc carrying his axe.

Numerous figures at the bottom of the hill had taken notice of him and stopped what they were doing to watch. Soon, several more did the same and the trend continued until dozens of orcs observed the spectacle.

"We have a treat for tonight's dinner!" one of his captors yelled to the crowd which cheered at the glorious news. Soon enough, Dalinil was being paraded through the camp, presumably so that every orc could see what would be in their stew pots tonight. They wound their way through the crowd, all the while being inspected by its inhabitants, some of whom either poked or jabbed Dalinil.

With each taunt, Dalinil felt anger rising within him. He observed everything, taking mental notes of the camp's layout, various weapons, and whatever else he could remember. He inspected visible food stores, supplies, locations of families, and the terrain itself. He realized that he wasn't just planning his escape, but he was planning the destruction of the entire camp.

Orcs yelled slurs and insults at him as he passed by them. He briefly thought about yelling back but decided it was best not to provoke a fight when he was vastly outnumbered and without his weapon. Regardless, the urge was there and it was very strong. *If I did have my axe... things might be a bit different.*

He wondered if he could escape by using the Threads. His instincts told him that he could, but he still felt apprehensive. He could probably even kill a few dozen orcs, but there was no safety—nowhere he could escape to rest. *I bet Cor'il could easily escape... or set everything on fire while trying.* The Threads wore on him. They bolstered his physical abilities to incredible heights and cleared his head, but they also eventually took their toll. He could force his body to ignore things like cold, heat, and fatigue but the effects were still there, even if they were suppressed. They would eventually catch up to him.

He'd had to learn this fact the hard way, and he still didn't know his limits. He knew that there was a level he could maintain without the adverse effects but he had not quite found it yet. He was also not disciplined enough to use only *some* of the Threads' power—he used all or none.

One of the orcs behind him jabbed his back with something sharp. He was trying to walk slowly—attempting to buy himself more time to think. Unfortunately, in his opinion, thinking was not what he was best at. Cor'il would probably know what to do. Kendra would *surely* know what to do. He wanted to cut them all down—he knew he could defeat them. Most people would probably mistake his confidence for mere braggadocio, but Dalinil truly *was* that confident in his abilities.

But, then, he would probably end up dead. As mighty as he might have liked to believe he was, he really couldn't win this one—there were most likely more orcs about. It was probably a good thing that they had taken his axe. At least now he was only mildly tempted. But his anger was still there, even if it only burned low and slow within him.

The orc camp was rather shoddy and poorly organized. The few shelters that existed were ramshackle, dilapidated-looking structures made from whatever the orcs could find. Dalinil swore that he saw bones built into one of them. The orcs apparently camped wherever they wished so, as Dalinil was marched through the camp, he had to constantly wind his way around fires or step over piles of trash and, sometimes, orc leavings. Any notion of the orcs being civilized was quickly discredited.

The orcs appeared to enjoy this camp. They carried on with their activities but stopped to take notice of a human being paraded through town. He passed a crude forge of sorts, and the smith stopped what he was doing to view the spectacle. The orc smirked and grunted as the group passed. With a forge so poorly constructed, Dalinil wondered how the smith could make anything at all. But he also realized this meant that these orcs had probably been here a while—everything looked established.

He was led past a large area that was clear of any encampment. The orcs were using this part of the forest to spar and train. Some of them attacked trees while others attacked each other. *Cor'il would have a hissy fit if he saw them attacking trees.* He grinned, imagining what Cor'il would do. Would this get him angry enough to retaliate?

Cor'il knew better how to finesse the Threads than Dalinil did. The half-elf, and that still seemed bizarre to think about, could create elaborate effects at which Dalinil could only marvel. Sure, Dalinil had some skill. He could shoot fire and he even summoned lightning once, but he could not weave the tapestries that Cor'il could. There was a part of him that was understandably envious of Cor'il, only partially allayed by the fact that Cor'il himself had admitted to Dalinil that he did not have full control. Dalinil had to admit that he was glad he had never accidentally caused the Threads to go haywire.

And Dalinil had found ways to increase his own skill. For the most part, he eschewed the colored Threads for the black Threads. The black Threads gave him nearly any ability or effect he wanted—power and versatility that was far superior to the colored Threads, which seemed to specialize in their effects. When certain colors were not present in the area it was severely limiting, but not if one clung to the black Threads.

Out of curiosity, Dalinil embraced the Threads. His vision blurred a bit, but the lines of power were as sharp and vibrant as ever. He saw a few red, green, and even a couple of white Threads, but the black Threads dominated this area.

In the distance, he saw one of the skeletal monsters and felt his body refuse to move. Instead of fighting the effect he embraced it, accepting the fear. He felt his conscience travel down one of the black lines to where the creature was, reaching out to it until his body relaxed and he could move again. But, this time, something new happened—something unexpected. He felt his mind touch its mind and, for a moment, he could sense surprise and even fear within it.

He abruptly dropped the connection to the Threads and his vision came back into focus. He had unintentionally stopped walking and had not felt the flurry of jabs in his back until now. One of the orcs yelled at him, punching him across the face to get his attention. His head swam but he fought to stay standing and clumsily began moving again in the direction they led him.

Dalinil reflected briefly on the skeletal creature—the *Threadfiend*. For a moment, he wasn't sure how he knew what it was until he realized that it had *told* him as much. He had connected with it, somehow, and it had communicated with feelings and thoughts, but not with any particular language. That had never happened before! Certainly, this would have to be something to explore later, once he escaped this awful place. He wondered if Cor'il knew any of this.

Dalinil closely inspected the orc that had struck him. He was ugly—as they all were. He had a horn jutting from the side of his head—something Dalinil had seen before but did not believe was very common. From what he had seen these past months, orcs did not always share the same set of traits.

The most noticeable feature, however, was that this one was missing his right eye. *When I get my axe back you'll be missing more than just your eye. I promise you.* He once again suppressed his anger, saving it for later.

Several minutes later the orcs stopped him in front of a hut. This structure was more elaborate and better constructed than the others Dalinil had passed. It was surrounded by a ring of stones and two torches burned on poles on either side of the entrance. The roof was made of animal skin draped over haphazardly piled sticks that came together in the middle. It, like the others, looked as if it would collapse at any moment. *Well, they know how to make fire. I guess that's good for them. They don't appear to be completely uncivilized, I suppose. Just mostly uncivilized.*

"Chieftain!" the orc with hair shouted. "We have a prisoner!"

"Dinner!" one of the other orcs replied.

Dalinil looked behind him to see quite a large group of them had formed. Scattered amongst them were goblins, jumping up and down, howling excitedly.

Soon an imposing figure emerged from the hut. Clad in furs and random bits of armor, it stood at least a foot taller than Dalinil. Jewelry dangled from its large tusks—even its horned helm was decorated.

"Chieftain Torgath," the orc with hair said, bowing its head, "we have brought you a prisoner."

Torgath squinted and glared at Dalinil then leaned forward to within inches of him, and sniffed. He pulled his head back, grinning savagely.

"Excellent, Gromgar," he replied. The chieftain's voice was low and gravelly. "I do enjoy killing my dinner. Fear makes the meat tastier!"

"I will see you dead," Dalinil responded, "long before you have that chance."

Several gasps could be heard from all around, including Torgath.

"So, this one speaks, does it?" Torgath inquired.

"Yes, chieftain." Gromgar nudged Dalinil as he stepped forward. "One of the reasons we brought it to you. It is a curious thing."

"Tell me, boy." Torgath stepped forward, walking around Dalinil as if inspecting him. After he'd made his circle he stopped and stared at him. "Where and how did you learn to speak our language? I have never met a human who knew how to orcish."

"Orcish?"

"You speak our language. Very well, too. Many of my tribe speak it worse than you."

Dalinil stopped. Sweat beaded up on his forehead as he realized that he had indeed not been speaking the Common Tongue. *But how can this be?*

When he had first encountered the orcs in the forest he had incorrectly assumed they were speaking Common when he had been able to understand them. He only now realized that they had not. And neither was he.

"I'm smart," he replied. "I picked it up after a few months. It's a simpleton's language for fools and idiots. Even a baby could learn it." Dalinil had this orc chieftain slightly off balance. He saw no problem with prodding his adversary.

Torgath growled, then laughed and turned his back on Dalinil. The hulking orc started to walk back to his hut, but suddenly turned around and savagely attacked. Dalinil embraced the Threads quickly enough to command them to strengthen his body before the orc's sizeable fist connected.

The blow still knocked him to the ground, but at least nothing was broken. In fact, he felt very little pain from the blow. Dalinil got up and calmly wiped the dust from his breeches. His jaw did hurt slightly but he ignored it, staring Torgath in the eyes.

"If you wish to fight," Dalinil continued, "then let's fight."

"This human has spirit!" Torgath announced, raising his arms into the air. The crowd cheered. "It wants to fight!" The crowd cheered louder. "You never actually had a choice in the first place, human!"

Torgath raked his clawed hand at Dalinil who immediately ducked and then jumped backwards. The crowd formed around the two, cheering and creating a makeshift arena with him and Torgath in the middle.

Torgath swung again, missing but knocking Dalinil off balance as he clumsily dodged the blow. He stumbled backward, staggering into the wall of orcs that pushed him back into the ring while making sure to get in a few blows of their own.

The chieftain came at him again, swinging his fist and growling. His haphazard armor clanked metal against metal as each swing barely missed Dalinil. Torgath grabbed for him but Dalinil once again proved too agile for the brute and jumped out of the way.

Dalinil embraced the Threads, feeling the rush of power flow through him. Torgath swung again and this time, Dalinil blocked with his arm and kicked the orc back. He laughed, feeling anger rising within him, and he realized that he was beginning to *enjoy* this. His confidence returned and so did his rage.

But Torgath was undaunted. He held out his right hand. Two goblins quickly emerged from the crowd struggling to drag a large axe behind them. They lifted it as best they could, giving it to Torgath who laughed and hefted it in the air as if it weighed nothing.

Dalinil quickly scanned the crowd for his weapon. He soon located the broken-tusked orc who was still holding it. *Alright. I've seen Cor'il do this before. It didn't seem too difficult.* He reached out to his axe with black Threads, pouring all his concentration into the effort. For a brief moment, the Threads resisted, but then they snaked their way to the weapon and yanked it from the shocked orc's grasp. It landed in Dalinil's left hand just in time for him to block Torgath's two-handed swing. The response from the crowd was immediate. At first it was shock, but it soon turned to anger.

The Threads bolstered his strength almost before he commanded them to do so. He felt an inner fire burning as he blocked another attack, then another. He swung his axe, but Torgath moved just in time and his weapon instead shattered a rock. Thunder roared overhead.

The orcs in the crowd started chanting, but Dalinil was not paying attention. Instead, he watched as Torgath swung again. Dalinil ducked and punched the orc in the stomach, feeling whatever armor was under the orc's furs crumple from the impact. Torgath stumbled backwards with a brief look of surprise on his face. It was soon replaced with anger and rage, and the orc growled savagely.

I guess I have gotten your attention now, haven't I? But there is no need to draw this out. You're not worth my time. I could kill every last one of you brutes without a care. How dare you treat me like this!

Dalinil summoned more energy from the Threads. He gathered every black line available and wound them all into a thick rope darker than night itself. The cord's energy pulsed more rapidly as Dalinil let loose his rage, letting the power fuel his anger. He wrapped his other hand around the axe and swung.

His first swing missed, as did his second. His third, however, shattered the chieftain's weapon when the orc tried to block his savage attack. Torgath had no time to react as Dalinil's next swing buried itself in the orc's chest, spraying blood high into the air. Dalinil pulled it out and brought it down again, this time caving in the chieftain's skull.

The orc's body collapsed in a heap on the ground next to his weapon. The crowd fell silent as Dalinil brought his axe down yet again. He yelled insults and profanities in orcish, hacking at the corpse repeatedly until it was nothing more than a pulpy mess scattered about the ground.

He then turned to the crowd, glaring at them until he found him—the orc with one horn jutting from his head. The orc that had struck him. Using the Threads, he pushed the other orcs aside and approached it. It was trying to look stoic but Dalinil could see the fear and hatred in its eyes.

Both disappeared when Dalinil struck the orc with his own fist, sending the brute flying backward. Its body rolled down a small hill and rested at the bottom, unmoving.

Dalinil held onto the Threads in case he should be attacked, but none of the orcs stepped forward. They all stood still and stared in a hushed silence, fear and surprise in their eyes.

"I am going to leave now," he announced. "If you want to stop me you are certainly welcome to try. I will cut you down like I did your leader and I will enjoy it!" His words sounded savage and angry in the orcish tongue, and he meant every one of them. He almost hoped that he would meet resistance.

None of the orcs made a move. They looked at one another, dumbfounded and afraid.

"Alright, then," he said in the Common Tongue. He turned to leave but found his way unexpectedly blocked. He grinned and raised his axe.

The orc was dressed in purple robes—not fancy or ornate, but certainly not the rags that the other orcs wore. Just as Dalinil was about to bring his axe down, the orc held up its hands. This one did not seem as tough and muscular as most of the others did. Instead, it was meek and humble as it bowed before Dalinil.

"Please, chieftain," it pleaded. "Lower your weapon. This tribe now belongs to you."

For a moment, Dalinil stood with his axe still raised above his head. He so badly wanted to strike this orc down and tear through the crowd with his weapon—to slaughter them all and revel in the combat. But, instead, he lowered his axe and released the Threads. The fires of rage within him diminished, a mere candle compared to the pyre it was just moments before. A grin escaped his lips as he looked around at the crowd.

"Well, now, *this* has possibilities."

Chapter 9

"Are you sure this is an actual shortcut?" Cor'il asked. He sat atop his white stallion nervously, trying not to be jostled too much by the animal. He was still uncomfortable atop the horse but was slowly getting used to riding—even though it may not have looked like it. At the very least he was finding ways to be less sore at the end of the day. They hadn't raised horses in Kuranthas—there had been no reason to have them, since nobody traveled outside of their lands. It was just one of the many things he'd had to become accustomed to.

"Quite sure, my boy!" Orvaril replied cheerfully. "You may have noticed the lack of a road here. Do not worry. It is perfectly normal—for places without roads, that is!"

Currently they were traveling through a meadow, which was a welcome change. The previous two days had been nothing but walking the horses through rocky, difficult terrain and wading across two deep streams. For a supposed shortcut, it certainly seemed to be a lot more trouble than expected.

Even Kendra was perturbed about the slow pace, and she was sure to remind Orvaril about it at every opportunity. He took it in stride, however, and every jab slid off him like water off an oiled cloak. In fact, he seemed rather amused about it all.

What mattered most to Cor'il was avoiding danger, but he was also anxious to return home and, like Kendra, he was skeptical of just how much of a shortcut this really was. The past two days had been slow so hopefully, now that they traveled on easy terrain, they would be able to move more quickly.

Several times, he had felt something. It was a sinister, cold sensation on the edge of his consciousness that disappeared as soon as it emerged. Whenever he felt it he looked about, expecting to see a grotesque, hulking beast charging at him. Instead, all he saw was rustling trees or disturbed bushes. Even now, he still wasn't sure if it was just his mind playing tricks on him, but the sensation was as real as the sword at his side. It almost felt like a connection to something that he could not explain. For now, he felt it best not to speak of it and cause unwanted concern.

"Ah," Orvaril exclaimed, pointing ahead of them. "That clump of trees over there. That would be a perfect spot to stop and rest for a while!"

Kendra squirmed atop her horse. The blouse of her green dress was a sickening, dull brown color where she said an orc's blood had soaked in. She was obviously uncomfortable and Cor'il suspected she might be in pain, even though she insisted she was fine. *The Goodness, mayhaps some of it is* her *blood.* He hadn't considered that until now.

"Aye," Kendra agreed. "I could use a quick rest."

Judging from the position of the sun, it was still mid-morning. Orvaril didn't look tired and Cor'il didn't feel fatigued. He was suddenly more than a little worried about Kendra, though. The more he watched her, the more his concern grew. She moved very slowly and carefully and, though she tried to hide it, Cor'il noticed her wince a few times.

"I'll ride ahead and scout," Cor'il suggested, urging his horse forward to a trot and heading for the clump of trees ahead. He rode around the perimeter of the area once and when he was satisfied, he hopped off his horse and wrapped the reins around a tree branch. The horse whinnied and began eating the tall grass.

"Easy there, Sky," he whispered, patting him on the head. His hair was coarse and dusty. Cor'il looked around, half-expecting to see something dangerous crawl out of the dry creek bed on the other side of the trees. He grew tired of always being suspicious of his surroundings, but it had kept him alive thus far.

Fortunately, the area appeared to be safe. He embraced the Threads and was immediately greeted by the vibrant, shining lines of all colors. Black Threads, however, were nowhere to be seen. Satisfied with his assessment, Cor'il set to weaving a few simple wards and placed them in a crude perimeter around him, encompassing the trees. He had just finished his weaves when Orvaril and Kendra slid off their horses next to him.

"This looks like a nice enough place," Orvaril said, glancing around. He sat down in the shade of a tree, leaned back against its trunk, and closed his eyes. "If only there were some serving maids nearby to provide me with a cold ale."

Kendra slid her satchel off her shoulder, and though she tried to hide it, winced as she did so. She sat down carefully and sighed, laying back and staring up at the sky.

Cor'il sat next to Kendra, fidgeting a bit. He pulled a pear from his satchel and ate it, nervously chewing while eyeing Kendra for any sign of an injury. He didn't understand why she wanted to hide it from him and Orvaril, but there was obviously *something* wrong.

"Hey," he started, "Kendra?" Her eyes remained glued to the sky and she did not reply. Sometimes she did this—gazed at the sky and ignored all else—and Cor'il had learned quickly to simply leave her alone until she snapped out of it. He drew back and looked to the sky, watching as fluffy white clouds floated overhead. When he had finished eating, he leaned back on his elbows and relaxed, feeling the warm summer breeze toy with his hair. He closed his eyes and for a moment, imagined he was back home in Kuranthas, lying by the pond in the clearing, and letting the sun dry the water from his face.

"No."

Cor'il snapped out of his daydream. Kendra still lay on her back, eyes still fixed on the sky.

"No, what?" he asked, quite confused.

"No," she responded, still gazing upward, "I do not need your help. Yes, I took a nasty orc claw or two back at the farm the other night. But I'll be fine."

"I wish I was as sure as you." Cor'il sat up and turned to face her. She finally shifted her gaze from the clouds but only glared at Cor'il momentarily. "Some of that blood on your sleeve looks fresh."

"Quit being so damned nosey." She spared a scolding glance his way and then stared back up at the sky. She started to clasp her hands behind her head but winced and folded them in her lap instead.

Cor'il fidgeted a bit, carefully inching closer and hoping she didn't notice. He couldn't believe what he was about to do—it was probably going to earn him a punch in the face. Regardless, he took a deep breath and poked Kendra's arm with his finger.

"You son of a three-legged horse!" she screamed, clutching her shoulder as she leapt to her feet. "What in The Abyss was that for?"

"I told you!" Cor'il also leapt to his feet, pointing at her. "If you were 'fine' then that wouldn't have hurt."

"You jabbed at my shoulder!"

"I barely touched you!"

Orvaril glanced briefly their direction, grinned, and closed his eyes with a sigh.

"Did I get hurt? Yes." Kendra pointed to her shoulder and further down her arm. She also pointed to her stomach and one of her legs. "Do I need you worrying about me and poking me? No."

"Kendra," Cor'il calmly interrupted. "Your arm is still bleeding. It's been two days."

"It's *fine*."

"No, Kendra, it's *not* fine!"

"Would you two quit fighting already?" Orvaril still had his eyes shut. "Kendra, let the half-elf help you."

The look on Kendra's face said it all. She stared at Cor'il, mouth slightly agape, in confusion and surprise. Cor'il looked back at Orvaril who, even though his eyes were still closed, smiled as though he knew exactly what was happening.

"Oh, don't be so surprised," Orvaril continued. "Given the events of the past year, it became apparent rather quickly, my boy. Besides, I think it's utterly fantastic!"

"How observant," Kendra quipped.

He was still smiling. "It really wasn't difficult to figure out—especially with those ears." He paused a moment to execute a needlessly dramatic sneeze. "Though I've no idea why you hide them. I think it's wonderful. I've never met an elf but I've met half of one!" Orvaril laughed, apparently finding himself quite humorous.

"So, theoretically, if my wounds are as bad as you think they are, then what exactly can you do about it? When last I checked, you were not a healer."

"Actually," Cor'il replied, "I'm not entirely sure. Mayhaps I can get a better look at it and bandage it better?" She had a point. He did not know anything about treating wounds. From where he sat, however, something obviously needed to be done. "And if it really *is* bad enough, then we should find a town with a healer and let them help."

Orvaril sat up and opened his eyes. He didn't say anything but now seemed more interested, as if he was watching a play.

Kendra sighed, looking annoyed, but she reluctantly unbuttoned the top two buttons of her blouse. Cor'il looked away shyly.

"Treeboy," she laughed. Cor'il detected a nervous undertone. "You're the one who wanted to see, so you're going to have to actually *look* at it. I am not going to show you anything you're not supposed to see."

Cor'il sheepishly looked back at her, still feeling awkward. He regretted pushing the issue, except that she really *might* need help. However, he found himself suddenly nervous.

Kendra slid her shoulder out of her sleeve. It was oozing blood and had soaked through the meager strip of cloth she had been using as a bandage. Cor'il carefully, and nervously, untied the cloth and dropped it on the ground. He looked closer and noticed that the cut was deep—too deep to leave untreated.

"So," Kendra began, "what do you think, oh sir healer?" She gibed, but Cor'il paid the sarcasm no attention.

"It looks pretty deep." He couldn't exactly tell how bad it was, except that it was indeed deep and it was still bleeding after two days. Part of it had scabbed over some, but it looked as though the scab had broken several times. *Probably because she keeps using the arm. The other scratches don't look so bad, though, so that's encouraging.*

His knowledge of medicine was limited to that which he had learned back home from Eleanor Farnham. Admittedly, that was very little. She had not been the most pleasant of people to be around and had only helped him and his friends with minor cuts and scratches when they got into trouble.

"Are there any others?"

Kendra sighed. Cor'il wasn't sure if it was irritation, frustration, or sadness.

"Yes," she grumbled. "My side, right here." She pointed to her left side, just above her hip. "And you don't need to tell me it's pretty bad. I already know. But I'm not letting you see that one. You'll just have to trust me."

Cor'il nodded, relieved. He would have felt awkward anyway.

"And another one across my chest which—"

"I understand." Cor'il became more concerned. She was admitting to injuries beyond those he expected. Orvaril even looked a little worried.

Cor'il looked around at the vegetation, hoping to find something he recognized that could help either clean the wounds or stop the bleeding.

"Where are you going?" Kendra asked, pulling her sleeve back on.

"Mayhaps there is some wildbud or dog's breath nearby. If I remember correctly, both of those can help a bit." Hopefully his memory served him well. Cor'il walked around the tree line, carefully inspecting the ground for either plant. He was careful to stay within his warded area which, upon a cursory glance, appeared to be untangling slowly. He took a moment to tighten his weave and then continued his search. He didn't have the time, however, to do a thorough job since his mind was preoccupied.

"Have you found anything yet, Cor'il?" Orvaril called. Cor'il thought it best not to be shouting back and forth, lest they attract unwanted attention. Though his wards *should* keep them relatively concealed he did not want to test their effectiveness. "I say, my boy! Have you found anything yet?"

"Not yet!" Cor'il yelled back, annoyed. He sighed and continued his search along the tree line but was, thus far, finding nothing but dandelions and a few daisies. He reached the end of the warded area and stopped, looking out over the meadow beyond. He could see quite far and watched as the tall grass and flowers swayed in the soft summer breeze. *Well, it doesn't appear as though I am going to find any helpful plants around here. And I would prefer not to venture too far looking for them.*

He, in fact, was not entirely sure what he would have done with each plant anyway. The truth was, he couldn't quite remember what they did, and he recalled Mistress Farnham mixing them with other ingredients to make a paste.

He watched as a family of rabbits hopped through the tall grass, but then his eye caught something else. Had they just appeared or did he fail to notice them the first time? Either way, a group of orcs was not a good thing, and they appeared to be headed in their direction.

Cor'il immediately hurried back to Orvaril and Kendra. The horses were happily munching on the abundant supply of grass around them and Orvaril appeared to be asleep. Kendra had one of her daggers—the black one—in her hand and was fidgeting with it.

"There are orcs headed this way," Cor'il whispered.

"How many?" Kendra asked, holding her dagger up to the sky. She squinted and ran her thumb along its surface.

"I don't know. More than just a couple. They're moving pretty quickly."

"Then we should probably get moving, too, I suspect."
Orvaril apparently wasn't asleep after all. He sat up and rubbed
his eyes. "Don't you think?"

"I don't think we have the time," Cor'il replied. "They're
moving awfully fast. If we leave now and they notice us... do you
think they'll chase us?"

"I don't know." Kendra got up and hurried toward the
trees. "Orcs seem rather unpredictable if you ask me."

"So," Orvaril stood up and dusted himself off a bit, "if we
aren't going to flee, we are going to fight them?"

"We might have to." Cor'il called upon the Threads and
they appeared like shining beacons, clear and sharp as sunlight
while the rest of the world blurred and distorted a bit. He
bolstered his wards, doing his best to tighten the weaves to keep
them from unraveling again. "But I am unsure of how many there
are. They most certainly outnumber us—I'm just not certain how
badly."

"I don't understand, then. What are we supposed to do?"
Cor'il wasn't paying close attention to anything except his labored
control over the Threads, but it sounded as if Orvaril might be a
little worried for once. "You know," he continued, "simply so that
I can prepare."

Cor'il understood weaving a pattern that would not undo
itself was difficult. In fact, he'd not managed it yet, but he knew it
was possible. The book spoke of weaves that could last for
thousands of years without anyone touching them. He had trouble
getting his to stay tight for just a few hours.

He saw Kendra returning and dropped the Threads—
where had she gone? There was nothing more he could do at this
point anyway. Hopefully his work was good enough.

"They indeed *are* traveling quickly!" she panted, out of
breath. She looked very pale. "I don't know how many there are,
but they're mounted on what appear to be huge wolves." She
leaned up against a tree as she tried to catch her breath.

"An army?" Orvaril asked.

"I don't think so," Kendra replied in between gasps. "Mayhaps 40 or 50 mounted orcs."

"That is too large to be a scouting party, isn't it?" Cor'il himself felt a touch of fatigue. He had expended a lot of energy just setting up his wards. It wouldn't have taken so much effort if he hadn't messed up several times.

"No," Orvaril replied. "It sounds more like a raiding party to me."

"So what do we do?" Kendra asked.

"We stay put and hope they pass us by." Even Cor'il himself could hear the uncertainty in his own voice. He hoped the others had not paid as close attention.

"I think the treeboy has lost his mind," Kendra laughed nervously. She pushed off of the tree and moved to stand next to Orvaril and Cor'il. "They will see us for sure, and will probably run us down."

"I agree with the lady," Orvaril added. "There simply is not enough cover here. A thin strip of trees in the middle of a meadow—no, we can't hide here."

"I am hoping we won't have to hide," Cor'il assured them. He tried very hard to stay calm and confident, but there was a large part of him that was uncertain.

"What do you mean?" Orvaril's voice held curiosity but his face showed overt skepticism. His eyes darted to the horses. This might have been the first time that Cor'il had ever seen him even remotely out of sorts.

"I have set a few... enchantments in place. If they work properly, we should be effectively invisible to the orcs. I wove them when we first got here."

"Wait," Kendra interrupted, "*if* they work properly?"

"Well, yes," Cor'il replied. "I've never done anything like this before. I've warded off an area around us that the orcs *should* feel compelled to ignore. We're not exactly invisible but they should fail to notice us.

"I must say, my boy, that you are not inspiring a lot of confidence in me—"

"Nor me," Kendra agreed.

"But, as I was going to say," Orvaril shot Kendra a scolding glare, "I am going to trust you."

Both Cor'il and Orvaril looked at Kendra. She certainly did not look happy and was nervously fidgeting with her dagger. Several moments passed.

"Fine," she growled begrudgingly. "But if your little magical ward things fail, you're going to bathe them in fire or something, right?"

"Sure," Cor'il replied. "Yes... I guess so." The truth was, he was already tired and he hated the thought of slaughtering other living creatures—even orcs.

"So what is our plan?" Orvaril's voice was now calm. Any doubt seemed to have vanished. Cor'il wished the same held true for Kendra.

"Well," Cor'il looked around. "I suggest we keep to the trees and remain as quiet as possible. There is no need to give the orcs a reason to investigate."

"Very well," Orvaril responded. "That sounds about as good as we're going to get!" Yes, he sounded as upbeat as always. Just the sound of his voice lightened Cor'il's heart a bit.

"I hope you know what you're doing, treeboy."

So do I.

Chapter 10

Kendra crouched in the thin line of trees, leaning against one for support. She clutched her black dagger tightly in her right hand, ready for a fight. She was sore and tired and, as much as she hated to admit it, weak from blood loss.

She really *had* hoped that her injuries, though rather serious, would heal over just enough until she could find help. Cor'il was right, though. Her wounds were still bleeding and were not healing. Traveling on horseback all day didn't help. *Damn that boy! I hate it when he's right!* Though she wasn't exactly sure why that was. She suspected it was less because he was right and more because she was wrong.

Now she was forced to trust him and whatever magic he had apparently mustered. If this didn't work, they were going to have a fight on their hands. They should have fled. They should have gotten on their horses and fled south. In fact, even now, she had to restrain herself from doing just that. She knew she would be leaving her friends behind but, hopefully, they would come to their senses and follow her. On the other hand, if these wards of Cor'il's didn't actually work, she knew what he could do—even if he didn't want to.

Cor'il had his hand on the sword at his side. She had not seen him use it much, but knew that he was decent with it. But his hand was shaking a bit and his gaze was fixed on the approaching orcs. Hopefully he was thinking, coming up with a new plan—something better than simply sitting here and hoping that the orcs would pass them by.

Orvaril, on the other hand, looked as calm as ever. In fact, he had a smile on his face and Kendra could hear him humming quietly. She wasn't sure if he was annoying her or distracting her from her fears. If he was worried, she could not tell. In fact, he almost seemed... excited? Kendra wished that she shared his sentiment. *It must be nice to be him.*

He held no weapon. His lute was still strapped onto his back. Kendra knew that he could use it as a strange but effective bow, but he made no move to use it. He proudly stood amongst the trees and stared out at the band of orcs that grew ever closer. Kendra could hear them now, and she could count at least 20. *No females and children in this group. These are definitely warriors. But where are they going?*

The group itself was spread out, taking advantage of the meadow's open space. They were not in any type of formation that she could determine, and each orc shifted its position in the group as it saw fit. Kendra tried hard to remain calm, so as not to overexert herself. Regardless, she was beginning to see small spots dotting her vision and it was becoming difficult to catch her breath.

All three horses apparently shared her feelings. They were beginning to get skittish. Kendra hoped that the animals would not give them away with any undue noise. She briefly wondered if she untethered them and they ran, if the orcs would give chase. *But then that would leave us without mounts, and then it would take us longer to get to a healer to help you, stupid.*

"Well," Cor'il whispered, "we're about to find out how well my wards work." There was little confidence in his voice.

The first orcs in the pack were probably only two hundred yards out and were approaching quickly. Kendra checked her daggers. Including the black dagger in her hand, she only had three left. Even if she had a hundred, she was not a warrior. Neither was Cor'il. Orvaril *certainly* wasn't, though she wouldn't be surprised if the man was able to charm them with a special song and dance. The very thought, under other circumstances would have brought a grin to her lips.

"As the orcs approached, the three friends crouched in the safety of the trees," Orvaril sang in a whisper. "Waiting it out, filled with doubt in the quiet summer breeze."

To The Abyss with it. It's too late to do anything now, so I guess we just stay put and wait. This was not Kendra's normal course of action.

"And as they hid in the trees," he continued singing, "letting out nary a wheeze, the orcs did pass them by without so much as a sneeze."

"Would you shut up?" Kendra growled. "We don't need the orcs hearing us singing."

"Of course not, milady," Orvaril retorted. "Because, certainly, there is not enough room for all of them to join us. Plus, I don't believe that orcs have the best singing voices in the first place. I think they would take better to the spoken word."

Kendra glared at Orvaril who, quite innocently, smiled back. Cor'il didn't seem to notice and was not paying attention to either of them. He was watching the band of orcs approach, his hand still on his sword.

Two of the orcs split off from the group and headed toward the clump of trees. Scouts. If the two scouts discovered them, they would alert the rest of the group. Kendra realized that she was holding her breath. She tried to calm herself, ironically, by reciting Orvaril's stupid song in her head. It gave her just enough of a focus to relax her a tiny bit. But it was an annoying tune, and she quietly cursed Orvaril for having planted it in her head in the first place.

It wasn't long before the two orcs—each one mounted on a frighteningly large wolf, stopped at the trees. Both wolf and orc alike sniffed the air and scrutinized their surroundings. Kendra found herself slowly moving closer to be within striking distance, ready to pounce if necessary. She was always very fierce if she got the drop on unsuspecting foes.

Cor'il looked at her with a both confused and disapproving stare. She shrugged and kept sneaking forward, moving quietly through the leaves and underbrush. She was much more used to the terrain of a city, and she felt a bit awkward trying to sneak through sticks and leaves. Nevertheless, she managed to get very close without being detected, but just that little bit of walking had tired her.

They sat in saddles atop their wolves. The saddles themselves appeared to be of better quality than most everything else the orcs had on their persons. Their riding skill surprised her, and they kept very good control of their panting wolf-mounts, who responded quickly and without resistance. Kendra had watched some of the finest trainers break horses back home. It required considerable skill, knowledge, and patience, and she found herself shocked that these brutes had managed to domesticate such wild beasts.

One of the orcs grunted and uttered some guttural noises, then urged his mount forward, skirting the edge of the trees. The other orc did the same but in the opposite direction. Kendra ducked behind a tree to stay out of sight. Orvaril slowly did the same, looking annoyed. Cor'il, however, did not move. He probably wouldn't be easy to spot, but he was making no special effort to hide. None of it would matter if the orcs spotted the horses.

Several tense moments passed with Kendra whispering to herself to calm her down. She figured that the orcs probably *would* spot the horses once they got to the south side of the trees. There just wasn't enough cover to hide one horse, let alone three. They were also such noisy beasts.

She felt sweat bead up on her forehead as she kept her eyes glued to both orcs. She noticed that the main group had paused about 20 or 30 yards from their hiding spot. *They must be waiting for the scouts to report. Interesting. I'd have thought that those were more advanced tactics. Their group is sizeable. Surely a small clump of trees would not cause them hesitation... unless they suspect something. Cor'il's wards had better not fail.*

Surely Kendra had learned more about orcs in the past few days than in the past year. Though still savage and brutal, they appeared to function at a higher level than she had originally assumed. This made them far more dangerous.

Several more tense moments passed as she continued to observe the two scouts. They were taking their time. They obviously sensed something but could neither see nor hear any danger. It appeared that Cor'il's wards worked—in a half-assed fashion.

Finally, the two scouts met up on the other side of the trees. They grunted and snarled some more and, when they were done, urged their mounts back to the main group. Kendra quietly moved back to where Cor'il and Orvaril stood.

"I think they worked," Cor'il whispered, obvious elation heavy in his demeanor. "The wards, I mean."

"Indubitably!" Orvaril exclaimed, though in a hushed voice. "Unless they actually saw us and are merely going back to the main group to muster their forces!"

"You are quite the optimist," Kendra responded sarcastically, though she realized Orvaril had a good point.

"I like to think of myself as an optimistic realist, milady."

"How is that being optimistic?" Kendra kept her eyes on the orc pack, which remained stationary for the time being. She, once again, felt the urge to get on her horse and ride south as quickly as she could. Surely the orcs saw them and were about to storm their position at any moment. She was mistaken—Cor'il's wards hadn't worked, and they were about to be set upon by the entire group of orcs.

"Because," Orvaril continued, "I am optimistic about our chances of defeating the entire group if they attack."

"But then," Cor'il interjected, "that is not being very realistic, now is it?"

Orvaril only winked at Kendra in response. How could he be so nonchalant at a time like this? They should go—all of them. How could Cor'il and Orvaril not see what was going to happen?

"We really need to go," she pleaded. "They are all going to come back and kill us. They know we are here."

"Nonsense!" Orvaril rebutted. "They would have attacked us when they had the chance—and alerted the rest of the group at the same time."

"I think you are underestimating them," she growled. "I don't think orcs are as stupid as everybody assumes—at least not *all* orcs.

"She could be right," Cor'il added. "We could be falling for a trick of some kind."

"You two worry too much." Orvaril waved his hand, dismissing them. "Trust me, we are going to be fine. Cor'il, whatever magic stuff you worked earlier appears to have succeeded. As long as we remain here, we will be unharmed. In fact, this reminds me of an old tale about the Battle of The Murkriver Bridge. It's an old story, dating back a few hundred years, but it was quite the battle!"

Kendra watched Orvaril and listened to him drone on about the supposed fight between two cities—each group trying to keep the other from advancing across the bridge, with neither committing to the fight. It was a fairly entertaining story, actually, and when he was finished, Kendra somehow felt a little better. Cor'il had also been listening and appeared more relaxed.

"But," she replied, "wait a minute. That story has absolutely *nothing* to do with our situation. Nothing at all!"

"Correct, milady!" Orvaril laughed. "But, as you can see, the orcs have passed us by, we are all safe, and you two didn't notice!" He laughed and pointed. "You two were too busy listening to that ridiculous story... that I just made up, by the way." He stuck his tongue out at Kendra and laughed.

Kendra looked outside of the trees and saw the group— now just dark shapes in the distance—moving away from them. She looked at Cor'il who, gazing back at her, had the same dumbfounded look in his eyes. They both looked at Orvaril who, by now, was cackling with laughter and, apparently, was quite proud of his endeavor.

"Also," he added, "I think I'm going to add it to my repertoire because it is a *fine* story, if I do say so."

"Well, it had me enthralled," Cor'il agreed.

Kendra could feel the collective tension fade. Cor'il was smiling and she could feel herself grinning a bit. Orvaril certainly was talented.

"You are quite the storyweaver, Orvaril."

"Well, milady, I do my best. However, I suggest we don't tarry any longer. Fortune has thrown us a line and I suggest we grab it."

"I couldn't agree more," Kendra replied.

"This might hurt," she heard Cor'il say. Then she felt his hand on her shoulder, followed by intense cold and then warmth that racked her body. Her vision blurred and she saw spots. She staggered forward until she rested against a tree.

"What," she stammered, "have you done?" She labored to turn thoughts into words. Her entire body felt cold and sluggish, as if she were trying to wade through quicksand.

"I was trying to help," Cor'il said, his voice full of worry. "I... I'm sorry, I think—"

Kendra leaned against the tree and slumped to the ground, letting the darkness take her.

"The sure way to differentiate between an ogre and a troll is that the former is ugly, while the latter is uglier."
—Darian, *Out and Beyond*

Chapter 11

"You have done extraordinarily well. Do not listen to the doubters. Your power grows and your control improves. You will soon become the most powerful being in the Realm and you will command respect from everyone. Do not let others pull you down. You don't need anyone else."

"What?" Cor'il asked.

Orvaril looked at him quizzically.

"I didn't hear what you said."

"I'm afraid," Orvaril responded, "that I did not say anything at all."

"I was sure I heard someone say something."

"I can assure you," Orvaril continued, "that I, myself, neither heard nor said anything. And she," he pointed to Kendra, "is still sleeping. Mayhaps it was a bird?"

"You don't need them."

Cor'il looked around him. Kendra was still unconscious and Orvaril was busy twisting several tall blades of grass together. It looked as though he was trying to make something, and he seemed quite focused.

I do need them.

Cor'il wasn't sure if he expected a response but, regardless, he didn't get one. He waited for several minutes, staring into the distance. He was left with nothing but his own ruminations and the sounds of a few crickets.

He felt guilt over weaving the Threads on Kendra without her consent. At the time, he had not thought about anything except trying to help her. He knew she would not have let him do so, had he asked her. Now that he thought about it, however, he realized that it could easily be considered a trespass, and that he probably should not have done it. He wanted to wake her up to apologize but, instead, sat calmly amongst the trees and let her sleep. She was going to be very angry when she woke.

The wards he had weaved earlier were steadily coming undone. He had not yet figured out how to keep them from unraveling without his intervention. He could keep them functioning if he paid constant attention but that also took concentration and energy.

Cor'il fidgeted with the ring on his finger, twisting it around absent-mindedly. He'd long since given up trying to take it off—it wouldn't budge. In fact, and he knew it was silly, the harder he'd tried to remove it the more obstinate it had seemed.

"Cor'il," Orvaril whispered after a while, "it appears that she is coming to."

Kendra stirred a bit, mumbling nonsense and groaning until she finally opened her eyes and stared at the two of them. Cor'il smiled.

"How are you feeling?" he asked.

He never saw Kendra's fist but he certainly felt it. He grunted and tried to catch his breath, bent over from her considerable blow to his stomach.

"It appears that the lady Kendra is feeling better!" Orvaril laughed. Cor'il, doubled over in pain, unsure as to what was so amusing.

"What was that for?" Cor'il wheezed.

"For doing whatever it was that you did to me!" She slowly sat against a tree, catching her breath.

"Hopefully," Cor'il gasped, "I helped mend your injuries."

While Cor'il recovered, Kendra glared at him uneasily.

"Well," she finally continued, "don't do it again! I didn't ask for your help—I didn't need it!" Kendra cautiously stood up and brushed off her skirts, testing her balance. She moved her arm around and checked the rest of her injuries, apparently surprised, but obviously still angry.

"It appears to have worked," Orvaril said.

"Mayhaps," Kendra added. "A bit. At least the bleeding seems to have stopped. But I already told you before that I didn't need your help."

Cor'il eventually caught his breath and stood up, keeping a couple of feet between himself and Kendra. Orvaril still looked amused—as if he was stifling laughter.

"You're welcome, I guess," he said.

She glared back at him but said nothing.

"I'm absolutely starving." She riffled through her satchel, sat down, and started eating.

"Mayhaps, milady, we should get going and eat along the way? I'm not sure we should—"

"Good idea," she replied. "You two get the horses ready and I'll eat while you do that."

Cor'il and Orvaril exchanged confused glances and then made their way over to the horses. It appeared that neither one was willing to argue with her.

All three of the animals were still skittish, which made it difficult for Cor'il and Orvaril to tend to them. After a few food-related bribes, however, the horses finally calmed down enough to let them near.

"It appears that we are not the only ones who were spooked by the orcs," Cor'il observed. "Still, I wonder why these horses didn't make much noise during the whole thing."

"Indeed, my boy. They seem quite well-trained. They are remarkable animals."

They stood in silence for a few moments. There really wasn't anything that needed to be done to the horses, but Cor'il thought it best to give Kendra some space. They had no tack, no saddles, and no saddle bags to check. The bridle and reins were easy enough to slip on and adjust. The horses provided only minimal resistance.

"Don't worry about *her*," Orvaril gestured behind him with his thumb. "We both know how stubborn she can be. I am sure that she is, underneath the angst and... rather formidable appetite, quite grateful. I'm not going to say that what you did was right but, if it were a choice between her living and dying, you made the right choice."

Cor'il nodded. *But what if I had weaved the construct wrong? Could I have hurt her or worse? Should I have done it at all?*

"You did fine."

Receiving a compliment from a voice speaking from inside his head did little to allay his fears. In fact, it only concerned him more. Antina had spoken to him and Dalinil from inside the room deep under Elston and that had been enough to cause him concern. And, now, he was hearing voices *again*.

Get out of my head.

"No."

Yes. You are not real.

"I am as real as you."

"Is something troubling you, my boy?"

Cor'il quickly snapped to attention. Kendra was approaching, still with a scowl on her face. How long could she stay mad at him for helping her?

"Nothing but the usual," he subtly gestured toward Kendra. Orvaril smirked.

"Are you two finished playing around here?" Kendra grabbed the reins of her horse and led the animal out of the trees. Cor'il shook his head, shrugged, and followed her while Orvaril chuckled from behind. Cor'il glanced back at him and glared, but the man didn't stop. In fact, he only laughed harder.

"They are going to slow you down, those two. They will only hold you back."

They are my friends. They would never.

Cor'il hopped onto his horse and gently nudged him in the sides with his heels. He was still getting used to riding a horse, but he felt more confident every time he rode.

"It may not be their intention, but they will merely get in your way."

Cor'il thought it best to ignore this voice. Whether it was an actual voice inside his head or just his own thoughts, he didn't see either as favorable. He didn't recognize the voice as his own, however. It was distorted and muffled, as if it was speaking into a pillow. He would need time to make sense of it all and right now was not that time. Hopefully it was just his imagination brought on by recent events.

He shivered, feeling the now familiar chill accompanied with a disturbing susurrus. He immediately looked around him but there was nothing out of the ordinary. He wondered if the voice he was hearing was somehow related to this newfound paranoia. It wouldn't do to be looking over his shoulder for the rest of his life, nor would talking to himself be a good option.

After several moments of traveling, they crested a small hill and stopped short. At the top, where the hill leveled out, lay numerous corpses—orcs and wolves. Out of the six dead orcs, three of them still had their weapons sheathed. The other three had drawn theirs, but that apparently had not helped them.

And, again, the ghostly whispers invaded Cor'il's thoughts. As with those he'd heard back at the clump of trees, they said nothing coherent.

Cor'il looked around, hoping to catch a glimpse of who or what had killed the creatures, but found nothing. Kendra and Orvaril were doing the same, looking just as confused as Cor'il felt.

"There is no smell," Orvaril offered, "and no flies yet. I'd say this just happened recently."

"Would we not have heard a battle?" Kendra asked. "It seems unlikely—"

"That one is still bleeding." Cor'il pointed to one of the orcs, blood still oozing out of its wounds. "I don't know how it's possible—" He paused, unsure of what to say next. "This definitely happened recently."

"Well that's lovely," Orvaril added. "There is something out there that can kill six orcs quietly and it's roaming nearby. I am beginning to think I should've stayed in Elston."

"Whatever it is, it's efficient and quiet." Kendra urged her nervous horse onward. Cor'il and Orvaril followed close behind.

Cor'il thought back to when barbarians were the biggest threat to the Realm. Orcs and goblins replaced that danger. Now, though, there was something else out there.

Were the barbarians even real? If history has lied to us all along then are they, too, a figment of a storyweaver's imagination? I wish there had been more time to speak with Antina. I have so many questions.

He waited a moment to see if the voice would reply, but was met with nothing. He sighed in relief as he pulled alongside Kendra. She appeared lost in thought and didn't notice him.

"I apologize," he started, unsure of how to proceed with the touchy subject. "I should have asked you before weaving the Threads on you. I could have fumbled the weaving and caused you harm. I could have made everything worse—and I did so without your consent."

"Yes," she replied, "you could have." She continued to look straight ahead. He tried to read her expressions to determine how she was feeling, but her face was a blank page.

Orvaril rode up on the other side of Kendra, but he appeared to be more concerned with inspecting his horse's neck than anything else at the moment. He was humming a tune that Cor'il did not recognize and he was not actually paying attention to where his horse was going. Instead he was sifting through its mane with his fingers.

"But," she continued, "you didn't." She glared at him still. "But you could have."

"But I didn't."

"But you could have."

"So, you are still mad—"

"Yes, I am still mad at you!" She turned her gaze away, staring ahead of her and leaving Cor'il confused. He felt like he should say something, but he resisted the urge and kept quiet. He briefly considered putting some space between him and her but, instead, continued where he was. He took it as a good sign that Kendra, while still angry with him, was not actively trying to avoid him. *Abyss, at least she's not trying to kill me.*

"But she might."

Cor'il was about to argue with himself again, but thought better of it and resisted. Kendra remained silent as well, never shifting her gaze from the landscape. It unnerved him—knowing that she was mad at him, but not knowing *how* mad. What Cor'il would have given to know what she was thinking!

Or mayhaps not. He was confident that, whatever she was thinking, he would probably not like it. Still, she would hopefully come around soon, and even if she didn't immediately forgive him, she might at least cheer up a bit.

But he was thinking too much about this, wasn't he? Her anger would fade. Mayhaps, once he was more adept with the Threads, she would grow to trust him. Mayhaps he would grow to trust himself.

The truth was, her injuries were still there. Cor'il had not been able to use the Threads to heal them. In fact, he had done little more than stop the bleeding and dull some of the pain. He simply didn't know enough about any of it—weaving a healing construct and how the body worked.

The book had only hinted at any of it, which was where he had gotten the idea in the first place. He had actually gleaned little information from the text on the subject. Despite his hope that the next pages would explain more to him, he had found that was indeed not the case. This was not uncommon—as with many other aspects of the Threads, the book never fully explained *anything*, and Cor'il was always left to experiment and to learn on his own. Unfortunately, it had offered much less information on healing than any other subject.

This was usually not a problem since he could find a secluded spot and test his weaves without risking harm to anybody. Healing was different. With healing, he obviously needed a test subject. *That wasn't the reason I wanted to help*

Kendra so badly, was it? Her wounds needed attention and I was helping her!

"There are always acceptable losses."

What do you mean?

The voice did not answer, and Cor'il became increasingly worried. He had always conversed with himself, sometimes talking to himself out loud to organize his thoughts. In fact, it was something his friends had routinely teased him about. This, though... this was certainly disturbing.

They rode in silence for quite a while. Orvaril, at times, looked as if he was going to say something but, instead, he kept to himself. Cor'il couldn't think of anything worthwhile to say, and it made him uneasy. Aside from that, he was simply afraid to attract Kendra's attention.

She didn't *look* angry. In fact, she didn't look like *anything* at all! Cor'il decided that he would have felt better if she'd kept a constant scowl on her face rather than a blank look.

"What," Orvaril exclaimed, "is *that*?"

Cor'il turned his gaze to the direction Orvaril was pointing. Kendra hesitated briefly and then did the same. They stopped their horses for a moment and Cor'il squinted to focus. It appeared to be a tower or spire in the distance, off to the north a bit. It glinted in the afternoon sun and jutted up from the landscape where there was nothing else but hills.

"I don't know." Cor'il continued to scrutinize it, but from here, he could not see much detail. "A structure of some sort, I suppose. But there appear to be no settlements nearby."

"A spire in the middle of nowhere does not make any sense." Kendra was inspecting it, too, obviously intrigued. It was good to hear her speak.

"Mayhaps we should camp there for the night?" Cor'il suggested.

"It's a bit off our path," Orvaril replied, "but I should certainly like to see what it is.

They both looked at Kendra who finally turned her gaze back to them. After several moments, she nodded her approval.

"It's certainly better than making a camp out here in the open," she said. "Especially if another group of orcs decides to come passing by. Mayhaps there is shelter nearby. It most certainly is a curious object."

"*Good. Excellent. You can feel it, can't you?*"

"*Feel what? I don't understand what you are talking about.*"

"*The spire calls to you. It needs your help. There is something dreadfully wrong nearby. Can't you feel it?*"

Cor'il felt nothing except confusion and frustration. Out of curiosity he briefly embraced the Threads and, during that short time, found that every shimmery line seemed to be pulsing toward the tower in the distance. Cor'il shivered and suddenly felt hesitant about their current destination.

"*Yes, you do feel it, don't you?*"

He kept quiet, however, and they urged their horses forward, turning north toward the tower. Cor'il tried to ignore the voice inside his head, but its ominous portents were difficult to dismiss. It spoke as if it was knowledgeable about things he could have not known.

As they rode, Kendra seemed to soften a bit, sometimes sparking conversation on her own and other times, simply replying tersely to something Orvaril said. Cor'il took it as a good sign that she was no longer glaring at him, nor was she drowning him in sarcasm. He was careful, however, to treat the situation gingerly and not overstep his bounds. Orvaril obviously noticed the continued tension and tried to lighten the mood when he could.

The spire still loomed in the distance but it became more obvious with every minute that it was not a natural part of the landscape. And, while Orvaril and Kendra did not seem bothered by it, Cor'il couldn't help feeling that they were headed toward something terrible. Possibly fantastic, but terrible.

The Coming Storm

Chapter 12

Kendra rode between Orvaril and Cor'il, nearing the spire at a decent pace. Each time they crested a hill and it came back into view, there seemed to be something new about it—a feature she had not noticed before. It had been a longer trek than any of them had anticipated, for it was larger than they had at first thought. As they topped the last hill, they all three marveled at its sheer size and complexity as it hovered before them.

The Goodness, it's not even rooted in the ground! How is that possible?

She was the first to reach the top of the plateau, overcome by curiosity about this monolith. The ground was flat and covered with flowers and tall grass except for the area around the spire itself. The ground there was a rocky, rougher terrain.

She got off her horse, keeping hold of the reins, and stood in front of it. Not only was it floating in the air but it slowly bobbed up and down slightly, never touching the ground.

Whatever it was, its color was a creamy white hue and, if she had to guess, it was 100 feet tall. It wasn't terribly wide— mayhaps about the width of one of the long tables back at the Gryphonwing Tavern. And it narrowed toward the top, ending in a point of sorts. She moved close enough to touch it, but she hesitated. Carved into the surface were ornate runes and designs that pulsed with blue radiance at seemingly random intervals. And each pulse started at the object's base and traveled up to the very top.

"Well, now," Orvaril marveled, "isn't that a sight to behold! It's a giant's toothpick!" As always, the man found himself to be funny, and he had a large grin plastered on his face. Kendra found herself smiling a little.

Cor'il was the first to touch it. He put his palm on the surface and, though everyone was apparently expecting something to happen, nothing did. He slowly pulled his hand away with a disappointed look on his face.

"I wonder where it came from," he said, inspecting his hand.

"It appears as though it might have emerged from the ground itself." Orvaril pointed to the area beneath the spire. "Look there. The ground looks like it has been churned up and the affected area is roughly the same shape and size as the spire here."

"But wouldn't there be a hole left behind?" Cor'il asked.

"Indeed," Orvaril continued, "that is rather perplexing." He rubbed his chin between his thumb and finger, still inspecting the area. "If anything, it appears that the ground caved in behind it, mayhaps?"

"And why is it floating?" Kendra asked. "And why is it here? Why does it pulse, and what is its purpose? And—"

"Milady," Orvaril interrupted, "I think you're getting a bit ahead of yourself. There are indeed many questions to be asked, but I am not sure we are going to get any answers."

"The Threads," Cor'il replied. "They are keeping it aloft." He was staring off into the distance again as he was apt to do from time to time. It always gave Kendra the shivers when he did so. It was as if he was staring right through everything—including her. What made it even more uncomfortable was the slight glow in his eyes when he did this. "But it's a very tight, intricate weave that I am unfamiliar with."

She watched as he walked around the spire, staring at it intently and ignoring everything else around him. He nearly tripped several times on the rough, rocky terrain, but never took his eyes off the spire itself. He stopped once he had made a full circle around it, then he came out of his creepy trance.

"It's ancient," he continued. "Whoever performed this weave did so a very long time ago."

"Elves?" Orvaril asked.

"Older," Cor'il replied. "*Much* older. This weave has barely loosened and will probably last for several thousand more years."

With all his talk about magic—or whatever he wanted to call it—Kendra was reminded of the dull pain in her arm and in her side. Sometimes the treeboy exhibited knowledge and skill far beyond his years, and that surprised her. Other times she could put no trust in his abilities. He had, in fact, healed her injuries a little, for which she was deeply grateful, but she was still not happy about the way he had done it, nor would she trust him if he wanted to do it again.

He obviously understood her anger and frustration to some extent. She had gone out of her way to make her feelings abundantly clear to him. But she was a bit conflicted. She recalled her feelings when she had awakened in the barn after being attacked by goblins—she had been angry that she'd had to rely on someone else to help her. When Cor'il had told her that he had only moved her to safety, she had felt relieved, but she had also been annoyed with herself for feeling angry in the first place. Even now, she was still conflicted about the whole thing.

Once again, she felt angry for having to rely on someone else to help her, and Cor'il was right—she would have refused his help had he continued insisting. Her pride may have ultimately cost her in the end. She was too accustomed to relying only on herself and being the only person she could trust. Weakness was having to rely on those around you, wasn't it? Not having a choice in the matter added a whole new layer of frustration, but could she really blame him for what he had done?

Certainly, I could blame him if he had messed up and made things worse. But he didn't mess things up, did he? My injuries do feel a little better and, at least, the bleeding has stopped.

Kendra was jolted out of her thoughts as the spire pulsed with blue energy that, once again, traveled from the base up to the top of the object. They all three watched it in silence. The horses, to Kendra's surprise, remained calm, nibbling on the grass around them.

"Did anyone else hear that?" Cor'il asked. He was concentrating on something.

"Hear what?" Orvaril looked perplexed.

"It was a low hum. It happened when the blue light pulsed up the spire."

"I did not hear anything." Kendra tried to listen for whatever sound Cor'il had heard but heard nothing. "You must be imagining things, treeboy." She knew that was probably not true but it was a force of habit to be skeptical.

"I definitely heard *something*."

They stood in silence, still staring at the object as it hovered just about a foot or so off the ground, bobbing slightly in a slow, rhythmic pattern. It pulsed again and, though Kendra herself did not hear anything, Cor'il most certainly reacted.

"There is definitely a hum when it pulses," he said.

"Does it mean something?" Orvaril asked. He produced an apple from his satchel and bit into it.

"I do not know," Cor'il replied. "But the Threads seem to respond in unison with every pulse. It's difficult to explain."

Kendra led her horse over to the left of the object and wrapped the reins around the branch of a large, flowering bush. The horse happily munched on the bush for a bit before deciding the grass was tastier. Until now, she had not named her horse but decided on "Brute." She had put far too much thought into it these past days and thought it was best to stop anguishing over it. It was a completely inappropriate name for such a slender mare and she smiled each time she thought about it.

Her stomach growled and so she, too, bit into an apple. She sat down on a rock and watched Cor'il as he inspected the floating spire. Orvaril joined her after he tethered both his horse and Cor'il's by hers. Cor'il had named his "Sky" and Orvaril dubbed his "Dummy." Kendra had to admit that Dummy was a decent name since the horse was by far the most scatterbrained creature of the three.

"So," Orvaril said, sitting next to Kendra, "what do you think?"

"About what? That?" She pointed at the spire. "I think I like your description."

"That would be quite a large giant now, wouldn't it?"

"Indeed." She could not finish her apple fast enough. She threw the core down the hill and pulled some dried meat from her satchel. She knew that it was the same dried beef and venison that she had always eaten but, given how hungry she was, it tasted so much better than normal. Orvaril took notice and muttered something under his breath, then laughed. She didn't bother asking him to repeat it.

Cor'il continued pacing around the spire, touching it and staring at it for quite a while. Every so often, Orvaril would make a joke at his expense and they would laugh. Cor'il did not seem to hear them, or if he did, he did not care. He was very much enthralled by the hovering object. Whatever he saw was apparently more exciting than what Kendra could see. She lay down across the rock and gazed up at the clouds passing by high above.

"I've never seen or heard of anything like this," Orvaril muttered.

"I am getting all too used to hearing that phrase from a lot of people." Kendra turned her head to look at Orvaril. Though his demeanor was the same as always, he looked puzzled as he gazed at the floating spire.

"Yes, I suppose so."

At some point, Kendra must have nodded off because she awoke to a dusky sky and a campfire roaring nearby. She sat up and stretched out her back, which protested with a pop. The smell of something cooking caught her attention and her mouth immediately began to water. Her ravenous appetite had apparently returned.

"Good evening, sleepyhead!" Orvaril laughed. Kendra moved over to the fire where both Cor'il and Orvaril were cooking something on sticks. "I caught us a couple of plump rabbits in a small clump of trees not far from here. I thought, with you eating everything in sight, that we might need a little fresh food."

"I can't argue with that," Kendra confessed.

"Just make sure," Cor'il replied, "that you save some for the rest of us." A look of concern swiftly crossed his face as he averted his eyes from her. She laughed, however, and he relaxed.

"Mayhaps," she replied, "if I'm feeling nice, I'll let you have the burnt parts!"

"What burnt parts?"

"Yeah," Orvaril joined in. "What burnt parts? We are professionals with the finest cooking implements!" He held aloft his stick for emphasis, then laughed.

"We'll move on tomorrow," Cor'il added. "We could probably stay here for a month and not figure this thing out—whatever it is."

"Do you think there are more of these out there?" Kendra asked.

"It's very possible. Mayhaps we'll run into another one and we can discover more about them. For now, however, I'm more interested in getting back to my homeland than tarrying here for too long."

"And don't forget the orcs!" Orvaril added. He was currently sampling the rabbit, but appeared to have singed either his fingers or his mouth. "We'd most likely be seeing them again if we stay here."

Now that Orvaril had started eating, both Kendra and Cor'il began cutting chunks of meat off the sticks until there was nothing left. It wasn't long before Orvaril and Cor'il were both dozing off. Though Kendra tried to sleep, she found herself wide awake, staring up at the sky. There were a few, wispy clouds hovering high above in the starlit sky, but they were formless and only served to obscure some of the stars.

She moved her left arm around a bit. It felt a little tight and was a bit sore, but otherwise seemed fine. She thought it looked much improved but couldn't be sure in the flickering fire light. She really *was* grateful that Cor'il had helped her, but her pride still got in the way and she was still angry at him. Or mayhaps it was the realization that mayhaps she was not as independent as she thought? But she had made it this far on her own, hadn't she?

Not only that but, yes, he had simply snuck up on her without letting her know what he was doing. It was true that he could have made a mistake and made it worse—she hadn't even thought about that at first. But, when she stopped to consider it, that definitely worried her even more. Lack of permission combined with the possibility of making things worse—she felt queasy thinking about it.

Was I too harsh with him? He really seems sorry that he did it. And he did help—I most certainly feel better but... but what? Why is this so difficult? Why am I so conflicted?

Kendra decided that it was better to simply not think about it. Mayhaps the issue would go away on its own and things could return to normal. The truth was, she didn't know quite how to react anymore. If she couldn't rely on her independence, then she would *have* to accept help. Would it have been different if Orvaril had been the one to help her?

Aye, it would. But why?

She would not enjoy accepting help from him, either, but she felt that she could somehow get past it easier if she had to. Orvaril was a much worldlier person. He knew things and he was a seasoned traveler. Cor'il, on the other hand, still reeked of naiveté and inexperience. She fully realized that she was being petty, and that irritated her even more. *So, I'm irritated with Cor'il and I'm annoyed with myself for being irritated with Cor'il. I bet the storyweaver would have a wonderful time with this mess.*

She turned her thoughts to the floating spire not far from where she lay. They were continuing their eastward journey tomorrow, but she couldn't help dwelling on this place. There was something about it—something they were overlooking. It was a puzzle with a missing piece, and that frustrated Kendra. She very much enjoyed puzzles of all kinds and didn't like feeling defeated by one—especially not a puzzle of this magnitude.

Sitting up, she stared at the obelisk as it floated just a couple of feet off the ground. It still pulsed with blue energy and, though she tried, she could not discern any visible pattern to the bursts. She watched it for a good long time, hoping mayhaps something would become apparent. Cor'il hadn't been able to figure anything out, and Orvaril didn't seem to care, so mayhaps a third pair of eyes would notice something they did not?

The patterns and symbols on the surface were not any language she'd seen before—not that she *understood* any languages other than the Common Tongue. If it was a language, it was a very elaborate language with elegant symbols that flowed formlessly from one to the next. She really hadn't put much thought into the object at first, somehow believing that Cor'il would magically figure out what it was. And he had tried, but after several hours of circling, poking, and prodding, he came up empty and gave up. He looked exhausted when he had finally finished.

Orvaril muttered something in his sleep and shifted. Frustration turned into extreme curiosity as Kendra stood up and walked away from their little camp. She found herself leaning against the spire, looking back up at the stars. She felt it rub against her back as it bobbed slightly up and down. The surface was smooth like ivory, but solid like stone. It radiated no heat from the blue pulses, nor did it make a sound even though Cor'il had insisted that it hummed.

She tried pushing it to see if it moved, but it did not budge. She scraped at it with one of her daggers, but she could not mar the surface even a little bit. She even, on a whim, tried lifting it but it did nothing. She moved aside some of the smaller rocks beneath it, hoping to clear part of the hole from which it had apparently emerged but saw nothing but more dirt and rock.

Kendra knelt down and moved some more rocks aside, only to uncover more of the same. It appeared as if there was no opening to speak of. She held a stone in her hand, inspecting it as if it were a clue. There was nothing remarkable about it. She dropped it back onto the ground and stood up with a sigh, wiping her hands on her skirts.

"A giant obelisk in the middle of nowhere," she mumbled, "pulsing with blue light and *floating*." She circled around it once, looking for anything that stood out. "Created by... who? And serving no apparent purpose whatsoever."

Like Orvaril, she could recall no stories or tales about this sort of thing. Orcs and trolls were one thing but *this*... this was entirely different.

Kendra turned to look at the object once again. The glyphs and symbols pulsed. She followed the light up the spire with her eyes.

"What are you hiding?" She began walking around it again. "What is your purpose and who made you?" Kendra dug deep into her memory, trying to bring up stories that might have even hinted at something like this. She had been taught by some of the finest scholars in the Realm of Sorloth and, yet, she came up with nothing. What good was such an advanced education if it missed something like *this*?

For a fleeting moment, she felt homesick. It wasn't a common occurrence but it happened from time to time—most often when she used her hairbrush. Home seemed like decades ago.

If this... thing is outside of any scholar's recollection, then this obelisk is either very old or very new.

Kendra found a rock to sit down on, staring at the obelisk once again. A blue pulse shot up the spire until it disappeared at the top. She watched several of these pulses over the span of a few minutes and felt her mind focus in on the structure. She shut out everything else—crickets, the breeze, the crackling fire, and Orvaril's snoring. Everything around her felt distant but the spire seemed close enough to touch. She was used to this—she did it often, but she had never tried it when looking at something other than the sky.

For an instant, she could see the surface of the structure up close. She could almost feel its smooth surface and, surprisingly, she thought she felt heat from each pulse. It *felt* much like heat, but she knew it really wasn't. She watched several more pulses light up the structure and dissipate at the point.

But the glyphs on the side seemed to almost rearrange themselves in front of her as they writhed and swirled on the surface with each new pulse, until they finally rested in a different configuration altogether. Kendra still could not read them but, somehow, she understood something about them. They conveyed not so much a meaning as a feeling within her.

It was at that moment when a blue beam of light shot outward from the tip of the spire, aimed at the ground nearby. It was a narrow beacon, and it disappeared from view—obscured by trees and part of the hill itself. Shocked and surprised, Kendra blinked and it was gone.

The symbols on the side of the obelisk were as they had been before, and Kendra now felt nothing from them. As quickly as she had discovered the structure's properties, they were gone.

But the message it had conveyed remained within her. Directions.

Chapter 13

Kendra carefully walked amongst the scarce rocks and trees. Only a sliver of moon shone from above, so she moved slowly, trying not to twist an ankle or accidentally fall. Cor'il's little glowing sword trick would've come in very handy right about now, but neither he nor Orvaril had stirred when she tried to wake them. Nothing short of a stampede of horses would rouse them.

Kendra had given up trying to get their attention and had set out on her own to investigate the obelisk's mystery. The symbols had directed her to a spot not far away but, due to the rough terrain and the darkness, the going was slow. *It would have been nice for the glyphs to actually tell me what I am looking for. It's one thing to know where to go, but another entirely to know what you will find when you arrive.*

She found herself humming one of Orvaril's songs as she made her way through the darkness. At least, she assumed it was his—she'd certainly never heard it before he had sung it. The words were utterly ridiculous, but the tune had firmly implanted itself within her mind. In any case, it kept her suitably occupied. She merely wished that she could see better in the scant moonlight.

She froze several times when she thought she had heard a noise. Once it had been a bird that had set her heart racing when it took flight just a few feet from her face. Another time, something had been moving in the grass. She had seen no danger thus far, but she made sure to be careful anyway. There was no telling what dangers lurked beyond her meager vision. She was reminded of the goblins in the forest by the barn and she shivered.

Looking back, she could easily see the smoldering campfire at the top of the rocky slope, Cor'il and Orvaril still sleeping nearby. She felt sure that she had walked much further than that. Up ahead is where the glyphs had told her to go— assuming she hadn't simply imagined that part. No, she hadn't.

But I didn't imagine it. For a moment, it was as crystal clear to me as when the skies show me a path. I wonder if another Cloudseer could have seen what I saw. Is there more to Cloudsight than what the stories have hinted at?

She didn't like to think about her Cloudsight, and she certainly kept it secret from others. In this capacity, she felt a kinship to Cor'il. Her abilities brought back painful memories of her home and worse, her parents. Every time she thought about her "gift," she was reminded of them, and a bad taste bubbled up in her mouth. She wondered how they were getting along without her. *Probably the same as always—most likely cheating someone out of their money like they did when I lived under their roof. Certainly not a fitting profession for someone of their status.*

She often wondered why her parents had acted the way they did. They had plenty of wealth and stature, and they didn't need to exploit their daughter's gift. Yet, somehow, they still managed to make all the wrong decisions. Mayhaps no level of wealth or status was good enough in their eyes.

Her life with her parents in Alarantha certainly had not been a rough existence by any stretch of the imagination. Her parents had showered her in extravagant gifts from every realm. She'd never had to lift a finger, and she had received the finest education. Sometimes she missed that life—longed for it, in fact—but she eventually came to realize that she had been nothing more than a tool to them. They didn't love her. They never had.

She carried only one thing from that life. Her hair brush was a silly thing to hold onto, but it was a positive memory from her homeland. The ruby set into the back was certainly worth a lot, but that was not why she kept it. It was a gift from her Uncle Sten—the only family member who she truly believed cared for her. Her parents had given her many gifts but they were hollow—none of them truly mattered because those gifts came from people who were merely trying to use her. Uncle Sten's gift, however, had meant something to her. It was a token of love, not a bribe.

Kendra slid down the slope, catching herself and balancing against a thin tree. Looking around, she still couldn't see anything that stood out to her. She also couldn't see the campfire from this side of the hill.

Cor'il, Orvaril, and Dalinil were her family now, but Dalinil was so distant. She worried about him, even if the other two didn't seem concerned. Though she had hoped he would come with them on their journey, she had not been surprised when he had declined the offer. What *did* surprise her, however, was how cold he had been. It troubled her and she had spent a lot of time trying to figure out why he had changed.

She was a bit more cautious with her descent now. She made sure to hold onto the trees as she slowly felt her way around in the darkness. *This certainly would be much easier if these mysterious things would happen in the daylight.*

She didn't want to risk forgetting the information she had gleaned. She also wasn't sure if Orvaril and Cor'il would want to linger over something she herself considered just a gut feeling. Cor'il was adamant about returning home and Orvaril was excited just to see Kuranthas. Kendra was not sure she could convince them to spend more time here if she waited until dawn. Until just a little while ago, she herself hadn't wanted to tarry.

The slope began to level off and Kendra stopped at the bottom. *Oh, look. More of the same—rocks, some grass and a few trees. If this turns out to be nothing I am never going to believe another pulsing obelisk ever again.*

She couldn't help but giggle. She was frustrated, yes, but that thought made her smile. *I've been lied to by an inanimate object! Oh, if* this *gets out, I'll be laughed at from here to Alarantha!*

She was absolutely where she was supposed to be—where the obelisk had directed her. There was no doubt that the pulsing blue object had sent her to this very spot. However, she saw nothing remarkable here. *Mayhaps, if it weren't so damned dark, I could more easily spot whatever it is I am supposed to be searching for. Bloody Abyss, I don't even know why I am searching for something... that I don't even know what it is.*

Kendra paced. She inspected everything around her as best she could. She was currently at the base of the plateau, atop which was their camp and the spire. *Climbing back up there is certainly going to be a pain in the neck. But, hopefully, it'll at least be easier to see by then.*

She stared at the hillside some more, backing up to get a better view and nearly tripping over a fallen log and several rocks. She sighed and sat down, despondent and irritated. *I'm glad that I trekked out here in the middle of the night to nearly break a leg while stepping over a bunch of bloody rocks. Thank you, mysterious spire, you have taught me a lot.*

Thoroughly exasperated, she was about to give up when, suddenly, the pieces fell into place and she began to figure it out. She hadn't been stepping over rocks and boulders, but she had been stepping over *rubble*. She got up and inspected the area more closely, and it began to make sense.

Suddenly, instead of useless stones, she saw fallen pillars, weathered stairs, and what appeared to be remnants of statues. She now saw the hillside much differently. For a moment, she almost believed she could see everything as it once had been, piecing together all the broken stone and admiring it in its original form. Suddenly, in her mind, she stood before a grand staircase, lined by pillars and ornate statues, which led *into* the hillside!

She ascended crude, half-buried steps leading up several feet until they ended at what appeared to be a cave. The mouth, which wasn't very large to begin with, was mostly blocked off by shattered rock and dirt that had collected.

A quick inspection revealed a gap that Kendra carefully slipped through. Once inside, she found herself in total darkness. The floor was solid and as she ran her right hand over the wall, she felt a smooth, unyielding surface. *Well, so, now what? You can't see a fool thing in here and you haven't got a torch, do you? For someone who insists on being prepared you certainly slipped up on this one.*

The way ahead was completely dark, yet Kendra slowly moved forward, still feeling along the wall to both guide her and keep her balance. The footfalls of her soft boots echoed on the solid surface but was the only sound in this empty place. Despite the fact that she didn't know where she was or what she was doing, she was positive that she was in the right place. *If only that stupid spire had provided me with a light source.*

"Hello?" she called out, hearing her voice echo. "If there is anyone else in here, and I hope there isn't, do you have a torch I could borrow?"

She was met with only the sound of her own breath and her footfalls. She slowly walked further into darkness. It wasn't long until her hand brushed against something. It felt smooth—like the rest of the wall—but it was cold and protruded outward into what felt like a spherical shape.

She moved her hand over the surface of the object, looking for any clues as to what it was but, aside from the object itself, there was nothing else. She tapped on it with her fingernail and with a pop, it flooded the area with a brilliant glow!

"The Abyss!" she shouted, squinting and covering her eyes in the bright light.

Once her vision adjusted, she inspected the area around her. She was indeed inside a tunnel or hallway of some sort. She looked back at the tunnel's entrance which was only about 10 feet back. Ahead, the light illuminated about 10 feet and then disappeared into more darkness. The tunnel itself wasn't very wide, but Kendra couldn't touch both walls at once. All surfaces were of the same material as the obelisk, with no seams or joints. There were, however, no pulsing runes or designs on any of the surfaces.

"Alright, then," she whispered, "Let's see where you take me."

She cautiously continued down the tunnel, her gaze darting to and fro, as if something was going to surprise her. As she walked, she could feel the passage sloping downward, descending. The construction of this tunnel was certainly different than the crumpled stone outside, as if they were built during two vastly different times—or by two different civilizations entirely.

Once she got to the edge of the light, another globe sprang to life, providing more light for the next 10 feet or so. Kendra, ever curious, stepped back a few feet and watched the globe wink out, disappearing in the darkness. When she stepped forward it lit up again.

"What *is* this place?"

Kendra briefly considered going back to get Cor'il and Orvaril, but quickly decided against it. It would be a difficult hike back up the hill in the dark, and what happened if she could not find it again? *And that's assuming I could even wake them up at all. I think Cor'il was so soundly asleep that he might have actually been drooling.*

No, it would be better for her to continue by herself. She took a few more steps forward and then stopped, dumbfounded, as her surroundings suddenly lit up as if by daylight.

Kendra stood a mere few feet from the edge of a precipice. She moved closer and stared into a vast cavern that opened out into an expansive cave below. Globes of light illuminated what appeared to be an entire, vacant city. The buildings in the distance, if that's what they truly were, were all slender and elegant and made of something white—probably the same construction as the spire outside and the tunnel behind her. Some of the tops of the structures reached almost as high as the ceiling which was a mere few feet above Kendra's head currently.

She gasped, unable to do anything except marvel at what lay before her. *I've never seen anything like this. I bet nobody has.* There was neither noise nor movement below, and Kendra found herself fascinated by what she saw. She had no idea how long she had simply stood, staring at it all.

Finally, she came to and looked around her for a way down into the city. Both paths to the left and to the right were blocked by the cavern walls. To her left, however, she saw a small pillar. Crafted out of the same smooth, white stone-like material as the hall and spire, it stood about four feet high and had a divot about the size of a coin toward the top where it came to a point.

Kendra ran her hand over the surface and used her finger to trace around the indentation. It was circular, shallow, and smooth just like the rest of the pylon. She tried lifting it but it wouldn't budge. Thinking it might be a lever, she tried pulling and pushing it but, again, it remained obstinately still.

"Alright, then," she muttered, "I'm not sure what your purpose is, but this can't be all that difficult to figure out." She searched the ground around her and quickly discovered a circular, blue gem nearby. It was difficult to miss once she saw it, but Kendra wondered how she had overlooked it in the first place. It stood out like a gortog in a pack of wolves.

The gem was smooth and slightly cool to the touch. Kendra turned it over in her palm and held it aloft, letting the light sparkle through its many facets. For a moment, she wondered how much it would be worth if she sold it, but she quickly dismissed the thought, laughing at her habits.

"Well, my friend," she said, "there is no question what your purpose is. I really should like to take you and sell you but, instead..."

Kendra carefully placed the brilliant blue gem into the divot on the pylon, twisting it a little to make it fit. She took a step back, expecting something miraculous to happen, but was crestfallen when nothing immediately did.

Well that *was rather anticlimactic. Surely there should be—*

The pillar sprang to life. First the gem lit up in a bright blue glow, pulsing slightly. Its glow spread to the pillar itself, flowing down the object like rivulets of water running down a window in the rain. It was not long before the entire object was aglow in runes and patterns much like the spire at the top of the hill.

At the same moment that the gem stopped pulsing, a shimmering blue path of light appeared that led down to the city below. *Well, now, that is quite handy! But it looks rather steep.*

Kendra once again stopped to admire everything laid out in front of her. This was a wondrous place full of fascinating new things. Again, she thought about returning to camp and fetching the others but, also again, she decided better of it and cautiously put her right foot onto the path of light. It was slippery, and she yelped and nearly fell backwards as her foot was pulled out from under her. She backed away and inspected the path closer.

There was a shimmer that periodically raced down the path, starting at the top. It was rhythmic, happening about every 10 seconds. She put her hand on the path and now she could tell that it wasn't slippery after all—the path somehow moved her hand forward on its own!

She found a rock and placed it on the path. The rock moved down the shimmering light automatically at a pace that appeared to be a brisk walk. She watched it travel for quite a distance before mustering the courage to try it herself.

Well, if a rock can do it, surely I can!

She cautiously stepped onto the path, letting it lead her. The motion was smooth and constant as the path moved her along its winding trail. The descent was not actually as steep as it appeared, and Kendra never actually had to lean or steady herself as it brought her down the cliff to the ground.

As she descended into the city, she tested the path's durability by stomping on it, and even jumping once or twice. It was as solid as the ground itself, but was also smooth. It had no support of any kind and took her out over open air, leading down to the edge of the city.

When she stepped off the path, Kendra found herself just outside the city, standing on a flat floor of dirt and stone. She looked behind her at the top of the cliff to where she had stood just moments before, and marveled at what she had discovered. Beside her was another small pillar like the one at the top of the cliff. Also, like the other pylon, it held a blue, spherical gem.

The city before her was immense. Some of the ornate, delicate-looking structures reached up to the cavern's ceiling while others were much shorter. The city floor began a few feet from where the path ended, becoming a smooth, solid surface that had a marble-like appearance as it swirled with various colors and patterns.

Kendra took a deep breath and stepped onto the surface of the city, feeling a bit guilty for stepping on such a beautiful surface, afraid that she would scratch or scuff it.

Other than the noise she was making, the area was completely silent. It was eerie, but there was a part of Kendra that enjoyed it. For all she knew, she was completely alone and was the sole person to have seen this place for... well, ever. It was exciting, fascinating, and a little creepy all at once.

Could elves have built this place? It seems rather unlike what I've heard of them, especially since they are supposed to dwell in forests. Now dwarves... this seems much more like their type of home. But what of their craftsmanship? Do these structures speak of dwarven skill and knowledge?

But the stories she had heard growing up—from books, storyweavers, and even her parents—always told of massive dwarven cities beneath the mountains. Dwarves worked in stone and steel, presumably not delicate, ornate materials such as what Kendra was now walking amongst. Besides that, she had never heard of a dwarven path or bridge made of pulsing blue light. If the stories were true, dwarves had little time, let alone skill, for magic.

"So," she whispered, "if neither dwarves nor elves built this..."

Kendra stopped to look around again. She was about 15 feet from the blue path behind her now, but was still not close to any of the buildings yet. She had started out by moving as quietly as possible, afraid that someone might hear her but she quickly realized that, in a ghost town, there was nobody to care whether she made noise.

"So, who *did* build this?"

Chapter 14

As she walked softly, amid stark silence, Kendra hesitated often. She was no less cautious now than she had been when she had first arrived, though she had yet to see any signs of danger.

Cities are deserted for a reason. Nobody simply leaves an entire town behind on a whim. Yet, everything appears perfectly preserved. What happened here?

Walking slowly down what appeared to be the main road, she paid close attention to everything around her and was ready to arm herself if need be. Thus far, however, she was met with only silence.

The city was well-lit by streetlamps and lights on the buildings. However, instead of the usual lamps or torches, every device contained one of the glowing orbs that cast a steady light without flickering. Each structure was lit sufficiently to see its entirety, even all the way up to the top of the tallest building. She wasn't sure, but she thought she could see the cavern's ceiling.

The buildings were arranged in an orderly fashion, with a layout very similar to a city like Elston. Some structures were as large as a traditional city block and rose high into the air while others were much shorter or smaller. They all exhibited the same shape, however, with each building starting out wide at the base and becoming slenderer toward the top.

As she walked, she admired many things about this wondrous place. She passed several waterless fountains, many of which were sculpted to look like unicorns, pegasus, and other mythical beasts. *Not so mythical anymore, are they? Though, I guess, I've yet to actually see a unicorn.* Likewise, there were numerous sculptures that depicted sea serpents, multi-headed beasts, and even a dragon.

She passed structures that did not look like dwellings. What function they served, however, she could only guess. They stood lifeless and still just as with everything else down here, captured in a pocket of time. Everything appeared in pristine condition—there was no dust, no chipped or broken sculptures, and no signs of decay.

There was also no way in—none of the buildings had so much as a front door.

The only thing missing is people to live here. Any sign of life at all would be fantastic. Unless, of course, whoever lived here considered me a threat or was hostile. Still, I should like to know more about this place.

"Hello!" she called as she made her way further into the city. Again, she was met with only the echoes of her own voice and the soft footfalls of her boots on the hard ground. She found her caution fading and her pace quickened a bit as she passed each building.

Each glowing sphere reacted to her by casting more light when she got within a certain distance, then each one dimmed once she had passed, but they never winked out entirely. It was eerie—the way this place reacted to her, as if it could think for itself.

It's as if the city has been... sleeping. Was it waiting for someone? How do I wake it up? Or, the better question, do I even want to wake it up?

The answer was obvious. Kendra felt an overwhelming desire to discover everything about this place. Caution and hesitation were quickly being overpowered by curiosity and wonder. This was one big mystery and Kendra wanted the answers. Thus far, the deeper into the city she ventured, she only found more questions, oddities, and wonders. It had been overwhelming at first, but now, she embraced the unknown, taking in everything she could while she explored.

Kendra found her pace slowed a bit, sometimes, as she took more time to look around. She began inspecting things up close, running her hand over the smooth surfaces and admiring the natural beauty of the structures and roads. She passed under a high bridge that connected two buildings on either side of the road. It was beautiful, but it looked delicate and frail. The archway under which she walked was tall; the smooth, slender pillars rose up to meld into the bridge itself, high above.

The road before her was flat. In fact, the entire landscape was very uniform and devoid of any varying terrain. She couldn't be sure, but she figured that this was by design—this city seemed meticulously thought out and deliberately planned down to every last detail. Ahead, in the distance, she noticed a triangular structure rising up and ending in a spire.

"Well," she muttered, "That's as good a place as any to head toward." She was under no illusion that she would find any answers, but it was nice to set a destination. Realistically, she would find more questions. But this structure, once she had been able to spot it, stuck out like a like a sore thumb—a slanted, angled building amongst tall, slender structures.

As she got closer to the building she could see everything more clearly. It stood alone in what appeared to be the center of the city. When Kendra finally stepped out into the empty plaza around it, she hesitated, unsure if she should continue. She looked behind her, unable to see the entrance, the cliff, or the blue path.

How far have I walked?

The structures at the edge of the clearing were all just a few stories high and were less grandiose than most of those in the city. Looking out over the area, Kendra could tell that the city essentially formed a ring that surrounded the triangular building in the middle, with this open space in the middle.

With nothing but an empty, open area between her and this strange structure, Kendra stepped out into the clearing and approached it. As she got closer, she could see that it was a triangular archway with a spiral protrusion at the top. It was blue and not rounded or soft-looking, with hard corners—a stark contrast to all the white, rounded, slenderer buildings that Kendra had passed during her exploration.

As she grew nearer, she noticed that the structure's surface had seams, crevices, and areas that jutted outward. Whereas all the buildings down here were smooth and looked as though each one had been carved from a large, white stone, this archway appeared more industrial—as if it had been cobbled together from various, haphazard materials, all connected to each other in a seemingly random fashion. With every step, Kendra's curiosity grew. Before she knew it, she was looking up at the object, attempting to see the very top of its spire.

You really are an oddity, aren't you? But you are nothing like anything else in this place. Why are you so different?

There were no light orbs nearby—they ended where the clearing started—yet the structure itself gave off a blue glow that, while not very intense, somehow lit the area very well. Kendra wasn't sure if she had missed this earlier or if it had just begun glowing as she had drawn closer. It was certainly within the realm of possibility that it had responded to her like the rest of the city had. That seemed to be the way everything down here worked. *Well, at least the lights are still alive. Nothing else seems to be functioning down here except this... whatever it is.*

Kendra walked through the arch and explored the other side. Then she walked around it until she was looking at one of its angled sides. Upon closer inspection, she was surprised to see that the structure was not merely built on the ground, but it emerged from *within* it!

It took Kendra a couple of minutes to slowly circle the entire structure and scrutinize it closely. Once she had finished, she stopped next to it and looked up at the top once again.

I guess the next logical place to explore is up.

She began climbing up one of the angled sides, hoping to be able to find out more from a higher vantage point. It was an easy climb due to the fact that there were plenty of surfaces and seams to grab, even though the angle was steep, but she took her time, careful to inspect the structure as she ascended. Several times, she stopped and simply looked out over the city or looked closer at the object's surface.

She had only been climbing for a couple of minutes when the ascent became steeper and the grips fewer and further apart.

She found a small ledge on which to stand and took a moment to stop and look out over the city again which, as she now saw, was laid out in progressively larger rings that encircled the structure she was now climbing. The city was still lit by the glowing orbs but their light had dimmed considerably. Regardless, she could still see much of the city in fine detail.

The tallest buildings obscured parts of the city, but she had climbed high enough to still have a decent view. There were several larger streets that led straight from the outer city into this plaza while smaller streets intersected them, forming the rings. Everything looked orderly and clean from up here.

I can only imagine what this all would look like if it was completely lit and operating. I would bet that it is quite beautiful. This puts to shame every city I've ever seen. It certainly makes Elston look like a run-down, chaotic mess. I bet The Blacksmoke would argue that idea, though.

She wanted to climb higher and get a better look but, even if she'd had proper climbing tools, she didn't think she could make it much further up the structure's steeper angle. She continued admiring the beauty from where she was, unable to pry herself away.

And then she saw movement.

She noticed someone moving into the plaza, emerging from the buildings. Exactly who, or what it was, was difficult to see at this distance in the limited light. She almost called out to get their attention, but instead, thought it better to stay put and remain quiet. They were getting nearer and, soon, she would be able to see them better.

Her heart raced as she was filled with both excitement and fear. At first, she thought that Orvaril or Cor'il might be wandering around down here. Surely, if they woke up and found her gone, they would come looking for her. She quietly found the watch in her satchel and, by the light of the structure, saw that it was still early morning. The sun wouldn't even be up for another couple of hours which meant that they were both most likely still sound asleep.

"Who are you?" she whispered.

After several moments, her patience paid off. The figure continued moving through the open plaza toward her. She watched as it paused every so often and then resumed its approach. Kendra climbed down a bit for a closer look. She found a small ledge about 20 feet from the ground and stopped abruptly, finally able to see the horrible truth.

This was not a *who* but, instead, a *what*.

This creature was an abomination; it was a twisted mockery of life itself. It stood upright and walked on three legs, each of a different length. It had two arms coming from its left side and another arm from its right. Instead of hands, each arm ended in one large claw. Where its eyes should have been, instead, it had tentacles. It lumbered across the clearing slowly, ambling nearer.

She could hear it, now. It wheezed and snarled, though Kendra could not see if it even had a mouth. She looked away and closed her eyes, shivering uncontrollably. Her heart was pounding inside her and she felt her hands start to sweat, causing her to grip the side of the building tighter.

She heard the thumping of its three feet on the smooth ground below as it approached the base of the structure, but then, those sounds ceased. Afraid but also concerned, Kendra opened her eyes to make sure she was still safe.

Her stomach churned and she gasped, seeing the creature standing directly below her. It had stopped at the base of the building and appeared to be sniffing the air. *Has it found me? Does it know?* Though it did not seem to notice her specifically, she believed that it knew something was amiss.

It brushed the surface of the building with the tentacles on its head. Kendra could see now, that some of those tentacles ended in eyeballs. She nearly threw up and clamped her eyes shut again, still shaking. She took a deep breath and tried to calm down but only found herself shivering even more.

She wasn't sure how long she clung to the side of the building with her eyes closed but, when she finally opened them, the thing had vanished. Her gaze darted all around but she could see no trace of the creature. At first, she had a terrible feeling that it might have climbed up the building but, after a quick look around, she found this to not be the case. It appeared that she was, once again, alone. She wasn't sure if this made her feel better or worse.

Not alone. That thing is probably somewhere in the city now, and if it detected me it might be waiting. Or, worse yet, she realized that there might be more than just one roaming about. Suddenly, the city's beauty had vanished, replaced now with a terrible horror. What once was a beautiful wonder had been transformed into a haunted graveyard.

Eventually, the shivering subsided and, once she had calmed herself a bit, Kendra began cautiously climbing down the structure. She kept looking about her to make sure she was safe, expecting to see that horrible monster waiting for her at the bottom. Once she reached the ground, with that... thing nowhere in sight, she moved quickly to get out of the open space and back into the city proper where she could use the buildings for cover.

The smooth and slender qualities of all the buildings now became a hindrance to her. Were she back in Elston, she could travel the rooftops to safety but, here in this city, that was impossible. Even if she *could* climb one of these buildings, the distance between the rooftops was substantial—certainly too far for her to jump.

The silence that was once so serene and beautiful no longer held those qualities for her. Now it was eerie, abandoned, and dangerous. Even though the intense silence would make it easier for Kendra to hear something approaching, she would almost have rather been able to hear minstrels playing a raucous tune to keep her mind off the horrors that may lurk around every corner.

"Just remain calm," Kendra muttered to herself, "and let's just get out of here as quickly as we can. You only saw *one* of those things. There is no proof that there are any more out there." She was comforted by her own words, even if she didn't truly believe them. Hopefully, if there *were* more of them down here, their numbers were small. Nevertheless, she moved quickly—darting from building to building and always making sure nothing was sneaking up on her.

I don't remember hearing any stories about something that hideous when I was young. She quickly ran across one of the smaller side streets and paused behind a building, looking around to make sure nothing had seen her. *I wonder if that thing was something new. Or something very, very old?* Surely tales of a creature like that would spread like wildfire, so why had she never heard of it?

You'd never heard of an underground city like this before, either. No dwarves created this.

No. This was all something *nobody* had heard of—something new. She wondered what Orvaril would say about this. He'd probably improvise and pull some story out of his ass but he, too, would be just as dumbfounded as she was.

"Weird, tentacle-laden creatures with three legs and three arms?" he'd say in his matter-of-fact manner. "That's nothing. Wait until you see the ones with multiple heads and 15 butts!"

She wanted to laugh but couldn't.

Don't lose focus. It's time to go.

Kendra briefly caught her breath behind a building and then quickly moved on. *So far, so good.* She made her way back to one of the main roads and then out of the city. Finally, she found the path of light and made her way back to the top of the cliff, letting the light automatically move her up to the top. On the way up, she wondered what would happen if that monster stepped on the path. Would it catch up to her? Once out of the city and back at the entrance, she took one last look down, watching the lights all wink out one by one as the city resumed its dark slumber. Then she hurried out of the tunnel and into the morning light. She had never been so happy to see the sunrise.

Chapter 15

Cor'il had been staring at the obelisk for at least a half an hour before he saw Kendra come scurrying up the hill. She was out of breath and appeared to be frightened.

"Well that is intriguing," Orvaril had said when Kendra finally calmed down and told them what had happened. Cor'il could see the man was very interested in her story. Cor'il, too, was *extremely* interested—so interested, in fact, that he suggested they all three investigate.

"There is absolutely no way I am going back down there!" Kendra argued.

"But I need to see it." Cor'il replied. He was trying to contain his excitement because he could see that Kendra was obviously disturbed. "It could answer some of the questions I have and—"

"No, you don't need to see it. Or, well, if you do that's fine. *I* don't need to see it again." Kendra was adamant. She sat down on a nearby rock and scowled at the two of them in silence.

"So," Orvaril piped up, "We should probably be going anyway." He pointed to the north.

"Riders," Cor'il replied.

"Orcs?" Kendra got up and looked with them. She couldn't see much since they were still a way off, but they appeared to be headed toward them.

"I'm not sure," Cor'il finally said. "But that would be my guess."

"Even if they *aren't* orcs," Orvaril added, "I personally would prefer not to have to deal with them. Orcs, men, whatever. They can all be hostile."

"Do you think they could be brigands or thieves?" Cor'il had spent so much time trying to avoid orcs that he had forgotten the dangers that people could pose.

"I don't think we should wait around to find out." Kendra shouldered her satchel and made her way toward the horses. "The possibility of meeting peaceful travelers this far off the road seems pretty small."

"Agreed." Orvaril moved to do the same.

Cor'il, however, stayed with the obelisk and, placing his hand on the smooth surface, began to concentrate. He took control of every Thread in the area and began to tie them around the object. Through closed eyes, he could feel each line of energy, especially the black Threads, which sickened him and made him want to throw up. More and more often he detested using them, but they were very powerful and versatile.

"Come on, treeboy," Kendra shouted. Cor'il ignored her. "We need to leave *now* not tomorrow."

"Just give me a little time," he replied. "I think I can get this thing to work. He could feel beads of sweat forming on his forehead as he worked to push the Threads through the structure. During the time he had spent inspecting it yesterday, he had learned little about it. However, when he had woken up this morning, it was as if it had puzzled itself out in his head, and he now knew at least one function of it—it was not just a structure, it was a *device*. And Cor'il suspected that he could use it!

"Whatever you're going to do, my boy," Orvaril added, "you should probably try to do it quickly. I doubt we can outrun these riders if they get too close."

Cor'il continued concentrating. He was unaccustomed to channeling the raw power of the Threads this way, and this device was... fighting him somehow. There was not much weaving involved but, instead, he had to force the Threads into the device itself. It would function only if the proper colors were applied in a specific order, and Cor'il was finding out the order as he went. It wasn't until just this morning that he had discovered this process and he hadn't expected it to be this laborious.

"Listen," Kendra said. Cor'il felt her arm on his shoulder. "Nobody can move mountains. Don't kill yourself trying to get this thing to—"

Cor'il opened his eyes and saw the device begin to light up. The glow started at the bottom and worked its way up, changing colors as it traveled. When the illumination reached the top of the spire, it stopped, and two blue lines traced themselves on the surface of the obelisk. They, too, started at the ground and worked their way up, stopping about 10 feet off the ground and meeting in the middle.

Cor'il stepped back and he heard Kendra gasp. Orvaril hurried over and gazed at the spectacle.

"Should we," he began, "oh, I don't know, be worried?"

"Hopefully not," Cor'il responded. Orvaril, for the first time, actually appeared concerned—mayhaps even worried. Cor'il grinned and winked at him. He felt exhaustion taking over and he would need to rest after this, but he was confident that his efforts had paid off. The obelisk required minimal concentration from him, but the initial expenditure had been monumental.

Once the two blue lines of light connected, the surface shimmered. The smooth, white surface of the obelisk itself distorted and blurred until it was unrecognizable. There was a low hum and a buzz as the area within the blue lines filled with light of the same color. There was a loud, thunder-like roar and the blue area separated like curtains to reveal trees beyond.

It worked!

"What," Kendra gasped, "am I looking at?"

"Kuranthas," Cor'il replied. "This is a doorway to my homeland—I think. No, I'm pretty sure."

"Amazing, my boy!" Orvaril clapped Cor'il on the shoulder and approached the newly-created portal, scrutinizing it as if he didn't believe it was real.

"You opened a doorway to halfway across the Realm?" Kendra joined Orvaril in examining the portal. She sounded skeptical but was captivated nonetheless. She looked back at Cor'il as if to say something but, instead, turned back to the portal in disbelief.

"I don't know if this device has any other functions," Cor'il replied. "I suspect that it might but, as we apparently don't have the time to tarry, I suggest we make our way through to the other side.

"Good work, my boy!" Orvaril fearlessly walked through the portal. Cor'il watched as the surface shimmered and distorted slightly as Orvaril appeared amongst the trees on the other side. The man looked back at him with a stupid grin on his face and waved enthusiastically.

Kendra led the horses through with her and appeared near Orvaril on the other side.

Cor'il took a deep breath and stepped through. For a brief moment, he felt wet and cold, as if he had just jumped into a lake, but that feeling quickly subsided and he found himself standing amongst the trees next to his friends. The horses were a bit skittish but otherwise seemed fine.

Cor'il turned around and looked at the obelisk he had just stepped through. It was identical to the device on the hilltop as was the portal contained within it. He concentrated briefly, unraveling the simple weave he had created. The Threads untied themselves and the weave fell apart. The moment he did this, the Threads were thrust out of the object and the doorway collapsed, instantly winking out of existence. The obelisk's glow faded and the buzzing hum was no more.

The three of them stood in silence for a moment, looking around the forest and unsure of what to say or do. The horses found some scrubby grass to munch on and happily did so.

"Well," Orvaril finally said, "that was quite handy." He began slowly walking around, exploring the area. "How did you learn to do that, my boy?"

"It's not something that I can easily explain," he told Orvaril. "Sometimes things just... become apparent to me. I looked at the spire again this morning and I just knew. I suspect it also has other uses."

"*The Great Machine does indeed sometimes reveal information to Threadweavers. That much is true.*"

Be quiet.

Cor'il waited for the voice to respond and was surprised when it didn't. He sighed in relief and looked around, unsure of just *where* in Kuranthas they actually were.

"So," Kendra said, "This obelisk has been here, in your homeland, all along and you never knew about it?"

"As far as I know," Cor'il replied, a bit flummoxed, "it *wasn't* here. I certainly don't remember anyone speak of seeing anything like it. But Kuranthas is a big forest. I am not sure that I've ever been to this part of it. I don't recognize this hilltop."

"*I've been here. Long ago.*"

Cor'il truly was unsure. The people of his village did not travel or explore very far so he did briefly think that this structure could possibly have been here all along without anyone knowing about it.

"*No, it was not here before. Not here. Nothing here. Empty hilltop. I would know.*"

The voice sounded unstable and mayhaps a bit frustrated, and Cor'il was becoming more irritated and distracted by it.

Alright then let's have it. Who are you? At first I thought I was going mad, but you... know things. You aren't just me thinking to myself and I am not imagining you.

"*Has it not been obvious, boy? Do you not recognize me?*"

Antina?

"*Correct!*"

But, how?

"*I've not figured it all out myself but that's not important.*"

No, it is important! I want you out of my head!

Cor'il was met with silence. Suddenly, as if he recognized the area, he knew which direction they should head and he began walking down the hill.

"My home is this way," he said, pointing. He soon heard Kendra and Orvaril following with the horses. "Kendra, once we've arrived, I can ask Dornan Jardov to look at your injuries." He paused a moment but then continued. "If that is what you wish, of course."

"Home. Heading home. But not your home, I sense. They hate you. They all hate you. They will not be happy to see you return. They will tell you to leave, they will. And you deserve it. You're a monster!"

Cor'il ignored her. She had her moments of lucidity in between her periods of madness, but they were few and far between. He wondered if she had been like this before she died. After all, she had been alone in that chamber for 200 years. How would that affect a person? She had seemed clear and rational at that time.

"That would be very nice," Kendra replied. She caught up to Cor'il and walked beside him. Soon Orvaril, leading the three horses, was also nearby. "I would appreciate it. Though everything is slowly feeling better on its own."

"So, my boy, how do you know where we are going?"

"I don't, really."

"But I do! Home. We're going home. Your home. It was your home but now it is nothing. Nothing!" Antina burst into cackling laughter and faded into the back of Cor'il's mind, for which he was thankful.

They walked for a spell, keeping themselves occupied with small talk and listening to Orvaril tell terrible jokes. Cor'il felt ashamed for laughing at some of them— the man's puns were awful.

"I suggest," Kendra finally said, "That we stop for a few. I'd like to rest and eat something."

"Very well," Orvaril agreed. "The lady's idea is a good one. I agree completely!" He secured the horses to a tree and leaned against it. "It certainly would be easier if we could actually, you know, *ride* the horses... being that's what they're for."

"You know as well as I," Kendra said, "that this area is too rough. We don't want one of them breaking a leg." She sat and pulled a carrot from her satchel. She seemed oddly uneasy, and constantly stared up at the trees. Cor'il sat down next to her but remained quiet. He began to watch the trees, too, unsure of exactly what he was looking for. If she was spooked about something, however, it would be wise for him to be cautious as well.

"We are being followed," she whispered.

"How do you know?" Cor'il scrutinized the trees closer but still saw nothing.

"I don't—not for sure, anyway." She bit into the carrot. "But I've got a strange feeling about this place—as if we shouldn't be here. Mayhaps I'm still a bit shaken from earlier, but I've learned to trust my instincts. There is someone out there."

"Someone or *something*?"

"Hopefully neither." She took another loud, crunchy bite. When she was done, she got up and dusted herself off, discarding the carrot's leaves.

Cor'il watched her walk slowly amongst the trees. She stepped over Orvaril who appeared to be asleep already, and then she walked past the horses and, finally, back to where Cor'il sat.

"I don't know who you are," she yelled. "But I know *where* you are!" Her gaze was fixed upward, at a large branch of a tree nearby.

Orvaril's eyes shot open and he looked around him, a bit confused. He gave Kendra a quizzical look that she ignored.

"We will not harm you, but we also do not like being followed. Please come down so that we may speak with you."

At first, nothing happened. Cor'il watched above him, waiting for something to descend upon them and attack. He stood, his hand on his sword, and waited. For a few moments, all was quiet. Nobody moved nor made a sound.

"I promise," Kendra finally said, "that we just wish to talk."

Suddenly, from up in one of the larger trees, a figure leapt from one branch to another. It jumped down to a lower branch, then slid down the tree's trunk and turned to look at the group. Orvaril leapt to his feet and stifled a yawn, attempting to look as if he had not been caught off guard.

Before them stood an elf. Cor'il gasped. He looked over at Kendra who appeared just as surprised as he. Orvaril was unreadable. His face was completely blank.

With blue eyes and short blond hair, the elf's face was slim and delicate. He had two swords—one on either side of his belt, and a bow and quiver were slung across his shoulder. He took several cautious steps forward and then stopped.

"I apologize," he said. His voice was low but soft—almost soothing in a way. "I am a stranger in this land. You three are the first people I have encountered, and I had to exercise caution."

Cor'il was giddy. He was meeting an *elf*!

"So then," Orvaril interrupted. "Where are you headed... um..."

"My name is Alannin Stormbriar and, to be honest, I am not really sure. I know neither where I currently am nor where I should be headed."

"This," Cor'il gestured around them all, "is Kuranthas— my homeland. We are traveling to my village."

"You're certainly welcome to travel with us, friend elf." Orvaril bowed awkwardly, as if he at first thought it a good idea and then suddenly reconsidered.

"It would certainly be preferable to you spying on us," Kendra chided. She still appeared suspicious. Cor'il was merely glad that they hadn't run into goblins or an abomination such as the one Kendra had supposedly seen.

"An elf! Oh, an elf! They have returned after all! But what of the dwarves? Have the dwarves returned, too? It all begins again! It can only end the same and you'll have to do it. Yes, you'll have to end it all! Or the other one—the other boy could do it. Two of you there are. Strange times!"

Cor'il ignored the voice. He pushed her back until she was little more than a whisper.

"I have a companion," Alannin said. "Would it be alright if she joined us?"

"I don't see why not!" Orvaril exclaimed. "The more the merrier! Where is she?"

"She is... rather shy." Alannin looked around briefly but did not see her. "Ilvania!" he called. "Ilvania, come!"

Cor'il heard rustling amongst the bushes. A gray and white wolf leapt out of the undergrowth to stand at the elf's side. Cor'il jumped back, startled. Kendra and Orvaril both did much the same, obviously unsure of what to make of the animal.

"Oh," Alannin started, "do not worry. She will not harm you unless, of course, you mean to harm either her or me. She is very smart and well-behaved."

Despite what the elf told them, all three of them still hesitated until, finally, Cor'il got up the courage to approach. The wolf sat, her tongue hanging out, and allowed him to pet her. He still felt uneasy but was, for the moment, convinced that the wolf was not dangerous.

"Well, then," Orvaril exclaimed, "mayhaps we should be going? Seeing as how none of us knows exactly how far away your village is, of course."

"*Oh, but I know! I do! Tomorrow. We'll reach it tomorrow. And we'll see just how you're welcomed back... if you're welcomed at all.*"

Suddenly, Cor'il felt a knot well up in the pit of his stomach. Mayhaps this wasn't a fantastic idea, after all.

Chapter 16

Cor'il awoke to the sound of Orvaril laughing. He sat up and rubbed his eyes and, for a moment, forgot where he was. The moment he remembered, he felt dread well up within him. He was starting to have second thoughts about returning home. *But I've come this far, haven't I? No, I cannot run away from this. This was my home.*

He felt as though he was forgetting something important. Sure, he was uneasy because he did not know how his family and friends would react to his return, but it felt like there was something more to it. But what was it? It would be easy to simply explain it away as nerves or anxiety, but Cor'il *knew* that there was something he was forgetting—a memory looming on the fringes of his mind that toyed with his emotions.

"Good morning, Cor'il!" Orvaril motioned him over to the small fire he was sitting by. Sizzling over the fire were two, plump rabbits. The wolf, Ilvania, eyed them intently, though she never made a move to snatch them. Orvaril stoked the fire with a stick while Alannin inspected one of his swords. It was shorter than Cor'il's, but it was sleek and elegant. It appeared much better made than Cor'il's own blade.

"Alannin, here, has caught us some breakfast." Orvaril grinned. "He's quite a good hunter!"

"You are the loudest man I have ever met," Kendra growled. "How is anyone supposed to get any sleep between your constant snoring when you're asleep and your babbling when you're awake?" She sat down next to Cor'il and winked at him. "Is there any time of the day or night when you *don't* make any noise?"

"Pardon, milady. But I would advise you then to both fall asleep and wake up before I do!" He chuckled, obviously amused by his own advice. "It's really that simple."

"Gee," she scowled, "thank you for the advice."

Cor'il watched Kendra produce her hairbrush from her satchel and run it through her hair a few times, as she did most mornings. When she was done, she held it securely in her hand instead of putting it back in her bag. She inspected it and scraped away some dirt with her thumbnail, then polished the inset ruby on the back with her sleeve. This was not the first time Cor'il had watched her care for it this way. He was puzzled both by how opulent the brush was as well as how attached to it Kendra seemed. He wondered from whom she had taken it.

The day was already steamy and Cor'il's tunic stuck to his chest. Dull, gray clouds obscured the sun overhead and threatened rain.

"It appears," said Orvaril, "that we are in for a rather unpleasant day. Summer in Cygil can be quite unpleasant, I'm afraid."

"Then let us make the most of it." Alannin began cutting chunks of meat off the spit with the small knife he had pulled from his belt. Cor'il realized suddenly that the elf did not have a satchel or rucksack of any kind. He certainly traveled light, but he also seemed to have everything he required.

"Aye!" Orvaril exuberantly exclaimed. "Let us!" He wasted no time cutting off a chunk of rabbit and stuffing it in his mouth. "It's hot!" he yelled through a mouth full of meat, as he began waving his hands in front of his surprised face.

After Orvaril had calmed down, they ate in relative silence, except for Orvaril who alternated between humming to himself and telling jokes. Cor'il focused more on just what he would say to his friends when he saw them. He had no idea how they would react, or even how *he* would react. *What does one say in a situation like this? I'm probably making a mistake. I shouldn't have come. No. Even if this is a mistake, I need to close the book on this—if that is what this truly is.*

Cor'il, once done with breakfast, quickly gathered his things. With as sticky and hot as it already was, he refrained from putting on his cloak and, instead, he slung it over the satchel on his shoulder. He approached his friends who were still lounging around the fire, picking at whatever was left of the rabbits.

"It appears," Alannin said, "that Cor'il is ready to go already."

"What's the hurry, treeboy?" Kendra grinned and tossed a bone into the fire. She wiped her hands on her skirts which, much like Cor'il's cloak, were in rather bad shape. Kendra's clothes had a lot more blood on them, though.

"Don't be so hard on him, Kendra," Orvaril answered. "He's obviously eager to return home. Were we traveling to *your* homeland, I am sure you would feel the same way."

"I seriously doubt that I would even care to see Alarantha again," Kendra scowled.

"While that is true," Cor'il explained, "I would also like to point out that, should it rain, it would be nice to have some shelter, regardless where it is."

Cor'il knew that was a terrible reason to get them moving. The truth was that he *was* very excited to return home. He was also anxious and troubled—more so than he thought he should be. What was he worried about? He had most certainly put his past behind him and come to terms with his exile, but he felt as though there was something else.

"I know what it is you are afraid of, Kuranthian."

I don't believe you. You rave like a woman gone mad and you tell untruths. You haven't the slightest inkling what I am afraid of.

Antina's voice fell silent.

"Cor'il!" Kendra shouted. Cor'il suddenly noticed that his friends stood around him with concern on their faces.

"Are you alright, my boy?"

Cor'il hesitated, quite unsure of what had happened.

"Of course," he said, "why wouldn't I be?"

"Oh," Kendra retorted, "possibly because you were walking around mumbling nonsense to yourself."

"You nearly stepped in the fire." Alannin was busy burying the glowing embers under a pile of dirt. "We all tried to get your attention but you apparently didn't hear us."

"Or you were ignoring us," Kendra joked. "It really was quite odd." While she may have been joking, Cor'il could sense worry in her voice.

"Don't worry, my boy!" Orvaril clapped Cor'il on the shoulder and laughed. "We all have a little crazy in us sometimes! Or all of the time... the point is—"

"Some of us, more than others," Kendra added. She pointed to Orvaril who bowed in reply. "If the fire is put out, I suppose we should be moving along before Cor'il lapses into another unintelligible tirade." Cor'il noticed her worried glance linger on him before she looked away.

Though Cor'il grinned along with the rest of his companions, he did so nervously, to hide his concern. *Mayhaps I am going mad,* he thought. He took Sky's reins and led him up a small hill. The others followed behind. He could hear them talking about him in hushed whispers, and he quickly turned his attention elsewhere.

He didn't blame them for talking about him. He realized that his behavior was odd. If they knew that he was conversing with a voice inside his head—real or no—they would think him to be crazy. *"Madder than a five-headed duck trying to eat a biscuit",* Ben Falhar used to say. Cor'il had never been quite sure what exactly it was supposed to mean, but he did have to admit it sounded crazy to him.

What made it worse was that he was following the directions of the voice in his head. It... *she* had told him in which direction his village lay and that was all that he had to go on—but he suspected her information was accurate. Thankfully nobody had questioned how he knew where to go, even though he himself frequently did.

Orvaril handed Dummy's reins to Kendra so that he could play a tune on his lute, eventually singing along. The pit pat of rain drops on the leaves soon accompanied his song and he put the lute away, continuing to sing without it. It was a warm drizzle—not at all the cooling rain Cor'il had hoped for. He considered putting on his cloak simply to keep the water off him, but thought better of it, preferring to stay as cool as he could. He suspected that he would be uncomfortable no matter what he did.

"If you happen to see milady fair," Orvaril sang.

"So," Kendra said. The three of them had closed the gap behind Cor'il. "How close are we?"

"I am not certain."

"And what sort of a welcome would you expect for us when we arrive?"

"Of that I am not certain as well."

"And also be sure," Orvaril crooned, "don't mention the maidens lusty and bare."

Overhead, a large bird took flight, squawking loudly. It alighted on a branch not far away and paused. Finally, apparently unsatisfied with its new perch, it took to the air and disappeared above the trees.

"Are you sure," Kendra continued, "that you actually *did* live in this supposed village?"

Orvaril stopped singing for a moment to laugh, but soon resumed his song. Alannin smiled, but Cor'il could read worry on his newfound friend's face. Either nobody else was concerned about Cor'il's behavior anymore or Alannin was simply the only one who was bad at hiding it.

"You are," Alannin started but then paused a moment before continuing. "You are... half-elven?"

"Aye," Cor'il replied. "I have been called that."

"And this village we head toward," Alannin continued, "is it an elven village?"

"It is a human village."

"I have never seen a human village. I am intrigued."

"How can you not have seen a human village before?" Kendra patted Brute's mane. Cor'il still smiled every time he thought of naming such a dainty horse "Brute."

"Where I come from," Alannin explained, "There are no human settlements."

"You can't help but trip over people around here," Orvaril laughed, momentarily pausing during his song. "Well, not around *here*, obviously, but... you know what? Never mind." He resumed singing. Cor'il suspected he was making up the words as he went along. Nevertheless, his own mood seemed to slowly be improving.

But he could feel himself getting more nervous. He wasn't so much afraid of his return anymore; he simply wasn't sure how he felt. It was raining harder, now, and the sky had darkened a bit. The air, however, was just as oppressive as it had been earlier, and Cor'il could tell that everyone was uncomfortable.

It wasn't until an hour or two later that they crested a hill and looked down upon a gentle slope that ended at a babbling creek. Cor'il sighed, relieved to see familiar terrain.

"I know this place," he said. He felt his eyes tear up and he discreetly wiped them on his damp sleeve. "My friends and I used to come here as kids and stomp around in the water. Sometimes, we would try to catch crawfish."

As a kid. Was it really that long ago? A few years at most. It nearly felt like yesterday to him. Over to the right, upstream, was the large rock in the middle of the water that they used to pretend was a boat.

"Further up the creek," Cor'il reminisced, "there is a deeper pool where we used to swim and play 'Drown the Rat.' Alton always ended up being the rat. He was a terrible swimmer and—"

Cor'il paused.

And what? Am I forgetting something?

"Come," he continued. "We are close, now."

"You really don't remember, do you? You will—soon enough."

Cor'il ignored the voice. He didn't want to worry his companions further with another mumbling episode.

"Suit yourself. You'll find out soon enough."

They descended the hill and crossed the creek. After walking a bit further, Cor'il spotted the familiar buildings of his home off in the distance. Both excitement and hesitation coursed through him and, even though he felt like emptying his stomach, his pace quickened. Sky kept with him, carefully traversing the rough ground with relative ease.

"It would be best if I went in first and made sure it is okay to allow you in. Kuranthians are a welcoming sort, but only after they overcome their initial suspicion."

"That sounds like a fine plan, my boy! We'll wait here... in the rain... getting wetter. Don't worry about us. We'll be fine."

Kendra jabbed Orvaril in the ribs with her elbow. He grunted, but kept a grin on his face.

Cor'il left Sky with the other horses and headed toward his home. The foliage became sparser and began to give way to signs of civilization. However, as Cor'il got close, he knew that something was terribly wrong.

Charred husks were all that remained of houses and stores. Some were mere skeletons of buildings while others were no more than piles of rubble and ash. The area was completely devoid of any foliage, and it looked more like a clearing than a village. His stomach knotted up and his heart sank within his chest.

And then he saw the bodies—charred and barely recognizable as having once been human.

He slowly walked into the deserted, ruined village, trying to hold back tears and failing. He wiped them away and continued looking around, hoping for any sign of life. Bodies were trapped underneath rubble—most were burnt and broken—nothing more than bones, blackened and crushed. In some cases, only shadows on the ground were visible—scant markings of where a body once had been.

From what he could tell, they had been like this for a long time. His head swam and his vision clouded as he walked down what used to be the main street through town. Everywhere he looked was more of the same—destruction and death.

If I had been here I could have stopped this. I could have saved my friends.

"Are you so sure about that? You know full well what happened here, but you're unwilling to accept it."

Shut up! You know nothing!

Cor'il wiped his eyes again and found the spot where his house had once been. There were two walls still standing but they were badly charred and broken. He stood where his bed was, now, there was nothing but dirt, rubble, and ash. He did not see a body anywhere in the rubble. *Mayhaps father is still alive?*

"Fool. Not alive. Nobody alive. All dead. Burned, broken, battered... destroyed. Nobody alive!" Antina burst into laughter until she faded away.

Finally, unable to take any more, Cor'il sank to his knees, stared at the ground, and sobbed. The only place he had ever called home was no more. At least, with exile, there had always been a possibility of returning. Now, there was nothing to return to.

"I will find out who or what did this," he sobbed, "and I will make sure they pay for what they did. I promise!"

"Oh, but you really don't *know, do you? You think you can find whoever destroyed your home but you already have found them. Look inside yourself!"*

No! Shut up! I did not—

He stopped, staring at the ground in disbelief as the memories came flooding back all at once.

"Yes, you see it now. I saw the memory a while ago but did not understand the significance until recently. You have

forgotten what you did… what you have become. This was your doing—your anger, your rage."

Cor'il remembered now. He remembered showing off to his friends—making colorful sparks in the air as they watched and laughed. He remembered losing control and feeling the heat as a surge of energy overtook him, sweeping him up in a current like a raging river. *Was that how it happened?*

"Or were you angry about how everyone treated you—how they looked at you and whispered things about you behind your back?"

He had unleashed a concussive wave of fire that day. It had consumed everything, knocking down houses and engulfing everybody in the town. It had exploded, shattering brick and bone, tree and rock. He had heard their screams and watched his three best friends burn to cinders in front of him. He killed them. He had killed them all.

He had not been exiled. His village had not forced him out. He had murdered and destroyed everything, all because he could not control the power within him! Or the anger. All because he had used it like a toy.

"Ah, you see it too, now. Yes, terrible, but not unexpected. But that is behind you now; it is in your past. The future is what is important now. You can use this knowledge to become what you should be."

Cor'il shut her out. He felt anger, sadness, and rage inside him. He had no way to right this wrong. There was no target to hunt down, no orcs to seek out, and no vengeance to exact. It was him. It had been him all along, and he had to live with that knowledge.

I'm dangerous.

"Yes… yes you are. And the Realm needs to know it. You wield immense power just as I once did. How does it feel? Does it make you feel superior? Like you can change the world? Or destroy it?"

It makes me feel sick.

"I'm so sorry, Cor'il."

Cor'il looked up to see Kendra standing in front of him. There was deep sadness in her eyes. She knelt beside him and put her hand on his shoulder. Cor'il could hear his other companions approaching. He tried to stop crying but he couldn't. When he slowly stood up, tears rushing down his face, Kendra hugged him, holding him tightly as he sobbed.

"Do you think anyone survived?" she asked softly.

"No," he replied. "Nobody survived. They are all dead."

"How can you be sure? Mayhaps some of them—"

"Because *I* did this!" Cor'il yelled, pushing her away. "I killed them all! I couldn't control the magic and I killed them!"

Cor'il heard several gasps from around him. He couldn't face his friends. He was too afraid to look them in the eyes, so he continued looking down, watching tears drop from his face onto the dirt.

"It wasn't your fault, Cor'il." Kendra's voice was soothing. At that moment, she reminded him of motherly Eleanor Farnham. Of course, she was dead, now. *Everyone is.*

"Not everyone. Not you. You are important. You dropped the stones into the well, but what you did can be undone, still. Reverse this. Set the world right."

Cor'il collapsed and sat down for several more minutes with memories running through his mind. He would never taste one of Corinne Bailey's pies again. He would never see Lena, Brand, or Alton again. This was not exile. This was destruction. Only the steelwoods remained standing in the area, now.

Several more moments passed while he sat on the ground. Eventually, the tears stopped, replaced with frustration and anger. He balled his fists hard enough to dig his fingernails into his palms. The pain was real, and it was a reminder to him that he could somehow accidentally do this again.

"I have to go," he said, standing up. He wiped his eyes on his sleeve again and sniffed through a runny nose.

"Where are we going?" Orvaril asked.

"I don't know, but I am going alone."

"Now you wait a bloody minute, treeboy!" Kendra's once soothing voice was now dripping with anger. "You're not going to run off and—"

"Kendra," Cor'il said calmly. "I killed everyone here—even my three best friends."

"It was an accident," she said.

"Aye," he replied, grabbing Sky's reins. "You're right. And I don't want to risk having another one. If I were to lose control again, there is no telling what could happen."

"Especially considering that you wield more power now than you did then."

"I must be alone, at least until I sort some things out. I need to learn how better to use the Threads. They still fight me sometimes, and I can't risk putting any of you in danger."

Cor'il climbed up on his horse's back. Kendra mounted Brute as well. She had a scowl on her face, glaring at him.

"I am sorry, my friends," he said. "But this is something I *must* do." He fought back more tears as he realized that he may never be able to see them again. *This is for the best. I can't risk their lives if it should happen again.*

"We could simply follow you," Orvaril piped up. "You know, at a distance."

"I am sorry, my friend, but this is something I must do alone—at least for now." Cor'il urged Sky down the rough, blackened road at a slow walk. There was no sense in hurrying when one had nowhere to be. He looked straight ahead of him, trying not to ignore the death and destruction all around him.

"Come on," he heard Kendra say from behind him. "We're going with him."

"No, milady. We must let him go. I believe he may be right—that he needs to do this on his own."

"Stuff it, storyweaver."

"Milady," Orvaril replied calmly. "Trust me. If our paths are meant to cross in the future, they will."

"Damn you, treeboy!" Kendra shouted.

Cor'il did not look back. It would have broken his heart. The rain was still falling, but Cor'il barely noticed it as he left his friends behind, headed toward uncertainty just as he had done a year ago. Only, this time, things were not as simple as they once were.

Chapter 17

Garwin Greenbriar cowered behind the barn, desperately trying to catch his breath in the light of the full moon. He looked around him, but nobody was there—though he could hear their voices in the distance, barking orders to one another in the darkness. They were not going to give up. They had a tracker—a large, round man who had more hair on his chest than on his head. Garwin had only seen him once and he had barely escaped.

Of course, he was on foot and the Red Swords were on horseback. He could sooner outrun them as he could escape the moon above. There was at least a dozen of them, mayhaps more, and he was no warrior. He kept a small knife on his belt that he used for hunting—it would do him no good tonight.

He brushed wet, brown hair out of his face and wiped his sweaty hands on his breeches. *There* must *be a way out of this. Mayhaps I could talk to them—tell them I didn't do whatever it is they think I've done?*

The truth was, he hadn't the slightest idea why these Red Sword soldiers were interested in him. He was nothing more than a simple farm boy of 14 summers who helped his parents with their sheep and vegetables. *And can, apparently, command lightning… and disappear in one place and reappear in another. That's probably it. But I haven't hurt anyone or done anything wrong!*

He called it *jumping*, but there was probably a better term for his ability to disappear.

He briefly remembered that he had forgotten to let the sheep out into the field before he had fled. But his thoughts quickly turned to his parents and how they had offered him up to the Red Swords, demanding payment in return. He was shocked when he found out that they had sought out the soldiers themselves.

The sheep can go to The Abyss. He balled his hands into fists and pounded the ground. *And so can my parents. I'll show them! One day I will be powerful and command armies! And if they need my help with anything, they won't get it!*

His mind loved to wander. He constantly dreamt up complex stories in which he was the hero who saved his village from evil men. Of course, he'd had to leave Dunshire when he'd heard what his parents had planned to do. Thankfully, not many people recognized him here in Brambleton, which meant fewer people could point fingers toward his location.

He felt bad for his sister, though. Alana had been the one to warn him, and she had helped him escape before the Red Swords arrived at the house. He wondered if he would ever see her again. They had never gotten along well, but if he had had any doubt before, he knew now that she loved him at least a little.

The voices were getting nearer. *I need to get out of here.* Garwin wasn't very familiar with Brambleton—though his home was nearby, he rarely left the farm. He wasn't sure where in this village he could go where he would be safe. His original intent had been to hide in a barn nearby, but it was locked. The soldiers were heading this direction and, with a tracker in their midst, they would easily find him.

He had always been curious about trackers. Nobody quite knew why they were so good at finding targets, and most people did not have the proper skills or abilities to be one. Garwin had never met a tracker and, hopefully, he would not meet one tonight. And to think, he once wanted to *be* a tracker.

"The boy is definitely nearby, in the town up ahead," he heard the tracker shout. The man had a distinct, low voice that carried very clearly through the night air.

Garwin shivered as he looked around, peeking out from the edge of the barn. He could see flickering torches in the distance. They were spread out in a wide line as they combed the outskirts looking for him. He darted out from behind the barn, staying low behind a wooden fence, and headed toward a small road leading into town.

Thankfully, this late at night, everyone should be asleep. Though these soldiers, once they reached town, would probably wake everybody. *If my own parents would offer me up to these Red Swords, certainly strangers in this town would do the same.*

When he got to the end of the fence, he spotted a building across the road. It was too dark to tell if it was a house, but there was no light inside that he could see. Garwin darted across the street, fumbling in the dark, until he reached the house. The door was, as he'd feared, locked. He peered in the window, but saw only darkness. He desperately tried the door again but it would not budge.

"Keep your eyes open, men!" One of the soldiers shouted. "This boy is young but he could be dangerous!" They were still off in the distance, but they were getting closer.

Me? Dangerous?

Garwin spotted light approaching from further within the town. He heard the clopping of hooves on the dirt road and wheels crunching gravel beneath them. He looked around, frightened, and saw no immediate place he could hide. There was another building across the street—closer to town—but he could not risk crossing and being spotted by the approaching carriage. If they saw him they could tell the soldiers where he had gone.

He fixed his gaze on the house. *It will have to do. Time to try this again.*

The last time Garwin had tried to disappear he had ended up reappearing a few feet above a pond—a rather chilly pond, at that. Each time before that, he had met with similar results. In fact, the only time he had successfully reappeared *exactly* where he wanted to be had been shortly after he had accidentally discovered his ability.

Fortunately, he had never ended up anywhere dangerous, but that fear was very real. He stared at the house and concentrated, visualizing the exact spot where he wanted to reappear. In his mind, he could see it start out small and, then, rapidly approach him. It almost felt as if he was not so much going to it but, rather, he was pulling *it* to *him.*

Sweat beaded up on his forehead and began trickling down his cheeks. His hands shook and his vision distorted in a moment of nausea. The house and everything around it blurred and twisted in a spiral, distorted and impossibly bent. He felt himself yanked toward it and, as quickly as it started, it all stopped.

Garwin quickly looked around to find that he was now on the front roof of the house. Dizzy and wary, he sluggishly climbed around to the rear of the building and slumped down to rest.

Not perfect, he thought, gasping for air. *But better than most other times.* And there was the added benefit of not having hurt himself. *Hopefully this will throw the tracker off a bit. If I am not leaving tracks or signs of passing, mayhaps it will make it more difficult for them.*

Garwin wished he could master his jumping ability. If he was in control if it, he would probably have a much better chance of escaping. Even a short *jump* like this caused immediate, overwhelming fatigue that took a while from which to recover. Even if his life depended on it—which it might—he wasn't sure if he could *jump* again for a while or where he would end up if he did.

Garwin listened to the sounds of the carriage as it moved down the road, past the house. He peeked out to see its shadowy form—dimly lit by a lantern—now heading away from town and he breathed a sigh of relief. Whoever it was hadn't noticed him. He was safe.

Soon, however, he remembered the Red Swords. Escaping the carriage had been a huge accomplishment—but only briefly. He still needed to escape, and he feared that the soldiers would not be nearly as easy to evade as a carriage.

What if I fought them? Garwin was much better at summoning lightning than he was at *jumping. Mayhaps I could scare them into retreating or even defeat them.* The idea of standing up to them was appealing, however, he found that he simply could not do it.

The thought of killing anyone left a bad taste in his mouth. He remembered back to a day when he was seven summers and he had watched a squirrel eat a nut on the woodpile outside his house. Curious, he'd picked up a rock and had thrown it at the animal. His aim had been true and he had hit the squirrel, which stumbled off into the bushes and probably had later died. While his parents had praised him for his good aim, he had felt guilty and sad for weeks. Upon thinking about it just now, he found that he *still* felt bad.

The mere possibility of killing anything—especially another person—tied his stomach in knots. But what if *they* wanted to kill *him*? What then? Would he defend himself against them or would he simply let them kill him? Though he had constantly daydreamed about these types of adventures, he had never once considered that they could come to pass. *Some hero I am. Running scared!*

Not only did he need to figure out how to get off the roof, but he also had to figure out where to go next. He looked over the edge and saw that it was quite a drop. The roof hung slightly over a descending hill. If he dropped off the back, it would be a long fall and an even longer tumble that he was pretty sure would result in an injury.

With his heart still racing, he nervously scooted over to the front of the house and noticed a gutter that emptied out into the street. It was a crude, metal pipe that didn't look very sturdy, but he thought it would be safer to try climbing down that way instead of simply jumping off the roof. Exhaustion was setting in, and he was unsure of how much more he could take. He would need to find a safe place to sleep soon... if there was such a place. Worry crept further into his mind.

Taking a deep breath, he slowly climbed out over the edge and, gripping the gutter tightly, he began to shimmy down the side of the house. Immediately, he realized his mistake as the pipe began to creak and pull away from the building. Before he knew it, he was on the ground, dazed with pain shooting through his left leg and up his back. He couldn't help but cry as he lay in the grass.

"What was that?" one of the men yelled.

"It came from over there!" the tracker replied.

Get up! Stop crying and get up! Run!

Garwin slowly rose to his feet but fell to one knee as his left leg collapsed. He noticed several people had emerged from their houses and were now standing in the street, watching. Soon after, a man and a woman approached and helped him over to the porch stairs of the house where he collapsed.

"The Goodness," the woman exclaimed, looking him over. She sounded older, but Garwin's blurry vision could not make out many details. "What happened to you?"

"I," he stammered, "I fell. I was on the roof and—"

"The roof?" the man interrupted. "Goodness, son, what were you doing up there?"

"There are... there are soldiers tracking me—Red Swords."

"Red Swords!" The woman brushed Garwin's hair out of his face and dried his eyes with the corner of her nightdress. "What in the Realm would the Red Swords want with a young boy? You can't be older than 13!"

"Fourteen, actually." He sniffed, his nose running. "I have to go. I don't want—"

"Well," the man said. "You're not an orc or an elf, so I have no idea why the Red Swords would be coming after you."

"Clearly," the woman agreed. "I am Dolly and this is my husband Wil."

"I need to get away from here." Garwin tried to stand up without putting any weight on his left leg.

"I don't think you're going anywhere, son. Not with that injured leg." Wil knelt down and examined Garwin's leg. The boy winced from the pain. "It's most likely broken."

168

"Please," Garwin pleaded, "I need to hide, then. I don't want the Red Swords to find me." He was crying again, sobbing now.

"We'll do what we can, dear." Dolly stood up and, along with Wil, lifted Garwin to his feet. They helped him hobble into the street and toward a house closer to town and on the other side of the road.

The familiar sounds of horses and men broke the relative silence as seven Red Sword soldiers galloped into town with the tracker in the lead. Their torches lit up the night and cast flickering shadows about.

"Is that him?" one of the men asked.

"Aye," the tracker replied.

"Halt, by order of the Red Swords!"

Both the man and the woman stopped in the middle of the street, still supporting Garwin, and turned to face the soldiers.

"We are here for the boy—official business of the Red Swords as authorized by Captain Jarel Forsch himself. We demand that you hand him over to us."

The man dropped off his horse and removed his helmet. He had plentiful, curly black hair and a clean-shaven face. His left eye was stuck in a squint and he was missing several teeth.

"He's just a child!" Dolly shouted. "What harm can he do to the Realm?"

"This is not your concern, woman." The soldier approached and drew his sword. The blade was blood red. "If you do not hand him over, we will take him by whatever means necessary." He looked out to the others who had emerged from their homes to watch the spectacle. "Return to your homes!" he shouted to them. "This is official Red Sword business!"

"Surely," Wil added, "this is a mistake. This boy is harmless!"

"If you stand in our way, then you will be considered an enemy of the Realm," the man said in a monotone, emotionless voice. He pointed his sword at all three of them and inched closer.

Garwin was having trouble thinking straight. The pain in his leg was overwhelming and he felt faint. He briefly considered *jumping*, but he doubted he could concentrate enough. He feared that he would end up impaled on a tree branch or reappearing 30 feet in the air. There was no escape, and the Red Swords would hurt these kind people just to get to him. He had no doubt that this man would carry out any threat he made. But he also sounded... afraid? Did this man fear him?

"I repeat," the man said after nobody made a move. "Hand over the boy and no harm will come to you. If you resist, however, we will take him by whatever means necessary."

"Please," Garwin whispered, "I don't want you to get hurt. I thank you for your kindness." He could see no way out of this. He gently shrugged them off and clumsily made his way over to the soldiers. He was afraid and tired and all he could feel was pain.

"Ah," the man said, "smart boy. Now listen to me and listen carefully," he growled. "I'd sooner kill you and be done with it, but Captain Forsch has other plans. If you try anything—if you try to escape or you hurt any of my men, I will run you through myself."

Garwin nodded, tears running down his cheeks.

"What is so important?" Wil growled. "Why are the Red Swords scared of a child?"

The soldiers ignored Wil's taunts.

"I don't know what it is you can do," the soldier said, turning to Garwin, "and I don't give two shits. But the Captain apparently has something he wants from you so, for now, you get to live. Abyss, we may even help you with your... injury."

Garwin was lifted up and placed on one of the horses, his hands bound behind his back. His leg exploded in pain and his vision clouded. He couldn't be sure, but the soldier with whom he rode did not seem pleased to be sharing a horse with him. In fact, the man appeared scared.

"The Red Swords thank you for your cooperation!" the soldier shouted as his men turned their horses out of town and rode. "But in the future," he continued, "I would advise you to be quicker with your decisions. Not everyone is as patient as I."

Garwin heard several soldiers laugh as he turned his horse to join them.

Chapter 18

Three days had passed since Cor'il had split from his friends, and his anger, frustration, and sadness had not yet subsided. If anything, they were more intense. He remembered, now. He remembered *everything,* and nothing he did would allow him to forget any of it.

On the first day, he had ridden hard. He had gotten as far away as possible from Kuranthas and hadn't stopped until Sky finally showed signs of fatigue. Had he been able to, he would have continued through the night. While he didn't usually need much sleep, he slept even less, now, kept awake by his terrible thoughts and memories. When he *did* sleep, his dreams were filled with horrible visions both of what he had already done and what was possible in the future.

The paranoia had only gotten worse, made even more intense by the voice inside his head. At one point, before he could calm himself down, he found himself running wildly in a clump of trees, chasing someone—or something—that he couldn't even see, and screaming for it to show itself. He had eventually collapsed, sobbing into his hands. Worse, still, he was certain that he was being followed.

Setting out on his own had certainly been the right decision—of that, he was sure. He could not risk harming anyone else. The only option had been to leave. That didn't mean, however, that it wasn't painful to do so.

"You abandoned them. You left them in great danger."

I spared *them great danger. I cannot harm them, now.*

"But you are not the only dangerous creature that roams the land."

They can take care of themselves. Together, they will be just fine without me.

"You believe you are being followed—hunted."

I don't know what to believe.

The two following days had included long rides as well, but Cor'il had eventually slowed his pace. He did not want to hurt his horse, nor did he know exactly where he was headed. All he knew was that he was headed north, but he now began to feel the need to have an actual destination. He remembered The Densewood and, even though his friends might try to look for him there, it was the only place left that felt like home to him.

He had to find his way back. Cor'il was still largely unfamiliar with this land and was not too keen on sticking to the roads if those Red Sword soldiers were actively looking for him. At this point, he was in such a torrent of emotion that he simply didn't think he could control himself. His greatest worry, however, was that he wasn't sure if he wanted to avoid contact for his safety or *theirs*.

And now, here he was, aimlessly riding across the Realm, wondering if he would accidentally hurt someone else. He was alone, he was tired, and he was angry.

Cor'il snapped out of his thoughts and he found himself face to face with a rather large group of orcs. He had easily seen them coming—first the scouts, then the warriors. But he made no effort to flee or to hide. At this point he found that he did not care. He halted Sky about 30 feet from the group, defiantly staring at each orc.

If they want a fight, then I will gladly give them one.

"*And if they kill you?*"

Then so be it.

"*It is glorious to die in battle. That makes a true warrior. You are not a warrior. You are a Threadweaver and you shall not die this day. You should destroy them all, right now. Unleash the power within the Threads. These creatures are parasitic and insignificant. They are nothing but biteflies to you and should be crushed under your boot. You will shape the world. You will move mountains.*"

"If you know what is good for you," Cor'il spoke, "You will let me pass." He made sure to project his voice to sound as imposing as he could. He created a simple weave to make his voice louder and deeper so that all the orcs could hear him.

They moved to surround him on all sides, forming a large circle, and not giving Sky much room to move. The white stallion was skittish and nervously stomping his feet, whinnying quietly. Cor'il kept him steady, however, and remained defiant.

"It's okay, boy," Cor'il whispered, patting the horse's mane. A lesser-trained mount would probably have kicked him off and bolted by now, he suspected.

"We no let pass," one of the orcs replied. He had a single, black braid jutting out from the top of his skull and wore a bandolier on which hung several skulls. His mount, a large black wolf, snarled and drooled. The axe he held looked to be in better shape than the weapons held by the rest of the tribe. "We kill and eat both you and horse," he laughed.

The rest all laughed, too. Had Cor'il been in a different mindset, it may have sent chills through him. He remembered being afraid of orcs at one time. He squinted and said nothing.

This seemed to confuse the orc. His grin slowly faded as the two of them stared at each other, each refusing to yield. This continued for several moments until the orc finally urged his wolf slowly forward.

But the wolf made it only one step. In that short amount of time the chieftain realized his folly when Cor'il uttered one simple word.

"Dorinaus."

In a heartbeat, the very ground came alive, erupting from beneath the orcs. A hand made of dirt and stone surged upward from the ground and engulfed both orc and wolf. The chieftain screamed, but only for an instant as the hand closed around him. Blood and gore sprayed every direction, showering much of the orcish pack with the entrails of their leader.

Just as quickly as it appeared, the hand returned to the land from which it came, leaving a crowd of confused, stunned, and horrified orcs in complete silence.

Cor'il made no other move. He merely stared out at the circle of would-be attackers, scowling at them and almost daring them to advance. He did not want to admit it, but that had felt good.

"Yes! The magic spells—the words of power! They are so rarely used but can be so much more powerful than manual weaves! No, kill the rest. Kill them! How dare they attack you! They are not fit to walk this Realm! They are savages—nothing but mindless killers. Crush them under the weight of your boot and show them what makes a true warrior!"

"Chieftain dead!" one of the orcs in the crowd shouted, his voice filled with surprise. He looked around, confused and with fear slowly creeping in. "What do now?"

"You turn, and you leave!" Cor'il shouted, still amplifying his voice. "And you never bother me again. You turn around and flee like the cowards that you are." It took an immense amount of restraint for him to not kill the rest of them outright. He was angry, and it would be so easy to turn that anger against these orcs, but he stayed his hand.

The orcs, many of them bowing their heads, did not move. To Cor'il it appeared that they simply didn't know what to do or where to go. *Do they rely on their leaders that much?*

Cor'il did not move, either. He was now interested to find out what the orcs would do. Finally, after much waiting and staring at one another, several of the orcs at the edge of the pack slowly turned and began to leave. They looked both sad that their leader was dead and angry that Cor'il had killed him. Cor'il knew that the way he had dispatched their chieftain had broken them.

Most of them.

Four of the larger, unmounted orcs closest to Cor'il looked at each other, grunted, and then suddenly attacked. Cor'il drew his sword and quickly dispatched one of them, stabbing him in the throat.

"Sorigion," he said, pointing at two of his attackers. Shimmering, translucent spears of light appeared above his head

and impaled the two orcs, disappearing shortly afterward. Both brutes crumpled in pools of blood on the ground.

The remaining attacking orc glowered at his dead companions, but still leapt at Cor'il, knocking him off Sky's back. He fell backwards, landing hard on the ground. The pack of orcs cheered happily and clattered their weapons together.

Cor'il wrestled with the orc, completely outmatched in every way. One of the orc's thick, strong arms pinned him to the ground as the brute raised his axe above his head and wailed.

Instinctively, Cor'il channeled red and black Threads through his body and instantly felt his strength bolstered. He thought back to how Dalinil had done this many times and concentrated, trying to copy the same actions. He felt more strength flow through him, then more.

The orc brought his axe down, but Cor'il grabbed his arm and stopped the attack. He both felt and heard bones snap as the orc cried out in pain. Cor'il then, using his newfound strength, threw the now stunned orc off him and got to his feet.

He then dispatched the orc by caving in its skull with his fist.

The rest of the orcs, once again, fell silent, completely shocked and confused.

"Would anyone else like to challenge me?" Cor'il yelled, his voice dripping with rage. Anger and strength coursed through his body, along with a sickening feeling from the black Threads. He was breathing hard and had balled both fists tightly. "Well?"

They all began to slowly turn away, heads down in shame and sadness.

"No! You had your chance the first time," Cor'il growled. He created a weave out of the red and black Threads he held and set it loose upon the retreating pack, consuming them all in fiery explosions and leaving none alive.

"It feels good, doesn't it? They got what they deserved. You set them free and should be commended for being so generous! Do not have remorse—this could not have ended any

other way. A favor—you have done the Realm a great favor indeed! Have no remorse! No regret!"

Cor'il mounted Sky and looked out at the landscape. Charred and broken corpses lay in unnatural positions everywhere. Several bodies had been blown into nearby trees, left to hang from the branches until they were picked clean by scavengers. The pungent smell of cooked orc and wolf was awful, but Cor'il barely noticed. He looked at the veritable graveyard before him and felt... nothing.

No, he thought as he urged Sky forward, *no remorse.*

Chapter 19

Arcturas sat at the table, waiting patiently. Today would hopefully be the day that he and several others had been preparing for. Ilathri had finally moved.

The city now sat in an open field. There was a stream nearby but, Arcturas knew nothing else. He could only observe what he saw from within the city's walls, and that was often very little.

He sipped his tea carefully—it was still very hot. Next to him, Braelus fidgeted and fumbled with his cup, sloshing some of the green liquid onto the round table. He nervously looked up at Arcturas who simply grinned in response. Braelus really was eager to learn. That was always a good thing. He'd never seen a pupil so excited.

Also around the table sat three others—Barinar, Aleisha, and Salomil. Arcturas had specifically asked for their services today because he knew that he would need them. It was one thing to have as much knowledge as he did, but Arcturas knew full well the value of others' input. His knowledge was vast but he was no expert on many subjects.

Frustratingly enough, he wasn't exactly sure *why* he needed their knowledge—only that the Threads had urged him to seek them out. It was not something he dwelled on. During his many years, he had learned to let the Threads guide him but not control him—much like a strong river current. One need only listen to hear what the Great Machine suggested.

"Today shall be a very important day," he said, staring into his teacup. Little flecks of tea leaves floated about, hovering just below the surface. He rubbed his chin with his thumb and forefinger and briefly remembered that he had forgotten to shave.

"He is coming, then?" Aleisha asked. She was a truly beautiful woman—shoulder-length honey-colored hair and green eyes. She had a quiet, gentle demeanor that never failed to soothe

Arcturas with every word she spoke. Her specialty was artifacts, and there was no one more knowledgeable.

Barinar and Salomil were brothers. Both were slender and tall. Salomil had curly brown hair and a beard to match while Barinar was mostly bald, save for a few wispy strands of white hair. Both had extensive knowledge of various creatures and antiquities.

"I believe so," Arcturas replied. "The city has shifted. Ilathri has sought him out."

"But," Barinar replied, "why? You have already met with the Threadweaver, correct?"

"Aye, that is so." Arcturas sipped his tea which was bitter but had a slight licorice sweetness to it. It wasn't his favorite, but it would do. "I have met with *one* of the Threadweavers. There is another."

Everyone around the table fell silent, obviously shocked and confused.

"How is there another?" Aleisha asked. "There has always ever been only one."

"To have *two* Threadweavers is..." Barinar stammered.

"I thought," Aleisha continued, "that we were supposed to meet him when the city moved into the forest a little while ago.

"As did I," Arcturas responded. "And we should have."

That much was troubling. Never had there been a city shift that had resulted in nothing. They had previously been in a forest, awaiting the arrival of this... other Threadweaver, but he had never arrived. Arcturas could not remember this having happened before. It troubled him, but it was often not wise to dwell on things out of his control.

Control. Is it possible that this other Threadweaver is outside the influence of the Great Machine? What does this mean?

"Let us hope, then," Salomil added, "that this shift is not also a mistake." The man rarely spoke unless needed, so Arcturas could sense his palpable concern. "It is troubling to think that

Ilathri is seeking out a Threadweaver that does not wish to be sought."

"There is no evidence to prove that the last shift was a mistake." Arcturas suddenly had no desire to drink his tea. He swirled it around his cup, watching the bits of tea leaf move around in a circle, before he looked back up at his colleagues.

"Then what *does* it mean?" Salomil asked, scratching the back of his head nervously.

"I... cannot be completely sure. Things have changed—the path that was intended has now taken an unexpected turn, I believe."

"And what are we to do about it, then?" Barinar, too, seemed a bit unsure. He, like the other two, looked to Arcturas for guidance.

"We await this new Threadweaver's arrival," Braelus replied, much to Arcturas' surprise. "He is close, now. I can feel him. He brings waves in the Threads wherever he goes, they surrender to him completely."

He is *learning... and quite quickly.*

"Yet," Aleisha interjected, "there is something else, isn't there?"

"Aye," Arcturas replied. "There is. The Threads bend to his will—we have all felt that. Whereas Threadweavers traditionally work *with* the Threads, this individual appears to be able to, to some degree, *force* the Threads. But they also appear to influence his actions to an extent."

"I know nothing about how he should *use* the Threads," Barinar interrupted. "But is it not the way of the Threads to surrender to their influence?"

"That is the way I understood it," Salomil agreed. "Has this *also* changed?"

"You are both correct," Arcturas confirmed. "But this is... different. The Threads influence one's actions with gentle nudges. But I have sensed what appears to be more like pushes than nudges at times."

"Does this concern you?" Aleisha asked.

"A little. I have many theories as to the cause, which is why I have asked for your expertise—all of you. I am not sure how much time we will have with this one, so we need to make it all count."

"I will do what I can, Arcturas," Aleisha said. Barinar and Salomil nodded in agreement.

"He is going to have many questions," Salomil continued. "Will we be able to answer them?"

"I suspect that there will be some questions left unanswered. That is nothing new." Arcturas poked his finger in his tea, causing the flecks to swim around. It was still very hot. "Whatever information the Great Machine passes to us we will pass onto him."

"Things feel... different this time." Aleisha's face showed great concern.

"What do you mean?" Barinar inquired.

"It feels," she continued, "as if there is something else out there. That is the only way I can explain it, and I don't yet know what that is supposed to mean."

All three nodded. Arcturas could recount several times in the past when he had experienced something similar. It was the way the Great Machine worked and they lived in accordance. But Arcturas held back his knowledge about this new entity—the Dark Machine. He knew so little about it. To present its existence would probably result in wild rumor and misinformation—mayhaps even panic. Fortunately, Braelus also remained silent on the subject, but he gave his teacher a quizzical look.

"Mayhaps," Braelus suggested, "it has something to do with the dual Threadweavers?" He paused a minute, obviously collecting his thoughts. "This *is* the first time in recorded history that there have been two concurrent weavers."

This was something that had puzzled Arcturas for some time, now. He had not decided if it was a new danger or merely a new beginning. No matter how much thought he gave it, he never came to any conclusions either way.

"Your pupil proposes an interesting correlation," Salomil added. "Mayhaps there is more of a connection than we realize. Surely we have all considered this possibility."

"The truth is," Aleisha interrupted, "we seem to be entering uncharted territory."

"Or we have been there for some time." Barinar added. "And mayhaps we are just now realizing it."

"We have the opportunity to blaze a new trail," Aleisha continued. "But none of us is sure where that trail shall lead the world. Do we have the courage to walk that path?"

"Aye," Arcturas agreed. "But, lately, it feels as if the *trail* is leading *us*."

"There are others, sir," Braelus said, standing up. He looked both nervous and determined, as if he had something to say but was afraid to say it.

"Others?" Aleisha asked, looking quite puzzled. "Other *what?*"

"Can you not feel their presence, sir?"

"Whose presence, Braelus?" Arcturas clasped his hands in front of him on the table.

"Other people who can command the Threads, sir."

"Preposterous!" Barinar shouted. Salomil and Aleisha were speechless but both gasped in shock.

"Ah, the Threadspinners we discussed," Arcturas replied. "Do you believe they have something to do with our current state?"

Barinar, Salomil, and Aleisha all began muttering to each other in stout disbelief. Braelus started to say something but Arcturas could not hear him properly.

"Quiet!" he shouted. The other three immediately stopped talking. "Thank you, my friends. I apologize for my rudeness, but this is no time to lose all logic. Please, Braelus, continue."

"I," Braelus stammered, unsure how to proceed. "I began feeling... others a while ago. I don't know how much time in Ilathri has passed since then but, in the realms of the Threadweavers, I would guess it has been somewhere just over a year."

"I don't believe—" Salomil started, but cut himself off when Arcturas shot him a disapproving glare.

"At first," Braelus continued, "I wasn't sure what it was. Each new... Threadspinner... felt like a pinprick—like a tiny mote of light in vast darkness. A few have winked out, but many more have appeared to take their places."

Aleisha, Salomil, and Barinar all remained quiet, dumbfounded and apparently trying to process what they had just learned.

Arcturas closed his eyes and cleared his mind. He concentrated on the Great Machine and the Threads themselves. Though he knew not *where* the two Threadweavers were— locations were meaningless to Ilathri—he could sense them just the same. And one was approaching. Proximity to Ilathri was only revealed when the two were very close to each other.

But the familiar feeling of the Threadspinners was also there. Braelus had described it well—pinpricks of light in a vast darkness. He knew that this information would be troubling to the others.

"I promise, sir, that I can sense them. They are not nearly so bright a light as the two Threadweavers, but they nonetheless shine." He paused, unsure of what else to say. He seemed frustrated. "I assure you, while they do not command the full range of Threads, they are out there."

"I believe you, learner," Arcturas replied. "As I have felt them, too. This, also, is a very new development—unprecedented. We would all be wise to be mindful of this."

"And what do we do with this new information?" Salomil stood up abruptly and began pacing the room with his hands clasped behind his back. Aleisha watched him, worried. He had a temper—most everyone knew that. Arcturas had encountered it many times in the past. Salomil was extremely intelligent, but he became uncomfortable with both change and the unknown.

"We do what we always do," Arcturas calmly replied. He rose and put his hand on Salomil's shoulder. "We see what happens. For now, we have the Threadweaver's arrival, and he has a lot to learn. Mayhaps he can enlighten us as much as we can enlighten him."

"Aye," Aleisha agreed. "I sense no direction from the Great Machine with regards to these new... Threadspinners as you call them, Braelus. But if you have sensed these individuals then I believe you."

Every day my student surprises me just a bit more. If he is the only one besides me to sense these new Threadspinners, then he has made a monumental leap of ability.

Not only that, but the world had made a leap, too. One Threadweaver was commonplace. Arcturas had been shocked to learn of *two*. But, now, there were others out there—less powerful, but they still had command of the Threads. Would there be *more* Threadweavers yet to come?

"While this is a truly remarkable era, I encourage caution and careful observation." Arcturas sat down and pushed his tea cup away. It was only serving as a distraction which he did not need.

"Is there something in particular that concerns you?" Salomil also hadn't touched his tea. He had stopped pacing but still stood, gazing out the window.

"No," Arcturas replied. "Nothing specific. But you *do* remember our long sleep—when the Threads went stiff and unresponsive."

"You believe that could happen again?" Barinar looked worried. Arcturas knew that Barinar had been particularly concerned about everything involving the long sleep. It had shaken him and he was constantly in fear of another one.

"I have no reason to believe it will." Arcturas had no inkling what to expect, but another long sleep did not seem to be where events were headed. "The Threads are more vivacious than ever. I do not believe that we are headed for another long sleep. In fact, I believe just the opposite."

"What is the opposite of a long sleep, sir?"

"Well, Braelus, I believe the opposite of a long sleep is an awakening, for lack of a better term."

Everyone around the table stared blankly at Arcturas who, truthfully, only grasped at the concept as if he were trying to grab water in his hands. He felt that there was more to it—more than just additional, unexpected Threadspinners out there. It was something that he would have to ponder. Ultimately, if it was the Great Machine's will, he would gain that knowledge. Until then, he could only conjecture.

"Let us prepare, then." Aleisha stood up to leave. "As always, we shall do what needs to be done. These are... intriguing times, to say the least." She nodded and left.

"Aye," Barinar agreed. He also stood and left.

Salomil, however, lingered.

"You have concerns," Arcturas stated. It wasn't a question. It was obvious on Salomil's face.

"Aye, Arcturas. This is all wrong." He wrung his hands nervously and seemed distracted. "This is not how it should be."

"This is not how it has *been*." Arcturas rose, clasping his hands in front of him. "But that does not mean it is not how things *should* be. That is not for us to decide. The Great—"

"What if the Great Machine is fallible?" His brow furrowed, as if it pained him to say it. "We have always allowed it propel us, as if we were riding a wave to the shore. But what if that wave is, unbeknownst to us, actually taking us further out to sea?"

"Have you sensed something, Salomil?"

"I have not, Arcturas. But I am uneasy. Not only is there more than one Threadweaver, but we now have these... Threadspinners out there who are wandering about the world without our guidance and influence. Does that not trouble you?"

"I... do not know. It is certainly a lot to think about."

"It worries me, greatly."

This was precisely the reason that Arcturas chose to let the Dark Machine remain a secret—at least for now. He could only imagine the chaos it would cause.

"We can do nothing about it. For now, let us prepare." Arcturas ushered Salomil out of the room and followed close behind. The time was near.

Chapter 20

Ilathri's gates creaked open once again, as they had countless times in the past. On the other side of the wall stood a boy—probably of no more than 20 winters. Like those before him, he obviously knew not what was happening and, just like the others, it showed on his face. He held onto the reins of a white horse beside him.

Unless Arcturas was mistaken this boy was what the world called "half-elven" and, as far as he could remember, that was a first. It was the ears. Elves had traditionally more delicate features and longer, pointed ears. But this boy looked human—except for his ears.

It wasn't that Threadweavers were always human—far from it. In fact, Arcturas remembered reading about an orcish Threadweaver from many ages past, though he had long since forgotten the name. And there had certainly been elvish Threadweavers in the past, with Antina Delovine having been the most recent. *Intriguing that a half-elf would follow an elf in the art. But there are now* two, *aren't there? If only I was sure of where they both fit, it would help me gain some perspective.*

"I welcome you to Ilathri," he said. The initial greeting was always awkward for Arcturas, not knowing anything about the individual before him. In the past, he had tried a plethora of different greetings, but it never mattered—he always felt wooden and somewhat out of place. "I am Arcturas. Please, step through the gates. We have much to discuss, and I am unsure how much time we have."

"I—" the boy stammered. He looked around nervously, fidgeting with the hilt of a sword at his waist. "But... where am I?"

"You have found Ilathri or, rather, Ilathri has found you. Mayhaps the best place to start would be with your name. I do so like to know to whom I am speaking."

"I am Cor'il Silvermoon," he said, bewildered.

"Please, Cor'il Silvermoon, the city welcomes you. We have been expecting your arrival... but, I must admit, you're a little late."

"I don't understand."

"Nor should you," Arcturas chuckled. "Do not let it bother you."

Cor'il cautiously stepped inside the gates, leading his horse. He jumped a bit when they closed behind him, and a look of worry crossed his face. Though he followed Arcturas down the main road, his eyes darted nervously around the area. This was not unusual, and Arcturas would've been surprised if the boy *hadn't* been scrutinizing everything he saw.

"I have given this speech more times than I care to remember," Arcturas started. "Everything you see here is Ilathri—including me. We are the Threadkeepers and we are here to help Threadweavers such as yourself. We seek you out so that we may teach you the ways of the Great Machine."

"The Great Machine?"

"The Great Machine is the entity that is the source of the Threads. They are an extension of its influence upon your world. But we are getting ahead of ourselves. Let us get your horse to our stable first, and then we can begin."

Arcturas felt a familiar sensation and noticed that Cor'il was weaving the Threads. *Many things are different this time, it would seem.* In Ilathri, it was impossible to weave the Threads unless Arcturas himself allowed it. *Apparently, I am not the only teacher here.* He thought at first that he should be apprehensive, but with this boy weaving the Threads within Ilathri, he found that he was more excited than anything.

Arcturas led Cor'il to Ilathri's stable, behind which was a field of grass. Traliv, a husky man with shoulder-length black hair, took the horse from them and began tending to it. Cor'il seemed uneasy to let his horse go into the hands of a stranger, so Arcturas reassured him that everything would be fine. They then continued down the main road.

As they walked, Arcturas explained the basics to Cor'il—just as he had with Dalinil before. They talked about Ilathri, the Threads, and the Great Machine. Cor'il appeared both extremely intrigued and confused at the same time, but he also surprised Arcturas with his unexpected knowledge.

Because the town's layout had changed since the last shift, it took Arcturas several minutes to locate the home in which Cor'il would be staying.

It was the same home that every Threadweaver from ages past had used—including Dalinil.

"Feel free to make yourself at home, young Threadweaver. This house is specifically for you."

"Thank you, sir."

"Please, you may call me Arcturas. We have no need of formalities here and, if anything, *I* should be calling *you* 'sir'."

Arcturas could see the confusion on the boy's face. He suppressed a smile. They were *always* confused at this point, except Cor'il was different. Yes, he was confused, but Arcturas could also see that the boy was absorbing everything, and making sense out of some of it.

"I don't understand."

"Of course you don't. Whereas a king rules over his people and they look up to him, a Threadweaver is a *true* king. Except you don't rule over people. You rule over *the world*. You can do things that nobody else—well, *almost* nobody else can. For the first time in history there are *two* Threadweavers." Arcturas sat down in a chair and clasped his hands in his lap.

"Dalinil?"

It was now Arcturas' turn to be surprised. *So they've met! Truly extraordinary indeed! Mayhaps the Threads have brought them together. Surely it is more than mere happenstance.*

"Why, yes," he replied, trying to mask his surprise. "Yes, Dalinil. I was not aware that you two were familiar with each other."

"We met over a year ago," Cor'il replied.

189

He listened to Cor'il's story with wide eyes and excitement. The boy had already accomplished a lot and had great power within him. His tale was certainly captivating! *Truly remarkable!*

There were moments of concern, however, as he listened to Cor'il. At times, the boy seemed distracted and frustrated, and he occasionally mumbled to himself in an agitated manner. At first, Arcturas thought he may have simply been overwhelmed by the current situation, and he still thought this may be the case. But then Cor'il pulled the book out of his satchel and, though Arcturas tried to hide his surprise, he gasped, speechless, staring at the tome on the table. Its leather cover was worn, but the symbol on the front—that of the Great Machine—looked completely unmarred.

"I've... never seen this before," he said. He ran his fingers over it slowly, feeling the ridges, cracks, and divots that pocked its surface. "But I have heard of it. Honestly, I was skeptical about its existence. None of the others before you have had it in their possession—or, at least, they never told me they had it. It is an artifact straight out of legend, apparently become real."

He slowly opened the book, nervous with anticipation. The binding creaked slightly and he smelled the musty odor of the pages within—a smell like rotting leaves and soil. But the scent belied its true condition—the pages were all pristine—unaffected by the passage of time and usage.

"How long have you had this?" he asked.

"About a year, I think. I found it in a room at an inn."

No. It found you, *didn't it?*

The symbols scrawled on the pages were very familiar. Though he could not make use of them in any way, Arcturas understood completely what they said. They were the teachings of the Great Machine itself. *This* was how the boy already knew so much about the ways of the Threads. The Great Machine had been talking to him this entire time.

"Have you read through it completely?"

"Yes," Cor'il replied. "I've been reading through it a second time. It's... different this time."

"Remarkable," Arcturas mumbled, still inspecting the pages of the book. "You are full of surprises, Cor'il Silvermoon." He flipped through several more pages before finally closing the book and sliding it back to Cor'il who slid it into his satchel. "You may already be far beyond anything I can teach you. Yet, Ilathri has still sought you out for a reason, even if that reason is unbeknownst to me."

"But there truly *is* so much I do not understand about things I've done or seen. I am afraid that I will accidentally hurt someone else with the Threads."

"Adequate control comes with discipline. We can help you with that. We do not necessarily have all the answers, you must understand. We can show you the path and start you down it, but where it goes from there is entirely up to you. We cannot walk that path for you."

Cor'il muttered something under his breath, annoyed. His face twitched a little and he scowled. Then, as quickly as it had started, it passed. He then fidgeted with something on his finger.

Salomil, Barinar, and Aleisha entered the house together and sat down near Arcturas. They introduced themselves to Cor'il and as Arcturas could easily see, observed every word and action.

He had not consulted their expertise when the first Threadweaver—Dalinil—had come to Ilathri. It had not been necessary. However, for this unprecedented second Threadweaver, he felt that he must lean heavily on their expertise. This was how the Threads worked and, thus, how he worked.

"That ring," Aleisha said, after the pleasantries were over. "Where did you find it?"

"This?" Cor'il held his left hand aloft. The ring appeared as two vines intertwined around an octagonal emerald. "I found it in the Harpy's Head tavern."

"Can you take it off so that I can see it closer?" Aleisha asked.

"It won't come off," Cor'il replied. "It's been stuck on my finger ever since I first put it on."

"Fascinating." Aleisha approached Cor'il and abruptly grabbed his hand for a better look. The boy looked a bit uneasy, but he nervously let her inspect the ring. She tried tugging on it and twisting it, but it did not budge. "This ring appears to be enchanted."

"How?" Arcturas asked.

"I'm not sure what its purpose is," she replied, still scrutinizing the piece of jewelry, "but it has somehow bonded with him."

"Is it harmful?" Salomil asked.

"I don't believe so." Aleisha released Cor'il's hand. She ran her fingers through her hair and sighed. "Rings of this type can do a variety of things. Some of them require Threads to be channeled through the ring itself, but others simply function on their own."

"Why can't I remove it?" Cor'il asked. He tugged on it as if for emphasis.

"Some of them bond to a specific person," she explained. "And only that person can use them. Sometimes this happens with items of clothing or weapons. Have you any idea this ring's purpose, Cor'il?"

"No. I only know that I put it on and I've not been able to remove it." He put his hand down on the table, visibly restraining himself from toying with it some more. "It does not belong to me anyway."

"Oh, but I think it *does* belong to you, Cor'il," Aleisha continued. "If it has bonded with you, then it is now yours. It does not matter who owned it before you."

"Are you saying that the ring chose me?" Cor'il laughed.

"No, not at all. It did not seek you out in the same way that Ilathri seeks out Threadweavers, but you found it, and you are now bonded with it. How you came by it is not important—it is yours."

"I just wish I knew what it does. That seems to be a recurring theme with me."

"What do you mean, Cor'il?" Arcturas asked. He was leaning back in his chair, looking relaxed—a contrast to the other three, who looked more on edge. Arcturas couldn't wait to see what mystery unfolded next.

"There are things I've encountered that I can't explain. I don't know what they are or who created them."

The moment Salomil and Barinar heard this they stood up and leaned in closer.

"What?" they both said at the same time. Their eyes lit up like a fire and they both leaned in even closer with looks of childlike curiosity on their faces.

"What have you seen?" Barinar asked. His gaze did not leave the boy. Arcturas was reminded of the fanatical interest these two had in the world outside. He was surprised they weren't both drooling.

"Well," Cor'il continued, a bit nervous. "I found a large obelisk with symbols that glowed. At first, I couldn't figure out what it did but, when I channeled Threads directly through it, I was able to travel from that location to another, similar obelisk."

Barinar gasped. Salomil simply stared, remaining silent.

"Amazing," Barinar muttered. "Truly extraordinary. What else?"

"I'm not really sure," the boy continued. He appeared shy and fidgety, then muttered to himself in whispers. Arcturas could not understand what he was saying. It almost sounded as if he was speaking in another language. "My friend, Kendra, told me about a city lying underground that she discovered close to the obelisk. I did not get a chance to look at it but—"

"The Shapers!" Salomil shouted. The rest of the room remained silent. Arcturas knew little on the subject but he had heard that word used before.

"I don't understand, Salomil," Aleisha replied. She appeared confused.

"Don't you see?" he continued. "It is one of the cities of The Shapers—the original caretakers of these Realms! Surely you all are aware of them!"

"I am not sure we are, actually," Arcturas responded. "I know *of* them. I must admit, this is a huge stretch. Our books have only alluded to them and only in vague and cryptic references."

"Because we cannot leave Ilathri, we are left in the dark!" Salomil abruptly stood up, his frustration palpable. He began pacing the room and remained silent for several moments before continuing. "This boy's companion has found one of the Shaper's cities!"

"Salomil," Barinar retorted. "I know that you have been quite vociferous about the Shapers in the past but are you sure you are not simply trying too hard to connect this to them? We must not draw conclusions that may not be there."

"I don't understand," Cor'il interrupted.

Arcturas sighed.

"The Kai'Tan," he said, "are an ancient race of people we call 'The Shapers.' They are an obscure legend among Ilathri. We have very little information on them, and the bits and pieces we *do* have are just that—nothing more than fragments of stories. Most Ilathri know next to nothing about them. We have no way to separate fact from fiction."

Salomil rose and began pacing again. He rubbed his chin, staring at the ground, and slowly walked about the room.

"Many of us," Salomil grumbled, "in fact, either know nothing of the Shapers or do not believe the legends." He paused and looked at Cor'il. "But you... you say that you have found their ruins!"

"I did not say—"

"Right," Salomil interrupted. "My apologies. What I meant to say was that your friend very well may have found the ruins of one of their cities. What did it look like?"

"I," Cor'il stuttered, "I don't know. Kendra found it and we didn't really discuss it at great length. I wanted to investigate but we were forced to flee."

"I see," said Salomil.

"Cor'il," Barinar interrupted, "it might be prudent for you to return to that location and investigate the city for yourself. Ilathri cannot leave the confines of this city. We are limited in our knowledge of the world outside but, and I know Arcturas has felt this, there appears to be a storm brewing."

"Aye," Arcturas agreed. "I feel it. Something is different—something dark and unnatural."

Aleisha looked horrified. This was all most likely completely new to her. She was young still, and very knowledgeable about ancient artifacts and powerful objects, but this was all far out of her area of expertise.

It would appear to fall out of the realm of my expertise as well. Still, Barinar is right—there is something looming on the horizon. It's as if a stopper was just quickly removed from a vial, allowing its contents to escape ever so briefly before the vial was stopped up again.

"Cor'il." Arcturas motioned to Salomil to return to his chair. "Your friend may very well have discovered something important enough to steer the course of your world for eternity. Everything about your world feels different now—even the Great Machine. With the discovery of this Dark Machine I have come to realize that Ilathri's knowledge and influence is waning."

"What do you mean?" Cor'il asked. "What is the Dark Machine?"

All three of Arcturas' companions had the same surprised look on their faces as Cor'il. It was only then that Arcturas realized he had let slip word of the Dark Machine.

"I will explain it to you, Cor'il. For now, I ask that Salomil, Barinar, and Aleisha do as much research as they can to help me. There most certainly is a storm coming. And we are all extremely ill-prepared for it, I'm afraid."

Mayhaps we were not drawn to Cor'il to help him, but for him to help us.

Chapter 21

Kendra quietly rode atop Brute, keeping several yards ahead of Orvaril and Alannin who rode atop Orvaril's horse. Though it had been over a week since Cor'il had ridden out on his own, she still found that she was hurt, sad, and even angry.

Orvaril and Alannin happily chattered behind her, blissfully unaware of her mood. While they were often on different levels of conversation, she wished they would shut up and be as sullen as she was. Orvaril mostly babbled on about his usual legendary stories and Alannin asked incessant questions that didn't matter. Ilvania alternated between trotting alongside Orvaril's horse and running off on her own for hours at a time, sometimes reappearing with something dead in her mouth.

"Calm down, Dummy," Orvaril said. "Ilvania won't hurt you, I promise."

Whenever Kendra thought about how naming Brute might be odd she realized that Orvaril's naming his horse Dummy was just about as ridiculous, if not more so. Orvaril found the horse's name to be way much more amusing than she did, however. *Sometimes I simply don't understand that man. But he is, admittedly, entertaining at least—sometimes.*

The road from Kuranthas to Elston was lightly frosted with low-lying fog this morning. They were up early to travel, much to Orvaril's distaste, and the Realm itself appeared to be waking up slowly. Hopefully, it was safer at this time of the morning. Not even the birds were awake yet to sing. *Are orcs early-risers? Let's hope not.*

A fox darted across the road up ahead, quickly disappearing into the mist beyond. Every little bit of movement caught Kendra's eye and made her jump, for she still had visions of that horrible thing that she saw in the underground city. It haunted not only her dreams while she slept, but it also plagued her thoughts while she was awake. She had tried to explain it all to Orvaril and Alannin—to tell them of the overwhelming terror and revulsion—but they had shrugged it off as something that would pass. Ordinarily, she would have agreed with them.

But they hadn't been there. They didn't see what an unnatural abomination it was. If they'd seen it, they would feel the same way, I am sure of it.

Were there more? What if it got out? Could it get out? She started sweating and could feel her body shaking just thinking about it. The fear was still very real, and it was more intense than anything she had ever experienced in the past.

She closed her eyes and took a deep breath. They were headed to Elston now, where she could resume a life less dangerous. Alannin had agreed to accompany them until he figured out where he wanted to go.

At first, Kendra had suggested that he live among the trees of Kuranthas. She assured him that he would not be bothered by interlopers, but he had ultimately decided that it was better to go elsewhere. He even went so far as to tell her that Kuranthas felt "tainted."

Which, of course, brought Kendra's thoughts back to Cor'il and what had happened. There was no way that she could possibly understand what he was going through. The boy wielded immense power—power she could never dream of—and it threatened to consume him. And, even though his actions had been purely accidental, they were still terrible. *How does one cope with that? How does one come to terms with the fact that he, in an instant, destroyed everything he knew and loved?*

Kendra could not say for sure how she would feel. Certainly, something like that would wrack her with guilt for the rest of her life. She didn't think that she, either, could ever forgive herself for such an atrocity. She was a lot of things, but a murderer was not among them.

Additionally, Cor'il's distracted, muttering and bouts of random anger worried her. She missed her friend, but she also understood why he had left. She hoped that he would be able to shake his demons, and that she would see him again. She wanted the old Cor'il back.

What happens if he's unstable? Could he lose control and cause another accident? Could he possibly do it on purpose? What does that kind of power do to a person—even a good person like him?

Kendra hadn't even considered that before. Now that she had, she wished she hadn't.

The birds gradually began chirping around them as the sun rose higher in the sky. Kendra swatted at a bitefly as she listened to Orvaril attempt to explain a joke to Alannin.

"You see, my good elf," he explained, "The bar maid brought him a tankard with a cat in it instead of..." Orvaril trailed off and sighed. "Mayhaps I'll tell you another one later."

They descended a gentle slope and crossed a small creek where they stopped to water the horses and rest for a few minutes, but were soon on their way. As the sun rose and the fog began to burn off, they encountered more travelers and caravans, and ultimately joined a group of merchants for company.

The leader's name was Demerus, a rather gaunt man with dusty gray hair and a patchy beard. His clothes hung off him and he was missing two fingers on his right hand. Kendra was extremely curious about this, but she decided not to pry—at least, not immediately. The group of merchants seemed just as curious about Alannin as she was about them. Only one of them claimed to have seen an elf before, and even he was still in awe.

There were 11 merchants in the group, all headed to Crossroads. According to Demerus, there used to be 15 of them, but orcs had claimed the lives of four of their companions several weeks back. Kendra soon found that she was only half-listening to Demerus' story. Her attention shifted to the skies.

There were many times when the skies had fallen silent for her. In fact, many days, she didn't bother to try to glean any information from them, avoiding the disappointment altogether. But Kendra suddenly found herself without a clear direction, and she hoped that she could find an excuse to head somewhere other than Elston.

Actually, she found herself hoping that the clouds would somehow lead her to Cor'il. Instead, however, they gave her conflicting directions. She watched as they swirled and rearranged themselves into various forms—forms that carried meanings to her as if they were words on a page. Sometimes, the messages they conveyed were vague while, other times, they were clear and precise. Kendra was unsure if this was due to a lack of skill or if the clouds were purposely playing tricks on her. *Clouds... playing tricks,* she mused. *Well, now, that's a crazy thought.*

She tried looking away for awhile but, upon returning her gaze to the skies, she found much the same. Unable to make sense of it, she found herself getting more and more frustrated and swore under her breath. She closed her eyes and took a deep breath, trying to clear her mind. After several moments, she looked back to the sky.

She saw the abomination staring back at her. It was just a cloud but... there was something behind it—something ancient and sinister. She felt cold and found it difficult to move or look away. With her eyes clamped shut, she shivered and shook, trying to get herself under control.

"Are you alright, Kendra?" It was Elistray, one of the merchants.

"Yes, thank you," she replied, attempting to sound as normal as possible.

The fear eventually subsided once the cloud changed its form, but Kendra made sure to keep her gaze straight ahead, away from the skies above. She could see several of the merchants whispering to themselves and shooting a glance her way on occasion. Some of them had noticed her discomfort.

What good is that *supposed to do? What information am I to learn from* that? *Curse The Abyss!*

As much as she tried to avoid it, she couldn't help dwelling on their current situation. It consumed her attention, and she was unable to think of much else. She paid no attention to those around her, so when the caravan suddenly stopped she nearly ran into the wagon in front of her. Thankfully, Brute wasn't as distracted as she was. The horse skittered a bit and tossed her head, but stopped short of the wagon.

"What is it, girl?" Kendra patted the chestnut mare gently on the head and looked about. The rest of the caravan had stopped, though most of its members appeared unsure as to why. Kendra quickly saw it—about 30 men on horseback approached from up ahead, the banner of the Red Swords flying overhead.

Kendra felt a knot in her stomach as Orvaril and Alannin rode up alongside her. The caravan moved to one side of the road to allow the approaching group of Red Sword soldiers to pass. Kendra and Orvaril followed suit, moving their horses into the grass beside the road. Every instinct urged Kendra to flee but she held steady, knowing full well that the Red Swords would become suspicious and pursue her.

"Alannin," she whispered, "If these men see you they are going to capture you."

"Why?" The elf peered down the road to get a look at the approaching soldiers. "What would they want with me?"

"I've heard they don't like elves," she continued. "These... Red Swords don't like anyone who isn't human, and they don't treat prisoners well." She paused to look at the soldiers, then back to Alannin. "That's what I have heard, anyway."

"Aye," Orvaril agreed. "I have heard the same. I believe it is in your best interest to flee, Alannin. I think we can create a suitable distraction."

"Head for the tall grass." Kendra pointed off the road, to their right. Hopefully the grass and weeds would be tall enough to hide a person. "Then, if you can make it to the trees over there, you should be safe. I would stay off the road, though."

Alannin nodded but hesitated. At first, Kendra thought he was waiting for his wolf but then she read the sadness on his face.

"We'll try to escape if we can but, for now, you're in more danger than we are." Kendra made a shooing motion with her hands and scowled. "Now get your ass out of here! Go!"

Alannin slid off Orvaril's horse and, keeping low, headed away from the road. Orvaril immediately urged Dummy forward to the front of the merchant group. Kendra quickly followed, unsure of what to expect.

I hope he knows what he is doing. If we were smart we, too, would flee... and probably be run down by an army of Red Swords. But if we split up, we might have a chance!

Neither she nor Orvaril had anything to hide—they were not elves nor were they Threadweavers. However, from what she'd heard, the Red Swords didn't care if they had a reason for any of their actions. They were men, drunk on power and motivated by fear. Hopefully, whatever it was Orvaril had in mind would not get them into trouble.

Once they got to the front of the caravan Orvaril began playing his lute and singing. It wasn't a song that Kendra recognized, and it appeared that Orvaril was making up the words as he went along. It did not take her long to become familiar with the repetitive tune and she reluctantly began to sing along as the soldiers at the front of the group stopped a few yards from them.

Orvaril threw a surprised glance her way as she tried to keep up with him. She quickly gave up singing and, instead, hummed the tune. Orvaril grinned, apparently now satisfied with her performance. His fingers stumbled across his lute for a second but he quickly regained his composure and continued. The soldiers looked perturbed but took no immediate action.

Several of the men scanned the nervous caravan and three of them moved to the side of the group to begin inspecting each merchant, wagon, and horse. Kendra stopped humming and eyed them closely. She kept her hands away from her daggers, but it was a colossal effort to do so.

Each soldier wore a simple helmet and was clad in a shirt of chainmail covered by a tabard. On the tabard was the Red

Sword insignia—a downturned sword with a bright red blade. *Mayhaps a gortog's ass would be a better symbol? It certainly represents them better, I think.*

"By order of the Red Swords," the man in the lead proclaimed, "I insist that you stop singing."

Orvaril stopped his song but seemed amused.

"Why?" he asked.

"Because I find it annoying," the man replied.

"And what is the name of the man who finds my singing so offensive, if I may ask?"

"I am Commander Aldon Demovar, if you must know."

Kendra couldn't help but find the man's demeanor repulsive. He oozed conceit with every word and he puffed himself up as he sat on his white horse, looking high and mighty. He was obviously proud of his stature and his actions, and Kendra found herself growing more annoyed. She glanced behind her to see if Alannin was visible. He had disappeared completely.

"Feel free to inspect everything," Demovar said. Several more mounted soldiers rode alongside the other side of the group of merchants and began riffling through wagons and carriages, throwing things out onto the ground.

The men and women of the group all pleaded and protested but, ultimately, stepped out of the way of the armed soldiers. Some of them began to cry, obviously frightened.

"What exactly is it that you are looking for?" Kendra growled, after having watched the soldiers ransack these peoples' possessions for several minutes.

"That is none of your concern," Demovar tersely replied. Through his helmet, Kendra could see his smug, satisfied grin. *He's got no purpose except to bully these people and exert his authority. He's simply furthering the Red Swords' name and influence. These people are no danger.* "The Red Swords have authority to apprehend all sorcerous individuals as well as any elves, orcs, or anything else we find—for the safety of the Realm."

"On whose authority?"

"King Alzine's, of course. Now if you don't mind, girl, you need to step aside and let us do our duty."

Kendra stood by and watched as the *soldiers* continued their search. When one of the men in the caravan tried to stop a soldier from dumping a crate of fragile art, he was violently pushed to the ground and the crate was dumped on top of him. His wife cried out and tried to help him, but the soldier stopped her, his blade drawn.

Kendra looked to Orvaril, her blood boiling. He also looked none too happy. His fists were balled tightly in his lap.

"You don't find Threadweavers or elves by rummaging through the belongings of merchants," she growled. "What are you *really* doing?"

The man urged his horse slowly forward, coming close enough that Kendra could smell his stale breath and see the anger in his eyes. For a moment, she wondered if she had gone too far by questioning his authority, but decided that she didn't care. She could feel anger and contempt welling up inside her. These men could do whatever they wanted and nobody would stop them.

"You should learn not to run your mouth, little—"

Demovar moved to slap her face but was taken by surprise when Kendra ducked his blow and buried a dagger under his chin. He gasped and gurgled as blood ran down his tabard and quickly obscured the Red Sword symbol, now lost in crimson. She hadn't merely anticipated his attack. She had *expected* it—*hoped* for it, even.

"A title and a sword do not give you the right," she exclaimed, pulling her dagger from his throat. Orvaril stared, his mouth agape, with a complete look of shock and disbelief on his face. Aldon Demovar fell from his horse and onto the ground.

"Insolent bitch!" one of the other soldiers yelled. "How dare you!"

"She killed the commander!" another one shouted. Immediately, they all moved to surround her, weapons drawn, but she had already turned Brute around and was kicking her into action. Brute broke out into a gallop, nearly knocking a soldier from his mount. Kendra headed off the road and toward the trees she had earlier pointed Alannin to. Behind her she saw Orvaril following her, trying to catch up. In pursuit was a dozen mounted Red Sword soldiers.

Well, now you've done it. If only you had a brilliant plan to get out of this *one.* She was still angry. She wanted to turn around and fight the soldiers—to show them that they couldn't just step on whomever they wanted. But she and Orvaril were hopelessly outnumbered. She still felt immense anger, however now it was mixed with fear.

She kicked Brute with her heels, trying to squeeze every little bit of speed out of her. Brute was surprisingly fast, but Orvaril was starting to fall behind, and the Red Swords were keeping pace with him. The trees were still in the distance and she had to admit, she had no idea what she would do once she got there. It wasn't as if the Red Swords would simply give up because of trees, but mayhaps she could hide or use them for cover if she and Orvaril had to fight?

"Milady," Orvaril called out. "This doesn't look good!"

Something flew past Kendra's face and stuck in the ground up ahead. *They're firing on us!* The wind whipped through her hair and whistled in her ears as she urged Brute to go faster.

Another arrow flew past her and clattered off a large rock to her left. All her anger, her outrage, was now replaced with terror. She had killed the leader of this group of soldiers in cold blood and she had no idea what would become of her if they caught her—if they even wanted her alive.

She quickly glanced back and her heart sank. They had captured Orvaril! Four of the soldiers had hold of Dummy and Orvaril was holding his hands up in front of him. *You must stop! No, you have to keep running! You can go to Sulbar and rescue Orvaril if you can escape!*

Several more arrows whizzed past her. She yelped as pain shot down her back from her right shoulder blade. She kicked

Brute again, trying to squeeze every last bit of speed from the horse. She felt another piercing pain in her back and her vision began to cloud. Her grip on the reins was failing and she had trouble staying upright.

Brute slowed down to a fast walk as the pain intensified. She didn't have to look to know that she had been shot.

"This is it," she muttered under her breath as she closed her eyes and tumbled onto the ground. Darkness overtook her.

Chapter 22

Luc Isvarin dismounted, his chain shirt and sabatons clattering as he landed. He took off his helm, letting his shoulder-length blond hair spill out, and set it on the saddle's pommel. Then he knelt down to inspect the girl.

She lay face down in the tall grass, two arrows protruding from her back. She was soaked in blood and wasn't moving. To many of the soldiers it would not matter if she was alive or dead—she had not only dared to attack the Red Swords, but she had also killed their commander. She was a criminal and an outlaw and should be brought to justice.

Her companion, the singer, had surrendered peacefully once they had caught up to him. He had no weapons on him except for a quiver of small, crudely-fashioned arrows. They had not found a bow on him, though. Luc was glad, at least, that they hadn't been forced to shoot him as well. They were, however, careful to remove all possessions from him just in case.

He carefully pulled both arrows from her back, dropping them on the ground beside him. She made no sound or movement. Her dress looked as though it may once have been of quite excellent quality but it appeared that, even before she had tangled with them, it had seen a lot of wear. *You get yourself into trouble a lot?* Her horse stood about 10 yards away, chewing on the tall grass. It did not run, but it also seemed wary of him and his men.

Luc reluctantly rolled the girl over onto her back. Beneath the dirt and blood, she was a pretty one. She was, apparently, fierce and underhanded as well. Still, though she had attacked them, he couldn't help but feel pity for her. She had only been standing up for what she had felt was the right thing—much like the Red Swords had been doing.

Since the commander was dead, the burden of leadership now fell on Luc's shoulders. It was a position he neither relished nor wanted, but he would fill the role to the best of his ability. The men would obey him unquestioningly as he had already proven himself to them in battles past.

"How is she?" her companion asked. The only information his soldiers had gotten out of the man was that his name was Orvaril.

"It appears that she is dead," Luc answered, standing. And trying to sound emotionless. Killing a savage orc was one thing, but having to bring down another human always left a bitter taste in his mouth. Despite his efforts to the contrary, he felt remorse and sorrow. *We're besieged by orcs and other creatures of legend, yet we continue killing each other, and for no good reason.*

"No!" Orvaril yelled. The man shrugged off the soldier who held him and ran to the girl's side. He knelt beside her to see for himself. After a moment, he sniffed and wiped his eyes. "Damn you, Kendra," Luc heard him whisper. He looked up at Luc and the two of them exchanged sad glances. "The mighty Red Swords... ruthless killers of whomever they wish."

Finally, Orvaril stood. His shoulders sagged and he looked devastated, but he made no move to escape or to fight. Luc was glad, since he did not relish the thought of having to kill anyone else. He already regretted this woman's death. There was no need to add another.

The majority of the Red Swords did not share the same feelings as Luc—if any of them at all did. Many of them reveled in the violence, and they exerted their power on anyone they could find. Aldon Demovar had been one of those individuals. He had been a good leader, but he often went too far. He abused his station, as many other soldiers did. Luc felt differently, but any deviation from the other soldiers would most likely be seen as treason.

"We're taking her body with us," Luc announced. "Captain Forsch can decide what he wants to do with it or if it might be of some use to the Adjudicators."

The Adjudicators were a frightful lot. Luc could never figure out quite what it was that they did for the Red Swords. They sometimes acted as advisors, researchers, and executioners—at least, that is the conclusion that Luc had come to. Regardless, Luc tried to spend as little time around them as he could. They were not a group of people whose company he enjoyed.

"If I may," Orvaril said, "I will carry her back."

"Aye," Luc responded. He felt for the man, and he regretted how this turned out. But he could not let his men know his feelings—they would see him as weak and unfit to lead. It did not pay to have enemies in your own ranks.

Orvaril picked her body up in his arms and carried her back to the road where the group of soldiers currently held Dummy. The soldiers remained on horseback, eyeing him suspiciously as he approached them.

"What about her horse, Commander?"

Commander. How odd it sounds to hear them call me that... and so quickly after the previous captain's death. Is that something you have to get used to? Whether he would *truly* command their group remained to be seen but, for now, he was in charge.

He slowly approached the chestnut mare. The horse seemed unconcerned with his presence until he got to within a few feet. Once he got too close, the animal slowly walked further away, eventually stopping and staring at him. This went on several times before Luc realized that it was futile.

"We leave the horse here," he shouted. "No sense in wasting time chasing it down. Our prisoner can ride his own horse with the body."

"Aye," the soldier responded.

Luc walked back to the group, mounted his horse, and they returned to the road together, leaving Orvaril to walk with Kendra in his arms. When the group returned, several of the merchants gasped and looked horrified at the sight of the body. Two of them looked away, crying. Luc felt as if he should apologize to Orvaril or the merchants or *someone*, but he wasn't sure for what. In any case, it would undermine the Red Swords' stature, so he remained calm and quiet.

Orvaril laid Kendra's body over his horse and climbed onto Dummy's back, making no move to escape.

Soldiers surrounded their prisoner on all sides, making sure he could not flee. Several of the men scowled at him and had their hands on their weapons. He looked angry but kept his composure. Luc understood—the man just lost a friend, and his men had just lost their commander. Tensions were high and he had to keep order.

"No need to crowd him, men," he commanded. "He's not going anywhere. Did we find anything?"

"No, sir," one of the soldiers replied. He was a burly, large man named Orskahn, if Luc remembered correctly. There was never too much activity going on in the man's head, but he was as strong as an ox, and he never questioned authority. *Is that a good quality or bad?*

"Then we continue to Sulbar," Luc announced. "We will submit the prisoner for questioning by the Adjudicators and they can do whatever they need to with the corpse." Luc positioned himself at the head of the group and set them off at a decent pace. "Let's not tarry, lest the body begins to stink or we attract unwanted attention from orcs. You merchants may continue on your way."

Luc looked up into the sky and stretched, feeling uneasy and unsure of himself. He rubbed his neck with a gloved hand, trying to loosen it up. Though he understood that necessity of armor, he never enjoyed how restricted it made him feel.

The sky was a beautiful blue and the clouds that slowly floated by were a nice, contrasting, fluffy white. After a moment's respite, he felt more at peace. Somehow, he knew that something good could come from these events. Something good was *going* to come from these events. He soon began planning for when they arrived in Sulbar. Captain Forsch would want a report and, no doubt, be upset over the Commander's demise. If the girl hadn't already been dead, Luc knew she would be once Forsch had learned of what she'd done.

How did I let myself get mixed up in all of this?

"While we all may swim in different waters, we often wash up on the same shore."
—Source unknown

Chapter 23

Once the soldiers and the merchants had left and were well out of sight, Alannin cautiously rose from the tall grass and inspected the area. He had made it a fair distance from the road before the situation had deteriorated, but he wanted to make absolutely sure he would remain unseen. And, although he hadn't been able to see the altercation very well, he had heard everything all too clearly. His heart was heavy from the loss of his new friend, Kendra, and Orvaril was now a prisoner of these Red Swords.

For a few moments, his mind was clouded with grief and confusion. His thoughts dwelt on his companions and their misfortune. Kendra's death wracked him with sadness and grief. He had not known her for very long but, yet, he still felt close to her. Her death had been an unnecessary tragedy and he could not ignore his sorrow.

He was now left alone in an unfamiliar world without direction and purpose. Whereas, before, he was simply alone in the woods, he was now exposed in a dangerous land. On top of that, he was now aware that an entire group of people was dedicated to hunting elves. Of course, he'd heard about the orcs and other creatures about but this was a new enemy—one that would be more difficult to identify. His list of things to avoid was growing large.

Nobody ever said The Longing would take me to safe, hospitable places, I guess. But I wonder if there is a purpose to my journey. This land certainly seems to be in an awful lot of turmoil. Why would I be brought here, of all places?

Alannin looked around him and he noticed Kendra's horse, Brute, standing nearby. She seemed on edge, and every little sound spooked her. He understood, because he felt much the same way.

"Easy, girl," Alannin muttered as he slowly inched his way toward the animal. "I won't hurt you." The horse either didn't notice him yet or didn't care, because she made no move to flee. As he approached, still yards away, Brute looked up, staring directly at him, and slowly moved toward him.

"That's right." He continued his slow approach. "We'll be safer together." He stopped at a spot where the grass was crushed and stained with Kendra's blood. Sadness overtook him as he stared downward. He had never had a friend or family member die violently, and it was not something he could easily understand—even for someone he had known for only a brief time.

As Alannin paused, he felt the horse's nose nudge his arm. She snorted softly and nudged him again. He took the reins in his hand and sighed.

For several minutes, Alannin simply stood next to Brute as he tried to figure out what to do. For most of his life he had lived within a small group of elves that was comprised of his family and friends. He'd had a purpose—to hunt, build shelters, and help protect those with whom he lived. His mother and father had always done a respectable job of leading the group, and Alannin had made sure to help in any way he could. Together, they had thrived in safety.

Even when The Longing had overtaken him, Alannin still had a goal—his destination. Once he had arrived, however, he found that he did not have a distinct path anymore. He had been fortunate when Cor'il, Orvaril, and Kendra had found him because, at that time, even if he did not have a clear purpose, he at least had new friends who he could follow. *Being guided by a river's current is better still than being stuck in stagnant water, even if you know not where you are headed.*

But his friends were now gone—scattered and... worse. Alannin now found himself without purpose and it frightened him. He was where The Longing had taken him, but where was he to go from here? As he looked around him, he could think of no reason to travel in any particular direction.

Except one.

Though he realized that, sometimes, violence and fighting was necessary, he loathed both. He wished to avoid these situations, but found himself pulled in the same direction as the Red Swords. Unsure of just what one individual could do, he still felt the urge to try and save his remaining friend.

The one Red Sword soldier who had spoken with Orvaril had seemed remorseful and mayhaps even sad. Mayhaps Alannin could convince him to let Orvaril go free. Being an elf would create its own problems. If the Red Swords were holding elves as prisoners, then Alannin would surely be in danger. *That is a bridge I will have to cross when I get to it. I don't know what I can do, but I've got to try to do something.*

Brute did not protest when Alannin climbed onto her back. He patted her on the side of her neck and paused as hesitation crept into his thoughts. It would be so easy for him to ride the opposite direction. Mayhaps he would find other elves and they could start a new life deep within a forest where the Red Swords would not find them. He wondered how many elves had come through like he had, arriving where The Longing took them, yet disconnected from real purpose.

"Ilvania!" he called. He waited several moments, and when there was no response, he called again for his wolf companion. After several more moments of waiting Alannin sighed and urged Brute toward the road. Ilvania would catch up eventually. He was accustomed to her disappearing when she wanted, but he worried every time she did. Still, she always found him eventually. If he was fortunate, she would return with dinner.

Gravel crunched beneath Brute's hooves as she stepped onto the road at a slow walk. Alannin was in no hurry to catch up to the group of soldiers, for he was not sure what action to take if he did. Regardless, he knew in what direction his future lay. He would follow the Red Swords' trail and determine a course of action once he got there—wherever *there* was.

Certainly, this is the absolute worst idea I have ever had. I will need to disguise myself somehow—mayhaps a hat or a hooded cloak. He now began to wish that he had purchased some clothing from the merchants with whom they had been traveling. Hopefully, he would encounter more merchants or a town along the way. It was a great idea, though he soon realized both options would do him little good without any money. There had been no need for it back home. *Mayhaps I'll have something to trade when the time comes.*

The tracks of numerous soldiers on horseback were easy enough for Alannin to follow—especially when many of them were traveling alongside the road. The grass nearby was well-trampled and the road was pocked with hoof prints. He had encountered more difficult trails in the past, but he was careful to keep his distance and never bring the group into view. They did not appear to be moving swiftly, so Alannin made sure to keep Brute moving at a slow pace.

It wasn't long before Ilvania happily trotted toward him from further down the road. Her fur was soaked and she shook herself dry once she arrived alongside Alannin. The elf sometimes wondered, given her behavior, if someone else had domesticated her prior to him encountering the wolf. She certainly seemed accustomed to being around people and horses.

The first travelers he encountered were ecstatic to meet an elf. So ecstatic, in fact, that they gave him a spare, dark green cloak. With the hood up, he could hide his ears and blend in better. He hoped it would hide enough of his elven facial features to keep from attracting any unwanted attention.

Alannin had offered to pay them something for their generosity, but they would not have it. They had insisted that they did not require any payment—that they enjoyed helping people in need. When he inquired about the Red Swords ahead of him they confirmed that they had indeed seen the band of soldiers. The Red

Swords had not stopped their group for any kind of search or questioning, however, and they appeared to be in a hurry. Aside from being almost nearly shoved off the road, there had been no interaction.

Several times that first day, he had encountered travelers. Each time he asked them about the Red Swords ahead of him, and they all reported much the same thing. He learned that they were probably headed to a human city called Sulbar that was most likely their main encampment. Alannin's heart sank when he heard this news. His chances of finding and rescuing Orvaril had gotten smaller. His "wait and see" plan was getting more complicated by the hour.

Ilvania looked up at him and let out a whine. Alannin wondered if she could sense his frustration.

At night, he slept far from the road under whatever cover he could find. The first night, it was on the back side of a large hill. The second night, it was among some thorny bushes. On the third night, he made a bed in some tall grass. When the sun came up on the third day, Alannin's despair had grown even more. He was now certain that Ilvania could sense something wrong. She was nervous, and she stuck very close to him always, never letting him out of her sight. She wouldn't even hunt without him by her side.

It was just past midday when Alannin thought he saw a city on the horizon. He wouldn't have noticed anything unusual except that something was jutting up into the sky—something rather tall. From his vantage point, it looked like a tower or spire of some sort. After a few minutes, his keen elven eyes could make out more detail.

Though the structure was still a good ride away, he could see that it was unfinished. Movement around the building led him to believe it was currently being worked on. He got a little closer and could see that, indeed, construction was still underway.

He was encouraged by the sight. Not because he had gained any useful knowledge to formulate a plan, but because he at least knew where he was now headed. Hopefully he would be able to get an adequate layout of the city itself and find a safe way in. After that, he would have to improvise. *I am a fish that is a* long *way from any water, and I need to stay out of the Red Swords' cookpot.*

The sun was beginning to set below the horizon, but Alannin was determined to get as close to the city as he could. Besides, scouting the surrounding area would be safer at night when guards were fewer and nobody was about. This, at least, was something familiar. His skill as a scout was unmatched back home. Not only could he move around the wilderness largely unnoticed, but he was also very adept at detecting anyone or anything around him. And, in the dark, his vision was superior.

Once the city walls came into view, he stopped and found a place where Brute would be safe. The horse did not protest when he wrapped her reins around a tree, keeping her concealed within a nearby forest. Ilvania, however, refused to stay behind with Brute and, instead she went off on her own, disappearing into the night. Once the animals were taken care of, Alannin moved quietly through fields and trees until he was up against the outside of the wall.

The top of the wall was mostly dark. He could see a scant few flickers of torchlight scattered about and moving slowly, back and forth. Thankfully there appeared to be only one guard nearby atop the portion of the wall closest to him. Alannin approached and waited patiently for the man to pass by, then he cautiously made his way toward the city gates. All trees and foliage near the wall had been removed—most likely for better visibility and defense. The elf frowned as he stepped around a tree stump. *This tree was probably 30 or 40 years old, judging from the width of the stump. What a shame.*

The sturdy, iron gates were locked tight. Alannin had hoped there would be a gap he could slip through or that mayhaps he would be fortunate enough to sneak in when they opened, but he had no such fortune this night. After spending a good 10 minutes or so inspecting the gates, he headed across the road and continued walking around the wall, looking for a way in.

He wasn't sure how long it took, but he eventually circled most of the city, stopping briefly to inspect the north gates at the other side. He could not, however, find any way in. The walls were least 10 feet high and, though they were still sparsely guarded, Alannin was beginning to see why. This city was built like a fortress and, from what Alannin could see, it was only getting more secure with the construction of the tower within.

He could see the structure much better now that he was closer, and it was indeed still under construction. It rose above the city like a beacon and appeared to be situated near the center. It was brightly lit, and construction continued through the night. But it wasn't this spire that worried him so much as it was the construction being performed just outside the city to the east.

Once Alannin had circled around to the other side of Sulbar, where the road led east, he could see that it was a massive project, possibly larger than Sulbar itself. Much of the wall around the area was already built, but Alannin was nevertheless able to get a good look at everything. *The Red Swords are building another city. Only, it would seem, this city's purpose is a fortress.*

It wasn't long before Alannin noticed the Red Sword flag flying high above the partially-built structures, glowing in unnatural light. Within these new walls was a myriad of tents and ramshackle structures. Pinpricks of flickering light moved about the area as guards made their patrol rounds. Alannin dared not get any closer, lest someone notice him, but he had seen all that he needed to see. He darted across the road and slowly moved around the wall on the other side, but a noise made him suddenly stop and draw his short swords.

A figure approached from the other direction. Several moments passed before it noticed Alannin and drew its weapon. For a moment both Alannin and the other creature stood and stared, a mere few feet from each other but neither made a move.

Alannin had never encountered a creature like this before. In the dim light of the moon he could see rather well, but he still supposed his eyes might be playing tricks on him. It had tusks jutting from its jaw and its eyes were sunken back under a protruding brow. Its head held scant few hairs and it was wearing assorted skins, some of which had fur. The axe it held was crude and possibly made of stone.

It grunted a few times but, still, neither it nor Alannin made a move toward each other. It seemed to be just as surprised by Alannin as he was of it. It sniffed the air and squinted.

"You... elf?" it muttered in a guttural tone. Alannin was not quite sure that it was an actual question. He barely understood its broken Common Tongue.

"Aye," Alannin whispered back. "And what manner of creature are you?" Neither Alannin nor the creature lowered a weapon or shifted a gaze anywhere else.

"Orc," it said. "Torgin."

"Your... your name is Torgin, then?"

Upon further inspection, Alannin decided that this orc was male. But, having never encountered one before, he was merely making an assumption. From everything he had heard Orvaril and Cor'il say about orcs, he was curious as to why he hadn't already been savagely attacked. Though, from hearing Kendra talk, he got the impression that their assessments were somewhat at odds.

"I am Alannin," he continued, pointing to himself but being careful not to leave himself open to a surprise attack.

"You get out of way," the orc responded. "I kill you."

"Whoa, wait a minute," Alannin replied. "I do not wish you any harm. I am merely trying to—"

"Move." The orc slowly advanced, raising his axe and grunting belligerently.

Alannin slowly backed up, keeping distance between him and Torgin. He was confused as to why the orc would bother to speak to him if he was going to end up attacking him anyway. In any case, Alannin had no wish to fight the orc, but his options were quickly dwindling.

"I do not wish to fight you," he whispered. "Besides, we may attract unwanted attention with the noise."

"No noise," Torgin said. "Will kill real fast." The orc made a chopping motion with his axe.

Alannin heard a savage growl from behind Torgin and the orc instantly froze. He immediately recognized the source as Ilvania, though he could not see her. He had never heard her this angry before, and he wasn't sure what she was going to do. A look of terror crossed the orc's face.

The wolf slowly walked around to stop at Alannin's side, still growling, and never shifting her gaze from the orc. Her hackles were raised and she bared her teeth. Torgin looked intensely frightened but also bewildered.

"You wolf-friend," he said, his voice shaking. He must have noticed that Ilvania made no move to threaten Alannin.

"I would recommend," Alannin chuckled, now with confidence, "that you drop your axe. You will probably live longer."

Torgin immediately set his axe on the ground, his hands out in front of him. Alannin wasn't sure whether Ilvania could win a fight with this orc but, hopefully, it would not come to that. He sheathed both of his swords and patted his companion lightly on the head.

"Alright," Alannin whispered. "Now let's do it my way. It's time to talk a bit."

Chapter 24

The sound of construction was endless. Sometimes it seemed to go on even at night, and it was difficult to get any rest with the constant hammering and commotion. Fortunately, Orvaril was very adept at ignoring annoyances. Since being brought to this Red Sword citadel—or spire or whatever they called it—he had learned a lot about them merely by keeping his eyes and ears open. Unfortunately, he wasn't sure that any of what he had learned was going to help him.

He still felt sorrow for Kendra, and he did not know what they had done with her body. He hoped, however, that they were honorable enough to give her a decent burial somewhere. Luc seemed as though he might have seen to that. Mayhaps, if Orvaril was right about the man. He missed Cor'il and Alannin, but he was saddened by the fact that he would not get to talk to Kendra again. He hadn't even been able to say goodbye to her.

Orvaril's cell was very small and contained only a pile of straw and a chamber pot. Ironically, he remembered having been in worse conditions in the past when he *wasn't* a prisoner. Normally that would arouse a chuckle from him but, at this point, he wasn't sure there was any joy left in him. *No, you must keep a positive attitude. Your friend may be gone, but you can keep her memory. She would certainly want you to make these Red Swords pay somehow.*

Orvaril was not normally one for revenge but in this case, he may be able to make an exception. Just how he was going to do that, however, was another matter entirely. His cell's four walls seemed to have other plans for him currently.

Of course, the Red Swords had taken all his equipment. This was of no concern to him, however. Orvaril had never put much stock in material possessions. Items came and went but it was what you *were* that always mattered most. And he was very resourceful. He knew this to be true and, thankfully, the Red Swords did not.

Upon his arrival, they had waited a day before he had been brought out of his prison and interrogated. Luc had been present, and Orvaril was unharmed during the questioning. He had told them everything truthfully and cooperated as best he could, but he wasn't sure what useful information he could give them. They did ask him about whether he knew anything about Cor'il, and he lied accordingly when the conversation had come to that subject. The Red Swords were very eager to apprehend the boy—they fortunately did not know his name. They told him it was because Cor'il was a danger to the Realm, but Orvaril detected something else. Mayhaps they had ulterior motives. It was foolish to think that they did not.

"Here's your breakfast." A guard opened his cell door just wide enough to place a metal bowl on the floor. Floating in whatever soup he had received was a lump of crusty bread. The guard quickly moved on, paying Orvaril no more attention.

"We should chat again sometime!" Orvaril called after the man as he picked up the bowl and smelled its contents. It smelled just about as appealing as it looked.

The soup was more of a gruel, but it had lumps of something in it. Despite its rather rough consistency and abhorrent smell, it was palatable and didn't taste terrible, at least. *It's certainly not the* worst *thing I've ever eaten.*

Orvaril wondered if he could somehow convince the guards to upgrade his accommodations or find him something better to eat. He doubted it, but he had always been good at talking his way into and out of situations. He might be here a while and there was no sense in having a bad time of it. He'd already been here three days—or was it four? He didn't see a point in keeping track when there was nothing specific to wait for.

During his short stay, Orvaril had already discovered that most of these soldiers were nothing more than thugs and thieves, recruited into the group with the promise of combat and compensation. Most of them were rude, mean individuals who cared about nobody but themselves. They were disciplined enough to know how to follow orders, but they were certainly not ideal for a stable army.

Mayhaps that is what is intended. Or they are the highest quality that this organization could find. Thus far, the only tolerable person Orvaril had encountered was Luc, and he hadn't seen the man since his interrogation. Luc appeared to be the only Red Sword with a conscience. In fact, though he followed his orders, Luc gave Orvaril the impression that he did not necessarily agree with all of them. There was a... hesitation in the man's eyes.

Orvaril should have seen it coming—he should have noticed Kendra's mood and realized what she would do. He could have stopped her from killing the Red Sword commander and then everything would be fine. He wouldn't be stuck in this cell and, more importantly, she would be alive. But he hadn't done *anything*.

There was a part of him that simply hadn't believed Kendra would actually attack the man, but there was another part of him that had really *hoped* she would. Unfortunately, rational thinking did not prevail. But, despite his situation, Orvaril did not despair entirely. *Life is a series of playing cards thrown at me, but what I choose to do with those cards is still entirely up to me.* He felt that a new hand would soon be dealt to him. He merely had to bide his time and wait to see what cards he got.

The guards did not have any sort of pattern to their meanderings through the prison, nor did they drop off food with any regularity. They were always crass and violent with prisoners who caused trouble, and they appeared to enjoy making prisoners squirm or beg. Orvaril did not know how many cells there were down here, but he was pretty confident that they were all occupied.

The construction was brand new, though, and so was the towering spire under which the prison lay. Orvaril hadn't been to Sulbar in a while, but the speed at which this building seemed to have been constructed amazed him. It was not completed yet, but it was truly staggering how far they had come in such a short amount of time. There was also the camp being constructed to the east, just outside the city. Orvaril surmised that the Red Swords had essentially brought the city under their influence. It didn't take a genius to figure out that they ran Sulbar now.

After a while, three heavily-armed Red Swords came down the stairs. Orvaril's cell was almost directly across from the stairs, so he watched them approach. Their cumbersome armor clattered as they stepped off the staircase and looked down the hall.

"And what are *you* staring at?" one of them asked Orvaril.

"Overcompensation?" Orvaril asked in reply.

"You should be happy we're not here for you... this time," the guard sneered. "But that may change."

The three men walked past Orvaril's cell, and moved far enough down the hall that he could no longer see them. He could still easily hear them, though. They made noise enough for 30 men, let alone just three.

"Did you hear about the army in the West?" one of them asked. He had a quiet voice, but sounded as if he was trying to come across as tough.

"What army?" another one of them asked. "I haven't heard about any army."

"I heard two officers talking about it—whispering," the quiet one continued. They said there is an orc army massing in the West somewhere. He also said he heard that there are *mages* among their ranks!"

"Orcs?" the other man laughed. "Using magic? It sounds like rumor and exaggeration to me. If there *is* an orc force building up, then I am certain they will be no match for our forces."

"I think it's this one," the quiet one said.

"Aye," the third guard agreed. "Let's get him out of there."

Orvaril heard the three men unlocking a cell door which then creaked as it opened. He then heard the hushed pleas of the cell's occupant, but he couldn't understand exactly what the man was saying.

"If you give us trouble," the guard continued, "we'll have to get rough with you. And we'll enjoy it."

The other two men laughed and agreed.

"Captain Forsch wants to see you," the quieter man added. "He has need of your... abilities, or whatever you call them."

"And what if I don't cooperate?" The prisoner spoke loudly this time but his voice was shaky with fear.

"Then we'll cave your head in and find someone else," the quiet man grumbled. "Accidents happen. Now get moving."

"What does he want with me? I don't—"

"He knows what you can do; says he has need of your skills."

"You're going to have to choose, old man," the third guard threatened. His voice was very deep and gravelly. "You can join up with us or you can be executed for the safety of the Realm. We know that you can work magic."

So Forsch is collecting people for something—people who can do what Cor'il does. But why? Last I'd heard they wanted to rid the Realm of their menace.

Orvaril watched as the guards dragged the scruffy, gray-haired man past his cell. The prisoner struggled and fell to the floor, at which point one of the guards kicked him hard in the ribs.

"Get up, old fool," the low-voiced guard growled. They hoisted the gasping, coughing man to his feet and he looked at Orvaril—stared right at him. For a moment, the prisoner appeared to be limned by a brief but radiant yellow glow that vanished just as quickly as it had appeared. Then he disappeared up the stairs, dragged away by his arms.

Orvaril thought for a moment. He quickly came to a conclusion—that man was important. For better or worse. He was what Orvaril referred to as a "changer"—someone who could radically alter an event. If this man stayed alive, Orvaril was sure that he would be crucial to something important. What and when, Orvaril didn't know—he never did.

It was something that Orvaril had once tried to describe to others but he couldn't really explain it to himself. His mind worked in strange ways that even he did not understand. He had never been wrong as far as he could remember. He was now absolutely sure that he needed to be patient and just wait it out.

Which was difficult, of course. Having been in his cell this long, he had come up with half a dozen plans to escape. Though he was unsure if any of them would work, he had been just about ready to start trying them—until now. Instead, he sat down on the pile of hay in the corner, closed his eyes, and sighed. Waiting patiently was not a finely-honed skill for him.

He tried not to remember his brother, Daryl. The memories always came back at the least convenient times. Mayhaps, if he had listened to his instinct back then as he had just now, then Daryl would still be alive.

He always beat himself up about it—he still felt it was his fault. The stream had turned into a raging monster after the torrential rains, and he had known that they should have walked the extra distance to the bridge. Instead, they tried to cross on a fallen tree.

Daryl had not made it far when the stream engulfed the log and washed him downstream. He had disappeared under the water before Orvaril could do anything to save him. He *knew*. He *knew* that they should have crossed at the bridge yet it was *he* who suggested they save time by crossing over the fallen tree. It was an argument he'd been having with himself since he was 16 winters, and he wasn't sure it would ever end.

Which was much of the reason why he now beat himself up about Kendra's actions. He should have paid attention—he should have talked her down. *Mayhaps I should have been the one to act. I would probably be dead right now, but at least I wouldn't be haunted by these thoughts anymore.*

Orvaril felt uneasy. It was as if the Realm was a giant game of Capture and some of the pieces were beginning to fall into place while others were still out there, yet to be placed on the board. He was used to simply going wherever events led him and reacting accordingly, but everything felt... different. He *wanted* to act—to seize control, but he also knew that now, more than ever, he needed to be *here*. Right here, right now. *I just wish I knew* why.

Something was on the horizon. Something big. The storm was gathering and, when it hit, it was going to reshape the world. Orvaril could feel it, and it made him anxious.

Chapter 25

When Cor'il awoke, he was surprised to find that, instead of his bed in Ilathri, he was lying on a hillside, staring up at a radiant, blue sky. He sat up and looked around for the city that had once surrounded him, but it had vanished just as suddenly as it had appeared to him.

Confusion soon changed to disappointment and he got up, brushing off grass and dirt. He still had so many questions and so much to learn. In fact, he probably had *more* questions now than when he had first arrived.

He stared at the ring on his finger and played with it. It didn't move much because the leafy tendrils had spread out and gripped his finger in various places. Though obviously made of metal, they looked exactly as if they were parts of a real plant growing out of the ring itself. As obtrusive as this would seem, most of the time Cor'il didn't notice the ring at all. It was just one of the many things he still had questions about.

"I... I think I knew some of those people."

Antina's voice had been silent for much of Cor'il's stay in Ilathri—however long it had been. For the first day, she had been frantic—feeling out of place and not knowing where they were. She had babbled endlessly about feeling disconnected from something. After a little while, her blathering had changed and she began warning Cor'il how "these people" would betray him and lead him down a false path. She told him that they were not who he thought they were and that they were using him. After the first two days, however, she had stopped talking altogether.

Part of him wondered if she told the truth. Arcturas hadn't provided him with as many answers as he had been promised. Whether Arcturas and the rest of Ilathri truly didn't know the answers or were withholding them, Cor'il was unsure. Until now, Antina had not told him anything about having met the Ilathri before—only that she didn't trust them and that they were lying to him. One time, she had gone so far as to suggest that Cor'il kill them all.

"*I can't be sure. Have I met them before? Surely I have. They seem so... familiar. But they are false! Do not listen to them!*"

While he hadn't received all the answers he had hoped to get, he at least had more information now, and he might be able to act on it.

Cor'il glanced around until he noticed Sky standing nearby, eating breakfast. If the animal was confused about its surroundings, he did not show any sign of caring.

His thoughts turned to his friends. He had no way of knowing if they were okay, or even where they were, but he wanted badly to reconnect with them. Most of all, he wanted to tell them what he had discovered. The pain and anguish within him still remained, but he no longer felt as if he was a danger to his friends.

"*Your plan? Your plan is faulty. You've no idea what you're doing. The things those... those Ilathri told you are falsehoods. They're lying to you. They are using you. And, out of a book and some ramblings from them, you think you have enough knowledge to formulate an actual plan? You will doom us all.*

It was true. During his stay in Ilathri, he had been able to read much further into the book. While learning what he could from the Ilathri and combining that knowledge with the book, he had come up with his own plan. He knew about the Great Machine but, more importantly, he knew about the Dark Machine now. That had been a missing puzzle piece that he hadn't even known about in the first place.

You only delayed the outcome while you were trapped under Elston. You merely prolonged the order in the Realm with your crystals. It is you who didn't know what you were doing.

"No. Everything was in harmony. You only needed to take my place and the world would still be as it was! But you let *the crystals fall into the well. By doing so you let Chaos back into the world."*

"I also let Order back into the world." Cor'il approached Sky. "And I released the power of the Threads to everyone with the potential. I refuse to live the lies you created."

"A dangerous gambit and a fool's prospect. You barely grasp the knowledge to wield the Threads. What do you think will happen to all those individuals who do not even know about them? They're dangerous. There will be destruction. People will die. And even if—"

"Shut up," Cor'il growled. His sword was instantly in his hand as he broke out into a run down the hill and into the woods. Once he was among the trees, he stopped and looked around.

He had felt it again—the eerie chill that sent shivers down his back. He was being watched. He was certain now, and he wanted to know who was following him. His heart pounded inside his head as he caught his breath and looked around him. But there was nothing. He embraced the Threads and found no clues.

"Who are you?" he called. A group of birds hastily took flight from a nearby branch. He stood alone, amongst the trees, waiting for several moments with his breathing being the only sound. Eventually, his frustration took over as he turned to head back up the hill.

"Chasing ghosts and talking to yourself again. Fantastic. And you believe me to be the crazy one."

And, then, he heard it—rustling leaves and sticks snapping. He turned and ran to his left, hurdling a fallen log and dodging a low branch. He caught a glimpse of something—a brown cloak—as it disappeared behind a large rock. Cor'il leapt onto the rock and then down onto the forest floor, ready to fight.

But there was nothing. He looked around him for any sign of someone but, again, found nothing.

"Who are you?" he shouted, his voice echoing through the trees. "Why are you following me?"

The only answer was silence.

Frustrated, Cor'il sat down on the rock. It was becoming more difficult to stay calm.

"Footprints," he whispered to himself. Though not easily visible, Cor'il could make out several boot prints left in the dirt and crushed leaves. His heart jumped with excitement as he scoured the ground, finding four more before the trail went cold. *So I'm not imagining things, am I?*

The area where the footprints stopped was... tainted. Several of the plants appeared warped or twisted somehow, frozen in a silent, mangled torment. Cor'il touched one of them. Nothing about it felt abnormal but at the same time, everything about it looked wrong.

After heading back up the hill, Cor'il climbed up on Sky's back and looked around him again. He was concerned that he was being followed, but his elation was much more powerful.

He needed to return to Elston—the city was central to his plan. He also needed to find his friends to keep them safe. If anyone knew where his friends were, surely it was The Blacksmoke. While he did not relish the thought of dealing with the man, he had to admit that Blacksmoke certainly knew a lot about events in The Realm.

"I kept balance for 200 years. You ruined it."

I returned the world to what it was meant to be. I restored it.

"You let Chaos in while Order barely has a foothold on this world."

I aim to rectify that.

"There is something else—something you're missing. I can't quite remember what it is. It... it eludes me. But it, too, has touched this world. It is familiar to me. It feels... very old. If only I could remember!"

Yes, I can feel it, too. It's almost like an infection— festering, but hiding and getting worse.

Antina fell silent and, for the first time, Cor'il was disappointed. Hers were ramblings of a madwoman, but she had her helpful moments of lucidity. Besides, it was much more productive to have someone around to hear his ideas instead of just talking to himself... even if he wasn't entirely sure she was real.

He still had not come to terms with the fact that either he was going mad or that someone was trapped inside his mind—and she *was* mad. Neither was a preferable situation. He wondered, should he ever get used to it, if that was a scarier proposition. Real or not, for the foreseeable future, he was stuck with her.

The only way Cor'il could determine which way to go was by the sun. He figured out which way west was and pointed Sky toward it, but he stopped abruptly. Elston was mayhaps a week away but the pillar near Kuranthas—the *duratas* as Arcturas had called it—was much closer. Mayhaps he could use it to travel to another *duratas* closer to Elston.

He sat for a moment, mired in indecision. There were too many unknowns for easy answers to become clear to him. Eventually he turned and, at a brisk walk, directed Sky back toward Kuranthas. It was truly the last place that he wanted to be, but if he was right, it would be a shorter trip.

He now understood a lot more about the Threads, the Great Machine, and even the Dark Machine. But there were holes—gaps in the information that Cor'il couldn't explain. If he could just get a few key answers... but, then, he wasn't even sure what the right questions were.

Cor'il set out with Sky at a relaxed walk, making sure to keep an eye out for any approaching danger. Hopefully this risk would pay off.

• • •

"*What is* that?"
I was hoping you could tell me.
Cor'il hunkered down behind the broken rubble that used to be a Kuranthian home. Though he tried not to think about it, he couldn't help wondering *whose* home it had been. The ruins of the

town were completely unrecognizable. Those thoughts only led to sadness and despair, and he was not sure that this was a wound that would ever heal.

He remained hidden and watched from behind cover. Wandering about the ruins of Kuranthas was a twisted, misshapen creature. It almost looked as if a man and a bear had been somehow melted down and fused together. Just looking at it sent shivers down Cor'il's spine. He fought the urge to flee and, instead, continued observing.

The beast's head was hairless and it had several mouths that all sat at different angles. It walked on four legs and had two arms protruding from its back. The arms ended in clawed hands that appeared to each have more than five fingers or claws... or whatever they were. Its grey, mottled skin looked almost diseased and its breathing sounded labored.

He shivered in fear. Several times, he closed his eyes tight and ducked behind his cover, hoping the creature would be gone when he looked again.

The twisted monster kicked over some rubble and appeared to sniff the air, though it had no nose that Cor'il could see.

Soon, another creature emerged from the trees and made its way into the ruins of Kuranthas. This one was built like a giant snake but had two arms to help itself along. Its neck ended abruptly in one large eye.

This monster also had pale skin but it looked as if it had been scarred by fire. They both growled as they moved about, largely leaving each other alone.

"Wait. I should know these things. They are familiar to me."

Cor'il's skin crawled. He had to force himself not to look away. Fortunately, he had left Sky tied to a tree just outside of the ruins the moment he had sensed trouble. Hopefully the horse would not see these monsters and bolt. If Cor'il had this strong of an urge to flee, then a horse would, too.

He moved closer, hiding behind charred stone that he had shattered over a year ago. His whole body shook with fear as he tried to slow his breathing and calm himself.

"Closer? Why closer? Flee—you should run now. Are you daft? These things are not natural; they don't belong here. You don't belong here."

"Be quiet," Cor'il whispered. He found it difficult to concentrate with Antina rambling in his head.

"You can no more fight these creatures than you can kill a swollen river with a sword. They are monsters. They are a torrent of rage. They are..."

For a moment Cor'il cheerfully thought that Antina may have sunk back down to the depths of his mind as he embraced the Threads. When he did so he immediately noticed both creatures gave off a radiant, almost piercing light. In fact, he could barely make out their features.

"Madness. Absolute madness."

Cor'il heard a sound behind him, and he released the Threads. When he turned, he found one of them not even 10 feet away. It was big—twice his size—but it had no eyes. Though it was a hulking mass, it was closer to a normal human shape than the other two monsters.

Cor'il drew his sword and stabbed the creature as it approached, but it was like sticking an elephant with a toothpick. The monster hit Cor'il with its hand, knocking him back several feet and leaving his sword stuck in it. He staggered out into what used to be a street and tried to get his wits about him, unable to seize control of the Threads.

His vision swam and his balance was shaky. He backed up some more, hoping to give himself as much time and distance as he could. To his surprise, the behemoth stopped and began swatting at something in front of it. Cor'il could see only vague shapes through his blurry vision. *I hope it hasn't seen Sky!*

He desperately grasped for the Threads and finally managed to grab hold of them. Though his head was still foggy, he was beginning to see more clearly, and he watched as three skeletal creatures desperately tried to escape the reach of the monster.

It shrieked loudly and grabbed one of them, smashing its skull with one beefy hand. The other two fled, but the creature's arms stretched out unnaturally to grab them, slamming them into the ground as they tried feebly to fight back.

"*Madness,*" Antina repeated.

Yes, this is madness! It's terrible!

"*No, stupid boy,*" she continued. "*These creatures—they are Madness. They are born of Madness itself. I remember now! Madness has leaked back into the world! You should have listened to me but you didn't! And now, look at what you've done! I suggest you escape while it is busy destroying the last two Threadfiends. It is almost done with them and, when it is, it will come for you. It will not stop until either you or it is dead. Madness is uncontrollable and unstoppable!*"

It was good advice. When Cor'il looked around, he noticed the other two creatures closing in from further down the street. He needed to get back to Sky. He needed time to think.

Cor'il began weaving Threads, furiously tying and twisting and layering until he had woven a dome-shaped tapestry of Threads around him. Then he tried to calm himself—to force down the fear that threatened to consume him.

"*Yes! I remember! By keeping the balance of the Chaos and Order stones, I kept The Madness at bay—contained within its own realm! But you—you unbalanced them!*"

"You weren't trying to keep Chaos and Order out of the Realm, were you? You were keeping The Madness out!" Cor'il looped and tied off his weave, then he released the Threads. The world became crisp and clear again.

Yes! The Madness! Now you understand! The only way to banish it from our lands was to banish everything*! By keeping the Chaos and Order stones in balance the Madness stone was also kept in balance.*"

"But I didn't see any Madness stone," Cor'il muttered. The behemoth had destroyed the Threadfiends and now lashed out at Cor'il. His dome deflected the attack, shimmering with golden energy that radiated outward from the point of impact.

"There is no Madness stone. Madness is not a thing that can be touched or observed. It is felt and experienced. It will slowly eat away at you, twisting your existence and turning your own thoughts against you."

Sort of like you?

Antina's voice went silent, for which Cor'il was very thankful. Now he could try to figure a way out. The dome was immobile and it would not hold forever. Unfortunately, Cor'il didn't know how long it would *protect* him. At this point, he was just happy that he had been able to weave it properly. His head was still swimming and his chest ached where the Madness creature had hit him.

The monster pounded on the dome again, which once more pulsed outward with golden light. The other two creatures followed suit, surrounding Cor'il. The entire dome lit up as all three of them attacked, trying desperately to get at him.

Cor'il looked around, feeling frustrated and angry. He saw the ruins of his village—what he had done—and felt a burning sensation welling up within him. His insides felt as if they were on fire and his vision blurred more. His mind further clouded and he gasped for air. He could hear nothing and barely could see his own hands in front of his face. He recognized this sensation. It had happened before. He fell to his knees, and just as he was about to collapse into darkness, he spoke.

"Verifalimos!" he shouted, his voice echoing and booming through the trees.

The dome shimmered and then collapsed as everything around him exploded outward in a fiery, rage-fueled wave that nearly deafened Cor'il. Trees snapped and shattered, then burst into flame as the very dirt and rock around him shot high into the air.

All three creatures were thrown violently backward and then they, too, were consumed by impossibly hot fire. Cor'il fought to stay conscious.

Though weak and tired, he managed to stand, panting and gasping for breath. His strength slowly returned to him as he watched the remaining bits of the Madness monsters burn. He could smell the sickening, pungent odor of their seared flesh smoking around him as he staggered slowly back to where he had left Sky.

He stepped past smoldering ash that had been the largest of the beasts and noticed his sword, now molten slag, on the ground amongst the remains. For a moment, he felt vulnerable without it and he knew he would need to find another. Cor'il continued until he found his horse, still tethered to a branch outside of the scorched area. With significant effort, he grabbed the reins and climbed onto Sky's back, urging him forward. Cor'il breathed a sigh of relief as they left the ruins of Kuranthas behind.

"That was... impressive. But you had already done that once before, hadn't you? Yes... it was."

Be silent.

"You have great ability within you, that much is obvious. It appears I might have underestimated your talents but you still lack control. The Madness will consume this world and you along with it. Your level of talent or power won't matter. You destroyed the stones which were the only things keeping The Madness at bay."

I have a plan.

Cor'il clutched weakly to Sky as they slowly crossed the creek on the other side of Kuranthas and began their ascent up the hill. He knew the *duratas* was nearby, not just because he recognized the terrain but because he somehow could *feel* the spire. He tried to ignore Antina but she continued rambling.

"I had a plan, too. You only had to take my place in the chamber and the world would have been safe—removed from Madness and Chaos."

No. The cycle had to be broken.

"It was your duty. It was your place."

You would have me be a prisoner?

"Whatever it took. But the point is moot. We can't go back now. The Dark Machine has been let loose upon your world. It will consume everything, and these lands will be cloaked in darkness for eternity... until The Madness consumes it."

Cor'il tried to ignore Antina. She continued to speak of eternal darkness and chaos. It took all the concentration he could muster to ignore her ramblings and stay upright on his horse. Eventually, fatigue overtook him and he was forced to stop and bed down for the rest of the day.

He slept soundly through the night. When he awoke the next morning, Antina was eerily quiet. Had he so quickly grown accustomed to her mad notions of doom? Mayhaps it was better than being alone, even if he might still have been imagining her.

The *duratas* was not far now. He could feel its presence. Curious, he embraced the Threads and its presence grew stronger. He also felt the chilling presence of a Threadfiend, but he did not feel afraid as he had in the past. He felt uneasy and his movements became labored but, this time, he did not freeze up entirely. He thought that, mayhaps, these creatures had no effect on him anymore.

Sure enough, he spotted one floating between the trees in the distance. He watched it move about silently and then, suddenly, it was mere inches from his face.

Cor'il's body froze and he could not move at all, now. His breathing hastened and condensed in front of him. He shook as he stared into the empty eye sockets of the hooded Threadfiend.

"Kill it! Kill it now! It will devour you!"

It raised a bony index finger to its mouth and, for several seconds, everything was completely silent.

"Splintered..." it whispered. "Fix..."

"Fix... fix what?" Cor'il stammered, barely able to speak.

"Don't listen to it! It will trick you! It is pure evil!"

After a moment, Cor'il felt control return to his body, and the Threadfiend drifted away into the distance, disappearing entirely. He slumped to the ground and released the Threads, trying desperately to catch his breath as sound and color returned to the world around him. *I guess I'm not immune to them after all.*

He dismounted once he reached the *duratas* and led his horse over to the smooth, white obelisk. As before, it floated above the ground and pulsed with blue light, illuminating runes that were otherwise invisible. Cor'il closely inspected the object.

"Yes," he muttered to himself. "It appears that'll work... if I am understanding this correctly."

"What are you doing?"

"We are going to Elston," he said.

"Yes! To the well! We can set things right!"

"No," Cor'il continued. "I am going to find my friends."

"And then what? You'll simply sit by and watch as the world is consumed by Madness?"

Cor'il remained silent as he slowly ran his fingers over the smooth surface of the obelisk. He needed to be sure. Suddenly, he understood.

I told you, I have a plan.

Antina fell silent for a moment as Cor'il concentrated, channeling the raw power of the Threads into the *duratas*. It began to hum and several runes lit up with a bright blue glow. Soon a rift appeared in the air to the right of the obelisk. It expanded until it was large enough to walk through.

Cor'il could see into the chamber beyond. The walls were smooth and white—like the *duratas* itself. More importantly, the chamber looked much like the room in which Antina had dwelt previously. Hopefully, this *duratas* was close to Elston.

"Oh my... you are a clever one, aren't you? But what if you're wrong?"

"I'm not."

Cor'il stepped through the rift.

The Coming Storm

Chapter 26

The rift closed with a loud swishing sound behind Cor'il shortly after he stepped through. He found himself in a plain, rectangular room of mostly white. As with the room in which he had met Antina, the walls and floor pulsed every so often, illuminating ornate patterns and designs with a different-colored light each time. Though the ceiling was quite high, the floating *duratas* seemed to nearly touch it.

Aside from Cor'il's footfalls the room was completely silent. The only illumination was provided by the pulsing, glowing designs and several glowing orbs affixed to the walls. He stood for a moment and inspected his surroundings, hoping that the *duratas* had transported him to Elston, but there was no way of knowing where he was until he got out of this room.

"Why are we here? What can you possibly accomplish?"

"I need to find my friends," Cor'il muttered, still gazing about the room. It was not terribly large but it was empty. As it was, there was nothing but Cor'il and the obelisk that floated silently behind him. He found himself chuckling about the fact that, currently, his most pressing question was about the large amount of empty space in the room.

If he indeed had arrived at Elston, he then had to find The Blacksmoke, and he wasn't quite sure how to do that. Cor'il took a few steps forward, his footfalls echoing throughout the room, and scrutinized the wall before him. There were no cracks and no doors. He ran his fingers over the smooth, glossy surface, convinced that there was something he was missing.

He moved along every wall looking for signs of a doorway, but he found nothing. He made another pass but, again, came up empty.

"You're really bad at this, aren't you? Judging from the fact that you can't even find a way out of a room, I'm not sure I should put any confidence in you. In fact, I'm shocked that you were able to come up with this plan on your own."

Cor'il did not feel like arguing so he simply waited for Antina to offer up information instead of trying to pry it out of her. It was as if he could almost feel her smiling.

"This room was made for Threadweavers only," she finally replied. *"Therefore, you must channel the Threads just as you did with the* duratas *and if there is a door, which there should be, it will respond."*

"You could have simply told me."

"I figured you already knew. Sometimes, you seem to be very clever and, other times, you make me believe that your head is filled with stone."

Cor'il relaxed and embraced the Threads. He could sense each one—the bright light of gold, the cold of metal from silver, the heat from red, the earthy smell from green, the breeze from white, and the oily, sick feeling of the black Threads.

But was there something else? For a moment, Cor'il was sure he had felt something—either within the Threads or... he wasn't sure.

He gathered all the Threads into something like a braid or a rope and cast them out in every direction. The surface of the far wall shimmered and the outline of a door appeared. When he released the Threads, he saw that a door had swung inward, leading to a passage beyond. As he stepped into the corridor, an orb on the wall came to life, lighting the way ahead.

"What do you hope to accomplish?"

I need to find my friends and make sure they are well.

"That is not what I asked."

Harmony, then.

Another orb lit up ahead of Cor'il as he slowly traversed the passageway. There were no pulsing designs on the walls here, but the area appeared to be constructed in the same fashion as the room he'd just left. It was seamless and looked delicate—though Cor'il knew better than to assume that.

The passage curved to the right and then abruptly ended in a wall. Before Antina could interject Cor'il grasped the Threads.

His surroundings darkened and his vision blurred, but the spindly Threads of energy illuminated everything in a dingy but sufficient light. A quick inspection of the wall in front of him revealed a faint, almost undetectable, outline of a door.

He directed the Threads at the wall, pouring their energy into it. Almost instantly, the portion of the wall inside the outline began to fade until it disappeared entirely. Cor'il released the Threads and stepped through the small archway which sealed itself once he was through.

He stood in darkness only briefly before the familiar orbs illuminated themselves, revealing the passage beyond. The walls were of the same make and material as the room he had just left, but the passage ended in an archway. When he passed through he found himself on a wide ledge—to his left was a sheer wall of rock and dirt. To his right was a cliff, which quickly gave way to darkness. Fortunately, there were light orbs positioned along the wall to his left, springing to life when he was near, as he slowly made his way across to the other end.

His breath and his boots on the smooth rock ledge were the only sounds Cor'il could hear. When he reached the end of the ledge, he stood next to a small, white stone pillar that came up to his waist. It was round and had a flat surface, above which hovered a blue, spherical gemstone.

"I can tell that you know what this is, don't you?"

Cor'il recalled Kendra telling him and Orvaril about the desolate city she had found underneath the ground back when they had found the first *duratas*. This matched her description almost to the letter. Cor'il reached for the gem but hesitated.

"I need to find my friends," he muttered. "This will accomplish nothing."

"On the contrary. This could accomplish everything! *This is a city built by a civilization before us! There must be endless knowledge somewhere down there!"*

I need to find my friends. I must know if they are alright.

243

"But what if you didn't have to find them? What if you could bring them to you?"

How do you know that is possible?

"I don't. Your road leads down there. We have no way out of here as it is. You don't even know if we're in the right place!"

Cor'il gently plucked the stone out of the air. He was insanely curious, but he also felt a burning desire to reconnect with his friends. He took a deep breath and placed the gemstone in the divot on the side of the pillar. *If it'll keep you quiet...*

The chasm below him came to life, instantly illuminating an entire city. Cor'il stood above it all, in stunned silence, marveling at what had just happened.

"Just as Kendra had said," Cor'il gasped. "A city of the *Kai'Tan.*"

It was beautiful—white structures towering in the distance and glimmering in the magical illumination. Cor'il could make out, toward the center, the shadowy shape of the structure Kendra said she had climbed—the triangular, A-shaped building. *It's all just as she had described. Hopefully there won't be any of those* things *down here.*

"Are we going to just stand here, looking stupid?"

Cor'il looked around him and saw a blue, translucent disc of light hovering just off the edge by the pillar. It was large enough to hold probably 20 people, but looked almost completely immaterial.

He cautiously set one foot on the disc and the surface shimmered briefly. Two gentle pulses of light radiated out from his foot, repeating when he followed with his right foot. A few seconds after he first stepped onto the platform it gently moved forward, slowly descending into the city below. Above him, he saw that it was immediately replaced by another disc up by the pillar.

Cor'il grasped the Threads and quickly marveled at the complexity of not just the floating disc apparatus, but of the *entire city*! The Threads wound around and through seemingly every inch of the metropolis, permeating everything, and they lit up the city brighter than the light orbs themselves did with Cor'il's regular vision.

The weaves were intricate and complex. Cor'il could spend a lifetime down here inspecting them and mayhaps figure out how only a handful worked. At a glance, he could not determine even the basic function of any of them. They were designs and patterns that he never would have dreamed possible. He had no idea how some of them were merely holding together, much less functioning. They should have unraveled the moment they were woven yet, somehow, they were still immaculately spun together and had lasted countless years.

There was so much to take in—so much to consider all at once. Antina was quiet. Cor'il wasn't sure if she had access to any of his knowledge or anything he had seen in the past—at times he thought she might have access to his memories, but he was still unsure.

Cor'il released the Threads, and the rush of power and exhilaration ceased, leaving him feeling empty for a few seconds. His vision returned to normal and he realized that he was standing on the ground just outside the city. To his right stood another pillar that was identical to the pillar on the ridge above.

"In case you were wondering," Antina chuckled, *"you've been standing here like a wide-eyed fool for several minutes."*

Cor'il frowned but refrained from saying anything. In actuality, he had been wondering just that. He didn't wish to give Antina the satisfaction but, somehow, he figured that she already knew. It had been easy to become so distracted by the city's beauty and the mastery at which the Threads had been used throughout, that he had indeed lost track of where he was.

Cor'il picked up the floating stone and inserted it into the pillar, causing a familiar, translucent blue disc to appear on the ground.

He turned and slowly stepped forward, walking into the city with wonder and awe. He moved from the dirt ground and onto the smooth city street. The stonework was incredible—intricate patterns of different shades of white and gray fitted perfectly together so that he could barely see a crack between stones.

Yet, still, the city was dormant—quiet and unmoving, despite the amount of energy coursing through it. Cor'il walked amongst the silent structures, both admiring the precise architecture and looking for danger. Kendra had encountered one of those Madness creatures in a city like this. There might be danger lurking about here as well.

"This could be yours. Knowledge! Power! You would be an unstoppable force! You could shape the world and destroy any who stood against you! There is no one else left to seize this power—only you!"

"Be quiet!" Cor'il admonished.

"The Madness! You could harness its power and control it! You could—"

"What? I could what?" Cor'il stopped near a statue of a horse. Conversations were much easier when he could see the person he was talking to. "I could go mad like you?"

Antina was silent. Cor'il really had no idea what he was saying. He just wanted Antina to stop rambling. She made it difficult for him to concentrate on anything.

Or I'm already mad and this is merely the beginning. Is this how it starts, then? Mayhaps I'll start seeing hallucinations or other voices will crop up inside my head.

Cor'il remembered Alton's father once talking about a drink called *iscatan* that could cause hallucinations. As a child, Cor'il had always imagined that it would be exciting to try. In particular, he thought mayhaps he would see something wonderful like a unicorn or a dragon. The latter would have been exciting back then, but not so much now.

Assuming dragons truly exist. It seems within the realm of possibility, given the events of the past year. Cor'il waited for Antina to pipe up with some useless fact or mad rambling, but instead, she remained quiet. Cor'il found himself disappointed. He really was curious.

He passed building after building, each a quiet monument to an entire race of people who had apparently abandoned it long ago. His mind started trying to fill in the blanks—of which there were many—but the result was that which a storyweaver would tell. There was simply no evidence to answer any of his questions.

Cor'il did not need to use the Threads to be able to detect their flow. They were so large in number that he couldn't help but feel the energy running through every inch of this city. There was a particularly large concentration that dominated all others, however. It was obvious, and it was showing him the way—at least that is how it felt to him.

The Threads feel as if they are leading me deep into the city. But how can this be? Was this intentional? Is the city itself directing me?

"Grab them. Take them. Yes. Make them yours! They beckon to you and will not be ignored!"

Cor'il walked in silence, following the unseen path down one of the city's main avenues. Several times, he stopped and looked around cautiously when he thought he heard something, but as far as he could tell, he was still alone. The last time he was in a settlement this quiet, it had deceived him.

Listerville.

That very thought made him shiver. Instantly, he darted his gaze around the area, looking for the sources of sounds that his mind may have made up. While the Madness creatures he had recently encountered were truly frightening, the abominations in Listerville—creatures that had once been people—were even more disturbing. What could cause such a curse?

Cor'il was unsure of how long he had walked but, after taking several turns through the city's streets, he found himself standing in front of a large, white dome. It had no windows but there was a door right off the road. Yes, the Threads converged here, but why?

"It's a trap, boy. It's surely your doom. You are so powerful, yet so reckless."

Cor'il hesitated briefly, his outstretched palm just inches from the door. Then his hesitation dissolved and he pressed his hand onto the surface. He had prepared for disappointment but, to his surprise, something began to happen.

The portion of the dome around where he had touched began to dissolve in patches that began as dots and then grew. Cor'il peered inside and saw a dimly-lit foyer, in the center of which was a statue of some sort. He looked around him cautiously and, taking a deep breath, entered the dome.

"I am telling you it's a trap!"

The door rematerialized behind him.

Sean R. Frazier

Chapter 27

Captain Jarel Forsch ran a hand through his brown hair. He'd just had it cut not long ago, yet it seemed to already be past a tolerable length. He brushed it out of his face and shifted the papers on his desk, trying to remember just what it was he had last looked at.

It was immense—all of it. The management, patrols, and soldiers. There was so much to keep track of. Even with his myriad of assistants he found it difficult to keep everything straight. Agreements, supply lists, manifests, personnel lists... that was just the beginning. Defending the Realm was not easy and there were days when he felt as though the weight of the world might crush him. Quite often, he longed to return to the battlefield—to command soldiers on the front line. Battle was easier, clearer—kill the enemy while you avoid being killed. Black and white.

However, thus far, his efforts had been met with much success. His men had slaughtered numerous bands of orcs and had either killed or captured dozens of these so-called "mages." Fordaril had coined that term and it had somehow stuck. In fact, it had been The Snake's idea at the outset to bring the mages into the Red Sword fold instead of merely killing them all. He was useful; Forsch could not deny that.

Sure, there were some mages who refused to cooperate. The majority of those were run down and executed. They were all a danger to the Realm—even those in the Red Sword army. Forsch never forgot that. But, as long as they were afraid, they would fall in line. If the Red Swords could keep them down, they would remain tethered and obedient. And once Forsch had no use for them, they would be destroyed just as the enemies they cut down.

It was because of these harnessed mages that the Red Swords had made so much progress both with the recent construction as well as in combat. They were extremely useful, though their talents and proficiencies varied widely. They were tools to be used, but the trick was figuring out where each one fit within their ranks. Fordaril had underlings to make sense of all of that.

Not only had the Red Swords' physical numbers grown since the Spire's construction had begun, but their ability to build, organize, and defend had improved—all because of the mages. Many possibilities opened up when you controlled the ability to lift things through the air or to make an object disappear and reappear in a different place. And those were just a couple of the many abilities these tools possessed. One mage was worth at least a hundred men—mayhaps more.

Forsch rose from his chair, rubbed his eyes, and moved to the window. His new chambers toward the top of the spire afforded him an unprecedented view of the countryside in all directions. Construction on the several levels above him was nearing completion, and would hopefully be finished in the next few days. He looked forward to the absence of noise.

The Red Swords' compound behind Sulbar was also coming along nicely, but there was still much to be done. They were not keeping up with the housing needs of their soldiers and had been forced to bunk them in houses within the city itself. While Forsch himself had no problem with this, the citizens of Sulbar were unhappy and the Red Swords had a reputation to uphold. Forsch was not yet sure if he was ready to outright defy the Council, should it come to that.

Mayhaps you should just claim the entire city as Red Sword property. The Council may resist but either they will see the light or we will simply take it by force. He rubbed his chin, still gazing out the window. *That is not a decision to be made lightly but, still, it must be considered. Hopefully, they will comply with whatever needs to be done.*

He moved back to the desk, briefly wrote a note, then returned to the window and looked out into the darkness.

The lamps of Sulbar were dots of light that pierced the night, illuminating much of the city with their flickering flames. Beyond Sulbar's walls, however, the light stopped abruptly, allowing the darkness to take over. Forsch wondered if there should be some sort of illumination *around* the city—mayhaps large fires scattered about outside the walls? He wanted to see past the confines of the city walls. An army of orcs and goblins could be standing right outside the gates, sneering at him, and he would never know it.

He would make sure to get that rectified. Certainly, he would be a fool if he neglected to keep the city—*his* city—secure. But Sulbar was safe enough for now. He had other operations to consider. Construction of the Spire in Elston was underway. Progress was slower than here in Sulbar, but Forsch had plans to relocate some of his men—and mages—westward to aid in the construction. In addition, he would personally oversee the construction himself. The Spires would help keep each city safe from invasion.

King Alzine had been hesitant at first when Forsch had approached him about building a Spire in Elston, but eventually, the two had come to an agreement for the city's protection. He was a wise king and obviously wished for the safety of his subjects— especially considering the recent orcish incursions.

Then there was Ten Kings. He had sent two small contingents to negotiate the need for a Spire there as well but, thus far, his emissaries had not reported back to him. He was worried that they had been intercepted by dark creatures. As of late, rumors had spread of an army of abominations growing in the West. Mayhaps his men had run afoul of this force—if those rumors were true. If they indeed *were* true, then he would have to put them down. The Red Sword numbers and training could easily defeat whatever savagery they uncovered.

As he peered out the window his thoughts turned briefly to the past. It wasn't very long ago that the Realm's worst problem had been a group of bandits or petty thieves. Sulbar, anyway, had had no pressing issues. And, even then, Elston's only *major* problem had been crime, and King Alzine put most of the blame on a handful of individuals, probably led by the murderer who called himself The Blacksmoke.

Things had changed radically. Forsch recalled the first siege of Sulbar, when the orcs appeared seemingly out of nowhere and attacked the city walls. Many good men had died that day. In fact, Forsch considered that to be the day *he* died—the old him, anyway. It was the day that he realized the Realm was in great danger. He had been quick to form the Red Swords and he had not once regretted that decision.

Mistakes had been made, however, but the Realm needed protection—a standing army. To date, the Red Swords had driven back the monsters more times than he could count. They had protected people far and wide.

And, yet, they keep coming. They're like waves crashing against the shore, except that they appear to be growing stronger with every new day. Where are they all coming from? Probably Darovinia or Scorovia, no doubt.

This was why they needed *more* soldiers. Surely there would come a point where the orcs' numbers waned and the Realm could be safe again. He would chase them into the depths of The Abyss if that would ensure their defeat. He would make sure he had the numbers to do it, too.

And, yet, one of my commanders was killed... by a mere girl, no less. Not even a warrior! We will need to be more selective with whom we promote in our ranks. I will see to that. Fortunately, his replacement has been stout and trustworthy thus far.

He had long toyed with a plan to secure Darovinia—the northern Realm. Not only did they possess vast wealth, but they also had a large army. To bring Darovinia under his control, however, would be tricky. Brute force was not the way. Instead, he would have to be subtle and start from the inside. Once he had secured the Realm to the north, what next? *I'll cleanse the scourge from the surrounding realms once I've made this one safe. Spires will go up in cities across the realms to keep* everyone *safe. We will eliminate the threat from orcs* and *mages.*

Forsch felt the corners of his lips rise in a grin. He couldn't help it. He despised all threats to the Realm, and the very thought of banishing them all lifted his spirits. He was under no illusion—the protection of the Realm came first, but he was certainly not against the power and authority. They were both necessary to accomplish his goal.

There was a rap on the door.

"Enter," Forsch called. A wiry man entered the room and brushed his long, raven-black hair from his eyes. He bowed his head briefly and approached as Forsch turned to face him.

"Captain, sir," he began, nervously. He was young—probably having seen only 20 winters—and had a scar that reached almost all the way across his forehead in a jagged path. For a moment, Forsch's eyes fixed on the scar, unable to look away.

"What is your name, soldier?"

"Uh, Commander Derek Ironfist, sir."

"Ah, an Ironfist! I know your father Baramond—good man, he is."

"Yes, sir," Derek stammered, "I suppose he is, sir." He paused for a moment, as he shifted his weight from one foot to the other. "The Spire has spotted orcs in the countryside around Sulbar, sir. And mayhaps a troll or two. Though your watchers' vision from atop The Spire is very good, it is still difficult to tell. They might be ogres.

"How is it that my watchers cannot tell the difference?"

"Well, sir," he stammered, "Your mages' talents allow them to see better than normal, but they simply don't know the difference."

"Dispatch a small scouting party in the morning," Forsch replied. He was very matter-of-fact. His scouts would assess the situation and then they could determine how big a force they would need to eliminate the threat.

"We, uh, did that earlier today, sir." Derek's voice cracked slightly. This man obviously had some unsavory news to report. He was fidgeting with the edge of his cloak with his left hand. For a son of Ironfist, he seemed very sheepish.

"And?"

"They never returned, sir."

"I see." Forsch paced across the room twice, his hands clasped behind his back. Mayhaps his scouts had been foolish—mayhaps they had gotten too close to the orcs. While the Red Swords had large numbers, not every soldier was the best and the brightest. The Abyss, some of them were just downright stupid! "What does it appear that they are doing?"

"It is difficult to say, sir." He fidgeted some more. "The Spire says they are not roaming. They are either establishing a settlement or—"

"Or a camp." Forsch turned to look out the window again. Mayhaps he imagined it, but he thought he saw faint pinpricks of flickering light in the distance. "I believe the city is going to come under attack soon."

"Sir?"

"It is my belief that these orcs are establishing a base and will use it to launch a siege against Sulbar. We must send a force out against them to make sure this does not happen. It shouldn't take much. It always begins this way—it starts small but, if left unattended, can grow into a massive horde of invaders."

"But, sir, our scouts—"

"I see no need to waste more men's lives. I am sure we can dispatch an adequate force to take care of a few orcs to keep the city safe." Forsch turned and leaned against his desk, resting his hands on it. "Did the Spire indicate how many orcs there are?"

"No sir, they did not."

"Then we will send three hundred men—mixed cavalry, archers, and infantry." Forsch paused for a moment. "And I shall dispatch five mages with them. That should suffice."

"Yes, sir." Derek's apprehension quickly melted away into confidence. "Shall I give the order?"

"That will not be necessary," Forsch sat down at the desk and started writing the orders on a piece of paper. The inkwell was nearly dry. When was the last time he'd had it filled? "I will give the orders myself. By tomorrow evening the threat shall be eliminated."

"Excellent, sir. I have full confidence in our forces."

"That is good to hear, Derek. Would you like to lead the assault?"

"Me, sir?"

Derek's face lost all color. Forsch wondered just how experienced with a blade this man truly was. His father had served under King Alzine for a while and was rumored to be a skilled swordsman. In a time of relative peace, however, what experience could one truly gain with a weapon? And what would he have taught his son about combat? Derek was reliable enough and, Forsch assumed, he could probably lead adequately. *Is this a mistake? Mayhaps someone else would be more properly suited for this task. Or he'll be killed in combat and I can replace him with someone more suited to his duties.*

"Aye. Surely you are up to the task."

"I would," he stopped and, with much effort, swallowed, "I would be honored, sir."

"Excellent!" Forsch stood up and clapped Derek on the back. Then, with his arm around the man, he led him over to the door and opened it. "I will get these orders ready and we can talk about the details over breakfast. This will be a great victory for the Red Swords!"

"And the Realm!"

"Yes, Derek. And the Realm."

Chapter 28

By the time the sun forced its light through the leafy canopy, Alannin had already been awake for several hours, wiling away the time in pensive repose. When he lived amongst only elves, the typical elven sleep cycle was not an issue. But, when among humans or even orcs, the reduced need for sleep afforded him an abundance of extra time—time he sometimes did not know what to do with.

This morning, however, did not present him with the same dilemma. He had plenty on his mind to keep him busy for quite a while. Somewhere, through the trees and down a steep hill, was a group of orcs, goblins, and their kin—an army, as a matter of fact. According to Torgin, they had been camped in the valley for at least a couple of weeks, pulling in as many numbers as they could. In just the few days Alannin had been observing them, their ranks had swelled impressively.

He knew full well what the orcs were planning to do. Torgin had told him outright that they planned to take the city for their own, which left Alannin conflicted. There were people packed inside Sulbar's walls—people who would die. Also, Orvaril was somewhere inside. The Red Swords... well, they had not left a good impression on him.

At first, he had considered warning the city of the impending attack. When he had encountered Torgin several nights ago, he had learned that the orc was just a boy on a surveillance mission to scout the city. After talking with the orc for several minutes, Alannin had rejected the idea of warning Sulbar. First and foremost, his safety was in jeopardy. He figured that they would capture or kill him and not heed the warnings anyway.

He still wrestled with this decision, wondering if he was doing the right thing by not warning Sulbar. It didn't feel right, but he also didn't think it was *wrong*. Anyway, if Torgin was truthful, the Red Swords had slaughtered countless members of his tribe.

There appeared to be no lesser evil in this conflict. Alannin decided it was in his best interest to stay out of it.

Alannin carefully climbed down from the tree branch on which he sat, jumping down to the ground where Ilvania lay on her back, sunning herself happily. She briefly cocked one eye open, looked at the elf indifferently, then shut it again and repositioned herself.

"Ilvania," Alannin whispered. He nudged her with his boot and she slowly rose to her feet. If the wolf had a look of indignant disappointment, she was giving it to him right now. She slowly got to her feet, stretching and yawning, and followed closely behind Alannin as he made his way through the forest.

After stumbling into the orc just outside Sulbar's walls, the two of them had agreed to part ways peacefully. Rather, Alannin agreed that Ilvania would not tear Torgin apart. He had waited, and then followed the orc back to his tribe's camp, which lay just outside the forest at the bottom of the small valley.

He had then decided that he would keep an eye on the encampment. Ultimately, he wasn't sure why he was doing this except to try to help innocent people in Sulbar if he could. He had no love for the Red Swords, but Sulbar residents had no part in this conflict.

Each day he kept watch over the group from the safety of the trees, making sure to stay well-concealed from orcish eyes. He and Torgin had come to a minor understanding, but they were not friends, nor did the orc speak for his tribe. Alannin knew full well that any agreement they had made with each other had ended when the sun came up the next morning.

It wasn't long before his ears picked up the sounds of battle. His heart sank.

Alannin's pace quickened into a flat-out run—with Ilvania keeping stride next to him. He dashed between the trees, through creeks and over hills until he came to the forest's edge. He could see the backs of men—quite obviously Red Sword archers with their symbol emblazoned on their backs—standing at the top of the hill firing down on the orcs. He moved quietly along the tree line, staying hidden within the forest, until he could see out over the gradual slope.

The Red Swords had brought far too few soldiers, and they were getting slaughtered. The archers desperately fired arrows into the crowd of orcs, goblins, trolls, and ogres, trying to keep them from overrunning the now retreating soldiers. He thought he saw one or two men on horseback escape, but in the chaos, he couldn't be sure. The rest were mowed down by bloodthirsty orcs that reveled in their victory.

War drums thumped and mingled with the screams of man and horse alike until, in a matter of minutes, the archers, too, were overwhelmed—swallowed in a great sea of green and grey monsters. When the battle was over, the orcs dragged all of bodies back down the hill, throwing them in piles.

Alannin was sickened by what he had just seen. He should have felt pity for the Red Swords, and he might *truly* feel some. Any sympathy he had for their plight was quickly overtaken by his contempt for their intense hubris. They were overconfident fools. *Mayhaps this can work to my advantage.*

He observed the orcs a little longer, until they began cutting up the bodies—orc and man alike—for their stew pots. Disgusted, he turned back into the forest, but stayed close to the edge. He needed to be able to hear when the army was on the move—an action that he thought now might come sooner rather than later.

And he was right. As the sun began to sink below the horizon, he heard a great yell come from the orcs in the camp. It sent chills down Alannin's back and had him ducking behind a tree, his heart racing.

The drums soon started up again, and he cautiously moved closer to the edge of the forest to observe. The army was *enormous*! He didn't know how many men the Red Swords had in their ranks, but if they did not have a significant force, they were going to quickly be overrun. That concerned him greatly, but he had a bigger worry on his mind right now. He still needed to find Orvaril.

"Time to leave," he whispered to his wolf companion. She sat next to him, happily panting in the early evening summer heat. Time and time again he was amazed at just how docile she could be. Most wild animals would have lunged into the crowd of orcs outside the tree line but she sat patiently, staring at him as if she was his personal servant. He patted her on the head and scratched behind her ears. "Let's go."

Alannin took off through the forest, darting in between trees and rocks and dodging fallen logs and bushes with Ilvania close behind him. Alannin chuckled as she howled once. He hurdled over a fallen tree, jumped over a creek, and ran up the gentle slope on the other side.

Kendra's horse was still tethered to a tree, munching on whatever she could find on the ground. He quickly untied her and led her through the remaining woods, soon emerging into open ground.

The orcish army was moving at a marching pace. He could easily outrun them and prepare... for whatever it was that he was planning on doing. Sulbar was a big city, and the camp being constructed behind it was almost as large. His chances were slim, but he had to try to find Orvaril and free him.

Then, hopefully, Sulbar would still be standing when it was all over. He had no love for the Red Swords, but he certainly did not wish for blood to be spilled this day. To his surprise, that included the orcs. While he did not understand them, he did not believe that they deserved to die. If they were truly savage beings with a thirst only to destroy and kill, then he hoped for their utter defeat—but not until after they had served their purpose. Still, he had learned that they could be reasoned with, and that gave him pause.

When Alannin burst out of the trees and headed across the open countryside, he could only just barely see the army. There was no road to follow so they, too, were traveling across whatever uneven terrain was between them and Sulbar. *Excellent. I'm ahead of them. I just need to get to Sulbar first and... then figure out exactly what I'm going to do.*

Alannin pushed Brute as fast as she could go, but eventually had to slow down, fearing for the horse's safety in the waning light of the dusky sky. Ilvania caught up quickly, but appeared to be disappointed that she had to slow down for him. She kept running slightly ahead and looking back at him as if to urge him onward. Alannin smiled. He knew that she would be unable to stay away. He did not want to put her in danger, but it was reassuring to have her by his side.

The sky was dark when he finally arrived at Sulbar. He rested behind a hill, caught his breath, and surveyed the city. Either the Red Swords were afraid of the dark or they were expecting an attack.

The city's walls were lit up with fires every 15 feet or so. There were guards crammed onto the top of the walls, using the crenellations as cover. It appeared that most of them held bows. That tall tower in the center of the city was also lit up—every inch of it aglow with yellow light coming from strange, twinkling spheres of light that floated around it. It cast out a bright light that illuminated the area beyond the walls.

Like a lighthouse signaling incoming ships, it slowly rotated, casting effective daylight out into the environs below, but only covering about 50 feet at a time. Every so often, the light would stop rotating and, instead, move directly to an area. Upon seeing nothing, the light would then resume its circuit. *The Red Swords are prepared. It appears I underestimated them after their folly earlier today. But where are all their men? Mayhaps they are still not taking the orcs as seriously as they should be?* With Brute tethered to a small bush at the bottom of the hill, he moved forward, running to the city's walls under cover of darkness with Ilvania at his side.

Alannin hurriedly scouted the section of the wall before him, making sure he both kept his distance and dodged the tower's massive ray of light. He saw more of the same—men packed tightly together on top of the walls, waiting. He made his way back toward the relative front of the city and found some cover.

"Well, Ilvania," he whispered, "it appears that, for now, we must be patient and wait." He sat down behind a small hill and tried to relax. At least this gave him a little time to formulate a plan of some kind. He laid back against the hillside, clasped his hands against his stomach, and relaxed. It was time to wait for his distraction to catch up.

It was not long before he heard the familiar sound of the orc army approaching and felt Ilvania's tongue licking his face. He rolled onto his stomach and peeked out over the hill.

Sure enough, the army was in view and headed toward the city. The field of light cast from the tower at the center of the city focused itself on the army as it approached. The orcs did not hesitate. In fact, they only seemed to become more incensed. The drums started thundering again amidst the sounds of wolves, weapons, and various sorts of armor clattering.

Alannin could only watch for the moment as Red Swords began pouring forth from inside the city, positioning themselves outside the walls, probably in some kind of strategic formation.

The Goodness, there are a lot of them!

Alannin was unsure if he was referring to the Red Swords or the orcs. Man and orc alike just kept filing into the area in an attempt to show which force had the superior numbers.

Finally, the orcs stopped their advance, halting a good distance outside the city—far enough to avoid the archers on the wall or, at least, make it difficult for them to be hit. Alannin was surprised. He had expected the army to simply charge the city and try to overwhelm it, yet they stayed their advance. He wondered what the Red Swords were thinking.

Alannin continued to watch the mutual posturing. He was having a tough time sitting still and being patient. "Well, girl," he whispered to Ilvania, "as much as I hate to admit it, I wish this battle would get underway already."

He had not come up with any grand plan to find and rescue Orvaril, so he was going to have to improvise. There was no telling exactly what would happen during the course of this siege or even how long it would last, so he decided that any plan would be largely worthless to begin with. *Doomed to fail, as Aref would always say.*

He could use Aref's skill with a bow right now. He would've felt better with his good friend watching his back. Hopefully he could avoid a fight altogether.

Get in, find Orvaril, and get out. That's the plan.

The new area to the east was too ramshackle—too unfinished. It would be foolish to hold prisoners in a prison that was still being built. No, Orvaril was probably being kept somewhere in Sulbar itself. For once, he wished that he was wrong—it would have been much easier to move about in the unfinished Red Sword compound as opposed to the area where the battle was going to take place.

The main problem was getting into the city unnoticed. Their defenses were formidable, and there were still hundreds of eyes atop the walls and presumably more inside that tower. His best hope was to get into the city and disappear. *I'm used to trees, bushes, and rocks. Not buildings, streets, and alleyways. But a city isn't so different. Just keep your wits about you and don't get sloppy.*

From within the orcish ranks, a deep, piercing horn rang out. The horde howled and rattled their weapons in response. Alannin felt a shiver of fear course through him. He wondered if the Red Swords felt the same. *I wouldn't blame them. This is no army of mere men and horses. These orcs are savage and brutal... and smarter than suspected.*

Alannin remembered the orcs dragging the bodies of the fallen combatants—and their comrades' corpses—back into the camp to eat. That pretty much said it all. He could see neither remorse nor fear in them, no hesitation. They lived, they fought, and they died with the same demeanor for every situation. Had

Torgin been different than the rest? Sure, he had wanted to kill Alannin but, when faced with a situation he could not win, he did not press the attack. Were other orcs like him or was he unique?

One of the brutes—troll or ogre, Alannin was unsure— hefted a boulder and launched it at the city. "I presume that is how orcs start a siege," he mused. Ilvania looked at him with a blank stare, unfazed by it all. The battle had indeed begun.

The huge rock fell far short of the city's walls but Red Swords scattered to escape its path. Some were unfortunate and were crushed under its weight, while men trampled one another in a panic. The other giants, now advancing, followed suit, lobbing large tree trunks, rocks, dead animals, and chunks of the ground itself. Alannin watched from relative safety as many hit the city walls and several even cleared them, landing inside the city.

"They brought their own rocks," Alannin muttered. "The savages are indeed smarter than they appear... and more terrifying."

Red Sword archers returned fire. Alannin could see individual orcs and goblins fall to the hail of arrows that rained down upon them. He heard several shouts, followed by louder drums and clanking weapons. All at once, the horde howled and then charged. It was not an orderly advance. They ran at full speed, appearing intensely excited.

Then Alannin noticed that the ogres and trolls began throwing orcs and goblins over the city's walls. He assumed most of them died on impact, but he watched as some of them grabbed onto taller buildings and began climbing up or down them as soon as they landed. The wolf riders got out in front and were the first to engage the Red Sword contingent. They simply ran into them! *Or are they running* over *them?*

Several more volleys of boulders and debris flew overhead, hitting buildings, walls, and men. They tore a hole in the fortifications near the city's gates. Red Sword soldiers quickly moved to block the gap, putting themselves between the orcs and the city.

"Stay calm and do your job!" he heard someone yell.

"We will prevail!" another voice rang out.

But the horde pressed its advance, each orc fighting with no regard for his own life. Many orcs were being killed, but just as many men were falling—if not more. Red Sword soldiers continued to pour out of the city, but were being cut down just as quickly as they arrived. The orcs were using the boulders and debris as cover. *They brought their own projectiles... and they double as cover! These orcs are surprisingly crafty.*

The soldiers stood their ground but the orcs were an endless wave crashing onto the shore.

Just when Alannin was about to move closer, he saw a streak of lightning fire out from the top of the tower. With a clap of thunder, it forked into many bolts, dropping at least 50 orcs instantly. Shortly after, another burst fired out, killing more. But the orcs continued their fight, apparently undaunted. Where their companions fell, more orcs were there to take their places.

Alannin's keen elven eyes could see movement and shapes from within the tower with each bolt of lightning. *So the Red Swords have magic-users in the tower. It would appear that they are also quite crafty.*

Large pieces of broken stone and rubble from the shattered wall lifted into the air and fell on top of the army, crushing the creatures beneath, and, still the orcs fought on. Arrows clattered harmlessly off an ogre's thick skin as it hefted a tree, preparing to throw it.

Instead, the tree slipped out of its meaty hand, hovered briefly in front of the creature, and then impaled the brute through the chest. It gurgled and moaned, then stumbled and fell on top of several goblins.

Fire rained out from the tower, exploding when it hit the ground and sending charred body parts flying in all directions—several of which, Alannin thought, were human. Either they couldn't properly control their weapons or they were indiscriminate.

Several balls of light arose from the horde and whizzed chaotically into the city. Alannin watched two of them impact on the tower, exploding and sending debris flying. The others landed somewhere inside the city. Alannin was dumbfounded. *Do the orcs have magic-users as well? Truly, this battle is full of deadly surprises.*

Part of the wall near Alannin exploded, launching rubble in all directions. *That was nowhere near the battle itself. Did they mean to hit that part of the wall?* Mayhaps the orcs did not have very good control of their weapons, either, for which Alannin was grateful. Thanks to them, his opportunity had just presented itself.

"Ilvania," he whispered, "Go find somewhere safe and stay hidden." The wolf whined and refused to move. "Wait for me out here, girl. I promise I'll be back." Again, the wolf did not move. "Now go!" he said, pointing to the tree line in the distance.

This time, Ilvania turned and ran in the direction Alannin had pointed. He was dumbfounded. His companion was either very smart or... *or what? Is there something else?*

"Well," Alannin muttered to himself, "Let us see how this goes." He took a deep breath and stared at the breached wall. "This is either going to be the best idea you've ever had... or the worst."

That was what Aref used to say. It seemed that he always had some words of wisdom for every situation. This one was no different.

Chapter 29

"Stand firm, men!" Derek Ironfist shouted, his sword and shield in hand. The men around him were nervous and probably scared. He couldn't blame them—he felt the same way. The orcish drums pounded inside his head as men were cut down all around him. His ranks stood in reserve, waiting for the horde to make it to them.

But the orcs were falling, too. The trouble was, he simply couldn't tell which side was doing more damage. The orcs' numbers were too vast to even estimate—he had discovered that upon engaging them at their camp. It had been a bloody massacre and he had tried to avoid it. Somehow, the orcs must have either been waiting for them or had reacted more quickly than he had expected because they had been set upon instantly.

By the time they had been able to run, it had been too late. Derek himself had barely made it out alive along with just a few of his men on horseback. He felt somewhat guilty, having fled from battle, but he had needed to return to Sulbar to warn his superiors of the danger they faced. As it turned out, Captain Forsch had already begun preparations for defense, as if he had already known. *Was there a point to my men's senseless slaughter?*

The orcs were close, now, and it was time to focus. They had the numbers, but they were still mindless savages, and that would be their downfall. His men were smarter, better trained, and well-armed. The orcs could not equal their might.

Except that he and his men now suddenly found themselves in battle instead of waiting.

Derek dodged as an orc tried to take off his head. He countered with his bastard sword, slashing upward across the orc's chest and neck. He blocked another strike with his shield and kicked the attacking goblin in the head, knocking it backward into the sea of combatants. He cut down another two goblins with a single slash, and stabbed a third in the eye.

Mindless brutes. They die just like any other animal. We will push them back and hunt them down.

He blocked a club with his shield, but his arm was knocked out of the way, leaving him vulnerable as the orc struck again. Derek ducked and rolled backwards, coming to his feet. *Don't lose concentration! Stay focused! Even the tiniest snake can be deadly!*

He was letting his mind wander. Such a thing was dangerous. He had to stay alert. The attack had thrown the Red Sword ranks into chaos, and he no longer even knew if his men were following orders.

He swung his sword, but the orc blocked his strike with its club. Derek's sword got stuck in the crude, wooden weapon so he tugged sharply, pulling it out of the orc's hand.

His attacker screamed with rage and leapt at him, sending them both to the ground. Derek yelled and kept his shield between them, dodging fists and claws as best he could. Thankfully, his armor and helmet absorbed most of the beating, but he felt the orc's claws dig into his flesh once or twice.

Two of his men came to his aid, stabbing the orc several times and then kicking its motionless body off him. One of them fended off two more attackers while the other one helped Derek to his feet.

"Are you okay, commander?"

"Aye," he replied, stepping on the crude club while he pulled his sword free. "It's nothing a few days' rest can't take care of—when I can afford the time. Thank you."

The moment was short-lived as more orcs advanced. Arrows flew overhead and he watched them fall into the orc horde. They were not as effective as he'd hoped, but the mages in the Spire helped make up for that by eliminating huge swaths of enemies at once.

What he *hadn't* expected was seeing the orcs fire back with mages of their own. This changed everything, and he could only guess how Captain Forsch had reacted. *I'm sure he has a plan—even if he didn't expect it. He always has a plan.*

And how *could* they have expected it? The orcs were savage creatures. Nobody thought that they would have individuals skilled in magic. But they did, and that certainly complicated things. Derek did not understand how mages operated, but he had a feeling that theirs were more skilled than any orcish mages. The Red Swords would win that contest, too.

The city's wall had been breached near the gates, but the Red Swords were effectively blocking it with their forces while mages from the Spire worked to repair the damage. It was amazing how the stone appeared to replace itself, somehow shaping into a new portion of the wall. Derek had to admit that he found himself slightly jealous of the abilities these people possessed. Then again, those individuals were dangerous and unpredictable. Even the mages amongst them were not to be trusted.

He parried a goblin's swing, knocking it onto its back, and then stabbed it in the neck. He dispatched two more just as easily. They were weak, cowardly creatures, but they were overwhelming in large numbers.

Derek cut down two more goblins but immediately found himself facing three orcs. Three of his men drew in close to him and fought at his side. Overhead, several fiery objects sailed by. They impacted somewhere in the middle of the orc army, exploding in an inferno that sent bodies high into the air.

Derek lashed out at one of the orcs just as the soldier to his left was cut down by another orc's axe. His screams were cut short by a gurgling sound as he hit the ground, and he was quickly replaced by another soldier.

It was then that Derek noticed the ogre. It charged toward him, trampling allies and enemies alike while knocking countless others out of its way. The archers on the wall desperately fired a volley of arrows at the monster. While a few found purchase in its thick skin, the rest clattered harmlessly to the ground.

"Get out of the way!" Derek yelled, motioning to anyone who could see him. Then he quickly turned and fled, diving to the ground as the grey-skinned brute collided with the city's wall with a thunderous crash that carried it through the wall and into the city.

How are we supposed to stop that?

Soldiers rushed to attack the beast as Derek got to his feet and checked for injuries. The hole in the wall was clogged with men who were attacking the ogre and trying to prevent orcs from flooding past them and into the city. Derek wanted badly to kill the beast, but he couldn't get anywhere near it. Up on the walls, archers fired their arrows nearly point-blank at the monster, hoping to do what damage they could.

More shimmering projectiles ascended from the ranks of the orcs. They flew out over the city walls and exploded, echoing like thunder claps. The city's Spire responded with what looked like a storm of jagged ice shards that relentlessly rained down upon the horde, sending them scrambling for cover. This was followed by several explosions when the ground erupted nearby, killing both men and orc alike. Three more explosions rang out but two of them caught mostly Red Sword soldiers in their destructive path.

By The Abyss, some of these mages are incompetent! They're doing as much damage to us *as they are the enemy! Or is this destruction coming from the orcs?* He dodged an orc's swing and handily dispatched him with a quick stab to the chest. Using his boot, he pulled his bastard sword out of his fallen enemy. *Surely those last two weren't meant to hit where they did. If I find out who is responsible I will have their heads for this!*

Derek waded further into the fight alongside his fellow Red Sword soldiers. Everywhere around him, the only thing he could see was combat. It was as if this battle was consuming the entire countryside! For a moment, he wondered if the city was surrounded. The invaders had *started* the battle at the front of the city, but had it spilled over into other areas? Mayhaps there was a second force? At first, he rejected this idea, but the orcs had proven to be more resourceful than he—or probably anyone—had at first surmised. The Red Swords' goal had been to contain the fighting to the main gates, but it was like trying to contain ocean waves in a bucket.

To his right, an orc riding atop a wolf charged at him. He barely got out of the way in time as the orc swung a jagged sword at him, clattering off his pauldron, but still cutting into his left arm. With no time to check his injury, he hefted his shield, ignoring the pain that followed, and gripped his sword tightly. The orc turned his mount around and came back for another swing.

Just as Derek was about to try to cut down the snarling animal both the orc and its mount were struck by several armored bodies—Red Sword soldiers.

"Shit!" Derek yelled, jumping backwards and away from the now motionless pile of bodies. As he did so, he looked to his right to see a troll—he thought it was a troll—clearing vast swaths of soldiers with each swing of its giant club. Without thinking, he ran toward the giant, dodging debris and bodies alike. He cut down several goblins before he was stopped by two orcs.

They attacked simultaneously.

Derek used his shield to block the left orc's club but he stumbled backward from the force of impact. The orc on the right followed up by swinging its axe at him, but its attack was sluggish and Derek was too quick. He cut off the orc's arm and shifted his attention back to the other orc on his left as it moved to strike him again with its club.

It lunged, trying to tackle him, but Derek stepped away and hit the orc with his shield. After following up with his sword, he turned and ran at the troll, which was making short work of the soldiers trying to bring it down. While the monster bled from numerous cuts and gashes it did not seem to have slowed down much, if at all.

Derek finally made it through the crowd and looked up at the troll. It stood at least eight feet tall and had arms as thick as tree trunks. One large tusk protruded from the right side of its lower jaw and its skin was stained with dirt and blood.

He jumped aside as it swung its club at the crowd of soldiers. Most of them dodged out of the way, but a few were caught by the attack and flung in all directions. While the giant was readying for another swing, Derek stabbed at it with his sword, feeling the blade sink into its side. The troll howled in pain and brought its club down on him.

But Derek, in one motion, pulled his sword back and leapt out of the way, feeling the ground shudder next to him where the club impacted, leaving a small crater. He slashed at the brute. His sword, desperate to find purchase, harmlessly bounced off the creature's thick hide. He struck again with the same result.

"Fine, then!" he shouted, throwing his shield to the ground and gripping his sword with both hands. An orc charged at him from the side but was cut down by a soldier with a mace. He ducked under the troll's next attack and, coming up beside it, struck mightily into the giant's thigh with all the strength that he could muster.

The troll howled and lost its balance, coming down to a crouch. Derek stabbed it again, his bastard sword biting deep into the creature's flesh near its stomach. Three other soldiers joined in, attacking upward at its head with their weapons. It wasn't long before the creature fell. Several men cheered and banged weapons on shields, but the celebration was short lived as another wave of orcs and goblins threatened to overtake them.

"Is there no end to this vile army?" Derek shouted. He picked up his shield, and cautiously retreated, falling back to where the bulk of the soldiers was. The mages in the Spire were still trying to repair the massive breach in the city's wall but seemed to be having trouble—probably due to its size. Orcs were trickling through the gap and into the city despite the substantial number of soldiers that were trying to block their path.

We are not going to be able to hold this position. If too many orcs get into the city we will lose it. Arrows continued to rain down from the walls, dropping orcs and goblins, but there were always more right behind them to climb over their bodies and take their places.

All at once, the ground erupted as explosive orbs launched out of the Spire and impacted nearby. At the same time, the gap in the wall shimmered briefly. Derek noticed that the orcs could not get through the breach anymore—something was keeping them out. *Something invisible? The Goodness, these mages have strange talents! They definitely should not be allowed to run around the Realm without restraint.*

This gave the soldiers some breathing room as explosions came from both above and below. The light from the Spire still illuminated the part of the battlefield, allowing Derek to see some details he would rather have not been able to see.

The initial rush of excitement from bringing down the troll soon wore off, to be replaced with fatigue and a certain degree of hopelessness. Derek was not sure how long the battle had lasted thus far, but it had been longer than he was accustomed to. It felt like they were slowly losing, but he couldn't even be sure of *that*. No matter how many orcs or goblins or even *trolls* he cut down, there were always more. Surely there must be an end to it!

But the orcs just kept coming, like endless ocean waves slowly wearing down the rocks on the shore. The Red Swords were slowly being pushed back against the city's walls or out in the open to be flanked and cut down mercilessly. The Spire continued bombarding the invaders with all manners of projectiles and strange magics which, Derek figured, was about the only thing evening the odds. The orcs had stopped producing such effects, but it did not seem to matter. They had the numbers, and they were fearless.

The war drums continued thumping from somewhere in the distance. Derek had somehow forgotten about them but, suddenly, their cacophonous thunder rushed back to his ears, sounding as if the drums surrounded him. It was enough to shake his courage, but he held fast, determined to defend the city.

More soldiers flooded out from the city, trying to surround the horde but the orcs fanned out in response, once again surprising Derek with their tactics. He considered it very likely that the city was surrounded by now. The Spire was apparently unable to cover more than one section of the battlefield with its light and, once the orcs began to realize this, they started to spread out, taking the fight to many different fronts in order to gain an advantage.

If you underestimate your opponent, you have already lost. It seems we have done just that.

Derek couldn't help but be impressed. The orcs used radical tactics, they adjusted, and they certainly were not mindless. Brutal, savage, and rage-filled, yes. But not mindless. They were the deadliest opponents man had ever faced. Surely Captain Forsch could not have seen this coming. Surely, he was just as shocked as Derek was.

Several large, fire-covered projectiles launched from the Spire and landed somewhere in the crowd of orcs with massive explosions that set the area ablaze. If they could keep that up, this battle *might* end in their favor. Derek knew nothing about magic, but he assumed that it wasn't something one could perform tirelessly. *Just how long can they continue? How long can* any *of us continue?*

He could feel his muscles weakening—particularly his arms. Each time he swung his sword it felt slightly heavier than the last time. His shield was dented and bent, and he assumed that much of his armor was in the same condition. Somewhere along the way, he had taken a blow to his left leg and his side. Both throbbed with pain, but nothing felt broken. He blocked a goblin's feeble attack. Derek almost felt a pang of pity when he split the creature's head open.

The battle raged on and, while the orcs seemed to have the upper hand, the Red Swords were successfully keeping them out of Sulbar, now. Several of the larger ogres and trolls continued to throw orcs and goblins over the city's walls but, there should be plenty of soldiers within the city to handle that threat—assuming the participants survived the landing to begin with.

Just as Derek started to feel his confidence return, he heard the screams coming from *inside* the city and he knew that his assessment was terribly wrong.

Damn it. They found a way in!

Chapter 30

Alannin jumped to his feet and darted across the open ground toward the breach in the wall. He almost expected Ilvania to be sprinting happily next to him but she, of course, was not. She could be incredibly obstinate sometimes, but she always seemed to obey when it was the most important.

The way to the wall was clear. The men atop it had disappeared, possibly killed in the explosion or flung into the air to land far away. The fires nearby had been extinguished, and there was very little light in the area. *Perfect. That takes care of the first question—how to get in.*

He didn't hesitate when he got to the gap in the wall. He leapt over the rubble and darted inside the city, sprinting past several Red Sword soldiers who had come to guard the breach.

"Who was that?" one of the men yelled.

"Halt! Intruder!" another shouted.

Alannin heard clattering armor and weapons behind him, but he paid no attention. He would almost assuredly be able to outpace armored men and could no doubt lose them in the shadows. These men were not hunters or trackers. They were simple soldiers, and many of them were probably unskilled in anything but swinging a weapon or swilling some ale.

He rounded a corner, jumped up some stairs and turned down a side street. As he suspected, the soldiers gave up relatively quickly, and he was left alone in a strange city that was both inhabited by and surrounded by hostile forces. *Quite the situation you just got yourself into, Alannin. Smart decision. Now what?*

Alannin looked around. The city was mostly dark, with the only light coming from inside homes or shops. The street lamps had not been lit and most buildings were dark and shuttered. *Hopefully the people who live here are all safe.* He wondered if the Red Swords had thought to evacuate the city. They had obviously expected the attack, so hopefully they had prepared accordingly.

The streets were deserted. It was an odd situation—being able to clearly hear the cacophony of combat just outside the walls yet, inside, the city was empty. A quick peek down one of the larger streets gave him an excellent view of the men stationed toward the front of the city. The Red Swords were only guarding the main gates. They must have assumed the orcs would simply charge the front of the city which, thus far, was exactly what they had done. But if the orcs investigated the sides...

Alannin stayed behind whatever cover he could find, remaining hidden. He ran across streets and through small alleyways, keeping to the shadows. Hiding in a city without people really wasn't much different than hiding in a forest! He tried to move as quietly as possible, but he wasn't used to stealth on city streets. Fortunately, there was nobody around to hear his footfalls which were, admittedly, much louder than he intended. In his experience, you could not move quickly *and* quietly at the same time.

Yet, he remained ever cautious. His instincts told him to move slowly and stay alert but his feelings urged him to quickly get to that Spire. He did his best to avoid being reckless and moved methodically toward the city's center. *There could be soldiers about, or worse.*

He could move freely through the deserted streets, using the night itself as cover. Unless the fighting reached this far into the city, he figured that he should be safe.

His good fortune did not last long, however. As he was peeking around the corner of a building he saw two orcs who had just cornered something or *someone.* They both laughed and grunted, probably speaking in their own language, as they walked slowly into an alley. Just as they were about to turn the corner, Alannin shifted his weight awkwardly and stumbled into a small pile of trash, making enough noise to attract one of the orcs' attention.

One of the creatures turned and saw Alannin, then hefted its club and charged. Alannin regained his footing just in time to dodge the orc's swing, but then fell onto his back in the process. As the orc raised its club above its head, laughing, Alannin kicked it in the knees. The orc wailed in pain, dropped its club, and buckled to the ground. Alannin wasted no time, quickly dispatching the orc with one of his short swords.

His heart raced as he stood over the orc's body, remembering that the other one was still in the alley. He hurried across the street and peeked around a building to see that he was too late. The green brute was hunkered down over a corpse with its back to him. Was it... *eating* the body?

Alannin quietly ended the orc's life with a swift stroke of his sword, leaving it next to the chewed remains. Stifling the urge to vomit, and pushing back sadness, Alannin continued his trek toward the Spire in the middle of the city. He was more cautious, now, moving slower and making sure there were no orcs about. If he could avoid them, he certainly would. The city had just become more dangerous and more unexpected combat would slow him down.

As he neared the Spire, the din of battle grew louder. The urge to quicken his pace grew within him, but he suppressed it, not wanting to be caught off guard or to attract unwanted attention. Several times, he encountered multiple orcs and goblins traveling through various parts of the city. Some were setting fire to buildings while others were trying to break into them. Still others appeared to be searching for something.

Each time, Alannin stayed his blade. There were too many adversaries and not enough time—felling a few enemies would make no difference and would delay him. Soon the city would be crawling with orcs and Alannin did not wish to be around when that happened. The fighting was much louder now, and Alannin could see orcs and men further down the avenue in the distance. *And right in the middle of it all, of course, is that Spire. I suppose that is not unexpected. But it would have been refreshing to have been wrong... and I'm headed right for it.*

Once he got closer he ducked behind a small cart to get a better look at the scene ahead. Orcs and men were locked in a battle around the large tower in what looked like a writhing sea of armored and green bodies. If there were goblins in the fray, Alannin didn't see any.

How did so many of them get into the city? Did they breach the walls? Surely not this many survived being thrown over the wall by their brutes!

A crowd this large was going to make it difficult for him to get inside. He had originally hoped to somehow sneak into the building, but that plan would certainly fail now. He couldn't fight his way in, either.

Alannin made his way around the battle, sticking to the shadows and using buildings on the fringe as cover. He climbed up a gutter and onto the roof of a house to get a better look. Thankfully, the sound and chaos of the battle drowned out the considerable noise he made scaling the house.

From here, the skirmish appeared smaller than he'd thought, but there were still probably one hundred orcs and mayhaps just as many men. The orcs were trickling in from other parts of the city, converging on the Spire. Alannin hoped none of the trolls or ogres would make it into the city. The destruction would be terrible.

The main entrance to the Spire was a large, heavy door that was blocked in front by a sturdy portcullis. The Spire itself appeared to be constructed of heavy, bluish stone. *It was meant to be easily-defended—only one way in or out.*

High above, from the top of the spire, several crackling lightning bolts shot outward, exploding somewhere beyond the city's walls, quickly followed by several shimmering motes of light that did much the same thing. The field of light emanating from up high was now constantly shifting, presumably to cover different areas of the battlefield. *Or mayhaps they're looking for something? If so, what exactly are they looking for?*

Several bolts of energy burst into the crowd around the spire, killing orc and man alike.

The battle in front of Alannin was deteriorating into all-out chaos as both orcs and men charged into the fray from all directions in an unending stream of combatants. *This is quickly spiraling out of control. Even if I could fight my way up to the entrance I have no way of getting inside.*

Alannin wanted to be patient, to wait for an opportunity to present itself, but he felt the need for urgency. Every minute he waited seemed to make his objective more difficult to achieve. He carefully climbed down off the roof and, staying outside the area of combat, he made his way around to the other side of the Spire. Bodies of orcs and men littered the ground but the Red Swords appeared to be gaining the upper hand and were pushing the orcs back.

More shimmering projectiles launched from the top of the Spire but Alannin couldn't see much more than that from his vantage point.

Though the light was scarce on this side of the tower, he could still see fairly well. He slowly made his way around the exterior surface of the Spire, running his fingers along the wall and listening carefully for sounds of anyone approaching. His efforts produced nothing, and just as he was ready to give up, he heard a noise behind him.

It sounded like stone shifting and, as he turned to see what it was, he saw a door slowly opening. He hid behind the door as it opened, a sword in his right hand at the ready. When the door stopped, Alannin leapt out from behind it and put his blade to the throat of a disheveled, gray-haired man.

"P-please!" the man begged. "Don't hurt me!" He looked startled and immediately put his arms up in the air. He hadn't shaved in several days and looked as though he hadn't eaten in a week. "I'm sorry! I won't try to escape again!"

"Who are you?"

"R-Randall Rickton," he stammered. "I was told to help repair the wall—I'm just doing what I was told. Please!" He looked as if he might start crying. Alannin felt bad holding a sword to this man's throat but he had no way of knowing who would emerge from the doorway when it had opened. He lowered his blade, still keeping it at the ready just in case. He doubted there would be any problems with this individual.

"Thank you—you're not a soldier! You're an... elf!"

"Keep your voice down," Alannin said in a whisper. "Are you a prisoner?"

"Aye. The Red Swords captured me several months ago. Because of my talents, they—"

"Did they keep you in this tower? Alannin craned his neck to try to see past Randall. There were stairs leading both down and up.

"Aye. Below the Spire are the dungeons where they kept me. But I got out because I can... melt things. They have been using my talents and those of others to build the Spire and to defend Sulbar."

"And now they sent you out alone to rebuild the city's walls?"

"Aye. There is another breach somewhere on the south wall."

"And if you refuse?"

"Then they execute us." Randall averted his gaze, either ashamed or scared. "The Red Swords do not tolerate elves and orcs. I guess they have thrown us 'mages' into the mix as well. They say that it's for the good of the Realm, but I think they are afraid."

"Well, then," Alannin brushed past Randall and into the stairwell. "May you be well, Randall Rickton. My advice to you is this—use the breach in the wall to escape the city and be safe. I must free a friend of mine from the dungeons."

"A fantastic idea—

"My name is Alannin Stormbriar."

"Good luck, Alannin."

"And, for you, the same."

Chapter 31

"Welcome, visitor," the soft, female voice said. The glowing, light blue orb hovered atop the pedestal, gently pulsing.

"Hello?" Cor'il asked, sheepishly. He found himself in a small, circular room containing nothing but the pedestal and this blue orb that had materialized just above it.

"Hello," the pleasant voice replied.

Cor'il stared in awe, unsure of what to do next. He slowly reached out and touched the orb. His finger felt slightly warm as it passed into the glowing light. He then waved his hand through the orb which shimmered and stuttered slightly in response.

"Is there something you require?"

Cor'il paused, completely at a loss. What was he supposed to say? He stared a while longer, dumbfounded, as the radiant blue ball of light hovered before him, still pulsing.

"What are you?" he finally asked, unsure of what to expect next.

"I am The Catalog," the orb replied. "I am countless years of history and knowledge contained within a construct woven from the Threads."

Cor'il embraced the Threads, letting his sight dim but feeling the rush of energy permeate his body and fill him with life and decay at the same time. He had long since learned to accept the variety of sensations the Threads offered, but was unable to single out or ignore any of them entirely. It was much like having a room full of people talking all at once. At first it had been absolutely maddening, but he had grown accustomed to it over time.

"Oh, now, this is something wondrous. I have all sorts of questions I would like to know the answers to. Ask her about the Great Machine, or the Dark Machine! Or ask her about—

"Quiet down," Cor'il muttered to himself.

"I apologize, but I do not understand the request," The Catalog responded.

"Oh, uh," Cor'il stammered. It was quite strange talking to both this... Catalog *and* Antina—neither of which had an actual body. *It's like I am talking to two ghosts.*

The weave of Threads was even more complex than any of the others in the city. It seemed impossible to fit so many of them into such a tight construct. Every Thread in the city appeared to pass through this dome and wind into the knot that resided where The Catalog was located. Cor'il wondered how long it would take someone to create such a thing, or how to even go about knowing how to do it in the first place.

"What is this place?" It seemed like the best question with which to start. He released his hold on the Threads and the world returned to its normal self once again.

"This is the *Talados*, where The Catalog resides."

"No," Cor'il continued, "I mean, what is this city?"

"This particular city is called *Darvinon*. It is just one of five Kai'Tan cities that stretch across the land."

"Five cities of the Kai'Tan? Amazing!"

"Can you tell me more?" Cor'il was excited, and it was difficult to resist blurting out every question all at once.

"The Kai'Tan lived and thrived in these cities, and created a vast civilization over a long period of time. Here they studied the Great Machine and the Dark Machine and learned how to utilize the Threads to create wondrous works of art and powerful tapestries from the Threads. Each city became a focal point for the Threads, harnessing the immense power and producing complex constructs."

"How long did they live here?"

"Unknown."

"Where are they now?"

"Unknown."

"Why do you not know the answers to these questions?" Cor'il found himself already becoming slightly frustrated.

"I can only relay to you what information I was given by my creators. I am a construct of their making and, as such, I have limits. I do apologize for any inconvenience this has caused you, however. How else can I help you?"

"This Thread construct is almost worthless! What good is a catalog that doesn't know anything?"

Mayhaps I am simply asking the wrong questions.

"What can you tell me about the fate of the Kai'Tan?"

The orb pulsed several times quickly.

"The Kai'Tan civilization thrived in relative peace for a great, long time. They were master Threadweavers and, through their skill, managed miraculous feats. That was before The Breach. The Breach brought on the Dark Times during which the Kai'Tan were forced to confront a previously undiscovered and unexpected enemy."

"What enemy?" Cor'il felt his curiosity rise, excited to uncover part of the mystery, and he could feel his pulse quicken. It was as if he had just found a missing piece to a puzzle.

"Unknown."

His heart sank again, disappointed. There was a part of him that had expected that answer, but it was no less disappointing. He sighed, trying to decide which question to ask next.

"The Kai'Tan cities became centers for research on this new threat. Specimens were housed in specially-designed structures with barriers woven from the Threads to keep the enemies from escaping."

"And what happened to these... specimens?"

"Unknown. It is entirely possible that the creatures still live and reside inside the containment structures here in not only this city but the other four as well. To be sure you would need to speak with The Caretaker."

Cor'il paused to think about what he had just learned. Even though The Catalog did not have all the answers, it still had provided a wealth of information already. He was fascinated with this new knowledge and he could sense that Antina felt the same.

"The triangular building at the far edge of the city—what is it?"

"That is what is called a *Skurata*."

"What is its purpose?"

"I do not know its specific purpose. However, it works with the Threads. It can amplify them and possesses the ability to twist and alter them in many ways that cannot be managed without."

Perfect. That is exactly what I was looking for. I was hoping to discover something like that.

Having read the book as recently as a couple of nights ago, Cor'il had been able to piece together a possible plan to bring the Chaos and Order back into balance. Until now he wasn't sure *how* he would accomplish this task, since the book made only vague references to devices with this ability.

"I don't know if I like where this is headed. You can't simply play around with the Threads and hope that you succeed. You could end up dead... or worse."

I cannot stop the Chaos, so the only way to bring balance back is to ensure that Order has as much of a presence here as Chaos.

"You're a fool. It cannot be done. The very nature of Chaos is to be unpredictable. You've no idea what the outcome might be. What if the Chaos becomes stronger?"

"Do you have a better idea?" Cor'il muttered.

"I apologize. I do not understand the request."

"I do not even know what it is you are planning so that question is irrelevant."

Then stop bothering me.

"I think that I am done for now, Catalog. I thank you for the information. Would you be able to tell me what the Caretaker is and where it is located?" Cor'il still had an endless list of questions he wanted to ask but he also realized that time was short. Mayhaps he could return when he had the opportunity.

"The Caretaker is a Thread construct like me that resides over the city itself. It is located in a similar building near the city's center."

"Thank you." Cor'il stepped away from the pedestal and headed out through the door that had, once again, materialized before him. Outside, the city was shockingly quiet and still, and he felt alone once again. He fought the urge to stay and ask more questions, fearing he would never leave. Now that he knew what he had to do, his sense of urgency increased.

"So where did they all go, then? If this society was so skilled in the art of the Threads and so advanced, what happened to them?"

Mayhaps they found a better place to live? Or mayhaps there was a sweeping disease? The Ilathri spoke of the Threads basically going dormant—could that have had anything to do with it? I was really hoping The Catalog could have helped me with those questions. When I have the time, I will return for more information.

"You have the time right now!"

No, I don't.

Cor'il continued down the wide, open street, passing building after building—all of which were presumably vacant and had been untouched for who knew how long. He walked under a bridge and down a small slope, admiring countless statues and dry fountains—all perfectly pristine and quiet.

He found himself envisioning the city full of life. He couldn't even begin to imagine what the Kai'Tan had been like or what their lives had entailed. Of course, the Kai'Tan could've been three-headed creatures with 15 legs, so he was forced to imagine elves and humans inhabiting the city.

Cor'il embraced the Threads and watched them wind through the city. In the distance, he could see a bright, glowing spot that looked much like The Catalog, and he realized that was where he needed to go. He could also see the Threads intertwined within the *Skurata* in the distance. It would probably take weeks to scratch the surface of how it actually functioned. Fortunately, he did not need to know everything about it. He simply needed to know how to use it, and hopefully, that would not take much time.

Off in the distance to his right, Cor'il heard a shrill, inhuman scream. He gasped and leapt for cover behind a fountain.

"We are not alone."

Unfortunately, you are right. Thankfully it sounds distant—whatever it is. Do you think it is alone?

Antina did not answer. Shortly after, he heard another blood-curdling scream echo throughout the cavern, coming from another direction.

"I think you have your answer."

We should hurry, then. I do not wish to meet whatever horror lurks in this city.

"City? Or graveyard?"

Cor'il tried not to think about it any further. Instead, he quickened his pace and hurried to what he hoped would be a building safe from whatever dangers were about. The door materialized in front of him and he stepped inside.

"Do you really think you can do this? And, even if you succeed, what makes you think the outcome will be what you desire?"

I don't. But everything I know and everything I feel tells me that this is right. The Great Machine and the Dark Machine were not meant to be apart. I will make them whole again.

"And you think I am the barking mad one."

The door shut behind Cor'il.

Chapter 32

Orvaril was getting antsy. He found it extremely difficult to sit and wait, especially when there was a battle raging up in the city. Now would be a perfect time to escape, but he had learned to trust his instincts—for better or worse—and right now, they urged patience. So, he would stay put until whatever opportunity he was waiting for presented itself.

The rest of the prisoners were nervous and they were going on about the sounds of battle they heard from above. They desperately called out, demanding to be released, but their cries were ignored by the one guard currently keeping watch. This particular dungeon was rather well-constructed and appeared secure, though Orvaril was a better judge of taverns than dungeons. That being said, no dungeon was perfect. Each prison had at least one flaw that could be exploited by someone who had a keen eye.

Orvaril, in fact, even knew where his possessions were. Each time the guards deposited someone into a cell they put whatever belongings the individual had carried into a closet near the stairs. He could see the closet from here if he positioned himself just so.

"So tell me, kind fellow," he started, forcing himself to relax in the pile of hay. "What has everyone so worked up?" The answer was obvious, but he needed to get the man's attention somehow.

The guard was a rather plump man who seemed to almost be oozing out of his chain armor. He did not respond.

"Did the city run into a spot of trouble? Is there another child on the loose?"

The guard turned and glared at Orvaril.

"Just a few orcs," he grunted, "nothing to be concerned with. So stop running your mouth already."

"A few orcs, eh? And how many, if you don't mind telling, is *a few*? Do you need more fingers to count on?"

288

The guard only grunted a response. He leaned against the wall, chewing on a piece of straw and apparently trying not to pay attention to his prisoners. Orvaril thought the man might fall asleep on his feet at any moment.

Though he had all sorts of ideas on how to escape, Orvaril bit his lip and stayed in his cell. Several prisoners from down the corridor continued yelling that they were innocent or that they "wouldn't do it again." They only spoke up when there was an actual guard down here—which was not every day. Occasionally, one of them would feign an illness, but they mostly ceased that behavior after they found out that the Red Swords' idea of medicine was a sharp sword through the throat.

"Are you sure your estimates are accurate, my good man?" he snickered. "Everybody seems to be awfully worked up over just *a few* orcs. I mean, I can hear the clamor from down here."

The guard had apparently grown tired of the conversation, and now didn't even so much as look at Orvaril. Undeterred, Orvaril continued. The guard's attempt to ignore him, in fact, only made him more ardent about getting under this man's skin.

"Did you draw the short piece of straw, then? You got babysitting duty in the dungeons instead of fighting the few orcs in the city? It does sound quite boring to me. Or did you volunteer for guard duty because you're too cowardly to fight?" That might have been pushing it too far, but the words had already been said.

"It would be more tolerable," the guard growled, "if you'd shut your mouth."

"Not fond of conversation, then? Surely it would pass the time more quickly if you simply had something to do. Mayhaps cleaning the lint from your armpits or the wax from your ears?"

The guard, not surprisingly, looked annoyed, but he somehow managed not to get angry with Orvaril. He sneered at Orvaril who snickered and grinned back at him.

He wasn't sure why, but Orvaril was immensely enjoying his "special time" with the guard. Short of outright killing the man, this was the next best thing. In fact, Orvaril really *did* wish to kill the guard. He held contempt for every one of the Red Swords, now. They killed his friend and they abused people without any limits on their power. *Good of the Realm my ass. The Red Swords are only interested in the good of the Red Swords.*

But, since he couldn't really kill the man from his cell, he felt compelled to have a little fun with him instead. Meaningless banter and cheap insults were a welcome distraction right now. He only needed to keep himself, and more importantly, the guard occupied for a little while longer. He was sure of this.

"In all honesty, good sir," he continued, "this whole 'watch over prisoners in the locked cells who have no hope of escaping' job must be one of the lowest on the list. Was 'muck the horse stalls' already snatched up by some enterprising young lad? You could've applied for 'clean the privies.' I hear that is quite prestigious."

The guard grunted.

"Or," Orvaril laughed, "did you do something to warrant this job as punishment?" He got up and leaned against the bars, staring at the man. Now, he *wanted* to irritate the guard. "Or are you just incompetent and cannot be trusted with an *important* job?"

The guard moved faster than expected for such a rotund individual, and was pressed against the bars in a heartbeat, grabbing for Orvaril who had jumped back out of reach just in time.

"I will wring your damned neck you little bastard!"

Orvaril tried to stay calm, though he was a bit shaky. He certainly hadn't expected the guard to move that fast. He grinned though, still making sure to stay a fair distance away from the cell door. This was what he wanted, albeit, not quite this intense.

"To do that," Orvaril chuckled, "you'd have to open the door, good sir. I don't suppose you'd like to let me out, would you?"

"Nice try." The guard spat at Orvaril and glared at him, still leaning against the bars. "You're not getting out of here. You're going to rot—"

Someone hit the guard from behind and the man slumped to the ground, unconscious. Alannin stood over him and sheathed his sword. He looked around for more guards.

"At first," he said, "I didn't know how I was going to find you once I got down here." Alannin rolled the guard over onto his back and started searching his pockets. "But, then, I saw how furious this guard was, and I realized that only you could get someone so worked up."

Orvaril chuckled and nodded. He was relieved to see a familiar face. His spirits lifted and he felt his body relax.

"It's a talent, I suppose. Or a curse. I'm not sure, really. I suppose it depends on the situation?" While Alannin was busy searching the guard, Orvaril produced a key from his pocket and unlocked his cell door. "Don't bother looking for his key," he chuckled, "I took it from him the last time he was down here, a couple of days back."

"Yet you didn't escape?" Alannin stood up, confused. "Why not?"

"I was waiting for the opportune time."

"I would say there is no more opportune time than now. There is a large battle going on directly above us. We need to escape before it engulfs all of Sulbar." Alannin started for the stairs but Orvaril did not follow.

"Wait," he said. Orvaril knew that something wasn't finished. There was more to this—more to be done, but he didn't know what it was. Something felt... unfinished. "I think, mayhaps, we should free the others."

"An excellent idea," Alannin agreed, "but we'd best be quick about it. The orcs are fighting right outside this tower— directly above us.

"Here, take this key and go unlock as many cells as you can while I get my things from the closet over there." Orvaril stepped over the unconscious guard, nudging the man with his foot. "Looks like you get off lucky today, sir," he whispered, before moving to the storage closet door while Alannin set to work freeing prisoners. "If we free a few, they can let the rest out."

Orvaril opened the door and riffled through the shelves until he found his rucksack and, more importantly, his lute. He grabbed them and then turned to leave.

"All done here, Alannin. It's time to go." But something still felt unfinished. He watched Alannin give the key to one of the few prisoners he had managed to free. Several of them raided the closet for anything useful while two men began helping other prisoners out of their cells. *Whatever it is, I can't wait around for it this time. Hopefully it's not important.*

Orvaril briefly thought about his brother. What if it *was* important? It didn't matter. They had to leave.

"Alright, let's go!"

Alannin followed Orvaril up the stone staircase, keeping close to the pillar in the center for cover. "The door to the outside is probably about 20 feet up the stairs," he whispered as they slowly made their way up. Orvaril nodded. As they got closer to the door, Orvaril could hear faint sounds of fighting.

When they reached the landing, they discovered that the door was already slightly cracked open with a very large Red Sword guard standing watch. He had a heavy mace on his belt and his plates of armor gleamed in the flickering torchlight. Orvaril stopped short and ducked around the pillar, but he knew the guard had already noticed them.

"Dammit, Gorin," the man shouted. His voice was deep and echoed through the stairwell. "If you've let a prisoner escape, I'll—"

His voice was cut off, replaced with gurgling sounds. As Orvaril peered around the pillar, the guard's body tumbled down the stairs, making a terrible, clattering racket.

"You two are quite possibly the most conspicuous people I have ever met. You probably couldn't hide if you were invisible, and I had my eyes closed!"

To Orvaril's surprise, Kendra came around the corner, clutching a bloody, black dagger in her right hand. He was speechless. Alannin, too, was dumbfounded as he stood behind Orvaril, staring.

Kendra curtsied and grinned.

Unsure of what to say or do, Orvaril found himself simply staring at her, with so many thoughts swirling around in his head. He tried to speak but couldn't form the words.

"While I would certainly enjoy standing here and catching up," she said, "I would much rather do so with this place visible in the distance." She turned and climbed the few stairs to the landing. Orvaril and Alannin shot bewildered looks to each other and then followed her lead, utterly speechless.

"We should be able to sneak out this door," she whispered. Orvaril nodded, still unable to speak.

"The fighting apparently hasn't spilled into the rest of the city." Alannin said, as he peeked out of the door. "If we're lucky, there is still a breach in the wall out there." He pointed and then, without hesitation, he ran to the nearest building and disappeared behind it.

Orvaril looked at Kendra. He must have been smiling like a complete fool.

"I know," she said. "I'm very happy to see you, too, but we'll have to talk later. For now, let's just get out of here. I've spent enough time in this tower and I've no desire to stay any longer."

"I cannot disagree with that." Orvaril motioned with his hand out the door. "Please, milady, after you."

Kendra sprinted out of the door and into the darkness. Orvaril felt a wave of happiness wash over him and he sighed contently. Now *it all feels complete.*

He fled into the darkness, following Alannin and Kendra through the city. Though they tried to be stealthy at first, they eventually favored speed over caution. In fact, they recklessly ran through the streets and alleys, unconcerned, speeding past stray orcs and Red Sword soldiers without hesitation. Alannin seemed to know where he was going as he led them out of the city.

When they got to the hole in the wall, Orvaril noticed Alannin's wolf, Ilvania, sitting next to three dead guards.

"I told you to stay hidden, away from here," Alannin scolded, but he didn't sound all that upset. The animal may have disobeyed his command, but she had just made things easier for them. "Thankfully, this breach was not repaired," he added.

There was no activity in this area, though Orvaril could hear the battle raging elsewhere. An eerie, orange glow emanated from the front of the city where he could only assume the larger battle was taking place. They all three darted through the wall's gap and fled into the darkness beyond, only stopping to catch their breath once they found cover behind a hill.

"Where should we go now?" Alannin asked, trying to catch his breath.

"We're going to Elston," Kendra replied. "We have important business there, apparently."

"What do you mean?" Alannin inquired.

"The Red Swords. They want to claim Elston for their own, and we're going to stop them."

"That's ludicrous!" Orvaril exclaimed. "King Alzine won't let that happen!"

"King Alzine doesn't have an army as large as the Red Swords." Kendra was staring back at Sulbar as if scrutinizing it. "He won't have a choice. We need to get to Elston."

"Your horse is nearby, Kendra." Alannin pointed to a tree line in the distance. "But we'll need two more."

"I don't think that will be a problem." Orvaril had grown accustomed to the grin Kendra now wore. He knew she meant to misbehave. "I am going to steal back your horse, Orvaril, and I'll find one for Alannin."

Orvaril glared at her. He was not going to let her go back in there alone.

"Don't worry," she whispered. "I don't plan on staying. This won't be difficult. Just stay here and wait for me." Kendra hopped up and darted back toward Sulbar before Orvaril could argue with her.

"I sure hope that she knows what she's doing," Alannin groused. "I'd rather not lose her again."

"The scary part," Orvaril replied, "is that I'm absolutely sure she does."

Chapter 33

The battle around the Spire was getting larger, and it was starting to spill into other portions of the city. Buildings burned while orcs slaughtered everything in their path. Despite this, Luc felt that his place in the southernmost area of Sulbar was too far removed from the fighting. He couldn't help but feel useless.

As quietly as he could, he made his way down the desolate street, scanning the area for orcs that may have made it this far. Thankfully, he'd not encountered any, but he kept his longsword in hand just in case. His small contingent of men did the same—roaming the streets in search of strays. He knew what this was—a test of his leadership skills. It was obvious that Captain Forsch did not trust him fully to be commanding men at the front lines.

It was unsettling—how quiet the city was, away from the fighting. Thankfully, they had been able to move most of the city's inhabitants into the Red Sword camp outside Sulbar, but there was still a decent number of people who had insisted on staying in their homes, locked and secured as best they could be. While Luc did not see this as a wise move, he understood why they stayed, and he hoped that they would all live through the siege. *Hopefully we will drive back the orcs quickly and return to normal life.*

Would life ever be normal again? Things had changed so much in just the span of a year. If the orcs were numerous enough to mount an assault of this magnitude, they could do it again. Would they return with larger numbers next time? Were there other savage creatures out there somewhere that were worse?

"What if Sulbar falls?"

The very thought made him feel ill. It was something he hadn't considered until just now. After all, Captain Forsch was a smart man and an able leader. And the Spire, combined with their considerable force of mages, was powerful. Yet, for all of their planning, strategy, and power, the orcs appeared to be taking them to task. If Sulbar fell, then what of the other cities of the Realm?

Luc shook it off, trying to clear his mind. Thinking about it did him no good. In all honesty, he really *should* be fighting to save the city instead of lurking in the darkness, heading *away* from the fray. *The fight will still be there once you're done.* He had left some of his men behind to guard the civilians in the Red Sword camp, but they could be called into the fray if needed. Hopefully it wouldn't come to that.

Luc wondered if there was a better way. Mayhaps, the citizens could flee to the hills beyond Sulbar—that way, his men would not have to worry about them and they could help fight. But it was not Luc's place to question the orders he had been given.

Captain Forsch was a wise man, and a brilliant tactician. He had seen many battles against brigand and orc alike and he had emerged victorious every time. Surely he had a plan. Surely he knew what he was doing.

The din of battle was now very faint as Luc moved further away. It almost didn't seem real. As the sounds faded in the distance, Luc felt his shame grow.

He certainly did not revel in combat, nor did he even *want* to fight. He had not considered joining the Red Swords until he had encountered a small group of goblins on his farm outside Greemish. They had already killed three farmhands and were in the process of eating them when Luc had discovered them. He had chased them off with only a tree branch for a weapon. It had been a sorrowful day when he enlisted, leaving his wife Nadya to tend to things at home, but he knew it had been the right decision. The Realm needed an army.

He saw her whenever he got the chance—usually when Red Sword business brought him close to his home. At first, all had been well. Nadya was taken care of and was well-protected while he served the Red Swords' noble cause. That wasn't to say that she was in any more danger now, but Luc also hadn't known the magnitude of the orcish threat when he had left her.

Without realizing it, Luc had inadvertently broken into a full run. He caught himself and slowed down a little to rest.

Though his chainmail was not as cumbersome as some of the heavier armor his men wore, he still tired quickly if he pushed himself too much. He was getting sloppy and careless. If there *were* any enemies this deep into the city, they surely knew he was nearby with the noise he'd been making.

Lately, Luc had asked a lot of questions. After the incident on the road, with Commander Demovar's behavior and subsequent death, Luc had noticed things—things he did not agree with.

Truly, he assumed most large organizations had similar issues but, he figured, these problems were few and far between. The Red Swords, on the other hand, carried out questionable duties daily. After some investigation, Luc had learned that the Red Swords had attacked several towns and murdered innocent people. At first, he assumed that this was merely collateral damage in battle against orcs, but he soon discovered that the motives had been far less noble. As it turned out, money and fear mongering were at the heart of the attacks.

Luc had always looked to the sky for answers—just like the Cloudseers in children's bedtime stories and tales told by storyweavers. Even the ubiquitous *Out and Beyond* mentioned them constantly. Until recently he hadn't been entirely sure what to think of his ability. But, with the appearance of other elements from folklore—the orcs, for example—his view had changed drastically. He knew he was not alone, that there had to be others out there like him. He also no longer explained it away as being just his imagination. This Cloudsight had set him on the course he now followed. It was the single reason he did not feel completely ashamed of not fighting on the front lines.

In the distance, he heard an explosion. The sky burned briefly with hues of orange and yellow. He turned to look, but saw nothing except the radiant glow of fires in the distance. *I hope that wasn't from inside the city.* His pace quickened as he hurried through the dark, deserted streets, guided by moonlight and the faint glow emanating from the fight.

Finally, he arrived a few blocks from the stables and found precisely what he was looking for. He had to look carefully to be sure that his eyes were not deceiving him.

"You are about as quiet as a gortog playing with a wounded squirrel," the woman said unconcerned. She did not even bother to look over her shoulder as he approached from behind.

"It was not my intention to sneak up on you, milady. In fact—"

She charged him with supernatural quickness and, before he knew it, he was pressed up against a wall, with her wicked black dagger at his throat.

"In fact," he choked, being careful not to move, "I am here to help you. Your name is Kendra. Am I correct?"

She stood perfectly still and inspected him closely in the pale moonlight. Her face was as calm as the surface of a still pond, but there was anger behind those eyes. She could have just as easily turned and bolted as she could have slit his throat, and he had no idea which option she was going to choose. Either way, there would be nothing he could do about it.

"Aye," she said. Then she stepped back, slipping her weapon into an unseen sheath. "I recognize you. You're one of *them*."

Luc was bewildered. She was still obviously suspicious of him and, yet, she had put away her blade. She was obviously not threatened by him in the least. Luc, in fact, thought that *he* was more afraid. Scared or no, she did not take her eyes from him.

"You look very well for a dead girl," he said nervously. And then he immediately regretted it, hoping she did not take it the wrong way.

"Precisely what a woman likes to hear." Was there a slight grin on her lips? "That's the nicest thing anyone's said to me all day."

"Listen, Kendra," Luc had never felt this awkward before. What was he supposed to say? "What happened on the road…"

"Are you referring to the Red Swords bullying a group of harmless merchants and ransacking their possessions for no good reason?"

"A very accurate description, to be sure," he replied awkwardly. "Aye. That is what I am referring to."

"What happened was atrocious. It was a crime and the Red Swords should pay for it."

"Whether you believe me, I cannot disagree with you," Luc concurred. "Commander Demovar paid for his actions with his life. I think that's probably adequate punishment."

"Mayhaps." Kendra paused. Luc could feel her scrutinizing him. "Although I am certain that was not an isolated incident."

"It saddens me to say that I cannot disagree with that, either." Until now Luc hadn't realized that he'd been holding his hands out as if he was surrendering. He slowly started to lower them and, once he saw that Kendra was not going to kill him, he relaxed a little. "But," he continued, "we are not all bad. In fact, my fellow soldiers are out there, fighting to save the city right now."

Kendra nodded, still glaring at him.

"You put away your weapon already so I can tell that you don't mean to do me harm," he continued.

"Or I'm simply not afraid of you," she smirked.

"Fair enough."

"Alright, then." Kendra leaned back against the edge of a nearby well and folded her arms in front of her. "You said you were here to help me. Tell me how."

"You want in there," Luc pointed to the stables.

"Aye. But how do you know that?" Kendra was obviously surprised, and rightfully so. Then her shock turned to suspicion.

"The Red Swords took Orvaril's horse," Luc continued. "If I'd had something of mine taken from me, I would certainly want it back. And it just so happens that I have the key to the stables."

"A key?" Kendra laughed. "I hardly need a key—"

"The lock is rigged with a trap. Were you to trigger that trap... well, I'd just say that death by viper venom is rather uncomfortable, I hear."

"Okay, then." Kendra's face returned to a look of suspicion. She obviously still didn't trust him, but Luc couldn't blame her. Even *he* wasn't entirely sure where his loyalties lay. "How about we talk less and walk more, then?"

"Good idea." He turned down the nearest street to the right, with Kendra beside him. "If this battle goes the wrong way, the rest of us may be fleeing closely behind you."

"Hopefully that won't happen. If attacks like this are common elsewhere in the Realm, then the human population may very well be exterminated."

"There have been other... incursions—large, to be sure— but nothing on this scale. The attack on Elston would probably have been the next largest. I heard about it, but it doesn't sound as if it compares."

"It was probably much smaller. Elston was caught just as unprepared as Sulbar, but we had..."

"Had what?" Luc turned down another street. Kendra followed. She did not seem cautious around him anymore. She was confident. He wished he was as confident as she.

"We had more resources," she continued. "And the invading army was disorganized and probably much smaller."

The two walked in silence for a while, somewhat more relaxed. There were no orcs here yet. After all, this part of the city was far removed from the combat. *At least we've still got them relatively contained. Mayhaps that is a sign that we've got the upper hand?*

Luc desperately wanted to ask one question. How had Kendra survived? Even lesser injuries would have confined her to a bed for weeks. He still couldn't bring himself to remotely understand how she was alive. Mayhaps, someday, he would find out, but today was not that day. *Even if we were the best of friends, how do you ask someone that question?*

The horses were housed in several large, unassuming stables near the city's south wall. The area was devoid of houses or shops, and instead featured only the stables and a few much smaller buildings.

Luc lead Kendra to the second barn and unlocked the door. He found a torch sconce just inside and lit it, taking the torch with him. "There. That is where I had my men put him." He pointed to the third stall on the right where Orvaril's horse indeed was. They quickly went about preparing the gray stallion. Kendra then moved to the next stall and put the reins on the black horse within.

"Wait," Luc said, "what are you doing?"

"We have a friend who will need a horse. I'm sure nobody will miss this one."

At first Luc thought about stopping Kendra. *If anyone asks I will simply tell them that mayhaps an orc stole it... or ate it.* He wasn't even really concerned with making up an elaborate story when horse thieves were a frequent problem.

"The quickest way out of the city is through the South Gate. It's not as heavily-fortified and I can probably distract the soldiers. Just make sure you are not seen."

"That won't be a problem."

As Kendra led the horses out of the stables, Luc produced a dagger and jammed it in the lock on the door. After several moments, there was an audible popping noise. He wiped off the blade and then opened several of the stalls inside. Kendra smiled.

"What did you do before you became a soldier?" she asked.

"I have a small farm."

Luc took the reins of the black horse and walked toward the South Gate.

"And before that?"

"Got into trouble a lot."

He heard Kendra chuckling behind him.

Chapter 34

The floating, pulsing blue orb sprang to life when Cor'il touched the pedestal—just as the Catalog had done previously. Though he had been expecting it, he still gasped and took a quick step back. He resisted the urge to try to touch the ball of light, knowing full well that it was probably immaterial, like the Catalog.

"Greetings," a man's deep voice said. "I am the Caretaker. How may I be of service?"

"Uh," Cor'il stammered, "hello. I am Cor'il Silvermoon."

"It is nice to meet you, Cor'il Silvermoon. How may I be of service?"

"I wish to know about this city—*Darvinon.*"

The orb before him pulsed with shifting colors for a moment before replying.

"*Darvinon* is the first of the five cities of the Kai'Tan. During the height of the Kai'Tan civilization it housed approximately 250,000 individuals."

"Who were the Kai'Tan?"

"They were the Shapers. They were my masters. They created me from the Threads and appointed me the Caretaker of *Darvinon.*"

"But who were they? Where did they come from?"

"I do not know how to answer that question."

Cor'il sighed, frustrated. He began pacing. *What good is this Caretaker if I don't know the right questions to ask it?*

"*We're wasting time, boy. This silly orb does not have any information that is useful to us.*"

"Caretaker," he said. "Tell me about The Breach and the new enemy that the Kai'Tan were forced to fight."

"I do not have that information."

"What about the buildings used for research?" Cor'il growled. He clenched his fists and felt his fingernails dig into his palms. His frustration was coupled with disappointment.

The Caretaker pulsed rhythmically for a few seconds, then stopped.

"The Kai'Tan, when confronted with a new threat, were quickly overwhelmed," it said. "There were several buildings designated as containment facilities, and the Kai'Tan studied specimens within these structures. Powerful tapestries of the Threads were laid over the buildings for security, though my information shows that there were 15 reported accidents."

"Accidents? What kind of accidents?" Cor'il continued pacing. There was not much to look at inside this room, and he was having a challenging time asking appropriate questions.

"Accidents that resulted in the brutal, horrible deaths of some Kai'Tan."

"So," Cor'il continued, "whatever it was escaped?"

"Correct."

"Was everyone killed? Were there any survivors? Why is the city deserted?"

"Unknown. I do not have that information."

Cor'il continued pacing, his frustration rising. He had so hoped that the Caretaker would have the answers he sought but, thus far, he was still missing most of the pieces of the puzzle. The orb floated silently above the pedestal, awaiting Cor'il's next question.

"Can you show me where these research buildings are?"

The blue orb flattened itself into a large square, then it turned horizontally. Buildings climbed up from the blue surface and Cor'il could even identify the *Skurata* at the city's edge. Several small buildings began flashing with white light.

"These 10 buildings were designated for containment and research."

"And where am I currently?"

A tiny, shining speck of light appeared above a small dome-shaped building on the map.

"You are currently here, in the building of the Caretaker— the *Ssvaril*."

Cor'il inspected the map. The nearest flashing building appeared to be just a few blocks away—or whatever the Kai'Tan might've called them.

"What can you tell me of the *Skurata*?"

"The *Skurata* is located at the edge of the city. It is the triangular structure with the spire atop it. It has many purposes and many functions."

The map of the city focused on the *Skurata* which enlarged and slowly rotated before Cor'il. It indeed was a rather nondescript building. It was just as Kendra had described the one she had seen—a triangular archway.

Cor'il scrutinized the image for a few moments as it rotated slowly in front of him. There was no level of detail, so the shape of the building was all he could really see.

"What did the Kai'Tan use the *Skurata* for?"

The image of the *Skurata* disappeared and returned to its place on the map.

"The *Skurata* has many uses. The Shapers most often used it to create impossibly complex weaves—tapestries that simply could not exist without it."

"Such as the weaves of this city?"

"Possibly. I do not have such knowledge."

Cor'il thought back to his childhood and his favorite book, "Out and Beyond." He carefully recalled every story he could remember, hoping to glean some information about any of this. But he didn't remember the book mentioning the Kai'Tan, shapers, or anything else. He wondered how many more layers of history had been lost to time and Antina's gambit.

"What you want to do is impossible. You're going to get yourself killed or worse."

Exactly what would be worse than getting myself killed? Cor'il laughed to himself.

"Getting everyone else killed."

Cor'il chose to ignore Antina. With every little bit of information, he felt more confident in his plan, and now he knew how he could accomplish it. *But first, I want to investigate one of those research buildings.*

"Thank you, Caretaker. I believe that is all of the information I require." Cor'il could think of endless questions to ask the construct but he had neither the time nor the patience.

"You are welcome, Threadweaver. Feel free to return should you need further assistance."

The map morphed back into the familiar, pulsing ball of light which then winked out, leaving the room dimly lit by a few floating, illuminated orbs close to the ceiling. When he left the *Ssvaril*, the room behind him went dark and the door rematerialized, leaving him alone once again.

"Except you're not alone."

You don't count.

"That is not to what I was referring."

Cor'il felt a shiver run down his spine. Antina was right. There was something out there—or *multiple* somethings. He knew that, now, and his wonder was slowly turning to fear. He headed in the direction of the nearest research building at a brisk walk. He heard things in the distance or, at least, he *thought* he heard things. Regardless, as he was unsure of how to use the *Skurata*, he thought it wise to move quickly.

"You'll never figure it out, boy. It's well older than you are, created by beings who were much smarter and more knowledgeable in the art of the Threads."

Cor'il chose to ignore Antina. There was no convincing her otherwise, so there was no point trying. He was curious about just how much knowledge she had—she always *seemed* to know everything, but Cor'il was beginning to doubt that façade.

As he hurriedly moved down the street, he began to see the large, blue *Skurata* towering in the distance. It appeared to have a faint glow about it, but Cor'il wasn't sure if it was the *Skurata* itself or if it was just the ambient light about the city. When he embraced the Threads, the *Skurata* did not radiate the light and energy that he thought it would. In fact, no Threads connected with the structure at all. It appeared to be completely cut off from all of them. *How am I supposed to use it to channel the Threads if there are none connecting to it?*

"Hey, boy. Snap out of it. We're here."

Cor'il stopped abruptly and released the Threads, realizing that he had nearly passed by the very building he was looking for. The white structure before him was simple and unassuming, standing mayhaps two stories high. However, unlike most of the other rounded buildings he had seen in the city thus far, its edges and corners were more squared, like traditional buildings he was used to.

There was a jagged hole where the door should have been, and the area was littered with shattered stone and rubble.

"It looks like... something broke out of it."

"Yes, it indeed does. Any guesses?"

I was hoping you *would tell* me.

"You're not that *stupid."*

Cor'il cautiously stepped inside the building, but unlike with the Catalog and the Caretaker's buildings, there was no light. Whatever happened here must have been traumatic to the Threads. *Or there wasn't supposed to be light to begin with.*

"D'rosoco!"

A familiar mote of light sprang to life in front of Cor'il, its illumination allowing Cor'il to see out to about 10 feet around him. He was in a small, but empty room. The wall ahead of him was destroyed in the same fashion as the outer wall.

He moved closer to the hole and stopped as a voice rang out in his mind.

"Containment facility number 3: Breach detected. One or more specimens may have escaped. Extreme caution is advised. Please report this event to the Caretaker as soon as possible."

"Well, that certainly does not bode well."

"No, it doesn't," Cor'il mumbled, inspecting the hole in the wall. He moved his light over the surface to get a better look. The wall itself was at least a foot thick, made from the same smooth, white stone that these buildings shared.

"You don't suppose whatever made that hole is still in there, do you?"

Probably not. Which means it's most likely somewhere out in the city—if it is still alive.

Suddenly, Cor'il wished he knew *when* it had escaped—whatever it was. Would this have contributed to the Shapers' downfall, or was it more recent, having escaped *after* the fact? If the Caretaker was supposed to hold information about this city, why didn't it know what had happened?

Cor'il stepped into the building, urging his floating light forward. Ahead of him was a horrific menagerie, each creature still and unmoving as if they were a twisted display of vile artwork in a museum. At first, he thought they were all statues, but upon closer inspection, he realized his folly. They were flesh, and each creature floated inches above the ground, frozen in time somehow. He could not tell if they were alive or dead, but if one had escaped, he would have to assume that the rest could, too.

Fear overcame him and he gasped, backing up a few feet. His first urge was to run—to flee the entire city and leave it buried for eternity—but he shook it off, though his body began to shiver uncontrollably. He was familiar with this sensation. It was an irrational fear but, also, very real.

"So, the Kai'Tan discovered Madness. It must be an evil older than I had surmised. How foolish of me."

"What are you babbling about?" Cor'il grasped the Threads and aimed several weaves at one of the creatures, but none of them affected it. These beasts may as well have been the statues that he first thought they were.

Cor'il slowly walked forward, passing by several more of the monsters. Each one was vastly different from the next. Some had tentacles, while others had no appendages at all. He stopped in front of one that he considered closest to a normal, human shape. It had three arms and one rather large leg. Its head was buried within its chest with vacuous eyes staring out of its pale gray, mottled skin and its mouth wide open.

He slowly reached out his hand and waved it in front of the creature's face, but there was no response. Its blank eyes continued to stare straight ahead. If it actually saw him, it made no response.

"I, uh, wouldn't do that."

Cor'il reached out further, but his hand hit something solid. The air shimmered and rippled, briefly revealing a barrier of some kind. As he touched it again and again, it shimmered in response, but denied his hand any further movement forward.

When he embraced the Threads, the invisible prisons became evident. The weaves to create the barriers did not appear to be very complex. It was the other constructs that Cor'il didn't understand—the much more complex weaves that Cor'il presumed kept the creatures dormant. Cor'il found himself wishing that he had more time to study them all. Instead, he let go of the Threads, determined to avoid getting sidetracked. Though he still felt uncontrollable fear, he continued his investigation.

"Why exactly are we here? What are you hoping to accomplish? You're going to get us both killed. You're a fool and a child and I cannot believe you were entrusted with the ability to use the Threads! You are either going to bring about the end of the Realm, or destroy yourself!"

Cor'il did his best to ignore Antina's rant. He slowly moved past cell after cell, each holding a different, ghastly specimen. He found it difficult not to stop to inspect each creature out of both disgust and morbid curiosity. It was one thing to fight these monsters, but another entirely to be able to scrutinize them safely up close.

Then he came to an empty cell. A quick embrace of the Threads showed him exactly what he had feared. The weaves had been broken and only tattered, ineffective remnants remained.

"This," he muttered, "is why we're here."

"It got out. There is one of them loose."

"Probably more than just one of them. The weaves are failing for some reason."

"Or the Madness creatures have overcome them. Mayhaps these monsters are more complex than they appear."

"Regardless," Cor'il's pace hastened, "I wouldn't be surprised if more have escaped, and if more escape in the future." He moved down the aisle, counting three more empty cells before he reached the other end of the room.

"And if the other buildings held as many..."

"It is safe to assume that the other buildings were breached, too. It's time to go. If you wish to continue with your foolish plan, then be about it quickly. Otherwise, we should leave. We will be killed if we stay here much longer."

Cor'il nodded. He was getting too comfortable conversing with a voice inside his head, but he had to agree with her this time—there was no reason to delay. This city was deceptively dangerous. He returned to the front of the building and was surprised to see a weapon rack leaning against the wall to his left.

There was a lone blade on the otherwise empty rack, which he picked up and inspected. The scabbard was made of a pitch black, but lightweight material. It was cold like metal, but felt more like wood.

"Steelwood," he mumbled, as he unsheathed the sword. The handle was also steelwood, but was deep brown in color. The sword itself was very light and had tiny veins of red running along the length of the blade.

"And blood iron. That's one to hold onto. Very fortunate, seeing how you need a sword. You'd be hard-pressed to find a better weapon."

The pommel held a red, spherical gem—possibly a ruby—speckled with gold from within.

Cor'il nodded and sheathed the weapon. Once he had attached it to his side, he exited the building, cautiously looking around for any danger. He extinguished his light and moved out into the street, gazing ahead at the *Skurata* in the distance.

"*It's a long walk.*"

"We'll make it."

"*And you're sure about this?*"

"I am not worried about getting there. I'm worried about what happens once I've arrived."

"*I'm concerned about both.*"

Chapter 35

Kendra was the first to wake. The sky was still mostly dark, but that would not last long. The sun's first rays would greet the world soon. Autumn was approaching—probably in a month or so—Kendra could feel it in the remarkably chilly, damp air.

They were headed to Elston, of course. Once they had gotten enough distance between them and Sulbar, they had made camp in a small clump of trees. Having fallen asleep almost immediately when she laid down, Kendra had slept solidly all night. Orvaril was still asleep and Alannin was nowhere to be seen. His wolf was gone, too.

She stood up, stretched, and yawned, admiring the serene beauty of the quiet morning. The crickets were still chirping but otherwise, the world around her was quiet and still. She walked to the edge of the trees and looked out over the landscape, doing the same on the other side. She could see Alannin was walking toward their camp, carrying something. Ilvania happily trotted beside him, every so often nipping at whatever was in his hand.

"Breakfast!" he said, holding up a fat rabbit. "Killing it was arguably easier than keeping it away from the greedy wolf, here." He glared at Ilvania, but soon smiled. She sat patiently, panting, as her gaze shifted back and forth between him and the rabbit. "Don't worry, girl, you'll get your share. It probably won't be much, but you're not going to starve."

Orvaril snorted, rolled over, and started snoring while Alannin built a fire. Kendra watched, enthralled with the process. She had never really paid this close attention to his methods before. Cor'il would've simply started one with fire from his hand which, she admitted, while completely abnormal, was much more convenient. *Hopefully he is safe. When we meet again, I am going to smack him for leaving us.*

With a few sparks and some smoke Alannin ignited the dry blades of grass which then smoldered slowly. Once he had nurtured the fire enough, he then skinned the rabbit.

"You're awfully good at this," she said.

"It's how I've lived my life. My family and friends not only live *in* the wilds but we live *with* the wilds." Using a small knife, he removed the skin from the rabbit with surprising efficiency.

"If you don't mind my asking," she said, "Where is it you are from, exactly?"

"I used to live in a place we called Eleria."

"I have never heard of such a place. Is it far from here?"

"I am unsure," Alannin continued. "I was brought here through some sort of gateway. I don't believe that I lived on this world—your world—until just recently. It sounds strange, I know."

"I am not sure I understand." Kendra picked up a leaf and slowly tore at it, each piece ripping off along a vein until just a small stem remained. She picked up another leaf and repeated the process.

"I am not entirely sure I understand, either." When he was finished skinning the rabbit, he put his hand over the fire. Seemingly satisfied, he dropped the rabbit on the hot rocks which immediately sizzled. "This place feels very different than my homeland. I am relatively certain that this world and my home are in two entirely separate and very different places."

"Do you wish to go back?"

"I do not." He paused for a moment, inspecting the rabbit. The wolf lay on the ground, staring at the searing meat and quietly whining every so often. "I was summoned here. I am *supposed* to be here."

"How do you know?"

"It simply *feels* right. It's as if I once knew this place and have been away for far too long. I know that I have never been here... but it also feels somehow familiar."

Kendra was sure the look on her face was one of utter confusion. Alannin, however, did not seem phased by it at all.

Orvaril got up, ran his hand over the half of his head with hair, and sat down with them near the fire.

313

"You cooked me breakfast!" he laughed. "So, where's yours?"

"Cute," Kendra laughed.

"Okay, fine... fine," he continued. "I'll let you have a bite or two. I'm a very generous person, you know."

"Yes," Kendra replied. "That you are."

"Mayhaps the lady should have a touch more than the rest of us." Orvaril poked Kendra's shoulder. "I am sure that being dead is hungry work."

"We are very thankful," Alannin added, "that you are alive, Kendra. Orvaril over here was just about ready to take on the entire Red Sword army on his own."

"Aye. But instead, Alannin apparently brought a force of orcs for me?"

"Well," Alannin continued, "that's not entirely—"

"I wasn't dead." Kendra fidgeted with another leaf, folding it repeatedly in her hands. "I mean, how can I be alive now if I *had been* dead?"

"We were sort of hoping that *you* could tell *us*, actually," Alannin replied.

"You took two arrows in your back, milady. Both the Red Sword soldier and I were absolutely sure you were dead." Orvaril's usual smile disappeared.

Kendra had the urge to check for wounds on her back but she resisted. She had already done so numerous times, and had found absolutely nothing. *I should be dead, shouldn't I? Yet, here I am, just as alive as a cat in a room full of mice. How exactly am I to explain this?*

"Believe me," she said, "I share your curiosity and surprise." She threw the folded leaf on the ground and began picking at individual blades of grass instead. "I last remember falling from Brute, but even that seems as though it was just a bad dream. When I woke up, I was in a small room, lying on a bed. I found this dress folded neatly on a table along with my satchel." She herself wondered why she had awakened in those

314

accommodations. If she were dead after all, why would someone go through all the trouble to provide clothing, and place her in a bed? *Someone must've known.*

"And then you ran into us?" Orvaril asked.

"After a bit of exploration, yes. I had a few... things I needed to acquire first." She remembered rummaging through her satchel until she found her brush. After that, her next goal had been to find her weapons. Surprisingly, that had not been very difficult, especially since her black dagger appeared in her hand at a mere thought. Getting the three other daggers had been more difficult, but their previous owners were no longer able to care that they had gone missing.

Alannin lifted part of the rabbit with his knife. Apparently satisfied with its status, he flipped it over. The fire briefly sprang to life as the juices dripped from the meat.

Kendra could tell that neither Alannin nor Orvaril was satisfied with her explanation. She did not blame them. It simply didn't seem possible, and it frustrated her more than she could explain. She could not explain something which she was herself unable to comprehend.

Kendra could see the questions on Orvaril's lips but he did not ask them. They remained in an uneasy silence until breakfast was done.

"So," Orvaril began, dabbing his mouth with his shirtsleeve. "To Elston, eh?"

"Yes," Kendra replied, wiping a small bit of juice from her chin. "We need to be in Elston."

"Why, exactly?" Orvaril continued. "I can certainly use the coin, but I still don't understand—why Elston in particular?"

"The Red Swords are constructing another Spire inside the city and we need to ensure that it doesn't get finished." She decided to omit the part about her Cloudsight urging her toward Elston. She much preferred not to try to explain it.

"Why not?" Orvaril inquired. He picked the last bit of meat from a bone and then tossed the remains into the fire.

"Right," Alannin added. "I saw the Spire in Sulbar during the battle. I don't think Sulbar would have fared well without it. Mayhaps a defense like that is something every city needs."

"Defense," Kendra retorted, "is not its only purpose."

"What do you mean?" Alannin asked.

"I am not entirely sure," she continued. "But I overheard a conversation between two men—possibly high-ranking leaders, but I can't be sure. They were discussing the Spires and how they would bring the Realm under Red Sword control."

"Bring the Realm under Red Sword control?" Orvaril repeated.

"They are trying to build one in Ten Kings but have run into... issues," Kendra added.

"What kinds of issues, milady?"

"There is a horde of orcs that has massed in Ten Kings and completely taken over the city."

"That is terrible news!" Orvaril gasped. "When did this happen?"

"From what I heard, it's been at least several months." Kendra picked at the ground, pulling out blades of grass one by one. "They are led by a shaman who calls himself 'The Reaver' and, apparently, the horde's size is considerable."

"Where in The Abyss are these orcs coming from?" Orvaril threw a bone at a tree. It bounced off harmlessly, and Ilvania pounced. "Why are orcs flooding in from all directions but we've only seen one elf?" He pointed to Alannin.

"I remember Cor'il mentioning that," Kendra replied. "He said something about restoring balance to Chaos and Order. Mayhaps that is what he has set out to do. I don't know how—I'm not sure I even understood what he was talking about." *But he is also in Elston, I am sure of it. Elston is where we need to be. It is where our journey truly begins.*

It was true that the sky had suggested Elston for their destination, but she also had another motive. Cor'il was there—

she could... feel him. It couldn't be just a mere coincidence that he happened to be where they were headed.

"So, he's somehow going to bring more elves into the world?" Orvaril laughed, leaning back against a tree.

"It sounds far-fetched," Alannin replied, "but mayhaps it is not as crazy as you think. There is much about this Realm that nobody understands."

"And," Kendra continued, "mayhaps along with those elves, more dwarves and gnomes? I don't know if that's how it works. Cor'il speaks of strange things, even when he's only talking with himself."

"Those are just storyweaver tales, not—" Orvaril stopped short and then chuckled, shaking his head. "My apologies, I sometimes forget just what has happened this past year. But I've seen one elf and have yet to see a dwarf. And, as far as I know, *nobody* has encountered a gnome at all."

"Even in stories and tales, gnomes are rarely mentioned," Kendra replied. "We are living in a world that is very unfamiliar and new to all of us—especially Alannin. I would not be so quick to discount anything."

Orvaril nodded. He combed his hair with his fingers and sighed, shutting his eyes.

"Mayhaps we'll get to see a dragon," he chuckled, nervously.

"Don't get too comfortable." Kendra threw a small bone at Orvaril, hitting him in the head. Ilvania watched the bone closely, and as it landed, she scooped it up in her jaws. "We need to be on to Elston soon. I feel that time is running short."

"Aye," Orvaril nodded. "I feel it, too. Cor'il is there, isn't he?"

"I believe so, yes."

Alannin stood up and began kicking dirt on the fire and Kendra followed suit. Orvaril slowly rose and checked the horses over, making sure they were ready to go.

"We've got several days' worth of travel ahead of us," Kendra said, slinging her satchel over her shoulder. "Let us hope that we don't encounter any trouble along the way."

"Hopefully all of the orcs in the area are too busy with Sulbar to be much trouble." Orvaril hopped up onto Dummy.

"I shall name you Verishka." Alannin looked at his colt and stroked his mane before jumping onto the animal's back.

Kendra hopped up onto Brute as well, and pointed her back toward the road. It felt good to be atop her chestnut mare again, but better yet, she was overjoyed to be back among friends. That was something she would not take for granted again.

"Do you really think he can do it?" Orvaril pulled alongside her with a slightly concerned look on his face.

"I really don't know," she replied. "But, if anyone *can*, it is probably him."

"Nobody can move mountains, milady. What if he fails?"

"Then at least we'll be there to help him if he does."

Chapter 36

There was a high-pitched shriek somewhere off in the distance as Cor'il carefully made his way through the deserted city streets, cautiously keeping his keen eyes open for any danger. Startled, he instinctively ducked behind a building, trying to calm himself. He had already done this same thing countless times—each time he heard one of them yell.

"You should relax, boy. Mayhaps we should go far away from here where it's safe and there are no Madness monsters running rampant like a plague. If every sound sends you running for cover, it seems that would be preferable."

Cor'il shut his eyes and took a deep breath. That one sounded faint and somewhere far away. *Of course, there are* at least *four of them out there somewhere.*

"And most likely a lot more than that."

Cor'il tried his best not to think about that. He wasn't sure if he'd be able to deal with another one of those horrible creatures. He had been fortunate the last time, and it had taken a lot out of him. Since then, he'd learned a lot from the book, but no matter how confident that made him feel, he still feared these creatures. No amount of talent with the Threads would change that. *I'm beginning to think that, mayhaps, there is such a thing as luck after all.*

It didn't take long for doubt to creep in. He only had a partial plan about how to go about converging the Dark Machine and the Great Machine. Given what he had learned, he was almost certain that it was possible, but there was much he still did not know. *Should something go wrong or I lose control... I don't even know enough to be able to predict the consequences.*

He needed the *Skurata*—he knew that much. His task was impossible otherwise. The sheer amount of Thread energy required to merge the two would be more than any one person would be able to handle without killing the user outright. Even then, he wasn't even sure that using the *Skurata* would keep him alive through it all.

"Yes, this could fail and you could die. That sounds very glamorous, doesn't it?"

"If you have any better ideas, I'd love to hear them."

"I gave you my idea already."

"I am not going to be a prisoner of the Threads merely to keep a wound from getting worse. I would rather heal that wound."

And die in the process?

"I won't lie and tell you that I am ready to die. I would prefer to avoid that. But, should I die, it will be more meaningful than the 200 years you spent avoiding death."

Another shriek sounded from somewhere to Cor'il's right. It was distinctly closer now, and he felt shivers run down his back. Was he being hunted? He quickly crossed the wide street and headed down a much smaller avenue, keeping close to the buildings for cover. His left hand rested on the hilt of his new sword, which made him feel slightly more secure even though he knew that was silly. If he had to fight one of those beasts, his sword was probably not going to be of much use. Last time, it hadn't been.

He could not see the *Skurata* from this street—the buildings were too tall and the street was too narrow—but he knew where it was. If he used the Threads he would be able to feel it. As he continued his journey through the city, his mind worked relentlessly, trying to puzzle out just how this plan of his was going to work. It was as if he was building the bridge while crossing the chasm, except that he wasn't sure he had enough materials to finish it before he plummeted to his death.

In fact, he didn't even know how to operate the construct in the first place. He could try to work out the details before he got there but, the truth was, he didn't have anything to base his ideas on—how it worked, how to manipulate it, or even what the building truly could do.

There's no sense worrying about the fleas before you catch the dog. That's what Ben Falhar used to say. And, while he was right, Cor'il found it difficult not to take that advice. This was a big, powerful dog that could outright kill him.

Cor'il stopped for a moment to listen, sure that he had heard footsteps. He was greeted with nothing but silence, for which he was thankful, but also afraid. It was sometimes reassuring, though terrifying, to know at least whereabouts these monsters might be. He leaned his back against a building and exhaled, closing his eyes and trying to relax. Or was he trying to stall? The uncertainty was overwhelming and it didn't help matters when Antina questioned his every move.

Do you know something that you're not telling me?

"Would it matter? You have not listened to a word I've said this entire time."

What would you do if you suddenly had someone talking to you inside your head? Cor'il started walking again, his hand still on the sword's hilt. The pommel still felt cool in his grasp, even though his hand should've warmed it up by now. *You would have had me be a prisoner. And for what? To keep the world broken?*

"I would have had you save the Realm, you insolent fool! You've no idea how this structure works—you barely grasp the Threads themselves! This is not play time with a toy sword!"

Cor'il covered his ears though it did no good. He could not quell her shouting. She was angry—that much was certain. He'd never heard her this worked up before. He wondered how she would act if she could stand before him, face to face.

"I knew what I was doing! Though my weaves were unraveling, you could have easily bolstered them and the Realm would have been brought back to balance! I hope you die! I hope you are gutted by one of those... one of those Madness beasts—it will be a fitting punishment for your hubris! I had been manipulating the Threads for well longer than you have even been alive! Your actions here will not only fail to succeed, but they

will bring about a new Storm that will engulf every Realm and it won't stop until it has devoured everything!"

Antina *did* know something that she wasn't telling him—Cor'il was sure of it. It probably wouldn't have mattered to him even if she divulged it, however, because he was resolute in his determination to end this once and for all.

He did his best to ignore her. She continued screaming inside his head, but he focused on his real problem—how to manipulate the *Skurata*. He had no intention of turning back now. While Antina certainly had more experience with the Threads—and mayhaps even more knowledge—Cor'il knew that she had a very narrow view. It was the book. Everything he had learned from the book pointed him in this direction. It *felt* right. *That* was his advantage.

"*Stop!*"

"No," he growled, "I will not. I'm going to go through—"

"*No, you fool. Hide!*"

Cor'il froze in his tracks when he heard it—a low, guttural snarling combined with heavy footfalls. He immediately stepped into a small entryway to one of the buildings and stayed as still as he could. He realized that he had become too lost in his own thoughts and had failed to hear the creature. He needed to be more careful.

Whatever it was, it sounded enormous! For a moment, Cor'il thought that he could *feel* the creature's footsteps shake the ground. He tried to convince himself otherwise but, no, he *could* feel them! Each footfall sent shivers through his body as it caused the ground to shudder.

Antina fell silent. That was at least one good thing. Cor'il could feel his heart pounding inside his chest, even as he tried to remain calm. He wanted to close his eyes and to wish it away as a child wished away the monster under the bed. *That monster is real, now, isn't it?*

If he couldn't see it, it wouldn't see him. Or mayhaps he simply wanted to avoid seeing it altogether. The previous abominations he had run into were hideous in ways that he could never forget. They were truly frightening, cruelly twisted insults to life itself.

Cor'il wasn't sure how long he cowered in the doorway but eventually, the sounds trailed off into the distance and he was able to calm himself. Even once he knew that whatever it was had moved on, he remained in the doorway for a while longer, affording himself a little more time to not only make sure the way was safe, but also to possibly come up with more ideas on how to complete his task.

He was well aware that a few more minutes to think was not going to solve his problem, but those precious moments afforded him comfort. He cautiously peeked out from behind the wall. When he saw nothing, he wiped his sweaty palms on his tunic and resumed his journey toward the edge of the city, his heart still racing.

Occasionally, he caught a glimpse of the triangular, blue-hued building in the distance. He had covered more ground than he had at first thought, and the building loomed larger above him now. Both a feeling of elation and a feeling of dread welled up inside him when he realized his unexpected close proximity to the structure. Regardless of the outcome, his journey was quickly coming to its end.

I have to try. It must be me.

Or did it? What about Dalinil? If Cor'il failed, could his friend do what needed to be done? After all, Dalinil had the type of control that Cor'il could only dream of. Sure, his own skills with the Threads had improved by leaps and bounds, but he always felt as if he had to coax the Threads to do his will. It was as if they needed to be bribed or threatened. But Dalinil... Dalinil just seemed to work *with* them, effortlessly becoming one with each Thread as if it were a part of him.

Dalinil had no explanation, of course. When Cor'il had once asked him about his skill, he had said it just felt natural—the same as walking or talking. He could no more teach Cor'il how to use the Threads than he could teach a gortog to read, he'd said.

Cor'il, however, felt as if he were lifting something heavy every time—there was resistance.

"The other boy has talent. Talent is a wonderful resource but it can only take someone so far. The Threads are simply an extension of his body, and he uses them as such. He can run and he can jump but he will never be the fastest or jump the highest. He will never reach the heights that you will... if you don't die here, that is."

Though Cor'il had been trying to ignore Antina, he decided to listen to her once he realized that her anger had vanished. Her crazy rant had subsided and she was much more lucid, for now at least.

"You, on the other hand... you may be walking into a terrible mistake, but your skill with the Threads is developing. Though you may not realize it, you also have talent—it simply hasn't surfaced yet. The other boy was quicker to reach his level of competency with the Threads, but I believe that you can far surpass him."

"What makes you think so?" he asked. Cor'il wasn't sure he believed her but, as much as he'd like to think she was mad, Antina did, in fact, know a lot about the Threads—information that could not be gleaned from the book.

"He has a shallow view of what the Threads' capabilities are. Not only has he imposed limitations on himself, but he simply does not have a connection as strong as yours. While he is indeed capable of much more than he displayed, he will never attain the level of mastery that you will—even at the height of his power. The Great Machine and the Dark Machine have simply provided you with tools. How you use them is up to you."

Cor'il seized the Threads briefly and saw a clear path to the *Skurata*, then he quickly let them go and continued down the narrow street.

"Once you figure out how to properly use them, you will see. You will realize the insanity of your plan—if you live—and you will understand. Unfortunately for you it will be too late."

"Why don't *you* teach me how to properly use the Threads, then? If you know so much, that is."

"For each individual, learning is a different process. There is a plethora of people out there now who can use a very small portion of the Threads' power. Some may only see the red Threads or mayhaps only the green. They may not even know what they are doing or that they even have the ability in the first place. How you utilize the Threads' power is unique to you and I cannot instruct you in their use. You may push the Threads whereas someone else might pull them."

Cor'il's thoughts turned back to Dalinil. He had not spoken to his friend since they left Elston. At that time, he'd seemed troubled and distant. Hopefully, when this was over, they could reconnect. He then thought about his other friends and he hoped that they, too, were doing well. He needed to apologize to them for the way he left. Even now, he was having difficulty dealing with the fact that it was *he* who destroyed his own home and killed everyone. Cor'il remembered everything now as if it had happened yesterday and he fought back tears as he tried to focus on the task at hand.

A noise somewhere off to his left brought him out of his thoughts as he searched for its source. It had sounded like something breaking though, thankfully, it was not nearby. *So far, so good. I just hope my fortune continues and those things decide to keep to themselves. I really wish I knew how many were out there.*

A terrifying thought crept into his head. When Kendra had told him about the city she had discovered, she had described her encounter with something that sounded an awful lot like a creature of Madness. If that was true... *then it's not just happening here. If there are five Kai'Tan cities, then the situation could be the same in all of them. This city—Darvinon—could be just the beginning.*

Was it possible to contain them or destroy them all? There might be hundreds of these creatures in captivity, frozen in time. If the other cities were in a similar condition, then most of them were still imprisoned—for now. As far as Cor'il knew, none of them had escaped into the Realms. Hopefully, the same held true for the others. If that were true, however, where had those he'd fought in Kuranthas come from? Was there another source?

Suddenly, the platform that took him from the ledge above down to the city made more sense to him. It was a transportation system that those monsters probably couldn't operate.

But that was another subject on which Cor'il did not wish to dwell any longer. It was like climbing a mountain he had not yet encountered. *Worry about the obstacle nearest you. No one can be expected to move mountains.*

"Isn't that what you're planning to do?"

Cor'il's mind feverishly jumped between thoughts. He had too many problems to think about and no way to solve any of them.

He stopped walking, suddenly realizing that he had left the city behind him and he now stood in an empty, plaza-like area with only the *Skurata* up ahead in the distance. Whereas the streets of the city were smooth and seamless, the ground here was dirty, roughly-hewn stone. He hadn't expected the structure to be in the middle of nowhere.

"D'rosoco!" The familiar spec of light sprang to life above Cor'il's head and followed him as he moved toward the structure before him. He could feel his palms getting sweaty with each step he took. Now that he was close to his goal, his doubts surfaced and began to dominate his thoughts. He tried to hide his fears, hoping that Antina would not detect his hesitation. She thankfully had not interjected her presence for a while, but Cor'il was not so stupid as to think she was unaware.

One by one, he pushed his worries down, clearing his mind and trying to calm himself. He knew he did not have any solid plan for what he was going to do once he arrived but, if he let his nerves take over, they could be the end of him.

Instinctively, Cor'il grasped onto the Threads and observed them. Currently, only a scant few—one of each color—seemed to run through the dormant *Skurata*. At first, Cor'il found this odd, but with a little thought, he understood—why devote Threads to a magical device that is seldom used?

Certain pieces of the puzzle began to fall into place as he released the Threads and continued toward the *Skurata*. He quickened his pace, feeling not only doubt but also excitement. He still didn't know quite how he was going to merge the two constructs, but he was eager to try. He hoped he would learn from the *Skurata* once he figured out how it functioned.

When he finally stood before the massive structure, he stared up at it. It was not a solid, smooth building as he had thought. Now that he was up close he could see that it had different interlocking panels, grooves, and outcroppings.

Cor'il walked around the *Skurata*, scrutinizing it and trying to decide what to do next. Aside from the blue glow, the building appeared unremarkable. He knew that there had to be some way to bring it to life. However, there were no doors, levers, buttons, or anything else that would obviously allow him to activate it.

He walked around it again, this time alternating between his normal vision and the Threads, but he learned little. *How does this device activate? If only there were a button or even a gem to place somewhere.* He stopped and stared at it from the other side, looking through the center at the city beyond. He felt like he was back at the first obelisk, circling it and trying to reveal its secrets.

"So why the open, triangular archway under the *Skurata*?" he mused. Cor'il scratched his head and then rested his chin in his hand, still staring. "Mayhaps that's it."

His footsteps echoed as he cautiously walked beneath the structure, passing into the archway. Once he was directly under the *Skurata*, he felt it—he connected with the structure itself. He could somehow *feel* it, almost as if he were wearing it like a tunic. Immediately, he noticed two blue, pulsing motes of energy emerge from the structure. They floated quietly down toward him, coming to rest mere inches from either side of his head as he looked out on the city.

Tricky. Like several other things in this city, the Skurata must be able to sense a Threadweaver. That is the only explanation. But is it reaching out to me?

Cor'il closed his eyes and grasped the Threads. His entire body was filled with an overwhelming surge of energy produced by more Threads than he had ever before controlled at one time. Every inch of his body burned with the hottest fire he had ever felt and he screamed as he let go, exhilarated, but trying to catch his breath as the pain instantly subsided. His legs buckled and he dropped to one knee. For a moment, he could do nothing but stare at the ground, trying to understand what had just happened.

But there was something else—a connection to places far away. And, at that moment, he knew. He knew just as surely as he knew his own name.

"It has four siblings," he gasped. "I can feel them... sleeping—waiting for me to reach out to them." With Kendra's discovery, he had known that there was another, but now he knew of three more!

He stopped for a moment and ran a hand through his sweat-soaked hair. In the mere few seconds that he and the *Skurata* connected, he had become drenched.

"It's about time you came out of your stupor."

"What are you talking about?" Cor'il wiped the sweat from his brow.

"You became distant. You simply... disappeared for several minutes."

Cor'il wasn't sure how to respond. *Several minutes?* Surely Antina was exaggerating. But he remembered that time flowed differently in Ilathri. Could the same be true inside this area under the *Skurata*? Or was it the Threads themselves that had caused it?

"What do you mean by *disappeared*?" he muttered, not quite sure of even what he was asking.

"You were just... gone. I tried to speak to you but you weren't there."

Cor'il decided it was best not to dwell on it. During the brief time he was connected to the *Skurata*, he had learned a great deal. It was time.

The familiar mixture of fear and excitement raged within Cor'il as he closed his eyes and once again let the Threads course through him. He felt them flow through him and out of his body to connect with the *Skurata* where he could sense the Threads' power welling up.

His use of the Threads in the past had been a mere trickle compared to the raging torrent he now experienced. He felt Threads from miles away respond to his call—Threads he should not have been able to detect. Their energy filled him and threatened to wash him away in the current, but he redirected their power into the Skurata.

One by one, he reached out and felt the others, and they responded in kind. He felt each *Skurata* spring to life, answering his call. He connected with them and used their power to redirect the Threads to him and, ultimately, to this *Skurata*.

"Well, now you've done it."

Chapter 37

With his eyes closed, Cor'il felt both hot and cold at the same time. He could smell flowers and rotting leaves. He felt wind in his hair and water splashing on his face. And he felt the lonely, cold slippery surface of darkness and the warmth of the sun above. He could feel these sensations all at once. It felt the same as any other time he had channeled the Threads, except for the almost overwhelming intensity.

Much, much more intense, yes. But also the same.

Except it wasn't *exactly* the same, was it? No. There was something else—something he may have touched inadvertently in the past. Something that might have always been there, just out of reach. It was something that evaded him—elusive yet taunting.

It was something sinister. It was whispers in his head far worse than Antina's. Something in the haze clawed at him—just out of site and just out of reach but very real. Voices spoke to him, beckoned him to give into their demands. They invaded his thoughts and taunted his mind, promising him power and eternal life, but also a permanent grave.

Something poked and prodded at him, testing his resolve and his strength. It was subtle, yet relentless and always persistent. It coaxed him. It threatened him. It tried to trick him.

It wanted through.

All of Cor'il's concentration, every shred of his will was necessary to hold onto the Threads. It was like trying to cross a raging river without being washed away. He was filling the *Skurata* with power from the Threads and the raw energy that raged within threatened to overtake him. It was all he could do to simply contain it, let alone shape or control it.

Through the sweat, the pain, and the exertion he still knew that something was trying to break free. It wanted to consume Cor'il and flood into the world like a plague, washing over everything in its path. No matter how hard Cor'il tried to ignore it, he couldn't. But, in that very same fashion, it seemed unable to touch him.

It was Madness.

It could come close. Cor'il could feel the intense confusion and icy cold of its influence, but it could not harm him. Whatever The Madness truly was, it could not yet touch him, and it was livid. It growled and it raged, but despite its anger and resolve, its efforts were futile. Cor'il was in control, and he knew this fact.

He tried to ignore it, turning his full attention to the Threads as their energy continued to fill the *Skurata*. Though they surged and rapidly poured into the structure, each minute seemed a mere drop in an immense bucket. He opened his eyes.

Even as he looked around him, more Threads answered his summons, latching onto him, burrowing through his body, and connecting to the Triangular building all around him. The *Skurata's* shimmer began to alternate colors as more energy channeled into it.

The Threads began to pulse in unison, forming a rhythmic pattern of energy and light. The entire city in the distance was aglow, pulsing in time with the power of the Threads and providing Cor'il with burning energy.

"I'm beginning to understand!" he shouted.

"*Indeed you are. I hope you know what you're doing.*" Cor'il was a little surprised to hear Antina's voice again.

I can never hope to force the Threads to do my will. To command them is impossible. But, at the same time, I cannot give into the Threads and let them control me.

"*Indeed. You've seen what can happen.*"

Cor'il felt a pang of sadness and he almost lost his balance with the Threads. He quickly recovered, though, and continued channeling them into the *Skurata*.

"I must work *with* the Threads. I understand now!"

Cor'il began to realize that, yes, he *could* command the Threads, but they would always resist him to a certain degree. He needed to form and shape them, but he also had to let them flow naturally. It was the difference between trying to dam a river and merely directing the flow. Instead of outright resisting, Cor'il began working *with* the flow of the Threads, guiding them instead of trying to command them.

When the Threads responded in kind, he felt everything finally fall into place. It was as if he told the Threads what he wanted to do and they *helped* him. With renewed vigor and concentration, he guided their energy through himself and into the construct, feeling it fill up faster. He felt his ring getting warm and his finger began to ache. And, still, he felt the Madness poking and prodding at him, looking for a weak spot in his aegis, but finding nothing.

Its frustration was palpable. Cor'il continued to hear the unintelligible whispers in his mind, which soon turned into irate growls, and then screams. Instead of merely poking at him, whatever it was began to lash out angrily. Each time it was turned back. Each time his finger ached and the ring's warmth flared. Then, he understood.

Careful not to break his concentration, Cor'il slowly held up his hand and inspected the Threads running through it. They were mostly green Threads with a few strands of black, gold, and white. They did not run to or through the ring but, instead, the ring *contained* them in an intricate weave.

As he watched, the Threads formed a rope that contained one Thread of each color. It snaked out from the ring and wound itself around Cor'il.

He felt The Madness strike at him, only to be rejected once again. The moment that happened he saw the ring flare in a flash of light. *It's protecting me. But, I wonder, for how long?*

Cor'il continued to channel energy into the *Skurata,* but he shifted just a sliver of his concentration to the ring, gently poking at it with his will. Though the object did not respond in any way, he was able to determine one important fact about it.

It was made of Threads.

It was not just an item crafted and then enchanted with a magical weave. No, it *was* the weave! And it was confusing and powerful and amazing all at once! He wanted so badly to unravel the weave and inspect it, but that would destroy the ring and, along with it, his protection against the Madness.

"Are you sure about that?"

Cor'il looked again at the ring's weave. At first, he saw nothing, but he continued scrutinizing it and soon noticed a subtle quality—something unique that he had missed before. It was easy to overlook because it was cleverly hidden within the construct itself. That rope of multicolored Threads, it came... from *him.* Every other Thread he had ever seen had come from something around him—a tree, a rock, the ground, water, the sky—something else. But not these. *How can this be?* That had to mean that the ring... was part of him!

The rope pulsed with a prism colors, constantly shifting with each beat of his heart. Why had he not noticed this before? How was it that Antina had found out before he did? With each pulse, the rope got thinner and thinner until, finally, it was a Thread just like any other—except that each pulse was a different color, and the Thread itself was part of him.

"This is not something I have seen before. I don't know what it means."

Working to keep his concentration, he touched the rainbow Thread and felt warmth and tranquil safety. Unlike the rest of the Threads, this strand did his bidding without resistance. And there was intense power within! He followed the Thread's path where it integrated with the ring, but instead of unraveling it, he altered the weave. He spread it out, expanding the tightly woven Threads to cover more than just his finger. The weave itself wrapped around his body like a net that moved with him. He watched it shift and surround him like a blanket. The rainbow Thread-weave then settled inside him. It unnerved him to still faintly see it inside of his body.

It was as if this is what the weave had wanted all along, and he felt joy. The rainbow Thread remained, snaking throughout his body, but the rest of the weave he could no longer see. He felt no different, but the ring had vanished.

Madness struck out at him again. Not only was it repelled as before but, this time, Cor'il pushed back. He exerted his will against it and the voices retreated, silenced almost entirely. He knew they were angrier now more than ever, but he grinned as he pushed further out in all directions.

Then he shivered, feeling intense cold set in. He almost lost control of the Threads, but with his newfound knowledge came more control and discipline. He looked out at the city and saw them—Threadfiends. There were dozens of them and they approached from every direction, floating ominously toward Cor'il and gazing at him with their expressionless, skeletal faces.

Some were taller than others, but only slightly. For the most part, they were all nearly identical. For a moment, Cor'il took a defensive posture and prepared to attack, but he stayed his hand. If he needed to, he was certain he could obliterate them all at a moment's notice. Though he remembered how ineffective the Threads had been on Threadfiends in the past, the power he had stored up in the *Skurata* was already enough to level half the city if need be.

The Threadfiends quietly formed a ring around him and the triangular construct, as if to surround him and then attack. But then they stopped and stared at him with their empty eye sockets, their gazes never leaving him. Cor'il started to feel the familiar fear that accompanied the hideous creatures, but to his surprise, it subsided and then vanished altogether. He stared *right at them* and felt no urge to cower, no paralysis, and no cold. The energy of the Threads continued to flow through him and into the *Skurata* as the creatures stared at him with blank looks.

Finally, one of them floated forward a few feet and stopped. It looked at him and then looked up to the darkness that obscured the cavern's ceiling. It returned its gaze to Cor'il and then did something unexpected.

It nodded.

It then bowed its head and, keeping its head low, slowly floated back into the ring. Only then did it raise its gaze again.

Nobody can move mountains.

Cor'il still felt the other four *Skurata* scattered across the Realm. Not only could he feel them, but he knew where they were, now. But while they were out there, answering his call, they were still dormant and lifeless. He knew he was going to need them to link with this one, but how was he to connect with them? How did he activate them without being physically beneath each one?

The Threadfiends remained in a ring around him, keeping about ten to fifteen feet away. Suddenly, a third of them broke off and headed back toward the city. Cor'il saw why. His vision through the Threads caught the familiar, bright glow of one of *them*—a creature of Madness. It was big—possibly ten feet tall or more—and it was headed this way.

"If Madness can't get at you one way, it finds another. It may be Madness, but it is devious and clever."

It wasn't long before the Threadfiends surrounded the creature and assaulted it, attacking all at once with a coordinated effort. Cor'il remembered the fight back at Kuranthas. He remembered the Threadfiends being seriously outmatched and falling quickly to a creature much smaller than this one.

But this was different. He watched the skeletal creatures fight the Madness beast with a vigor and conviction that he'd not seen before. They tore and clawed at the behemoth, savagely trying to bring it down. It screamed, shrieked, and howled as it retaliated, flinging Threadfiends into the air and smashing others with its misshapen limbs.

Though they had no weapons, the Threadfiends appeared to be hurting it, but its attacks were taking a toll on their ranks, too. It picked one up and crushed its skull, discarding the body and moving on to another. That one was cleft in twain by the

Madness creature's sharp tail which it then swung around to destroy several other Threadfiends.

The fight raged for several minutes as Cor'il continued channeling the Threads into the arch. The *Skurata* was not even a quarter full yet and Cor'il had an impossibly thick rope of Threads flowing into it. He reached out to more and they answered from all directions. Once he added his multicolored Thread to the rope, it surged with immeasurable power.

A scant few of the Threadfiends returned from the fight, having finally defeated the Madness creature. They took their place in the ring around Cor'il and stared at him unnervingly. Again, one of them floated a few feet forward, looked at Cor'il, looked up, and then looked back at Cor'il. Then it returned to the ring and resumed its gaze.

Frustration quickly flooded in. They wanted him to do something, but *what?*

More Threads answered his call and added themselves to the rope. He reached out again and again, but finally no more responded.

Cor'il traveled down the rope flowing out of him and prodded the *Skurata*. He started at the top of the twisted spire, feeling the smooth, cold surface. Then he moved down to where the spire met the rest of the *Skurata*. He could feel every crevice, joint, and seam of the structure as his consciousness journeyed to the ground. Once there, he did not stop.

He sensed more—a lot more.

This is just the tip *of it!* He gasped. It was so much more than what he could see above the ground. In fact, it snaked throughout the entire city! While it was extensive, however, it still did not connect to any of the other *Skurata*, out there, in the distance! His wonder soon mixed with frustration as he reached another dead end.

The Madness beyond continued to lash out at him, whispering irate gibberish and shouting threats. Cor'il barely noticed it now. It had gone from being an angry gortog in a cage to a simple bitefly buzzing around a room. It was annoying, yes, but hardly anything worth paying attention to at this point. Ignoring The Madness made it more furious, but no more dangerous. Cor'il had much more important endeavors to focus on.

Unfortunately, he found that he was... stuck.

He continued to focus on filling the *Skurata* with the Threads, pouring vast amounts of energy into it while it slowly charged.

Again, one of the Threadfiends floated forward but, this time, it was joined by several others. In unison, they all pointed at Cor'il, then pointed up toward the ceiling. They then returned to the circle.

Cor'il probed the *Skurata* further, hoping to find something he had missed the first time. *What do they want? Why do they keep looking up there? What am I supposed to do?*

And then he knew. It became clear the moment he looked closer at the object. *This part is just the tip... just the top of it. And it needs to reach the others. And this city is connected to it. The entire city amplifies its power!*

With that, he stopped directing the Threads power at the *Skurata* and, instead, sent their energy *underneath* it.

The ground began to rumble. The shaking was gentle at first, but it soon reached a crescendo that should have torn the ground asunder.

The Threadfiends, still encircling Cor'il and the *Skurata*, nodded in unison.

This would change everything.

Chapter 38

Kendra's mood would have been far better if they could have avoided the senseless delays that constantly slowed them down. They had been waylaid by far too many things, in her opinion. The sky, in fact, confirmed her urgency.

Orvaril, naturally, seemed completely unconcerned about expediency. As usual, Alannin remained largely quiet on the issue, having agreed that they should move quickly to avoid danger but not so quickly as to carelessly invite trouble.

Kendra had lost count of the days that had passed since they left Sulbar and she became more anxious with every new day. They were close to Elston, but they could have already been there had they not been forced to hide from several groups of orcs. What made it worse were the Red Sword patrols—they twice had to actively avoid them. At one point, they had also stumbled quite accidentally into the most hideous of creatures—much like the beast that Kendra had encountered in that underground city.

Thankfully, Alannin had spotted it and they had been able to hide. Kendra could tell that both Orvaril and Alannin were as spooked as she had been, and they had waited a good long time for the monster to pass before they ventured out from the trees. Just thinking about it now sent a shiver down Kendra's back.

And then there was Orvaril who wanted to stop all too frequently to either relieve himself or to have a snack. Despite Kendra's constant urging, he ignored her requests to hurry up. That man could be so infuriating! Sometimes she felt like smacking him upside the head; he could be *that* difficult.

What Kendra found odd, however, was the lack of traffic on the road. Oh, there were plenty of travelers heading *toward* Elston, but these last few days, they had not encountered anyone traveling *from* the city. With as large as Elston was, there should have been a lot of people traveling back and forth. Since they had left Sulbar, however, they had only encountered a couple of smaller merchant caravans. That was days ago. Since then, all they had seen were Red Swords, orcs, and worse.

And all three enemies appeared to roam about, completely unchecked. *Sure, the Red Swords say that their purpose is to protect the Realm. They are either lying or they're doing a gortog's ass job of doing it.* The land had indeed become much more dangerous during the past few months, and Kendra didn't see the situation getting any better.

"Finally," she said. "We're almost there."

"Indeed, milady," Orvaril replied, pointing ahead of them. "Just beyond that hill in the distance, I believe."

"Hopefully," Alannin added, "it will be in better condition than Sulbar."

"I should hope so." Orvaril's tone was oddly sullen. He paused for a moment, looking as if he had something more to say. "Alright," he finally said, "I'll say it."

Alannin and Kendra both looked at Orvaril. They all stopped their horses.

"I don't think we should go to Elston," he said.

"Why not?" Alannin asked. He was obviously confused.

"I can't really explain it," Orvaril continued. Then he paused again before speaking. "I've got a rather ill feeling in my stomach. I think this is a mistake."

Though Kendra did not say it aloud, she felt the same way. Simply judging from the lack of traffic out of Elston, she guessed that her feelings might be warranted. While the clouds above often urged her in specific directions, those actions were not guaranteed to be safe.

"But Cor'il is in Elston," Kendra finally said. "Whether it's wise to continue is not a mystery—I feel that there is great danger ahead. But I assure you, Elston is where we *need* to be."

Kendra sighed. She wasn't sure how to explain it. At first, she had assumed it was just a feeling—an instinct. Between this and what the clouds told her, she knew that she should be in Elston because Cor'il was there. But it was just *how* she knew where Cor'il was that had confused her—until just a couple of nights ago, when she thought she had finally figured it out.

"When the treeboy worked his magic to try and heal me back before everything went to The Abyss... I'm not exactly sure what he did, but now I can sometimes feel him." That was the best way she could explain it. The sensation was always vague and it was only sometimes present but, when she *could* feel it, she was absolutely sure of it.

"So," Orvaril started, "you think, when he supposedly messed up his attempt to heal you, he may have created a... bond?"

"No," Kendra replied. "I mean, I think he *did* create some kind of bond."

"I am confused." Alannin looked puzzled.

"What I am saying," Kendra continued, "is I don't think that he messed up at all."

Both Orvaril and Alannin now looked confused.

"His weave—or whatever he calls it—didn't immediately work as he had intended, and I *am* still angry at him for doing it without asking first. I don't know how, but I believe his magic somehow kept me alive when I should have died. In addition, this connection between us was inadvertently created, probably unbeknownst to him. Whatever he did, it *worked*."

"Well now," Orvaril said after a few moments of ponderous silence. "That *is* intriguing. And you don't think he knew what he was doing?"

"I... don't."

"You don't sound absolutely sure," Alannin replied.

"Indeed. I must agree with the elf, milady."

"We should get moving." She nudged Brute and urged her forward, with Alannin and Orvaril quickly following suit.

Cor'il had certainly *seemed* to have been disappointed and confused by his attempt to heal her. It *had* worked, to a certain extent. If anything, his actions had stopped the bleeding and reduced the pain. It was the only explanation as to why Kendra had survived after being shot in the back—the magic was still there, and it had somehow kept her alive. The question was, had Cor'il known the results of the magic he had cast on her—both the healing *and* the bond?

When she had awoken in the Red Sword tower, she had been extremely shocked to find that the arrow wounds had completely healed up somehow, yet there had been a few cuts still visible on her shoulder. Now, however, even those were long gone. Evidently the treeboy had ultimately succeeded, even if it had taken a bit longer than he had intended. *He* did *mess up, right?*

She knew nothing about what it was that Cor'il and Dalinil could do or how they could do it. Cor'il had briefly tried to explain it to her once, but it had been more than she could grasp. The only thing she knew was that their eyes sometimes seemed to glow when they did it, though Cor'il's eyes had always seemed more vibrant than Dalinil's anyway. She had never determined whether he knew about this or whether anyone else could see it. She felt odd asking, so she avoided it. If anyone else had noticed, they had never mentioned it.

"Does anyone else hear that?" Alannin asked, stopping his horse. Kendra and Orvaril pulled alongside him, straining to hear.

"I hear only birds, the wind, and Orvaril's humming."

"I hear only my humming!" Orvaril laughed.

"I fear that your 'bad feeling' might well be warranted." Alannin grabbed the reins tightly and his face hardened. "We should move quickly."

They all three urged their horses forward into a slow cantor. Kendra could see the worry in the elf's face growing with every passing moment and her concern grew as well.

"Wait," she shouted, and brought Brute to a halt. Orvaril and Alannin did the same, confused.

"The ground," Alannin said.

"Is it a quake?" Orvaril asked.

"It feels like it." Kendra said, looking around. The ground was rumbling beneath them. Their horses shied and whinnied as

Kendra, Alannin, and Orvaril struggled to keep them under control.

"I cannot see any scenario where this is a good thing," Orvaril added. "Come, let us hurry!"

As they continued at their quickened pace, Kendra finally could hear it—the sounds of a battle. She flashed back to the first time the orcs had attacked Elston. They'd had considerably fewer numbers than the orcs at Sulbar but they had been no less savage, no less brutal.

"If it's orcs," Orvaril started.

"*If?*" Kendra sneered.

"Right. Well, do you think they have somehow coordinated with those other orcs from Sulbar?"

"How could they?" Alannin replied. "They're too far away, right?"

Kendra fully realized that the orcs at Sulbar had displayed surprising intelligence and ingenuity when attacking the city, and she hadn't even witnessed the siege itself. But Alannin had confirmed what she'd heard some of the Red Swords say about the orcs' tactics. The thought of them working with other groups so far apart sent chills of fear through her.

"Surely not," she said, rather unsure of her own assertion. Both Alannin and Orvaril clearly shared her apprehension.

She urged Brute forward a little faster. In the distance, she could see the hill that obscured the city from view. Once they topped it they would have a bird's eye view of the valley below. She felt the need to arrive as quickly as possible, but did not wish to see what she knew was happening.

Let's just hope that Elston fares better than Sulbar.

She noted, however, that none of them knew how Sulbar had fared in the end. Things had certainly looked bleak when they had fled the city, but the situation could have been worse. Even though the orcs had made it into the city, they easily could have been driven back. *Cor'il is in Elston. He will drive them back.*

Cor'il. She could still feel him, and she was completely certain that he was somewhere within Elston. That brought comfort to her, knowing that he was probably helping to defend the city. His power—the things he could do—would be instrumental in driving back the horde.

She had seen what he was capable of, even if he did not have confidence in his own abilities. For someone who supposedly lacked control of his magic, he had done a marvelous job cutting through the orc horde during the first siege.

The three of them looked at one another with deep concern as an explosion rang out from somewhere up ahead. Without a word, they urged their mounts into a gallop. The horses were more skittish now, but they still responded to their riders and continued forward. Ilvania kept pace, her tongue hanging out of the right side of her mouth as she jogged alongside them. Though the wolf was obviously enjoying the run, even she let out a whimper every now and then.

At least one of us can still manage to be happy, she thought.

"What are we going to do," Orvaril broke the silence, "when we get there?"

"Whatever we must," Kendra replied. "If there is anything we *can* do. Our best bet is to find Cor'il, and then help in any way we can." She wondered if The Blacksmoke had already fled. He was unpredictable and often surprised her. She would not be shocked if he had remained and was helping defend "his" city. She also would not be shocked if he used the siege as an opportunity to remove several individuals from his path and then hide until this whole thing blew over. *If it does blow over.*

Surely, Dalinil would be decimating orcs ten at a time. Surely, he would be helping to defend the city. Kendra missed her friend, and her spirits were lifted slightly with the prospect of reuniting with not only Cor'il but with Dalinil as well. It felt... broken to not all be together. She was getting used to not being alone all the time.

The din of battle grew louder. Screams echoed as the clash of steel clattered and rang in Kendra's ears. Even Orvaril had a worried look on his face now. Before Sulbar, something like this might not have felt so overwhelming but, after having seen the sheer numbers the orcs possessed combined with both their brutality and surprising tactics, everything now seemed much more dire.

And even if the orcs were turned back or destroyed, how long would it be until *another* horde descended upon Elston—or another city? The small towns would be overwhelmed by even the smallest band of orcs.

After another ten minutes, they finally crested the hilltop and looked down on the city. Though they were still about a mile away from the city itself, they could see everything from up here.

Kendra's heart sank and her stomach twisted. Elston was burning! A writhing sea of orcs surrounded it on all fronts. The bigger brutes—trolls and ogres—towered above the rest of the horde, lobbing whatever they could get their hands on—even orcs and goblins—at the walls.

"Let's go," Kendra commanded. She nudged Brute with her ankles and the horse responded in kind, galloping down the hill. She moved down the slope and headed toward a hilly area to the south of the city. It was much closer and she could get a better view from there. Orvaril and Alannin followed.

When they arrived, they left the horses on the back side of the hill, lashing the reins to some scrubby bushes. Kendra concealed herself in the tall grass and peered out at the battle. It appeared that Elston was putting up a decent fight, but two out of every four combatants appeared to be townsfolk with crude weapons desperately fighting off the horde however they could. *There is no way they can win with untrained civilians. The orcs are far too numerous!*

She saw small contingents of Red Sword soldiers fending off invaders where they could, but they, too, were outnumbered greatly by the orcs. The city guard manned the walls and blocked the south gates as best they could, but even from here, Kendra could tell that they would not hold forever. *Where is Dalinil? I assumed he would be out on the front line, cutting down the enemies.* She did not see him anywhere. Likewise, she did not see Cor'il, either, and her heart sank. She still felt him, however.

"We should do something," Orvaril muttered. "We can't sit idly by and watch Elston fall."

"Just the three of us, fighting an entire army," Kendra replied, "we would surely die. If we can get into the city, however, then we have a chance. The problem is—"

"Actually getting into the city, yes." Orvaril's face said it all.

"I know a way." Sometimes there were advantages to her relationship with The Blacksmoke. "The horses must stay here, however."

"Then let us hope they will stay safe," Alannin remarked. "We should probably release them from their tethers."

"Aye," Kendra agreed. She slid down the backside of the hill and freed the reins from the bushes and removed the harnesses. The horses, while obviously still nervous, did not flee. "Well," she continued, "I suppose they will run away if they need to. Goodbye, Brute." She patted her steed on the head and gave her a small hug. "Follow me."

Kendra continued down the backside of the hill and the others followed her to a rocky area further south of Elston. Kendra began examining each boulder.

"I always forget about this passage," she muttered, inspecting one of the rocks. "In fact, I've only used it once, and I'm quite unsure precisely where it is." She knew what she was looking for—she was close, but she was also frustrated and, with the battle going on, she was having a difficult time concentrating.

"Is there anything I can do to help?" Alannin asked.

"There is not."

"Then I shall patiently wait." Alannin sat atop one of the stones, tucked one knee up against his chest and waited. Orvaril paced nervously while Kendra continued her search.

"Here!" she said after several moments. She ran her right hand over the surface of one of the larger boulders and found it—the pressure plate. She pushed on it and the boulder shifted. A portion of the rock slowly slid back, revealing a dark passage beyond. "This would be our way in," she said, gesturing into the darkness.

Once inside the passage, Orvaril plucked one of several torches off the wall and, after producing flint and steel from his rucksack, lit it.

"How nice." Kendra whispered sarcastically. "He left me some torches." She found another pressure plate and, after pushing it, the passage sealed itself. "Quickly, let's go."

They hurried down the long passage in the flickering light for ten minutes. When they finally reached the end, Kendra ascended a short flight of stairs, but found that the door at the top was locked.

She produced several small tools and went to work, using them to probe the keyhole. There had never been a lock The Blacksmoke could find that she couldn't open, and it annoyed him to no end. She soon found the right position and popped the lock, pushed the door open, and they emerged inside a small, dark basement. She climbed the stairs to the empty room above. Once there, Orvaril snuffed the torch and hung it on the wall next to several others.

'Well, then," a voice said. Kendra could sense smug satisfaction in the man's tone. "You're late."

"My apologies," Kendra replied and turned around.

The Blacksmoke reclined in an overstuffed chair in the corner of the room, his brown fedora covering most of his face. He looked relaxed and comfortable—as if he'd been napping all day. He nudged his hat up slightly as he rose from the chair and straightened his cloak.

"It's quite alright, my dear," he joked. "I've not been waiting around *all* day. But one of my men spotted you earlier. And since I had once shown you this particular route into the city..."

"There is no need to brag," Orvaril interjected.

"My apologies, good sir. But I am just so damned good at it!" The Blacksmoke bowed and chuckled.

"Enough!" Kendra scowled. She was frustrated and anxious and every moment they spent posturing was a moment wasted. "We need to find Cor'il. You two can fight this out later if you wish."

"Cor'il?" The Blacksmoke rubbed his chin and looked wistfully up at the ceiling. "Oh, yes, the half-elf."

"Yes, him!" Alannin added excitedly.

"Oh, look!" The Blacksmoke circled Alannin, as if inspecting him. "I see you've found a *whole* elf!" he laughed. "And he's got a pet!"

Alannin's face was blank. He simply watched The Blacksmoke. Ilvania refused to sit and kept her gaze on the man, snarling.

"Cor'il," Orvaril interjected, obviously hoping to bring The Blacksmoke's attention back to the subject at hand. "Where is he?"

"Yes, I know—the boy. I haven't seen him." The Blacksmoke sat back down in his chair and reclined. "Are you sure he's in Elston?"

"He's here," Kendra replied, perturbed. The Blacksmoke could be so difficult! Usually he expected payment for his information, but this time, he didn't even offer the option. *Mayhaps he truly doesn't know Cor'il's location. That would be a first—I know something he doesn't.* "Where is Dalinil, then?"

"The blacksmith? He left," Blacksmoke replied with a matter-of-fact tone. "Quite a while ago, in fact. He even left a messy trail of... unfortunate corpses behind him."

"Do you know where he is now?"

"I do not." He shifted in his chair and produced a dagger, picking at the blade with his thumb, and testing the sharpness of its edge. "Would you mind calling off your puppy? I wouldn't want to have to harm her."

Ilvania had managed to creep up close to The Blacksmoke, and wouldn't take her eyes off him.

"Ilvania!" Alannin commanded. The wolf backed away slowly, keeping her eyes on the man in the chair. She came to a sit next to Alannin and uttered a low, quiet growl.

"As I was saying," Blacksmoke continued, "I do not know where this Dalinil went. Highly unusual for me to be left in the dark? Yes. Unheard of? Certainly not. I know that he headed out the north gate of the city on horseback. I lost track of him after that. If he emerges in a town somewhere, I'll know about it."

"Quite confident in yourself," Orvaril chimed in, "aren't we?"

"Why, yes," Blacksmoke replied with a wry tone and a smirk. "But you are quite accustomed to feeling that as well, no?"

"How nice of you to notice," Orvaril retorted, not even flinching.

"Well, this has been less than fun." Kendra moved toward the front door of the house. "But I would like to find our friend. He's here somewhere and he probably needs our help... and we need his." She opened the door and left.

Outside, she found chaos and turmoil. She could smell smoke in the air and hear shouts and screams. Several people ran past her in a hurry, mumbling in worried voices or crying.

"So where do we start looking?" Orvaril asked as he and Alannin emerged from the house behind her.

"Right," The Blacksmoke said as he, too, walked out into the street. "The man with half a head of hair is right. Where do we start looking?"

"You mean to tell me that you're interested in helping?" Kendra sneered. "What stake could you possibly—"

"My dear," he interrupted, "this is *my* city. If your friend can somehow help keep it in one piece—again—then I shall entertain the idea of trying to find a needle in a haystack. The question seems to be, which haystack?"

Kendra shot The Blacksmoke a confused glance. She was both happy and confused that he wanted to help. No doubt there was something else in it for him. He could always make the best of a situation and come out ahead of the game.

"We need to get above this," she said. "The rooftops are our best bet.

"Ah!" Blacksmoke exclaimed. "Then I *can* help after all!"

Chapter 39

The ground continued to rumble as before, but Kendra could tell that it was getting worse. Dust fell from the walls and the ceiling as the group ascended the staircase to the roof.

"Is the battle causing the shaking?" Kendra asked, frantically climbing the staircase.

"Doubtful," replied The Blacksmoke. "I would guess something else is at work, here. Whether it helps or hinders us, I do not know."

"My guess," Orvaril added, "is it is neither and both. It doesn't really matter, does it?"

They reached the end of the stairs and stood on a small landing with a short ladder. Space was tight and they were forced to hunch over while The Blacksmoke opened the hatch in the ceiling. Kendra wasn't sure what kind of locking mechanism he had created but it involved fast finger work.

Finally, with an audible click, the lock opened. The Blacksmoke opened the door and they all climbed up onto the roof. The clamor of the battle below assaulted Kendra's ears and the acrid smell of smoke filled her nose. She hurried to the edge of the building and looked out over the city. This building was near the city's center and, three stories up, she could see everything much more clearly.

"Why is so much of it burning?" Alannin asked, arriving on Kendra's left. His voice was quiet and sorrowful.

"Either to distract," The Blacksmoke said, "or to destroy."

"What good is conquering a city in ruins?" Alannin was nervously fingering the hilt of one of his short swords with his left hand. Kendra had never seen him this upset before.

"What makes you think the orcs mean to *conquer* Elston?" The Blacksmoke clenched his jaw and grimaced. His fists were balled. It appeared that he, too, was upset. It was a rare show of emotion for him.

"He's right," Orvaril added. "I do not think the orcs mean to capture Elston. I think they intend to *level* it."

The streets below writhed with orcs, goblins, and men locked in battle. It appeared that the entire citizenry of Elston was defending their city and, while they were an untrained militia, they seemed to be at least slowing the tide.

"We need to help somehow," Kendra urged.

"My dear, I don't see how the mere four of us can make any kind of a difference down there." The Blacksmoke tipped his fedora up a bit. He may have *said* the words but Kendra could see his mind working, formulating some plan that could make a difference and help defend Elston.

"Do you have anything rigged in the area?" Kendra began looking around the rooftop for something—*anything*—that she could use. "You know, traps or whatever you call them?"

"Oh, my *equalizers*? Yes, I have some. We can use them, but I am unsure as to how much of a difference they will make."

"We have to try!" Kendra shouted, almost in tears. She was having difficulty holding back her emotions. While she was not originally from Elston, she had essentially adopted it as the closest thing she had to a home. And it was being destroyed while she stood by and helplessly watched.

A building collapsed nearly a block to their right, sending dust and debris into the air and filling her ears with horrible noise. *Where in The Abyss are you, Cor'il? You're here somewhere! Why aren't you helping?*

Kendra's eyes scanned the city, hoping to catch a glimpse of magical fire or something else that would alert her to Cor'il's presence. But she saw nothing—no explosions, no half-elf flying through the air—nothing. Her heart sank. She wasn't sure if she felt better or worse knowing that he was here in Elston somewhere. If he wasn't up here, helping defend Elston, then mayhaps he was in trouble!

She had a dragonstone. With it, she could destroy a large area. For a moment, she considered lobbing it into the streets, but thought better of it. The resulting destruction would probably do more harm than good. *But if I can get close enough to the army outside the walls...*

They stood, watching, but unable to help. Kendra ran through every idea she could imagine, but came up with no significant way they could stem the tide of the battle. Four people in a fight this large? Most likely they would end up dead in minutes. No, their only *real* option was to flee. Every urge within her compelled her to stay—that an opportunity might present itself. War was just like the weather—unpredictable. This storm of chaos was no different.

The building shifted beneath their feet and they all four stumbled, struggling to keep their footing. Orvaril nearly fell over the edge but caught himself at the last moment. Even in this dire situation, Kendra wondered if he had exaggerated for dramatic effect.

Kendra hunched low to keep her balance. From here, she could see a throng of orcs fighting around the castle in the middle of the city. She could clearly see the beginnings of another Red Sword Spire, its construction obviously halted due to the fighting. It stood in the courtyard of the castle itself, partially constructed and nowhere near complete.

"The ground is shaking more," Alannin said, merely stating what everyone was thinking.

"I've felt quakes before." Orvaril put his hand on the roof, feeling the vibrations. "This feels much different."

"A new weapon?" The Blacksmoke asked.

"It's possible." Orvaril ran a hand through his half head of hair and grunted. "But I would place my bet on something else."

"What?" Alannin asked.

"If I knew, good elf, surely I would tell. But I don't. I cannot think of anything that could make the ground shake so."

What about anyone?

Suddenly, she knew—it was Cor'il. *Cor'il* was causing the ground to shake—he had to be. With every passing moment, her confidence grew—Cor'il was doing something to cause the ground to shake. But what? Her urge to flee quickly waned, replaced with a new resolve. He would make it alright. He would drive back the horde. They merely had to wait.

"We are going to wait here," she said. Her voice was calm and resolute.

"For what?" The Blacksmoke asked.

Kendra turned around, hearing a noise behind her. An orc crested the edge of the building, climbing up onto the roof. In one motion her black dagger appeared in her hand and she threw it, burying it in the creature's skull. The orc whimpered and fell backward off the roof as the dagger reappeared in her hand and she slid it up her sleeve.

Orvaril and Alannin both looked surprised while The Blacksmoke grinned.

"That," she replied, pointing toward the castle. Everyone looked on as, further into the city, the spire began to sway, followed by the castle itself. It was subtle at first but soon the tower crumbled and disappeared in a cloud of dust.

"That..." Orvaril stammered, "is not good."

"I disagree," The Blacksmoke retorted. "I'm rather on the fence, myself. I never liked that eyesore. I've been hampering its construction for weeks."

"Well," Kendra said, "At least we don't have to worry about the Red Swords' little toy anymore."

Orvaril and Alannin looked on, speechless.

"So this is how Elston falls, then." Orvaril picked up a rock and threw it into the throng below. Hopefully he irritated an orc with it. "We have a front row seat to watch the castle fall—the beginning of the end, I guess?"

"I wouldn't be so sure." Kendra watched as the castle continued to sway more violently now. Chunks of stone began to slough off and clatter to the ground.

"If the orcs destroy the castle—"

"What makes you so sure it is the *orcs*, Orvaril?"

"Well," he shouted, "because we would be fools to believe that Elston's own forces were bringing down its center of power. That's why!" He was angry. Kendra wasn't sure she had ever heard him raise his voice before, but as if it had never happened, he regained his composure. "What else would bring down the castle?"

"You forget," she grinned, "Cor'il is here... somewhere."

"So the half-elf is responsible for this?" The Blacksmoke sounded both irritated and intrigued at the same time. "What makes you think that? And, if so, why is he destroying the castle? And, how?"

"Well I don't know for *sure*," Kendra sneered. "But he's certainly not up here, lobbing fire and lightning. I've seen him do some pretty incredible things. It stands to reason that, if Dalinil is no longer in Elston, then Cor'il would be the only force that could do this."

"That is truly a stretch, milady." Orvaril muttered quietly to himself. "But, as we have no other hope, I suppose I am willing to entertain the idea.

"I don't believe we really have a choice," Alannin replied.

As if on cue, the ground rumbled harder, shaking the building underneath their feet. They struggled to remain upright, grabbing onto whatever they could find nearby. The castle continued to crumble, toppling over piece by piece. They watched helplessly, until it disappeared in a massive, choking cloud of dust.

"So this is it, then." The Blacksmoke looked on, grinding his teeth. "Elston has fallen."

The rumbling increased, becoming a violent shaking. Every building around them felt it and swayed in turn. A house to their left collapsed, falling on top of combatants in the area—orc and human alike. Kendra fell onto her backside, unable to stand anymore. Orvaril and The Blacksmoke followed soon after, with Alannin sitting down of his own accord.

"No," Kendra replied. "Not the end at all. Look!" She pointed.

From the thick soot and dust rose a familiar object that Kendra immediately recognized. Triangular in shape and glowing bright blue, it climbed into the air atop a mountain of dirt, stone, and rubble, slowly consuming everything in its path as it pushed its way upward. They all gasped in unison, watching it rise from the rubble of the castle. The terrible cacophony it created was enough to drown out even the sounds of battle.

Buildings fell as the mountain expanded, gobbling up the city from the center outward. For a moment, Kendra wondered if they should flee, lest they too be consumed by the ever-growing mountain. She could see the same concern on her companions' faces.

"What in The Abyss is *that*?" Orvaril yelled over din.

And then she saw him.

Cor'il was perched securely underneath the building, standing amidst a glowing blue aura with multicolored streaks of light encircling him. His arms were outstretched in a "V" shape, pointing up at the object—whatever it was.

"It's Cor'il!" she shouted, excited. "I told you he was behind this!"

"Great!" The Blacksmoke chimed in. "What in The Abyss is he trying to do? Help the orcs destroy Elston?

Kendra, while ecstatic to see her friend again, had to admit that she didn't exactly understand what Cor'il was trying to do. Hopefully he did not actually intend to destroy the city. *But, then, he has admitted that he does not always know how to control his magic. What if it's out of his control?*

"And there you go," she mumbled. "Nobody can move mountains. However, that is apparently of no concern for you, Cor'il... for you *create* mountains."

The mound of dirt, stone, and buildings continued to steadily rise higher into the air with Cor'il riding atop it until, suddenly, it came to a halt. Dirt and rock skittered down the side of the mountain, coming to rest at various points along the way. The sound of battle had all but ceased. It was as if everyone was dumbfounded and unable to concentrate on anything but what had just happened.

The triangular building atop the high mountain peak continued to glow. In fact, its intensity grew. And then it occurred to her—there was another one! If there was another one of these structures, then there was probably another city—right beneath Elston!

She watched, speechless, for several moments until the spire atop the structure glowed white. Then there was a blinding, brilliant flash of light followed by a wave of soothing warmth and a crackling boom—like thunder. In an instant, Cor'il was gone and the structure's blue glow ceased. An eerie calm descended upon the city, accompanied by silence.

It was as if nobody—not even the orcs—knew what to do. Either that, or fear had overtaken everybody all at once.

It was then that they appeared.

The first one appeared, screaming, from the triangular archway and barreled down the mountainside, into the city. It was followed quickly by another, and then another—each one a hideous, twisted abomination. Kendra recognized them, and she felt like vomiting.

Cor'il was gone.

Kendra felt the urge to flee, but she had trouble moving. She recognized this sensation. These creatures were not so different from the one she had encountered, and they were now being unleashed upon everyone down below in the streets.

"What are—" Orvaril muttered.

"We have to leave," Kendra commanded. "Now!"

"I agree with the lady." The Blacksmoke was already opening the door in the roof and he quickly disappeared into the building.

"But, what—" Alannin was unable to finish his question.

"There is no time," Kendra shouted. "Elston is no longer ours. We have to go *now*!"

Sean R. Frazier

Kendra followed The Blacksmoke, hearing the shrill shrieks of the mutated monsters as they poured out of the structure and cascaded down the mountain like an avalanche. *Damn it, Cor'il! Why would you set these horrors loose on Elston? You haven't saved it, you've destroyed it! Why have you done this?*

They shut the door behind them.

THANK YOU

Thank you for reading "The Coming Storm!" I hope you enjoyed it and, if you did, I only ask that you mayhaps spread the word to others who you think would enjoy it. Also, if you'd be kind enough to leave a review, I would greatly appreciate it.

<3,
SRF

An ancient enemy awakens in The Forgotten Years: Descent Into Madness

ABOUT THE AUTHOR

Sean R. Frazier is the author of the Forgotten Years series. He was inspired to write in elementary school but did not seriously consider publishing anything until he graduated college. Though he had grandiose visions of churning out nonstop novels, those dreams were shelved for a while... until now.

Sean lives in Missouri with his wife, two daughters, and menagerie of pets. He is a father, a husband, a gamer, a runner, and a total dork. His biggest aspiration is for his cat, Thor, to stop hating on him.

Made in the USA
Columbia, SC
26 November 2018